Praise for *The Damage*:

"A startling twist makes this taut debut a must-read."   —*People*

"Compelling . . . a taut drama."   —*Bustle*

"This is a raw, sharp crime drama that puts a family at the center of seeking justice."   —*BuzzFeed*

"A magnificent debut to rival the very best of Dennis Lehane, *The Damage* scores knockout thriller punches chapter after chapter. It's dense and exciting, as though Michael Connelly and Tana French had joined forces."
> —A. J. Finn, #1 *New York Times* bestselling author of
> *The Woman in the Window*

"A brilliant debut. One of the best books you'll read this year."
> —Shari Lapena, *New York Times* bestselling author of
> *The Couple Next Door*

"Wahrer weaves a brilliantly layered story of a horrific crime and how it forces each member of a loving family to confront the harrowing question of what kind of person they truly are."
> —Jeffery Deaver, *New York Times* bestselling author of
> *The Final Twist*

"Smart, suspenseful, and timely."
> —Gilly Macmillan, *New York Times* bestselling author of
> *The Long Weekend*

"Compelling, relatable conflict and well-crafted twists create depth in this thoughtful blend of family drama and mystery."   —*Booklist*

"A deeply humane and affecting psychological thriller by a debut author."   —*Kirkus Reviews*

"Readers can expect thought-provoking, well-plotted psychological suspense from a bracingly fresh voice."   —*Publishers Weekly*

"With twists worthy of a season finale of *Law & Order: SVU* . . . *The Damage* carefully and expertly captures the collective trauma of a close-knit family when one of its members is victimized, and the lengths to which they'll go to find justice and healing."   —*BookPage*

"A blisteringly smart and evocative novel, with enough suspense to keep you up all night. A powerful debut."
                    —Bruce Holsinger, bestselling author of *The Gifted School*

"A brilliantly-observed novel . . . a damning and humane exploration of family, brotherhood, and upbringing. To say I loved it is a wild understatement."
                    —Gillian McAllister, bestselling author of *How to Disappear*

"Delightfully unpredictable . . . I ripped through it in one sitting."
                    —Brian Moylan, author of *The Housewives:
                    The Real Story Behind the Real Housewives*

"A smartly written, deft thriller . . . hard to put down."
                    —Araminta Hall, author of *Imperfect Women*

"A magnificent novel . . . The storytelling is masterful and I was hooked from page one until that exquisitely satisfying final chapter."
                    —Charlotte Philby, author of *The Second Woman*

PENGUIN BOOKS

THE DAMAGE

Born to two hippies in a small town in Maine, Caitlin Wahrer left the state for college but returned to attend law school and practice law, where she worked on cases involving some of the broad issues she writes about in *The Damage*. She lives in southern Maine with her husband and daughter. *The Damage* is her debut novel.

Penguin Reading Group Discussion Guide available online at penguinrandomhouse.com

THE
DAMAGE

Caitlin Wahrer

PENGUIN BOOKS

PENGUIN BOOKS

An imprint of Penguin Random House LLC
penguinrandomhouse.com

First published in the United States of America by Viking,
an imprint of Penguin Random House LLC, 2021
Published in Penguin Books 2022

Grateful acknowledgment is made to Claire C. Holland for permission to reprint "Clarice"
from *I Am Not Your Final Girl* by Claire C. Holland. Copyright © 2017 by Claire C. Holland.
Originally self-published by GlassPoet Press, Los Angeles, CA, in 2017. Reprinted by
permission of the author (www.clairecholland.com).

A Pamela Dorman/Penguin Book

ISBN 9780593296158 (paperback)

THE LIBRARY OF CONGRESS HAS CATALOGED THE HARDCOVER EDITION AS FOLLOWS:
Names: Wahrer, Caitlin, author.
Title: The damage : a novel / Caitlin Wahrer.
Description: New York : Pamela Dorman Books / Viking, [2021] |
Identifiers: LCCN 2020045748 (print) | LCCN 2020045749 (ebook) |
ISBN 9780593296134 (hardcover) | ISBN 9780593296141 (ebook)
Subjects: GSAFD: Mystery fiction | Suspense fiction
Classification: LCC PS3623.A356495 D36 2021 (print) |
LCC PS3623.A356495 (ebook) | DDC 813/.6—dc23
LC record available at https://lccn.loc.gov/2020045748
LC ebook record available at https://lccn.loc.gov/2020045749

Printed in the United States of America
1   3   5   7   9   10   8   6   4   2

Set in Adobe Caslon Pro
Designed by Cassandra Garruzzo

For Ben

THE

DAMAGE

I.

MONSTERS

—◦—

I have known monsters and I have known men.
I have stood in their long shadows, propped
them up with my own two hands, reached
for their inscrutable faces in the dark. They
are harder to set apart than you know.
Than you will ever know.

CLAIRE C. HOLLAND, *I Am Not Your Final Girl*

1

The dying detective's house was a tall, dark blue thing with chipping trim and shutters. It loomed against the bright sky, set back from the snowbank lining the street. The house was dusted with last night's powder, but the black *23* tacked above the front door was brushed clean. There was room in the narrow driveway, but she parked on the street.

Julia Hall shifted in her seat to expose the pocket of her heavy winter coat. She crammed her hand deep inside until her fingers scraped the edges of the folded paper. As she pulled the note free, she willed it to say anything but the address she'd located—anything that would let her drive on, maybe never to find the house. There, on the crumpled sheet, she'd written *23 Maple Drive, Cape Elizabeth*, and here it was.

"Just go," she said aloud, then looked sideways at the house. Windows abutted the front door, and each appeared empty with the blinds drawn. At least he hadn't seen her talking to herself, then.

The wind blew the door from Julia's hand as she climbed out of her SUV. This winter had been bitterly cold. As she aged she found the winter a little less pleasant to weather each year. She pulled her hat tighter over her ears, then turned back to the car. Without thinking, she slammed the door hard. She winced as the sound rocked down the neighborhood street. She hadn't done that in years—she was thinking of her old Subaru, the one that demanded a rougher touch. The one she'd had three years ago, back when she had occasion to talk to the man waiting for her inside that house.

In spite of last night's flurry, the front walk was freshly shoveled. Had he done that for her? The path and steps to the porch were layered in salt, and she focused on the sound as she crunched her way up to his door. She shook out her hands and rang the bell. Before the chime had subsided inside, the door swung open.

"Julia," said the figure in the doorway. "How are you, dear?"

She was certainly better than he was, wasn't she? Because the man standing before her was Detective Rice, or at least the husk of him. His once towering frame seemed to have caved in on itself like a rotting flower stem. His face was sallow, and he had deep bags under his eyes. A Red Sox cap pushed down on his ears, obscuring what appeared to be a completely bald skull.

"I'm good, Detective Rice. I'm good."

They shook hands awkwardly, as he had leaned in as though to hug her.

"Well, would you like to come in?"

Every day since you called me, I've thrown up my breakfast was what she wanted to say. Instead, she smiled and lied. "Yes, of course."

"And please, you can just call me John," he said as he wobbled backward to make room for her to step inside. He seemed to have aged ten years in the last three, maybe from the cancer. Not that she was doing much better. For most of her life, Julia had looked young for her age. Somewhere in the past few years, that stopped. She looked thirty-nine now.

As Julia pulled off her boots, she surveyed Detective Rice's mudroom, a little voice in her head pointing out how strange it was to be in *Detective Rice's mudroom*. The bench she sat on was sturdy, practical. A few pairs each of work boots and dress shoes butted up against the base. The bench was flanked by a bucket of salt on her right, and a wet shovel leaned against the wall. To her left was the only curious feature: a petite shelf crammed with gardening books. She never would have guessed him to be a gardener when she met him all that time ago. It suggested an earthiness that she had missed.

"I don't know if I can," she said as she stood. "I think you'll always be 'Detective Rice' to me."

He grinned at her and shrugged.

She followed him down a narrow hallway lined with family photos and religious artifacts: there were various portraits of a younger Detective Rice and his deceased wife, Julia assumed, and three children; a crucifix and a dried palm; a picture of a grandchild, probably, next to a picture of Jesus.

Detective Rice said something muffled as he led her down the hallway. "What?"

He turned and faced her over his shoulder. "Was just saying you got a new car."

"Oh, yeah." She pointed her thumb behind her. "Guess I've upgraded since I last saw you."

She studied the change in his height. He was still a tall man, she thought as she followed him, but his illness had stolen several inches.

"I was thinking we'd sit in here."

He motioned to the first room they came upon. It was decidedly a *sitting room*: something that Julia only ever saw in the homes of older people. Like others she had seen, Detective Rice's had a buttoned-up air to it, despite its obvious purpose for hosting company. The room was staged around two big recliners with a small table between them.

Detective Rice motioned for Julia to sit in the chair on the right as he continued down the hallway.

She waited a few seconds, then poked her head out into the hall.

Another doorway on the right. Kitchen at the end. She listened but heard nothing.

She turned back into the sitting room. *Deep breath*, she thought, and inhaled.

She moved toward the picture window across the room. It looked out on Maple Drive and a big house across the street. A steady chill radiated from the pane, and Julia touched a trembling finger to the glass. There were few things as bleak as Maine in February.

The cold months were hard; always had been. Every year, Julia was faced with the reality of Maine's autumn and winter, neither of which ever matched the nostalgia-tinged versions that lived in her head. The snow usually started in December, lasted through April. And after *that* winter—after the winter she last laid eyes on Detective Rice—winters carried some kind of existential melancholy that had to be shoveled away with the snow.

"Endless, isn't it?"

She started when she heard his voice behind her.

He was in the doorway again, smiling at her. In his hands he held two mugs.

He was just getting coffee. She breathed out, probably with obvious relief.

He motioned to the chair again, and this time she sat. She accepted a mug and watched him settle into his own seat. The scent that met her nostrils was not coffee, in fact, but tea. She tasted it and found it heavily sweetened. That was a surprise.

"How are your children?" Detective Rice asked as he sipped at his drink.

"They're good, thanks."

"How old are they now?"

"Uh, ten and eight."

"You'll never be ready for them to grow up."

There was something about him that made it easy to forget he had children of his own. Grown children; grandchildren, judging by the pictures in the hallway. It wasn't his personality that made her forget—it was his profession. There was something about him being *a detective* that made her forget that he existed outside of that.

Julia nodded and waited for him to ask her how Tony was.

"I suppose you were surprised to hear from me last week."

That answers that, she thought. Something about his passing over her husband felt like a personal slight, especially given everything that had happened, and she felt herself suppressing a frown.

She *had* been surprised on Thursday, when she picked up her cell at the end of a long morning in court to find a single voice mail waiting for her. It was the mark of an easy day if she only had one missed call by noon. She shouted goodbye to the marshal at the door and pressed Play as she strode from the courthouse. The voice that had croaked out of her phone halted her midstep; it was slow but unmistakable. A voice she had come to dread. Years ago she had worked herself into a state of near panic any time the phone rang or her voice mail blinked, for fear that his voice would be on the other end.

"I was surprised to hear from you," Julia said. "And very sorry to hear that you were sick, too." She leaned toward him slightly, realizing she hadn't mentioned it since they spoke on the phone last week and he asked her to come to his home.

"What's your . . . prognosis?" There was no comfortable word, not that she could think of.

"Well, it's not too hot," he said in a voice like he was discussing the chance of another flurry. "My doc thinks my 'quality of life' is going to get pretty bad over the next couple months, and it might all go pretty quick after that."

Julia could hear the quotes around "quality of life," and she pictured Detective Rice sitting in his doctor's office in a dressing gown, saying,

"'Quality of life'? What the fuck does that mean? Just tell me when I'm gonna die."

She smiled at him warmly. "I'm glad to see that you're still able to be at home."

"Oh, well, we'll see."

They each took a sip.

"Well," he said, and laughed lightly. He shrugged.

Was he nervous?

"I appreciate you coming up," he said. "Like I said, I wanted to talk to you before, well . . ." He shrugged at himself.

"While you still have that 'quality of life.'"

Detective Rice laughed, let out a wheezing cough, and reached behind his chair. There was the squeaking sound of an ungreased wheel, and he pulled a portable oxygen tank around to his side. He held the mask up to his face and breathed, holding up a *One minute* finger to her.

Jesus Christ, I better not make him laugh again.

He began to put the mask away.

"Why don't you keep that on," Julia said. "I really don't—"

"No," Detective Rice said firmly. "Thank you, but no."

The mask in its place on the tank, Detective Rice sat himself back up. The wind whistled at the window. "I wasn't sure you'd come, after everything. But I needed to talk to you. Well, to say some things to you. And I think you have some things to say to me, too."

Julia had to push herself to hold his gaze. His eyes were watery pink, and hers wanted nothing to do with them.

"I really wasn't sure you'd come," he said again. "But you always were too nice to say no to anyone."

The sick ache in her stomach intensified. What was she supposed to say to that?

He didn't expect a response, it seemed, because he spoke again. "So. Back to the beginning?"

2

The first time John Rice saw Julia Hall, she was standing in her kitchen, barefoot, washing a pile of dishes in the sink.

Rice was about twenty hours into the investigation at the time. Until that moment, it had been twenty hours of ugliness. Nothing but the kind of evil only man knows how to execute.

He'd seen the victim, a young man named Nick Hall, at the hospital the night before. He hesitated to think of him as a man at all. Nick was twenty years old, yes, but he should have been on the last legs of his boyhood. Instead, there was a look in his eye like he'd never feel young again.

Rice didn't want to overwhelm Nick by interviewing him that first night, when he'd already given statements to a nurse and an officer. Rice just wanted to introduce himself as the lead detective on Nick's case and ask him to write out a statement. It always felt a little callous to ask victims to write it out, ask them to relive the crime so soon. It was for the best, though, for everyone. Made Rice's case stronger; made the victim's memory better. Not to mention, the beginning of the case was usually the easy part. Most of the time, the victim hadn't grasped what had happened yet. The mind was in shock, the body in survival mode, and there was little to no affect. Nick had been like this: surprised, a bit confused, but mostly flat. Better for him to relive it now.

And he had. Before coming over to the house, Rice had picked up Nick's two-page statement at the hospital. Nick's older brother, Tony, was there again. He'd been there the night before, too, and now he had the baggy undereyes of someone who'd tried to sleep in a hospital chair. Tony stepped out of the room and handed Rice the statement. Told him Nick was sleeping. Rice said he'd come back later.

Rice found Tony Hall's house without trouble. It was a pretty little thing in the rolling outskirts of Orange, unassuming after a drive past some of the other houses in town. Rice's sister-in-law lived in Orange, too, but closer to the town center. Like many towns in southern Maine, probably like many towns everywhere, it was like two different places entirely depending on where you stood. Town center was where the wealthier inhabitants of Orange collected, either crammed into cul-de-sacs in large, cookie-cutter houses (Rice's sister-in-law included), or in Maine's version of mini-mansions on sizable plots of land (these were the very, *very* wealthy). The greater part of Orange, though, was farmland. Little of it was active. The Hall address was there, two plots down from a giant, ramshackle place overrun with geese, complete with a barn the earth seemed to be taking back. The Hall house, by comparison, was small, old but well-kept, and charming, at least what he could see from the road. The driveway was full, so he parked on the street.

Rice climbed the steps of the open porch to reach the front door. He could hear voices talking over the doorbell, then the solid inner door swung open and Rice faced a short, spry-looking woman with salt-and-pepper hair. She looked his own age, late fifties, maybe.

She opened the outer door and said, "Hello?"

Rice introduced himself, and she immediately nodded soberly and said that her son, Tony, was still at the hospital with his brother.

"I'm not Nick's mom," she said. "Just Tony's

"Yes," Rice said. "Tony explained this morni

hospital. I'm actually here to see Julia, if she's av

Even three steps inside, the house held certain

enjoyed by many of the families Rice encountered

were gleaming hardwood running down to tiles i

hall was framed in a rich dark trim. The space immediately evoked a

feeling of safety and an impression that this was a deeply *functional* fam-

ily. As the thought revealed itself, Rice felt heat on his ears. He realized

quickly he'd made certain assumptions about what the Hall family would

be like, based on little information. The address in farm country, the

brothers with different mothers. The total absence of Nick's parents at

the hospital at a time like this. The consequence of the mandatory "sen-

sitivity training" the station had done back in the spring was not that his

biases disappeared—it was simply that he noticed them more often and

felt like an asshole for it.

The short hallway opened into the kitchen, where a younger woman

stood at the sink. The October sunlight spilled in through a window just

in front of her, making her white blouse glow and illuminating hair that

should have been just brown but seemed to contain strands of yellow and

red in the light. She looked almost ethereal, except that she was frown-

ing and rinsing a dish.

"Sorry," she said. "Sorry, I'm just . . ." She turned off the faucet and set

a glass casserole dish on the crowded drying rack. "There. I heard you

come in, but I just *had* to finish that."

She grabbed a dish towel off the stove and wiped her hands quickly

before offering one to the detective. Her hand was damp and warm, and

she said, "I'm Julia."

"John Rice," he answered. "Detective with the Salisbury Police De-

partment."

was a muffled thud upstairs, like feet hitting the ground.

"Shall I finish the dishes or go upstairs?" Tony's mother asked from the hallway.

"Yeah, if you could keep them distracted while we talk," Julia said.

"On it."

"Thanks, Cynthia," Julia called toward the hallway as her mother-in-law ascended the stairs.

"The kids are happy to have their gram over," Julia said as she pointed at the ceiling. "They don't really understand what's going on."

Julia looked young, so Rice guessed the kids were, too. "How old are they?"

"Chloe's seven and Sebastian's five. We told them their uncle is sick so their dad will be busy taking care of him, but . . ." She shrugged. Now, talking about her children, Julia looked bewildered. "They're too young to understand, and I think that's for the best."

"Sure is," Rice said.

—○—

"How can I help?" Julia asked as she passed Rice a mug of coffee in the cool morning air on the porch.

Rice had suggested they speak outside, out of the children's earshot, and Julia agreed. The two settled into side-by-side Adirondack chairs padded with nautical-looking cushions, and Rice set his mug down on the small table between them. The smell of his steaming coffee mingled with the citronella candle on the table. Acid on acid.

"Well," he said, "Nick was still asleep when I went over this morning, and your husband looked like he hadn't slept at all, so I thought I'd give them a couple more hours' breathing room before I put 'em through the wringer again. Tony said you could give me a family history for my notes."

Her face washed with relief. "Oh, *that* I can do."

Rice pulled a small pad and pen from his windbreaker. He would have to get into what she knew about Nick, but he'd ease her in first.

"Do you care where I start?" Julia asked.

He shook his head. He was glad for the excuse to stare at her while she spoke. Meeting Tony, who was undeniably handsome, Rice had expected an equally striking wife. And Julia Hall was pretty, yes, but there was a plainness to her that was hard to name, now that she'd moved out of the morning light. Her face was round and without significant definition; as she spoke, her features were the same from all angles. It gave her an air of straightforward honesty—what you saw was what you got. It also made her look younger than she likely was. Rice might have guessed she was thirty were it not for the fine wrinkles she already bore: crow's-feet at her eyes and lines hugging the sides of her mouth. This woman was a smiler and a laugher.

"So Tony's parents are Cynthia"—Julia pointed backward at the house, indicating the woman inside—"and Ron. They were married for a while before they had Tony. Ron is—" She paused. "Ron had a really tough upbringing himself and wasn't the steadiest dad. Ron and Cynthia were together until Tony turned seven."

She was choosing her words like a politician, or maybe a lawyer. Either job would be ugly on her.

"Ron wasn't, like, abusive or anything. Or maybe, well . . ." She paused again.

Rice held up his pen at eye level. "How about I put this down for a minute and you relax about Ron?"

Julia laughed and brought her hand to her face as if to hide behind it.

"Just a little background on the family dynamic can be helpful." He didn't always make a point to ask about a victim's family but regularly enough. More often in a case like this, where the victim's life would be turned inside out by the defense, looking for blameworthy material.

"I get it," Julia said. "I've worked with just about every family dynamic possible."

"What do you do?"

"I work in policy now, but I used to be a defense attorney—all juvenile and criminal cases."

Rice shifted to pull his right leg over his left. "Then you *do* understand."

She nodded. "And honestly, Ron would fit right in with maybe the middle of the pack, you know? He's an alcoholic—he has been Tony's whole life—and it was easier for Ron to mostly just fade out of the picture after he and Cynthia separated. Cynthia is so warm and loving; Tony got really lucky there. Nick didn't get so lucky with his mom."

"So Nick's side of this."

"Right," she said. "So Ron is their dad, and Tony was seventeen when Nick was born, so he was, like, maybe fifteen or sixteen when Ron and Jeannie got together."

"So what's Jeannie's deal?"

"She's an addict, too, and she gets a little . . ." Julia waved her hand over her head. The word *manic* came to Rice's mind.

"Do they know what happened?"

Julia shook her head. "They don't even know he's there. He doesn't want to tell them."

Her voice faded out, and she shrugged. Her face sank into that frown Rice saw all the time when people tried to hold back their tears in front of him.

"He's gonna be fine, Julia. It'll take a while, but Nick will be fine." Rice pulled a packet of tissues from his pocket.

"Nick is just awesome," she said as she accepted a tissue. "Tony loves him so much. Honestly, he made Tony the man he is, you know? Who knows what he would have been like if he hadn't had that little baby."

"What do you mean?"

Julia shook her head. "Cynthia says Nick being born softened him. When he was a teenager he was kind of a macho tough guy, and *so* angry at Ron, and kind of the world I think. And you've seen what he looks like, he has *handsome jerk* written all over him."

Rice snorted and concurred. Not only was Tony Hall fit, but he had magazine looks. The kind of face that made you dislike him, just for having what you didn't. Rice wondered what Julia would have thought of him when he was her husband's age. Rice had mild acne scarring on his cheeks that persisted to this day, but when he was younger the pockmarks made him look tough. That's what his wife had told him, at least.

"But Nick just melted his heart," Julia said, dabbing the tissue at her eyes. "Tony grew up to be warm and emotional and a good communicator, which is probably super cliché to say about your husband." She laughed. "But whatever, I know I'm lucky. And I know I have Cynthia to thank for some of that, but I really think it was mostly because of Nick. You probably won't ever meet the real Nick. He's funny, wickedly funny, and charming and just, like, sincere. But now, I don't know."

Behind them, Rice heard the kids come bouncing down the staircase he'd seen inside the house. Seconds later, he heard Tony's mother trailing behind them. The noise faded down the hall and into the kitchen.

Rice's hand returned the tissues to his pocket and reappeared with a small, silver tape recorder. "I know this is hard," he said, "but I need to ask you some questions about yesterday."

"Okay," Julia said with an exhale. "Nick didn't call us until after dinner."

3

That Saturday evening had been ordinary. Tony and Julia had been sitting on the front porch, watching the sky go pink. Their neighbors had spread a golden blanket of hay over the field across the street, and the view from the porch was like an oil painting. And then the phone rang.

As Tony sat in the waiting room, he tried to remember the caller's specific words. She said her name, Dr. Lamba, maybe. She was calling from York County Medical Center.

At that point, his first thought was of his father. *He's finally killed himself driving drunk*, Tony thought. *Please, please say he didn't hurt anyone else.* But the doctor wasn't calling about Ron. She was calling about Nick.

"Your brother's been hurt," she'd said on the phone. That was as specific as she had been.

Tony had asked if it was a car accident.

"No," she'd said. "Can you come see him now?"

Tony had gotten to him as fast as he could—he'd rushed out of the house, sped down the highway, jogged through the parking lot, only to be halted in the lobby. The energy that had pounded through him earlier was still trapped inside him, buzzing, buzzing.

He pulled his phone out of his pocket. Texted Julia,

ETA?

She was at home with the kids, waiting on his mother. He would feel better when she got here, he told himself. Or once they let him back to see Nick. But *would* he feel better then?

"Your brother has been hurt." The strange words had played over and over in his head as he sped to the hospital. Vague, yet grave. The doctor had given him nothing, besides that it wasn't a car accident. What, then? Alcohol poisoning? A bar fight? Neither sounded like Nick, but things could get a little wild in college. Oh, Jesus, not a school shooting. He would have heard something on the radio on his drive. Still, there in the waiting room, he pulled out his phone and opened the browser. "University of Maine Salisbury news." Nothing. "Salisbury Maine news." Nothing.

What else had the doctor said on the phone? Something about Nick's age. She'd asked how old he was. When Tony said Nick was twenty, she said something about him having a fake ID on him, so she'd wanted to be sure. Said Nick didn't want her to call his parents, and she wouldn't have to. He only wanted Tony.

"Mr. Hall?" An older woman in a white coat stood in the doorway. He launched from his seat and met her with a handshake. She said she was Dr. Lamba from the phone, her voice low and confident. He was relieved to detect no message of condolences in her kind, dark brown eyes. Nick could be fine.

Tony followed Dr. Lamba down a long hallway as she explained that Nick had come in earlier that day, late morning.

"And as I said on the phone, he only wanted us to call you."

As she talked, Tony found himself fixated on the scrunchy in her silver hair. It was velvety black and sat at the nape of her neck. They were approaching a new set of double doors. Above them read BEHAVIORAL HEALTH UNIT.

"Wait." Tony's eyes hung on the letters as they walked under them. "Nick's in here?"

Inside the double doors was a small room surrounded by chicken-wired glass and a heavy door leading into the unit. Dr. Lamba motioned for them to sit in two small black chairs to the right of the room.

Dr. Lamba put her hand on Tony's forearm and said, "Your brother was sexually assaulted last night."

Tony stared at her.

"Whoever did this to him beat him up pretty badly, so I wanted to prepare you for that. We've—"

"Wait. Stop. Stop."

Dr. Lamba paused.

Tony shook his head. "No. No, no one would do that to him, that doesn't—that makes no sense." As he heard the words he'd said, a strangely detached voice in his mind whispered, *No, you make no sense.*

"I'm so sorry, Mr. Hall," Dr. Lamba said.

He buried his face in his hands. "Please, no."

He felt her hand on his shoulder now. "The emergency department treated Nick's injuries, and the good news is that he could go home now if he wanted. But the other good news is that he took my advice and admitted himself to our mental health unit, to give himself a couple of nights here."

Through his hands, Tony said, "Could you stop saying *good news*?"

"Yes." The hand rubbed his shoulder in a circular motion.

Someone did this. The simplicity struck him like a blow. Tony lifted his face from his hands. "Where's the fuck who did this?"

"Nick has already spoken to a police officer." Dr. Lamba met his eyes again and held them as she said, "Please, focus on your brother right now. He needs you. Don't focus on this other person, that's what the police are for. Focus on Nick."

—◦—

Nick's face was ruined.

It was the first thought Tony had when he saw him. Nick was lying on top of the covers of his hospital bed, like he was watching TV at a hotel. But his face was all wrong—the shapes of it were off, just a fraction: his lip was split and swollen, an eyebrow was cut. He had bruises on a cheek, his forehead, his chin, like he'd fallen down a flight of stairs.

"Nick?"

Nick smiled at Tony and then winced, licked the scab on his lip.

Tony's voice went watery. "What the fuck?"

"I'm fine," Nick said, and smiled reassuringly.

Tony pointed at Nick's chest. "Can I?"

Nick raised his arms.

As Tony crouched to hug Nick, his vision blurred with tears. He wriggled his hands under Nick's back and laid his head against his brother's. When he pulled away, there were tears on Nick's cheek. They were Tony's—Nick's eyes were dry.

"Sorry," Tony said.

"For what?"

For crying on you, he thought. *For being weird when you're saying you're fine. For taking so long to get back to your room. For whatever happened.*

Instead, Tony said nothing. He turned to pull a chair to the bedside and saw that Dr. Lamba had closed the door behind Tony. The two were alone.

Tony said, "So . . . ," but he was lost in a barrage of thoughts. Should he ask what happened, with what words, did he want to know, was he being selfish, *how* could this have happened, was that the wrong thing to ask.

"Where's Julia?" Nick's simple question nudged out all the others.

"Home with the kids. My mom's heading there, and then she'll come here as soon as she can."

"Julia'll come here tonight?"

"Yeah, if you want—*only* if you want."

"Yeah, of course, I almost asked for her instead of you to begin with."

Tony rolled his eyes. "Oh, *okay.*"

"She wouldn't have cried," Nick said with a grin, then winced again. He brought a finger to the slit in his lip. Whispered, "Shit."

Tony watched his little brother. They must have misunderstood him. This wasn't someone who'd been *sexually assaulted.* Clearly he'd gotten his ass kicked. Maybe he made a pass at the wrong guy and the homophobic fuck beat him up, that was possible. Or he could have been mugged. But not that—not what the doctor said. Their banter was unfazed. They might as well have been play-squabbling over a game, like when Nick was a kid and Tony used to pretend he was losing to him at checkers. And Nick was calm—*so* calm. He must have told someone he was assaulted, and they took it the wrong way. That had to be it. Nick seemed—

A knock at the door cut off the thought. A deep voice said, "Sorry to bother you." It came from the large man standing in the doorway. He was in plain clothes, but it might as well have been a T-shirt reading "I'm a cop" under his windbreaker instead of the white button-down, no tie.

"I'm Detective John Rice," he said, stepping into the room. "I'm from the Salisbury Police Department. I think Officer Merlo said I'd be stopping by?"

Nick adjusted himself to sit higher in bed. "Yeah, hi."

Tony felt the tension of that first silence swell back into the room.

Detective Rice made his way to the opposite bedside in two steps. He had to be six six, maybe even taller. His face was weatherworn and wrinkled; Tony guessed he was in his early sixties. The giant drew two business cards from his windbreaker and handed one to each of them.

The detective shook Nick's hand like Nick was joining the police force. "Well, nice to meet you, Nick." He turned to Tony. "Are you the brother?"

"Yeah." Tony stood to shake his hand. "Tony."

"Nice to meet you." The detective turned his face and shifted back to Nick. "I'm not here to stay, just dropping off these victim impact forms."

"What are these?" Tony reached over his brother to take the sheets. They were forms with a few spots at the top for details like NAME, DOB, DATE OF CRIME and then blank-lined space.

The detective pointed at the sheets. "Nick gave a statement to Officer Merlo, and he already saw a SANE nurse, so—"

"A sane nurse?"

"Sorry," Detective Rice said with a cough. "A sexual assault nurse examiner, over in the emergency department."

Tony glanced at Nick. Nick was looking down, twisting his hands together in his sheets.

"Oh, right," Tony said dumbly.

"The SANE nurse usually gets a pretty good statement, so I want to let you rest. But I need to come back tomorrow. That okay, Nick?"

"Yeah," Nick said.

"Why do you need to come back?" Tony flipped through the sheets; they were all the same.

"To interview him. It's important in a case like this that I get a thorough, consistent statement as close in time to the event as possible. The sooner you talk about it, Nick, the better your recall will be later, and it'll help me do my job. For tonight, I need you to fill out a statement of everything you remember that happened, starting at the beginning of your day on Friday. It was Friday, yesterday, right?"

"That it happened?" Nick asked.

"Yeah."

"Yeah it was last night, late last night. So I just write all of my day?"

"Well, you don't have to get too into the weeds with stuff before din- nertime, I'd say. And I can ask you for more details tomorrow if I need to. I'll collect them"—he pointed at the sheets—"sometime tomorrow morning and review them before we talk. Can you get it on paper some- time tonight?"

Tony looked down at his brother again. For the first time since he'd arrived, Nick looked like he was close to crying.

"Yup."

"Attaboy. Tony, if you could just step out with me and confirm some contact info?"

Tony nodded.

"I'll see you tomorrow, Nick."

Tony and the detective stepped out into the unit lobby. Tony shut the door behind him as he went. "Is that written statement really necessary, Detective, because I don't think—"

"Listen," Detective Rice interrupted. "I understand that this is a dif- ficult time, I really do, but I promise you I don't ask rape victims to do anything that isn't totally necessary."

Tony winced at *rape victims*. It felt sharp, hearing those words in the place of Nick's name. Like the detective had hurt him on purpose to back him down.

"We're building a case," Detective Rice said. "You have to remember that. Best-case scenario is we catch the guy who did this, but catching him means nothing if we don't have evidence to prosecute. Nick's story is part of the evidence."

"Can I—" Tony's voice cracked; he was about to cry in front of this man. He widened his eyes so the tears wouldn't spill out over his lids. He exhaled sharply and tried again. "Can I help him fill out the statement?"

"It's better if he writes it down himself. A lot of the time, cases like this turn on whose side of the story is more believable. Won't do us any good if you write out his statement for him. But you can sit with him while he does it."

Tony answered the detective's questions about names, numbers, addresses of the Hall family, but all the while *rape victim, rape victim, rape victim* repeated on a loop somewhere behind his ears.

The detective departed, and Tony stepped back into the room. From his bed, Nick frowned at him. "Why did you shut the door?"

A hot, damp cloth of a headache crept from his temples, spreading over his skull and down his neck. "I just did."

"Why?" Nick fired the word so fast it was clear he hadn't even listened to Tony's response.

"Nick . . ." He stopped. There were no words. "I'm sorry, I'm not trying to baby you, I just wanted to ask him if you really had to fill out those forms tonight."

"So you *did* baby me, because it's literally writing words on paper, and I said I would do it."

"Jesus, Nick, is it so bad that I would try to baby you today?" Tony's voice had almost climbed to a shout.

The brothers stared at each other.

"So, what?" Tony said. "I'm supposed to pretend everything's fine?"

"I *am* fine," Nick said.

Tony shook his head. Looked down at the sheets in his hand. Looked at the words *VICTIM IMPACT STATEMENT.*

Nick stared at him. Said nothing.

"I don't know how to ask you what happened."

4

NICK HALL, 2015

This is what happened.

On the first Friday of October, Nick Hall got a text message from the boy he liked.

In the middle of an Economics 101 lecture, Nick edged his phone from his pocket to check his notifications. The screen listed the names ELLE, MOM, and CHRIS. As his eyes registered the final name, a rush of butterflies pummeled his throat. No question: a text from Chris was worth the risk of getting caught with his phone out in class.

Nick pulled the phone free and balanced it on his thigh, quickly flicking past the other messages.

Chris G:

Hey

That was it. No punctuation, no response to Nick's last text, no effort. But at least he had texted. And *hey* was kind of sexy, Nick thought, in the right voice. Chris would have said it in the right voice in person: the kind of *hey* that had an ellipsis after it. The text was only twenty minutes old. Nick couldn't respond yet; *too desperate*. Unless responding now would show Chris that Nick didn't play games and wasn't afraid to go after what he wanted. Yeah, Nick thought, maybe he *should* respond now. He glanced up. His professor was lecturing right at him. He grinned sheepishly and shoved his phone back into his pocket.

As a junior in good standing at the University of Maine Salisbury, Nick had the privilege of living in a shithole off campus as opposed to a dorm on campus. A single management company owned a number of houses on Spring Street, which generations of students had long dubbed Frat Row. Although UMS had no official Greek life, house parties were frequent occurrences on the street. Nick and three friends had rented the yellow house on Frat Row for their junior year. Their freedom from the tyranny of dorm life came at the price of sticky doors, a damp basement carpet, and tiny closets.

As evening fell on the first Friday of October, Nick stood in front of one such closet, considering his reflection in the cheap mirror hanging on the door. He was wearing fitted blue jeans and a short-sleeved button-down with little polka dots. Add his dark navy kicks and gray utility jacket, and this was his latest feel-good outfit. He'd worn it to dinner a couple of weeks ago, and Tony and Julia had both gushed about how good he looked. And they'd been right . . . so why did it look like shit tonight? He crossed his bedroom to his dresser, crouched down to open his T-shirt drawer. Ran his fingers over the soft cotton band tees on the left side of the drawer, contemplating a cooler look. Chris had that effortless I-don't-give-a-fuck thing going on all the time. It was the sum total of Chris's short Afro, his nose ring, his perfectly worn jeans, his attitude he wore like an aura. Nick had taken one look at himself and realized that he looked like he gave a fuck, very much so, and that was bad. He pulled out his well-worn Springsteen tee: it was faded white with his *Born in the*

U.S.A. album cover on the front. Just looking at it Nick could hear a crackling hiss, the pop of a needle, and then "Dancing in the Dark" was grooving out of his dad's record player. He was eight again; his dad was buzzed and pulling his giggling mother around the living room. They'd been fighting, but the Boss could cut through their bullshit better than anyone. It didn't matter what his mother had threatened (calling the cops, getting a divorce, "taking Nicky to my mother's and you'll never see him again"), and it didn't matter what his father had broken (a plate, a beer bottle, the window in the back door once). All Ron Hall had to do was drop the needle on that ancient record player and they made right up.

The music and any reminder of it infused him with a mixture of nostalgia, homesickness, and something like regret. It was the perfect shirt to take his look from *eager* to *brooding*.

As Nick reached for his top button, his bedroom door creaked open slowly. Mary Jo, one of his roommates, appeared in the doorway.

"You decent?"

"Not that it mattered."

She grinned. "Just tryna sneak a peekatha deek."

"Ew, get out!" He whipped the T-shirt at her, and she caught it with a shriek.

"If you still want a ride, Eric is picking me up in like ten or fifteen."

Nick grabbed his phone off the dresser. Three hours after Nick responded to the "Hey" text, Chris had suggested that they "meet for a drink."

Chris was a senior, twenty-two, and tired of house parties. Chris went out to bars. Nick wouldn't turn twenty-one until March of next year, so he was relegated to using a fake if he wanted to even get in to most bars, let alone get a drink.

Nick had responded:

Jimmy's?

Salisbury was located tantalizingly close to Ogunquit, which housed some of the best bars and clubs in southern Maine. Or so Nick had heard. All the places he'd tried to get into in Ogunquit had turned him away after one look at his fake ID. Jimmy's Pub, on the other hand, had let him in twice. Jimmy's was near campus in Salisbury; pretty divey, but it had everything you could want: dim lighting, cheap drinks, and a small, sticky dance floor. Chris hadn't responded yet, but what else was new?

"I dunno if I need a ride after all," Nick said to Mary Jo with a wave of his phone.

"Fuck Chris, okay? He's jerked you around long enough. Why don't you meet me and Eric after dinner? *We'll* go to Jimmy's with you!"

Nick's phone vibrated in his hand. He looked down to see Chris had responded.

It read:

Interesting choice. 10?

Nick couldn't help but grin. Mary Jo was right—Chris did like to jerk him around—but right now, Nick didn't care.

"As much as I'd love to third-wheel it," Nick said, "looks like I've got a date."

Mary Jo rolled her eyes. "What did he say?"

"He thinks I'm interesting, and he's meeting me at ten."

"Ten? TEN? It's barely past seven and you've been texting all day and he wants to meet you at ten. He's a *jerk*, Nick; he's not even pretending this isn't a hookup."

Elle's head appeared in the doorway behind Mary Jo. "I wasn't eavesdropping," their roommate began, "but if I had been"—she pushed her way around Mary Jo—"I would have an idea for you." She plopped herself onto Nick's unmade bed and brushed a hand through her glossy black hair. "*We* go to Jimmy's, have a couple drinks, maybe a shot, just get a buzz on but no more." She gestured *Stop* with her hand. "When Chris shows up sometime after ten—you know he'll be late—I'll leave you alone and you can tell him off!"

"I'm not telling Chris off," Nick groaned. "You're wrong about him. I mean you're right, but you're wrong. It's so good when we're together."

"But he makes you feel like shit when you're apart," Mary Jo replied.

She was right. They were all right. Even Johnny, their other roommate and a man of few words, once said of Chris: "Seems like an ass."

Mary Jo and Elle stared at him expectantly.

"Fine! God. A couple drinks to give me the balls to tell him to shape up or get lost."

Elle squealed and clapped like a child.

"Now get out while I change!"

⟶

It was 10:38 and not a word from Chris.

Nick had made good on Elle's suggestion that he have a couple of drinks: three since they arrived just after nine, though the first was a shot of tequila. Nick wasn't exactly in the mood to rip shots, but Elle had been so sweet to come with him, and Elle was all about shots.

The first hour had zipped by. Elle had ordered them into a booth across from the bar, and she made Nick sit with his back to the door, reasoning she'd have his full attention that way. Elle was the perfect friend to keep him out of his own head, and they lightly gossiped about their roommates and other mutual friends to pass the time. When Nick pressed his phone screen and it read 9:59, he steeled himself to his plan. He would tell Chris how he felt. They'd been doing this on-and-off thing—Nick was always on; it was Chris who was wobbly—since the end of last year. He was crazy about Chris, so why didn't they just do this thing already, for real?

At 10:03, every creak of the door behind Nick rocked him with a wave of adrenaline that crashed each time he craned his head and it wasn't Chris. At 10:16, he started to feel angry.

I'm a catch, he thought, *a goddamn catch, so he needs to act like it or cut me loose. No, or* I'll *cut* him *loose.*

By 10:38, Nick had looked at his phone maybe forty times. No text, no Chris. He contemplated telling Chris not to bother coming . . . but texting him anything at all would betray how much he cared.

"Okay," Elle said loudly, slapping her palms on the sticky table. "I'm calling it. I'm going to the bathroom, then we're doing another shot and dancing. And if he shows up at all, I'll kick him in the balls and we'll leave."

Nick smiled but couldn't muster a laugh. God, he was pathetic. Why did Chris keep doing this to him? And why was Nick letting him? "Just go, I'm fine."

Elle scooched her way out of the booth, then stood over him. "Two more tequila shots," she said, then turned away.

As Nick approached the bar, he knew the night would end one of two ways. If he was lucky, he and Elle would close down Jimmy's, drinking and dancing until staff started putting the stools up on the bar. If he was lucky, the night would be a surprise hit. More likely, though, was the second outcome: Nick would take the shot, half-heartedly dance with Elle for a song or two, then steal away into the bathroom to stare at himself in the mirror. He would watch his features grow pronounced and strange under the influence of the cheap tequila and poor lighting, and he would try to discern what it was about him that was so easy to reject.

The bartender deposited the two shots in front of Nick.

"Is one of those for me?"

Nick turned toward the voice to his left. The voice's owner was settling onto a barstool. Nick hadn't seen the man come in—he'd been watching the door for Chris, and he couldn't have missed a face like this. The man was uncomfortably handsome. He wore his hair longer on the top, so a dark curl drooped over his pale forehead. Light blue eyes, high cheekbones, a dusting of facial hair. *Ho-ly shit.* It might have been the lighting, or the first three drinks, but this might be the best-looking guy who'd ever talked to Nick.

"Uh," Nick breathed. The man waited with a sly grin. *Elle will understand if I give away her shot, especially to a guy who looks like this. Actually, she'll take credit, since she sent me up here in the first place.*

"Yeah," Nick said. "Yeah, I always buy shots for guys *way* out of my league, just tryna level the playing field."

The man laughed, and Nick swelled with pride. How he had managed to put *any* words together was beyond him. He slid one glass toward the handsome stranger.

"You sure *she* won't mind?" The man nodded in the direction of the bathroom. He must have seen Elle.

"Nah," Nick said. "She probably won't even make it back to the booth—she'll be out there dancing with some girl she met in the bathroom."

The man moved the shot glass in a tight circle on the bar. "So you two have an understanding."

"Oh, yeah," Nick said. What the man meant, Nick wasn't sure, but he kept his voice confident. He felt smart, cool—the opposite of how Chris made him feel. How was that possible when he was talking to a guy who looked like he was fresh off a modeling gig?

"I'm Josh," the man said, and lifted the glass.

"Nick," he responded. He threw his head back and felt the cheap tequila wash down his throat; it tasted like burnt rubbing alcohol.

"Whew!" Josh exclaimed, looking at Nick as though he'd poisoned him. "That might be the worst tequila I've *ever* had. You must be a poor college student to drink that shit." Josh leaned forward and pulled his wallet from his snug back pocket. "Next round's on me."

As he watched the handsome stranger flag the bartender, Nick realized he'd been wrong. There was a third possible outcome tonight.

—◦—

Sunlight beamed onto Nick's throbbing face. He began to roll himself over, and his brain swirled in his skull. Nick held still for a moment, trying to ease the sensation, but instead it spread. The pain seemed to pulse down his neck, shoulders, abdomen . . . *Oh. Oh my God.* Nick shifted and felt a hot ache deep inside him. No. *No.*

In his ear, Josh's voice from last night: "You like that?"

No, *STOP*, he thought, *I'm fine, I'm fine.* He sat up, head pounding, and the pain stabbed beneath his belly. *You like that? STOP.*

He was alone. It was a motel room, small and beige and stinking of cigarettes.

He pulled back the thin comforter. Blood. There was blood on the sheets beneath his thighs.

"Oh my God." His voice was a whisper.

Was Josh still there? He listened. Heard nothing.

"Hello?"

Still nothing.

"Okay," he whispered. "You're okay."

What if Josh came back?

A thought in his head, distinct from the voice that needed to whisper: *You need to get up. You need to leave.*

Nick swung his legs out of the bed and felt a sharp, stabbing pain as he stood; he heard himself whimper, and he felt like a child. The sensation dulled into an aching burn, and the pain in his head announced itself again.

Keep moving, the voice said, *you need to leave.*

There were his clothes on the floor—he grabbed his jeans and pulled them on, leaving his underwear on the carpet. Shit, he'd get blood on his jeans. How would he get blood out of his jeans? He pulled on his T-shirt inside out and snatched up his jacket. Nick could feel his wallet in the back pocket of his pants, but where was his phone? He fumbled for it in his jacket—the pockets were empty. He got down on his hands and knees, and his brain pounded on his skull, screaming at him not to tip so far forward. There it was, under the bed. *Grab it and go.* Nick reached, closing his hand on the soft leather.

There was a sound at the door behind him, and he yelped, bringing his head straight up and cracking it on the bed frame.

"Housekeeping," a soft voice announced.

Nick pushed himself out from under the bed and onto his feet. *Cover the blood.* He pulled the comforter up, turned as the door opened. The thin woman in black startled and said, "Oh, sorry, hon, they said you checked out."

"Sorry," Nick said.

She moved out of his way as he passed through the door.

"Honey," she said, "you forgot something."

He turned to see her pointing at his briefs on the floor. A woman he didn't know was staring at his underwear. Asking him to pick it up. Assuming—correctly—that he didn't have any on.

"Sorry," he said again as he grabbed them and folded them into his jacket.

Nick stepped into the chilled morning air and immediately spotted a cab parked under the MOTEL 4 DELUXE sign on the driveway to Route 1. Jacket clutched in his hand, Nick ran down the stairs and across the lot. His mind was still caught on the housekeeper. That poor woman. She'd see the blood. She'd have to strip the bed. Or would she—what would she do when she saw blood on the sheets?

The driver rolled down the front passenger window as Nick approached. Shit. He'd spent the last of his cash at Jimmy's.

Nick gripped the window. "Do you take cards?"

"Uhhh, yeah, I'll have to call it in, but I can take a card." Cabdrivers almost always registered annoyance at this question, but this man seemed worried. "Get in, kid."

Nick sat himself gingerly in the back seat. The blood. The blood might soak through his pants, stain the seat. He sat on a hand.

"You okay, kid?" The heavy man turned to face him. He was middle-aged and wore a newsboy cap.

"What?"

"Who did that to you?"

Nick felt himself flush deeply but said nothing.

"Your face," the man said.

Nick looked above the man at the rearview mirror. His reflection was wrong. His lip was split and there was blood crusted above his eyebrow.

Give your address. "Eleven Spring Street," he said. "Please."

The driver looked at him for a beat longer and sighed. "All right."

Would the housekeeper call the police when she saw the blood? Did the motel have his name? *Check your phone.* Nick pulled out his phone. The screen was loaded with texts. Chris had texted twice, apologizing just after midnight for getting "caught up," and asking, this morning, if he could make it up to Nick. At 10:59 last night, Elle had started a group message with their roommates announcing:

NICK GETTIN IT AT JIMMYS.

This was followed by a poor-quality photo of Nick sitting at the bar with Josh and a dozen messages from Mary Jo and Elle, and one from Johnny this morning asking,

Wait, what did I miss last night?

Nick's mouth flooded with saliva.

"Pull over," he groaned. The driver obeyed, and Nick opened the door and leaned out. The fresh, dry air washed over him and the urge to vomit was suppressed. He took a couple of deep breaths. *Stop thinking about it.*

He sat back against the seat, shut the door. "Sorry."

"It's fine," the driver said. "Rough night?"

Nick was silent, and the man drove on.

When they reached the house, the cabbie took his card and called it in. Handed it back.

"You should put something cold on that face."

Whether Nick said "Thank you" aloud or just thought it, he wasn't sure.

He got out and stood on the sidewalk in front of the house, legs locked. Maybe no one would be home to keep asking questions. But then he would be alone. *There's no right thing to hope for*, the voice in his head said neutrally. *You'll just have to go inside.*

As he stepped into the entry, he heard Elle's voice carry down the hall from the kitchen. "Nick, is that you?"

"Uh, yeah," he answered, horrified to find that tears had sprung up at the sound of her voice. It was like something inside him had disconnected at the motel, and her question—*Nick, is that you*—had snapped the piece back into place.

"What happened last night?" Elle asked gleefully as she burst into the hallway. Her face fell. "What happened to your face?"

A sob burst from his mouth.

"Nick, oh my God. Nick, what happened? What did he do to you? What did he do?"

They sank to the floor together, Elle holding the sides of his face.

"Johnny! Johnny!" Elle's voice sounded strained and hysterical.

In a rush of chaos, Johnny crashed halfway down the stairs, ran back up, and came pounding down with his car keys. Elle and Johnny yelled nonsense at each other as they lifted Nick by the armpits back to his feet. He knew they were taking him to the hospital.

II.

MESS

—∼

This mess was yours,
Now your mess is mine.

VANCE JOY, "MESS IS MINE"

5

I t took me a while to see just how badly Nick's rape had hurt your family."

Julia winced at the word. Three years gone and the sound of it still scratched at her ears. Detective Rice seemed not to notice that it had bothered her.

"Nick and your husband's family were a little rough around the edges, but what you and Tony had, that was solid."

She shifted a bit in her chair.

"Did you see it coming from the beginning? I certainly didn't."

"See what coming?"

"How bad it would get."

Julia shook her head. No, she had not.

The detective held her eye for a moment, then looked down into his mug. "Now, I always sympathized with victim's families. It's a natural response to being around people going through something tragic, one, and two, it made people talk to me more, and tell me more, see? Made me better at my job."

Julia nodded, a small frown forming.

"But in your case, well, I crossed a line. I sympathized a little more than I should have, with everything that was going on, and it made me unprofessional."

Julia stared at him intently now. She'd played out endless scenarios in preparation for this day, but this featured in none of them. *Where is he going with this?* She felt herself cock her head as he went on.

"The way it all ended, with me and your family and the Ray Walker situation, I mean. I've never felt good about it."

The skin on her neck prickled at Raymond Walker's name. She had known she would hear it today, and she'd heard it a thousand times before, but she still couldn't suppress her reaction to hearing it spoken. She shifted her weight and crossed her right leg over her left. A feeling was stirring in the pit of her stomach: an emotion so palpable it nearly felt alive and separate from her—some nagging, gnawing monster she had finally lulled to sleep years ago. At Detective Rice's phone call last week, the monster had cracked an eye open. Now, with a raised head, its tail swished in anticipation.

She raised her mug to her lips and sipped.

6

John Rice, 2015

Rice sat in his car looking over his notes and Nick Hall's written statement. A cold cup of Dunkin' sat in his cup holder, nearly full to the brim. It was Sunday, late morning. He'd gone to interview Julia Hall, read Nick's written statement, checked in with the evidence technician who'd processed the motel room, talked to the Assistant District Attorney. He'd done what he could to give Nick a couple of hours of sleep, but Rice needed to conduct a recorded interview before too much more time lapsed.

He flipped through the notes he'd taken when he spoke to Officer Merlo and the nurses the day before. So far things were looking pretty good—no obvious inconsistencies or eyebrow raisers in Nick's story. Sex cases often turned into a battle of he-said-she-said, or assailant-said-victim-said, in this case. A defendant would pick apart the various records of the victim's statements (to police, doctors, anyone) looking for inconsistencies. It wasn't always an effective technique, but on the right facts or with the right defense attorney, it could work to force a crap plea deal, a weak sentence, even convince a jury to acquit. But then, none of this mattered at all if Rice didn't have a defendant; he didn't even have a suspect.

The kid was consistent on a number of important points across the statements: Nick had a total of five drinks himself that night; he was confident he could identify his rapist, "Josh," if he had the chance to see him again; Josh had two drinks that Nick saw; and Nick remembered being hit over the head just after they entered the room at the Motel 4 Deluxe. Nick said the rest was gone, until he woke up Saturday morning beat up and knowing he'd been sexually assaulted.

Nick's memory lapse was a problem. Rice had already discussed it with the Assistant District Attorney who would be handling the case. She asked Rice to circle back to it during his interview of Nick. Make sure he couldn't remember anything at all about what happened in that motel room.

And he'd been drinking—drunk victims always complicated these cases. People would question Nick's ability to remember what the assailant looked like; question whether he'd consented on account of lowered inhibitions. But if they could find "Josh," the fact that the prick had beaten Nick up so badly should make it easy enough to prove that this wasn't a consensual situation. No one consented to having their face beat up during sex, did they? The choking—that was a sexual thing for some people, and Nick had been choked. But the SANE nurse had told Rice that her exam of Nick's body would support a case of nonconsent. And they had physical evidence, bloody bedsheets. Thankfully, the cleaning woman at the motel had taken one look at the sheets and told management, so the room had been largely preserved.

A sedan pulled into the space next to him. It was Lisa Johnson, from a local victim advocacy center. He'd been glad to hear from Merlo last night that it was Lisa assigned to the case. All the advocates were good, but he'd worked with Lisa before, and she was a favorite of his. He held up his hand to her and shuffled his papers back into the manila envelope marked *N.H. 10/2/15*.

"You're late," Rice said as he shut his door.

Lisa looked at him wide-eyed and then down at her phone. "I am two minutes early."

"Yeah but I was fifteen," he said with a grin.

Lisa rolled her eyes at him and smiled wide. "You are bad, always trying to make me think *I* am bad!"

Rice led Lisa to Nick's room in the BHU. She hadn't seen Nick since he'd come over from the ER the evening before. Nick and his brother were watching TV with the door open. Facing the doorway together, there was a strong resemblance in the brow, mouth, and shoulder spread of these two men, and Rice imagined he could picture what their father might look like as well. Lisa greeted Nick and introduced herself to Tony.

Tony was convinced to step out easily enough, leaving the professionals alone with Nick.

"Cleaner this way" was all Rice had to say. Since his wife was a defense lawyer, maybe Tony understood why. Somehow Rice couldn't see sweet-faced Julia cross-examining a victim about whether they were too embarrassed to tell the truth about a sex crime in front of a family member, though, so maybe not.

Nick had been lounging on top of his bed in sweats and a T-shirt. He switched off the TV and sat back against the pillows, suddenly looking pale.

"Sorry to have to ask you to talk about this again, Nick," Rice said as he pulled a chair toward the bedside. "This should be the last of the interviews for a while."

"It's okay," Nick said quietly.

"I just need to get a complete statement from you while your memory's still good; it might fade with time, so we should get the details down now."

Nick nodded.

Rice pulled out his recorder and set it on his chair's thin armrest. If they'd been able to do this at the station the interview would have been video recorded, but with the kid in the BHU for the next couple of days, Rice didn't want to wait.

Rice had Nick tell his story, starting with when he woke up Friday morning. Nick filled in the details of that day that had so far gone undiscussed: breakfast at home, a class called Business English, homework and lunch back at his apartment, Economics 101 class, then home again for the rest of the afternoon and early evening.

When Nick got into the part Rice already knew, he was consistent with his written statement and the shorter version he'd told Merlo when he first got to the hospital. Nick had planned to meet a guy named Chris Gosling at Jimmy's Pub. His roommate Elle Nguyen had gone to the bar with him, and Chris had never shown up. Instead, Nick met Josh. After some time at the bar, they took a cab to the Motel 4 Deluxe, where Josh was staying. They stepped into the motel room, and Nick felt a blow to the back of his head. Fade to black until morning.

"Okay," Rice breathed as he shifted to cross his legs. "Thank you, Nick. Do you need anything before I ask you some questions about your story?"

"Bathroom break? Water?" Lisa spoke for the first time in about twenty minutes.

"No." The kid wanted this over with, that was for sure.

"Okay," Rice said as he flipped back in his notes. "First, let's go back to the bar with Josh. He never gave you a last name?"

Nick shook his head.

"Could you say yes or no out loud?" Rice pointed to the tape recorder.

"Sorry, no. No last name. Just Josh."

"Can you remember anything he said about himself?"

Nick was quiet for a while and said, "He didn't really talk about himself, but he seemed, like, kind of rich, maybe like a business guy or something."

"How long were you together at the bar?"

"Well, if I could use my phone I could give you more specifics."

"By all means!" This was good news. Anything with a timestamp would be helpful.

Nick produced a black smartphone from under his bed covers. These kids were never more than six inches from their devices; it was probably going to give them all cancer by fifty.

"First off, I know it wasn't eleven yet when I went up to the bar to get two shots for me and Elle. I had been looking at my phone a lot waiting to see if Chris was gonna show up. He was supposed to be there at ten. It was sometime after ten thirty but not eleven yet."

"Good," Rice quietly prompted.

"And Josh started talking to me within, like, a minute of me being at the bar. He might have been just getting there, but I'm not sure on that. And we were still talking at eleven forty-two, since Elle told me she sent this right when she took it." He turned his phone toward Rice to reveal a photo of two men at a bar.

"Hold up, is this you and him?"

"Yeah," Nick said, an unspoken *Duh?* hovering in the drawn-out *h*.

Rice took the phone in his hand. "You have a *photo* of him."

"Yeah, I told that to the cop last night. He said you guys would get it from me."

For fuck's sake. Rice was going to chew out Merlo the second he saw that moron back at the station. What if something had happened to the photo? What if the kid hadn't brought it up again?

"Can you email me this picture right this second?"

Nick raised his eyebrows in surprise. "Yeah, sure."

Rice's heart rate began to come back down when the email from Nick loaded on his phone. He forwarded it to the admin with the directive:

PRINT.

When he looked up, Lisa was looking at him with wide eyes and a tight smile.

"Well, okay," Rice breathed. "So we have a picture."

"Yeah, it's a little dark and far away, but he's the one facing the camera more, and I'm the one turned away. Elle took it from over near the dance floor."

Rice studied the photo more carefully. The lighting wasn't great, but the figures were clear: two men at a bar, one facing the camera, the other turned away. Rice zoomed in on the face. Josh, if that was his real name, looked like Nick had described him: Caucasian with dark features; older than Nick.

"So, sometime between ten thirty and eleven you meet, and at eleven forty-two you're still at the bar, and he didn't tell you where he lived, what he did?"

"No." Nick looked crestfallen.

"Nick, I'm not blaming you. My point is, well, did he have you talking about yourself?"

Nick nodded. "He wanted to know all about me."

Rice took a long look at Nick's face. His cuts looked uglier today, darker, and his bruising was worse. There were purple lines on the left side of his neck now. Nick only remembered one blow to the head, but he'd been hit multiple times and choked. A man didn't just unleash on a stranger like this once without having done something like it before. And he'd probably do it again.

Nick had said earlier that Josh asked if Elle would mind Nick talking to him. Nick seemed to think Josh meant to ask if Nick's friend would be angry to be ditched for a hookup. Rice had other suspicions. This Josh— he thought Elle was a beard, a fake girlfriend. And he'd asked Nick if he'd "done this" before. Maybe he didn't mean going home with a stranger. Maybe he meant sex with a man.

Josh thought Nick was in the closet. Maybe he'd done this before, to men who didn't want to out themselves by reporting the assault.

"Do you need a break?" Lisa asked softly.

Nick shook his head.

"He just bought you the one drink?"

Nick's eyes shifted from Lisa back to Rice. "Yeah."

Rice glanced down at his notepad. "So you had a shot of tequila when you got there around nine, two whiskey ginger ales between nine and ten thirty, another shot of tequila, this time sitting at the bar with the man, and then he ordered you an old-fashioned?"

"Yeah."

"So if you met him around ten thirty or eleven, how fast did you have that last drink?"

"I dunno. I was kind of milking it, because it was disgusting."

Rice and Lisa both laughed.

Nick smiled. "I'd never had one before. But I drank the whole thing. I wanted to look like, you know. Like I drank real drinks."

"You finished it before you left?"

"Yeah."

"When was that?"

Nick looked back at his phone. "At twelve seventeen Elle texts the group chat that I just left with him."

Rice triple-circled Elle Nguyen's name on his notepad. Megan O'Malley, another detective in his office, was interviewing Nguyen, along with the other roommate who'd driven Nick to the hospital. A Johnny Maserati. Ridiculous name. Rice would call O'Malley from the car and follow up.

"Would you say you were drunk?"

"Is it bad if I was?"

Yes, Rice thought. "I'm just trying to understand how you were feeling when you left."

Nick nodded slowly. "Drunk. Not, like, sloppy."

"Okay."

"More just . . . tipsy, I guess."

"But you didn't black out, or brown out, or anything?"

"No," Nick said. "No, I remember everything until he hit me."

It was helpful to know what Nick could remember from earlier in the night, but, in Rice's view, it didn't mean the alcohol hadn't contributed to the memory lapse he was suffering. Maybe the blow to the head caused an injury that combined with the effects of the alcohol. If they could get enough to hand the case over to the DA's office, the state would need to find an expert.

"Okay," Rice said. "Who asked who to leave?"

"He asked me. And he asked me if I'd ever had a one-night stand before."

"He did?"

"Yeah." Nick looked to his side like he was remembering. "He asked if I'd 'done this' before. But I think he meant hooked up with someone I didn't know."

Or, maybe he was asking if Nick had ever had sex with a man before. This "Josh," he was carefully choosing who he brought back to his room.

"Okay," Rice said. "So you left at twelve seventeen, and you cabbed to the Motel 4 Deluxe?"

"Right. He paid for the cab with cash. That reminds me, though, I did ask him about Motel 4, because seriously? And he said something about his company paying for it and they're all about the bottom line. Like that was why he was in such a shitty motel."

"So he made it seem like he was from out of town?"

Nick nodded. Rice pointed to the recorder, and Nick said, "Sorry, yes."

"Did you ask him about why he was in town?"

"He just said business." Nick paused and flushed. "He said he didn't really want to talk business tonight." The kid's eyes began to well up as he shrugged.

Lisa passed him a box of tissues, whispering, "This was not your fault."

Once, a couple of years ago during an interview of a rape victim, the victim advocate had said something like that when the victim started crying. Afterward, Rice had told the advocate, a petite, quiet woman, that she really shouldn't say things like that during the recorded interviews— didn't want a defense attorney calling them biased or saying they were reinforcing the victim's version of events. The woman had looked at him incredulously and seemed to swell in size as she said, "I understand that you're building your case, Detective, but once this is over for you, it's not over for her, so if I see a survivor struggling with feelings of guilt, I'm going to tell her it's not her fault." Rice had been floored, and he never complained about anything a victim advocate did again.

Nick wiped his eyes, blew his nose, and looked back to Rice. He wanted to keep going. Tough kid.

"Can you walk me through entering the room one more time? Go slower."

"There's not much slower to go. We went up to the door, Josh already had a key card. He opened the door; we went in. I shut the door, then I felt him hit me on the head." Nick shrugged. "That's all I remember."

"What was happening as you walked up to the room? Anything between you two?"

"I was going there to hook up with him, if that's what you mean."

"No, well, I mean were you holding hands, talking, uh, kissing, anything?" Rice hoped his hesitance had gone unnoticed. He knew people were gay, it was a thing, it was fine, none of his business, but he had a hard time asking the more intimate questions.

"We had started making out during the cab ride," Nick said, "and he took my hand as we walked to the room." He paused. "We kissed outside the door before we went in. It was . . . I thought we were, like, really compatible, I guess I'm saying. I don't know why he . . ." Nick shrugged and took a sharp breath.

"What, ah, was the plan when you got inside?"

Nick looked confused. "Plan?"

"What had you wanted to do with him?"

Nick dropped his gaze to the tissue in his lap. "Just hook up, I guess."

"But what does that mean, for you?"

Nick's eyes hardened. "I didn't have a plan," he said. "I was gonna take it one thing at a time. I didn't know I needed a plan."

"I don't mean to say you did, I just had to ask." Rice's neck flushed with itchy heat. "I'm not blaming you."

Nick looked up at him. "I know."

"You see what he used to hit you?"

Nick shook his head. "I was looking the other way. And it was still dark in the room. It happened so fast."

"And that's it? You don't remember anything else?"

"I don't know what else you want."

"I want to find this guy, and when we find him I want to nail him. It could be your word against his. If you remember stuff later, that's fine, but it always looks a little . . ."

Nick dropped his gaze back to his lap.

"The sooner you give us information, the more believable it looks. Does that make sense?"

Nick stared at his lap and nodded, pulling the tissue to moist shreds.

"So nothing else?"

Nick shook his head.

"Did you, ah, clean yourself up at all at the motel?"

"I just got dressed and left."

"Okay," Rice said. The evidence tech had found a dirty towel in the bathroom. If Nick hadn't used it, maybe Josh had. If they were lucky, it would give them his DNA.

Rice asked Nick a few questions about the morning after, then turned off his recorder. Before he left, he had Nick hand off his phone and sign a consent form so they could pull the data off it, and another for his medical records.

"Thanks for your time, Nick. I know this was hard."

Nick shrugged like it had been nothing, but his eyes were tired.

Rice stuck his head out into the hallway. A nurse told him Tony's wife had shown up and they'd gone to the cafeteria.

"I'll stop by the caf on my way out," Rice said to Nick. "Send them back to you."

"I will wait with you," Lisa said.

Nick looked spent, but if he didn't want her there, he was too polite to say so.

7

When Detective Rice left, Nick and Lisa were quiet for a moment. Nick understood now why people called it "giving" a statement. With his words, he'd given away his energy. He lay back into the pillows behind him, staring down at the loaner T-shirt and sweatpants Dr. Lamba had given him. His eyelids felt heavy.

"Okay," Lisa said. "I will only ask once, but I must: How are you feeling?"

Coming from anyone else, the question would have bothered him. Might have even enraged him. But from Lisa, it was genuine. She knew he wasn't okay, and she didn't expect him to pretend he was. At the same time, she didn't look at him like everyone else did, like his life was over. To Lisa, all of this—police interviews and hospital beds and *rape*—was just something that happened sometimes.

Nick liked Lisa. He wanted to give her the truth, but he searched and felt nothing. "I don't know," he said.

Lisa said nothing, prompting him to try again.

"I keep saying I'm fine. I almost *do* feel fine. Like nothing." In his lap, Nick rolled the pieces of shredded tissue into a ball. During the nurse's exam in the ER, he'd felt like he wasn't there. It wasn't his body she was peering into. Wasn't him she was photographing, naked in a bright room. "Why do I feel so little?"

"Your body, your mind, they are protecting you. It is your way of easing into the knowledge of what happened. There is nothing wrong with you."

That was good. Nothing wrong with him.

That was the other thing he liked about Lisa. Not once did he see in her eyes what he had seen so many times in the past two days: second-hand shame at the sight of a man who was raped. He'd seen it in the cop's eyes, and the detective's. He'd seen it when they got to the ER, at the front desk. The woman asked why they were there.

"I think I was sexually assaulted," Nick said.

Her face had been surprised. Her eyes had flicked to Elle and back to Nick. "You were sexually assaulted?" she asked. Implicit was the question: *Did you mean to say that* she *was?*

To Lisa, nothing was wrong with Nick.

"The next part will be bad, right?" The day before, Lisa and the nurses had given Nick pamphlets and a folder of information specially made for rape survivors. Eventually, the deep freeze he felt now would thaw. Instead of his normal self, though, those pages said he might be depressed, guilty, sleepless, suicidal.

"Maybe," Lisa said. "It is truly a bit different for everyone. Dr. Lamba told me you will be seeing Jeff Thibeault when you leave."

The therapist. "Yeah," Nick said.

"Jeff is a wonderful man." Lisa's broad face spread into a pleasant smile, like she knew Jeff well. "I think you will like him. And if you don't, you find someone else. You choose who is on your team. You decide."

Nick nodded. That would feel good: to be in control. He hadn't felt in control since—well, since he left the bar with Josh. Elle and Johnny had taken him to the hospital. He remembered them talking over his head, Elle saying they had to go to the hospital, Johnny asking if they should go to the police instead.

"He's hurt," Elle kept saying. "He's hurt."

When he saw Elle in the apartment, a dam had broken in him and he'd cried too hard to talk. Too hard to say, *Yes, take me to the hospital; no, don't call the police*. Elle called 9-1-1 in the car on the way. And then suddenly, the tears stopped. He could speak again, but she'd already called the police, already told them Nick's name, the hospital they were driving to. So Nick grew calm again. He grew calm, and he made a plan.

"Your brother loves you very much," Lisa said.

Nick nodded. "Yeah."

Tony being so upset had been the worst moment so far, worse than every humiliation he'd felt seeing the housekeeper and knowing she would find his blood on the sheets; worse than the two-hour exam; worse than talking to the nurse, and the officer, and the detective, one after another. Nick had felt pain, actual pain in his chest, when they released themselves from that first hug and he saw that Tony had been crying.

"How old is your brother?"

"Uh, twenty plus seventeen is thirty-seven."

"Seventeen years apart!"

Nick gave his normal two-word explanation: "Different moms."

Lisa cocked her head. "Where is your mom now?"

"She's, ah, not good with this kind of thing." How could he explain? It wasn't worth the effort. "She gets upset. It would be hard."

Lisa nodded. Her eyes were curious, but she didn't pry.

"Tony takes care of me fine," Nick said, but he was underselling it. Tony was more than fine at taking care of Nick; he'd been doing it Nick's whole life. They weren't like any of the other sets of siblings Nick knew. They didn't fight. They were never in competition for food, toys, attention, anything like that. They hadn't grown up together: Tony had grown up without Nick. Tony was an adult in every memory Nick had of him. He was almost like an extra parent. He remembered Tony buying him things—ice cream cones and action figures. He remembered Tony taking him to the playground by Nick's house. He remembered them playing games, so many games, but not as equals. He'd always been the kid, and Tony the cool guy Nick wanted to be.

Lisa shifted in her seat. "Do you have questions for me, while I'm here?"

"What are the chances they'll find him?"

Lisa shook her head. "I don't know."

For some reason, ever since Nick had made it safely into the cab outside the motel on Saturday morning, it hadn't occurred to him that he might see Josh again. Even after the examination, the swabs, the questions, the photo he told the cop he had. He knew Elle had called the police. The police were there to solve crimes—solving crimes meant finding the bad guy.

They had a shitty photo of Josh. If his name even *was* Josh. They had whatever they got from Nick's body yesterday. So maybe they had Josh's DNA, but maybe not. Maybe they wouldn't find him. Maybe, after some time, the police would give up, and maybe one day Nick would wake up and he wouldn't remember any of it.

8

TONY HALL, 2015

It turned out, the taste of hospital food changed depending on why you were at the hospital in the first place. This obvious truth had not occurred to Tony the first two times he ate at a hospital: first, after Julia had given birth to Chloe, and again after Sebastian. On neither occasion had the food been *good* by any stretch of the word. But anything, anything at all, would have tasted fine on those days. Damp sandwiches, weak coffee, packaged pudding cups. They had all sated his need to eat something, anything, so he could get back to his new baby, his wife, their excitement.

Today, he'd have rather fasted. When Julia showed up to see Nick, the detective was interviewing him, so she started in on Tony, nagging him to eat something. *Nagging* wasn't fair—she knew how upset he was. Knew he wouldn't have eaten. So they'd gone to the cafeteria, and Tony had selected the blandest thing available: ham and cheese on white bread. With every bite he took, the soft bread stuck to the roof of his mouth. Eating felt wrong, so wrong that he felt the tickle of his gag reflex kicking in.

They sat together in silence, Tony working at his sandwich, Julia sipping coffee.

When Tony looked up, Detective Rice was walking across the cafeteria.

"We're all set," the detective said. "Thanks for stepping out for so long."

Tony nodded. The bite he'd just taken was at the back of his mouth,
resisting descent.

"It was no problem," Julia said for him. "It gave me the chance to
make him eat something."

"What'd you get?"

Tony took a sip from his Styrofoam cup. The coffee took the lump of
sandwich with it. "Ham," Tony said.

"I've had it." Rice nodded. "Not great."

Julia laughed. Tony cleared his throat, pushed the plate forward on
the table.

"Hey, Nick did great today. One of the hard parts is behind him now."

Tony nodded. Good to have it over. The detective had been in there
with him for hours.

"How long until the sexual assault kit comes back?" Julia asked. Tony
wondered if she'd told the detective that she used to be a defense attorney. She knew more than most people did about the world Nick was
stepping into. He grabbed her hand and squeezed it, grateful to have her.

"No promises," Rice said, "but probably about a month."

"Oh," she said. "I thought it would take longer."

Tony was surprised. A month sounded like a long time to wait.

"No," Rice said. "Not usually. Our crime lab normally turns them
around pretty quick. Since Nick's willing to prosecute and we don't know
who did it, we've already sent the kit up to Augusta." He hesitated. There
was something he wasn't saying. "We don't know if the kit will be much
use, you know?"

In his peripheral vision, Tony saw Julia nod.

Tony didn't know what that meant. Before he could ask for explanation, the detective spoke. "But, hey, Nick gave me a lead."

Tony's stomach fluttered. "He did?"

Rice nodded. "Yeah, I mean, no guarantees. But he has a photo of the guy."

"Oh my God," Julia said. They shared a glance. There was excitement in her eyes. A photo. A photo was good.

"So now," Rice said, "we share the bastard's face. See if anyone knows him."

⁓

When Detective Rice left, he took their silence with him.

Julia turned her body toward Tony. "Did you know there was a photo?"

"No," he said.

"Me neither. That's huge."

"What did he mean about the kit not being useful?"

"Oh," Julia said. She set down her coffee. "I think he means that there might not be DNA in the kit. The hope is that they got the guy's DNA. From Nick."

"I get it," Tony said. That was enough. He didn't want to think about that. "So if that takes a month . . ."

"I know," she said. "It's all going to take a long time."

"If they find him, what comes next?"

Julia picked up her coffee again. "I guess it depends. They might arrest him right away, might wait until they indict him, with a grand jury. I don't know how they make their decisions—I think every department does it their own way. I never had a sex case in Salisbury."

Tony frowned. "A sex case?"

"Oh." She winced. "That's what people called them. Sometimes. I mean a sexual assault case." She paused. "I'm sorry."

Tony turned his eyes back to his sandwich. It stung, to hear her say something like that. The words felt callous and gross.

"It's just shorthand for a case that involves a sex crime," she said. "I know what happened to Nick wasn't sex."

When Julia had been a defense attorney, she talked about a lot of her cases in broad strokes, but he couldn't remember her talking about any that involved sexual assault.

"So you've had one before in the towns you covered?"

"Nothing specifically like this," she said.

"But sexual assault cases?"

She hesitated. "Yes."

She hadn't talked about those cases at home. Maybe she'd been ashamed. He'd never thought about it before, but the thought of Julia defending rapists . . . it was off-putting, to say the least.

Not that she'd had much choice over the cases she got. That wasn't how it worked. She had been a court-appointed lawyer, paid by the state to defend people who were poor enough to qualify for a free lawyer. Mostly she talked about her juvenile clients—teenagers who'd been charged with crimes—but he knew she defended adult criminals, too. Then there were the parents in the child protection cases . . . parents who'd abused or neglected their kids so much that the state had stepped in. He knew she helped those people, but he couldn't understand how she could face them, why she would do that kind of work. So, she didn't talk about it. She and Tony got along best when they both pretended it wasn't part of her job.

Maybe she hadn't been ashamed to defend rapists. Maybe she just hadn't trusted Tony not to judge her for it.

And maybe she'd been right. That she could look those people in the eye and treat them like they were anyone else, regardless of what they were accused of . . . he might have judged her for it before. Might have judged her just now, in his mind a moment ago. But he was lucky, he realized. So lucky to have a wife who was calm in the face of darkness.

"How bad is it going to be?" he asked.

"For Nick?"

Tony nodded.

She looked at him like she was weighing how much truth he could handle. "Honestly," she said, "I think it's gonna suck."

9

The house was ready for Nick's arrival. Seb was all set up to sleep in Chloe's bedroom. There were fresh sheets on Seb's bed for Nick. Tony and Julia had even picked up some of Nick's favorite snacks on the way to the hospital. All that was left was to sit through a discharge meeting with Ron and Jeannie.

Whenever someone left the structure and safety of hospitalization, it was important to have a meeting where the patient and his people made a plan for what would come next. Julia had been to discharge meetings before, but always as someone's attorney. Nick's meeting felt different.

It was happening in a small conference room in the behavioral health unit. As they all sat around the sterile table, Dr. Lamba told the Halls about Nick's treatment plan going forward.

"We've connected him with a therapist about ten minutes from campus," she said. "It'll be easy for him to get a ride there when he eventually moves home."

Jeannie turned to her son with wide eyes. "You'll stay with us first?"

"Don't he have school?" Ron's question caught Julia off guard. Until that moment, he'd looked like he was on another planet, staring at the center of the table with glassy eyes. The subtext of his question was clear:

he didn't want his son coming home with them. Judging by the bready smell of beer wafting off him, he wasn't handling the news of Nick's assault well.

"My professors said I can take some time," Nick said. "I'm gonna figure it out as I go."

"Mummy can drive you to school," Jeannie said with a hint of baby voice.

Julia looked to Dr. Lamba, hoping she would deliver the news that Nick had already decided to come stay in Orange.

"Tony's house is much closer to the school and his new therapist," Dr. Lamba said.

And unlike your house, Julia thought, *it's emotionally stable.*

Jeannie turned to Julia. "But you have the kids."

"They're excited for their uncle Nick to stay with us," Julia said.

"So you knew."

Julia felt herself flushing. "Yesterday we talked—"

"Right," Jeannie said. "Yesterday. See, we didn't know yesterday." She motioned to herself and Ron. "We get a little meeting on his way out the door of the *hospital*. Been here since Saturday, we get the call Monday." She turned to Dr. Lamba now. "And I know, 'he's an adult, he makes his own decisions,' but did it occur to you that he is still a child mentally?"

Tony cut in. "What are you even *talking* about?"

"Not even old enough to drink," Jeannie said. "Not an adult in the eyes of the law."

"He is, though," said Dr. Lamba. Her face was calm, but a hardness had edged into her voice.

"You're all sitting here," Jeannie said, "pretending we're a little team, thinking we're too stupid to notice you've all been making the decisions for him without us."

"I'm making the decisions." Nick spoke so loudly that Julia started.

Jeannie shut her mouth.

Nick looked at his mother with a miserable frown. Even on the third day of seeing him with those bruises, his appearance was jarring. It was what her imagination did with the markings. Fists had pummeled his face. Hands had squeezed his throat.

Nick lowered his voice. "I'm making the decisions, and I didn't want to tell you yet. It was too much."

Jeannie's eyes spilled. She dug a tissue from her purse.

Under his breath, Ron said, "Who do you think put that idea in his head?"

Julia knew Tony would take the bait, but she put a hand on his thigh anyway, hopeful he'd let it slide.

"Seriously?"

"You show up on your high horse like you always do, tell him he don't need us—"

"You *wish* I told him; he knows he doesn't need you."

"Stop it, Tony!" Nick groaned and pushed his chair back. "I can't fucking breathe in here." He turned to Dr. Lamba. "Do we have to do this?"

"No," she said, "if it's not going to be helpful."

The room had fallen quiet, and with any other group Julia might have thought people were considering whether they could all behave and finish the meeting. But not with this crew. She knew the classic Jeannie exit was brewing.

"Fine," Jeannie said. "We'll go, then." She pushed her chair back and stood. "Cut right out of his life like you all wanted, until he's strong enough to think for himself." Tears streamed down her face as she moved to the door.

"I'll never forgive you," she said, maybe to all of them. "I'll never forget this as long as I live. No matter how hard you try to pretend it didn't go down like this, I will never forget, never forgive."

Jeannie opened the door and left.

Ron paused in the doorway and said loudly, "Typical," then followed her out.

No one spoke for a moment.

"And *that* is why I made you call Tony," Nick said to Dr. Lamba. He meant it to be punchy, and everyone laughed tightly, but Julia felt like crying.

Nick deserved better. He deserved to be cocooned in love, told nothing was his fault, promised he'd be kept safe. Instead, he had Ron and Jeannie.

And Tony. He had Tony, too.

10

John Rice, 2019

The descent had been swift after his retirement. Nearly overnight, John Rice became an old man, all dressed up and no place to go, just waiting for the young people to arrive—his daughter, his grandkids, and today it had been Julia. He had wandered the house he'd already cleaned, sweater tucked in, belt resting on the bones of his hips, straightening picture frames and waiting for the sound of her car.

When he saw her walking up the front path, he felt ugly and self-conscious, angry, hopeful, so many things. He welcomed her in like he'd pictured doing a million times, but he never came close to setting their meeting until a couple of weeks ago. It took that last appointment with his doctor to force himself to pick up the phone and try her old cell number. The Lord must have known how badly he needed to speak to Julia before his time came, because her number was unchanged. Now that she was here, it was hard to know where to begin.

When he had breakfast with his friends or called his daughter, he could cut to the chase of what he wanted to get at. This would be different: Julia wouldn't want to talk about where he was heading. He would have to force her along, almost like an interrogation. He would have to show her, on his own, that talk was her only option.

"The way it all ended, with me and your family and the Ray Walker situation, I mean. I've never felt good about it."

She sat in the recliner beside him, sipping at her tea in silence.

"I guess I should have known it would be a complicated case. Sexual assault cases have their unique challenges."

She nodded but kept her eyes on the floor in front of her.

"But it had felt so straightforward at the beginning. I couldn't believe how fast we found him."

In the week following Nick's attack, Rice and Megan O'Malley, another detective from the department, interviewed the motel staff. Collected the bloody bedsheets and a towel from the bathroom. Tracked down the woman who rented the room; she'd been paid to do it by a handsome man who approached her where she'd been panhandling near the motel. They interviewed the bartender at Jimmy's and a few customers who'd been there that night. Jimmy's was cash only, so there was no record of a name, and no one knew the man who'd called himself Josh— the man Rice now knew to be Raymond Walker.

That first week, O'Malley hit the books and made a couple of calls to try to figure out what kind of rapist they were looking for. Since Nick was beaten up so badly, O'Malley thought they were probably looking for one of two types of rapists: one driven by anger, or one driven by sadism. If their suspect was driven by rage, he'd likely have a criminal history and be known for outbursts. If he was a sadist, well, there were two types, but given the damage to Nick's body, he was probably the *overt* type—the type who tried to cause his victim pain. Ditto the criminal history, and probably low intelligence. These were imperfect generalizations, but they were a start.

All that said, they knew Nick's assailant was likely to be a guy who flew under the radar. A man whose charisma would blind people to his less-attractive characteristics.

When they did find Walker, the looks and the charm were apparent. At the time, Rice and O'Malley didn't know how far off they were on the rest.

11

The first few days with Nick in the house were long ones.

On Monday after the discharge meeting, they brought Nick to his apartment in Salisbury so he could pack up some clothes. Julia put on a CD in the car, and they drove without speaking, listening to Alicia Keys. They reached Orange and drove through the town center, past the historic manors and the elementary school. Past the two rival gas stations, the library, the park. Past the housing developments creeping into the country. They carried Nick out to the farmland, where their house sat on the edge of a field their neighbor owned.

The kids had been excited for a long-term sleepover with their uncle, but the uncle who arrived that Monday was not his usual playful self, and they quickly grew indifferent to his presence.

On Tuesday, Nick borrowed Julia's car and went to his first counseling session. He returned to the house raw and edgy, sniping at Tony and crying abruptly without warning. To his credit, he reserved these small outbursts for when the kids were outside or upstairs.

The next two days, Nick seemed like a ghost, drifting in and out of rooms, either unsure of how to interact with the family or too tired to bother. Although Julia worked from home, she had a home office, so at least she was out of his way during the daytime.

Her workspace was at the end of the hallway on the second floor with the bedrooms. Each morning, after Tony had left for his office in Portland and the kids had been delivered to the school bus, Julia took the stairs to the second floor and paused on the landing to listen. Nick had slept late each morning, once into the afternoon. After her daily check on Nick, she made her way down the hall to her tiny study, closing the door as quietly as she could.

The room had once been a large, mostly useless closet on the second floor of the house. Five years ago, Julia had returned from the movies with her best friend, Margot, to find that the outing had been a ruse: while she'd been gone, Tony had converted the closet into an office for her. At the time, she was pregnant with Seb, Chloe's stuff was everywhere, and Julia was trying—and failing—to do her new job in policy from home. In a single, frantic afternoon, Tony had emptied the closet, painted the walls lavender, and assembled bookshelves and a standing desk with an adjustable stool. He was covered in sweat when she got home from the movies.

Some days when Julia opened the office door, she swore she could smell the fresh paint again, and for a second she was transported back to that day. A day she had been exceedingly grateful to have a husband who had never met a problem he wouldn't try to fix. In truth, it was not always her favorite trait of Tony's.

On Friday, late morning, she was standing in the open doorway of the study, mind adrift in the history of the room, when she heard Seb's door creak open behind her. She turned and saw that Nick had gone down the hall toward the bathroom.

"Hey, good morning!"

Nick startled violently, spun to face her.

"Oh, jeez, I'm sorry." Julia stepped into the hallway.

His face ran white, but he brought a hand to his chest in relief. "It's fine," he said.

"I'm so sorry."

"Really," he said, before she'd finished saying the word. He smiled and rubbed at the back of his head. "Mind if I shower?"

"No, of course not."

He started to turn away, then pivoted back. "And I have counseling today."

"I know," she said. Julia could feel her cheeks growing warm, her body continuing to register what she'd done. She'd spooked him, yelling out like that. He was probably extra sensitive to things like loud noises right now. He'd suffered a trauma, and she should have known better. *Stupid*. "You can take my car again. I don't need it back until two."

Nick nodded.

She stood in the hallway for a while after he closed the bathroom door. It was invasive, she knew that, but she was listening for sounds of crying. There was nothing, and then the shower came on.

She went back to her study and closed the door.

⟜

A bit after two, Julia opened that door to a silent house. She called out and heard nothing. Wandered the house. The driveway was empty. She called Nick's cell, but he didn't answer.

Therapy could have run long. Nick might just be taking time to himself. He kept saying he was fine but she knew he wasn't. There was no way he could be. He was trying so hard to act normal for them. She wished he would stop—just let it out. No good would come from hiding how he was feeling, not from his family.

She should have been relieved to be alone—free to bang around without worrying about startling Nick or wondering what he was thinking.

She only felt uneasy.

12

Jeff's office was on a back road in Wells. The road was Route Something, Nick couldn't remember. He'd just followed the GPS both times he'd driven here. It was a road that snaked through the woods; the kind of road that invited you to roll down the windows, turn up the radio, and floor it. Nick had not done this on either drive to see Jeff. He came down the front steps of the building and thought absently that it was fall. The air, the leaves, the sky—everything was crisp in the fall. The world around him was sharp, and his edges had melted.

He took a deep breath, hoped the clean air would ease his headache. Talk therapy was supposed to help him "get through this." That's what Dr. Lamba had told him, and Jeff had repeated it. So far, the only thing he was sure it did for him was give him a throbbing headache, as if a vise were clamped at the base of his skull. He brought his hand to the spot where the pain was the worst, then his fingers climbed higher until they found the scab.

He'd found it in the shower, on Tuesday morning. In a way, it was the simplest of his physical injuries to focus on. It was a far subtler reminder than the private, intrusive ache that had finally faded away sometime that week. It had nothing on the stomach-wrecking course of antibiotics the hospital had prescribed him to fight off potential STDs, or the bruises on his face and neck that announced to anyone who saw them that he was a *victim*. The cuts and splits on his face were nebulous—they could have been from a bar fight or a drunken fall in the street—but the fingerlike bruising on his neck was damning. He had been choked . . . dominated. *Victimized*.

So the scab was nothing, but he still couldn't keep his hands off it. He found it while he was washing his hair: it was a crusty bump, near the top-back part of his scalp. He'd fingered it curiously through shampoo suds and inspected it a second time with slick, conditioned hands. As he rinsed his hair, Nick rubbed the scab until he felt it crumble away. *There*. That was better.

The next morning, he awoke in his nephew's bed to find that the bump had returned. It was softer and tender to the touch. He flicked at it with his middle finger until he felt it scrape clean. It stung that time, but at least it was gone. Just a day ago, *again* he'd caught himself searching for the scab at the back of his head.

The urge to pick at it while he sat in Jeff's office today had been brutal. He'd wedged his fingers beneath the edges of his thighs and tried to focus on Jeff's face.

Jeff was as Dr. Lamba said he would be. He was kind of old, older than Nick's dad, and had a deep, relaxing voice. He laughed and smiled a lot. He seemed smart but not in an in-your-face way.

"I'm a survivor of childhood sexual abuse," Jeff said in their first session, earlier that week. He said it without shame, like he might have said anything about himself. He had said it, Nick was sure, to make Nick feel less embarrassed about what had happened. Nick had not pointed out how different they were: Jeff had been a child. Nick had not.

Another thing that both Jeff and Dr. Lamba had said was that therapy would help Nick "own" his "story."

"Why would I want to *own* this?" Nick had asked Dr. Lamba over the weekend.

She'd tilted her head. "Because it's yours."

"What if I'm not ready?"

"Jeff won't ask you to talk about it much, not at first. You'll do it over time, and slowly, you'll practice talking about it. Eventually, you can decide what to do with the story."

This had been a strange way to put it, he thought now as he stepped into the parking lot below Jeff's office and checked his phone. He had a missed call and a voice mail, and even though he hadn't saved the number, he recognized it. Detective Rice had called him while he was in therapy. It was funny that the therapists thought Nick could process the story on his own terms. That was bullshit.

He scratched at his head until he felt the scab lift off under his fingernail. He flicked it onto the pavement, then he called Detective Rice back.

"We'd like you to come into the station," the detective said. "We have a photo lineup for you to view."

⟶

The police station was not what Nick had expected. He'd imagined his first sight would be something like a city precinct on a TV show: a bullpen of desks, maybe a cell where some town drunk would be sleeping off a bad night. The door to Salisbury's police station, instead, opened to a simple lobby. Sterile walls, linoleum tiles like a school. A white-haired woman sat across the room behind a desk and a thick pane of glass. She asked cheerily how she could help him. Nick introduced himself, and she called Detective Rice on the phone.

After a minute or so, Nick heard a door slam across the empty lobby. A petite, dark-skinned woman stepped from the doorway. She was really quite pretty, with long eyelashes and a bright smile. She was an officer—she wasn't in uniform, but it was clear from her posture and stride.

"I'm Detective O'Malley."

Nick shook her extended hand. "Nick."

"I wanted to take the opportunity to meet you," she said. "I've been working with Detective Rice on your case. Your friend Elle might have mentioned me."

Elle hadn't. They hadn't talked at all yet. Elle had texted Nick a few times, checking on him, but he hadn't responded. There was nothing to say.

"Let's go up and look at some photos."

He followed her up a narrow stairwell and down a hall to a small room where a heavyset man in uniform was waiting. Detective O'Malley waited in the hallway, and Nick stepped into the room. On the table was a closed manila folder.

The cop smiled and said, "Hi, Nick."

Nick returned the greeting.

The man introduced himself and handed Nick a sheet of paper. "These are instructions for the photo array," he said, and waved at the folder on the table. "Please take your time and read them."

When Nick finished reading, he lowered the sheet. The cop told him he could open the folder and look at the photos. "Leave it like that as you open it," he said, indicating how the folder was laid horizontally on the table. "So that the top of the folder blocks my view."

Taped in the folder was a grid of photos of men's faces. Two down, three across—six in all. They weren't mug shots; they looked more like headshots than anything. Each photo had a numbered label in the corner.

There, at the bottom left of the grid, was Josh. The photo was like a magnet; Nick's gaze fell on it almost instantly. No stubble in this picture, but the light eyes, the high cheekbones, even the single dark curl on his forehead.

"Call me Josh," this man had said to him, nearly in a drawl, the name had spilled so slowly from his mouth.

Bile rose in Nick's throat. His picture looked like a business portrait. He looked important. Nick could feel the cop staring at him.

"He's here," Nick said, and his voice sounded sad. Was he sad?

"Which one, Nick?"

The moment was so surreal that something in Nick's mind detached and spoke, separate from himself. It was an indifferent voice, pointing out a simple truth. *This will be the moment you will always identify as the one from which there was no turning back. Not the report. Not the forms. Not the interviews. This moment.* Nick turned and looked behind him, expecting to see the detective in the doorway, but the door was closed. Nick turned back to the table.

"Him," Nick said, and he placed a finger on the hollow of Josh's throat. "Number four."

"Where do you recognize him from?"

Nick lifted his finger from the photo. "That night. At the bar."

"Can you be more specific?"

Nick looked up at the cop. His fleshy face was relaxed, but his bright eyes were trained on Nick's. This man—the police—they needed him to say it. To say it *again*, to *another* person. The more people he told, the bigger it got, and the further it slipped from him.

"He's the man who assaulted me."

"How confident are you?"

The officer's eyebrows jumped and fell so quickly Nick might have missed it if he'd blinked. It wasn't a real question. This was a script. The officer knew what Nick would say. There was only one acceptable answer.

Nick looked down at the photo. "Positive."

13

John Rice, 2015

Say what you will about its part in the decline of American culture, but social media was a beautiful thing from a law-enforcement perspective. It could show you who knew who, what people called themselves, where they were at a specific point in time. People would post incriminating photos and statements that could be screenshotted and placed in a file long after a post was deleted. Rice would never get sick of seeing what social media could do for them next. Just now, it had delivered him a rape suspect.

O'Malley had put the photo of Josh and Nick at the bar on the station's Facebook and Twitter accounts and asked people to share it. In the post, she called Josh "a witness to a crime." He and O'Malley had talked over the wording of the post for a while in advance. What they knew of Nick's assailant was that he was calculating, charming, and violent. To them, he smelled like a serial rapist. He was handsome, white, possibly well-off. Most of this added up to a guy who people probably didn't see as a monster. Maybe he seemed a little *off*; on the flipside, it was even possible he was well-liked. It was doubtful people saw him as the kind of guy who could be a rapist. If someone who actually knew Josh saw the photo of him with the caption "suspect in a rape case," they'd think, *That couldn't be Josh, even if it does look just like him.* But "a witness"? *Yeah*, they'd think, *that could be Josh in the photo.* And that morning, Rice walked into the station and learned it had done the trick.

The evening before, a woman called the tip line and said that the man in the photo on Facebook looked like her coworker, Raymond Walker. "What did he witness?" the coworker probably asked.

His own life go up in smoke, if Rice had anything to say about it.

An officer had hopped online and found a work headshot of Raymond Walker. Compared it to the photo at the bar. Things looked good.

When Rice got in that day, he called in Nick Hall for a double-blind photo array. Nick identified Walker's headshot.

Rice plugged all of this into the warrant he was drafting at his computer.

When he was done, he emailed a draft to the Assistant District Attorney for her comments. Then he called Raymond Walker's office.

Walker played dumb when he came on the line. Rice had identified himself to the secretary, so Walker was already on the defensive. Rice introduced himself politely, addressed him as "Mr. Walker."

Ray's response to Rice's credentials was: "All right?"

"Your name's come up in an active investigation."

"Oh, that's surprising."

Rice couldn't help but smile. You'd think someone who was actually surprised to find himself on the phone with a detective would ask *What kind of investigation?* But Walker already knew that. "Is it?"

Annoyance edged into Walker's voice. "Yes, it is."

"I'd like you to come in and answer some questions today."

A beat, and Walker said, "That might not be possible, I usually work late."

"So do I, Mr. Walker." Rice paused. "How about you swing by whenever you're off work tonight. Maybe we can clear all this up."

"I'm not sure I should do that," Walker said. "It's nothing personal, but without knowing why you want to talk to me . . ."

"'Course it's your call," Rice said. "This would just be your chance to give us your side of the story, before we have to go further."

There was a pause, and Walker said, "I'll be in around six."

Rice caught O'Malley's eye across the bullpen. Gave her a thumbs-up. "See you then."

14

Far off beyond the fields, the leaves were starting to turn. Sprays of red and orange dusted Julia's view from the road as she walked the kids home from the bus stop. Most of the trees would explode into their fall colors in a week or so, and there would be bare limbs all around before October was up. It wouldn't be long before the soft, springy plants in the garden were stiff and gray. The only way to survive what was coming was to harden and wait.

They were halfway back to the house—Seb chattering about school, Chloe whining about the walk—when Julia heard a car approaching behind them. She turned to see her own car coming down the long country road.

When Julia announced that it seemed Uncle Nick was coming to pick them up, Chloe squealed. They paused on the side of the road to wait for him.

Nick pulled up and apologized for being late.

"It's fine," Julia said. It really was—it was beautiful outside, and the kids had been dressed for the temperature—and she was too relieved to see him to care. Something about him going radio silent had unsettled her.

Julia loaded the kids into their seats and climbed up front with Nick. His face was drained of color, and he acknowledged her with nothing more than a flick of his eyes.

"Uncle Nick, where were you?"

Nick glanced up at the rearview to look at Seb. "I had to go to counseling."

"Why do you need counseling?" This time it was Chloe.

Before Nick could speak, Julia gave Chloe the party line. "It's to help him feel better after his accident."

Seb chimed in. "Did Grammy Hall do counseling after *her* accident?" That was a new one, apparently about Tony's mom's car accident the year before. Julia glanced at Nick apologetically. Kids had a way of pulling at the threads you most wanted to leave untouched.

"Sometimes getting in an accident is very scary," Julia said. "And so it helps to go to counseling to talk about it and feel better. So you feel less scared."

They pulled into the driveway as Chloe said, "Uncle Nick, are you scared?"

Nick put the car in park.

Julia spoke. "Kids, why don't you—"

Nick put his hand on her shoulder.

"Yes," he said, and he turned to face his niece. "Yes, I am scared."

He was right to tell them the truth, but it frightened Julia to hear him say it. It was part of a greater truth Chloe and Seb hadn't learned yet: there are things that can't be fixed. Maybe part of what Chloe was trying to understand was why Nick would need help from some other source, from outside their house. With her perfect life, Chloe had no reason to know that there were some things her parents could not make better.

15

Rice barely made it back to the station before six. While he'd been at the courthouse, O'Malley had set up the small conference room for their interview with Walker. Minutes after Rice arrived, the secretary called back to the bullpen, said Walker was there. Rice sent Merlo down to bring Walker to the conference room while O'Malley double-checked that the camera and mic were working.

They switched up their routine on occasion, but generally, Rice played good cop to O'Malley's bad. Counterintuitive on first thought, maybe, to have the female officer not playing the good cop, but the reasoning was simple: one detective was there to apply pressure, and the other was there to look like a lifeline. Most of their suspects were white men like Walker, and white men were more apt to believe that Rice could cut them a deal for cooperation. Rice had sex, age, and color on O'Malley. Wasn't right—just the way it was. So they used their differences to their advantage. And for her part, O'Malley enjoyed getting to treat a guy like Walker like she thought he was a guilty piece of shit.

They let Walker sit in the room for eight minutes before they joined him. They would watch the video later to see how many times he checked the clock behind him, fiddled with his phone, got up to look into the hallway. For now they waited in the bullpen. Rice slid a couple of unrelated printouts into the file to bulk it up.

Rice went in first. Walker had sat in the chair nearest the door, leaving one seat opposite him and one beside him.

"Mr. Walker," Rice said as he stretched out a hand. "I'm Detective John Rice, and this is my colleague Detective Megan O'Malley."

As she often did when they worked a suspect together, O'Malley posted herself in the doorway without a handshake or a word. She leaned against the doorframe and crossed her arms.

"Raymond Walker," the man said, "but you already knew that."

Rice laid the folder down on the table and took the seat across from Walker. "Sorry if we kept you waiting."

Walker smiled. Even under the fluorescents he was good-looking. "I'm sure you were busy," Walker said.

"Very," O'Malley said.

Walker looked sideways at her and then back at Rice. "Am I in some kind of trouble?"

The annoyance from the phone was gone. He was back in control of himself.

"You tell us," O'Malley said.

Rice held up a hand at O'Malley in an unspoken gesture that said, *Quiet.* "Well," Rice said, "we're trying to figure that out."

Walker's face shifted to that of a brownnosing child trying to please a schoolteacher. "How can I help?"

"Do you know why you're here, Mr. Walker?"

"Not a clue."

Rice pulled a photo from the file and slid it to Walker. "Do you recognize this man?"

Walker studied the picture. His eyes were narrowed ever so slightly, like he was working out what to say. It was a sweet picture of Nick Hall;

Rice had asked Tony for a recent photo for the file, and Tony had emailed him one from the past summer. Nick was bare-armed and grinning, his wet curls plastered to his forehead. He looked like he'd just climbed out of the lake behind him and pulled on a tank top. In the photo, Nick looked like he was on the cusp of manhood but still a boy in many ways. Rice would use the word *man* this evening, with Walker. It had occurred to Rice earlier that he could use his own biases to his advantage.

Walker spoke. "What's this about?"

"It's a simple question," O'Malley said. "Do you recognize him or not?"

Walker kept his eyes on Rice and smiled apologetically. "I think I have a right to know why I'm here."

"You're only here if you want to be," Rice said. "You're free to leave any time. Let me ask you this—if I told you this man says he knows you, how would you explain that?"

Walker dropped his gaze to the photo again. He was stalling—was he smart enough to know he was trapped with any answer? An admission that he knew Nick was further evidence that Nick had correctly identified him; a denial was evidence that he was a liar, since they had the photo at the bar to prove that the two had met. Anything feigning uncertainty and Rice would ask him if he always forgot the people he slept with. Then Rice would throw him the lifeline of consent—yeah they'd slept together, but it was consensual, right? And then they had him, because someone knocked out cold wasn't consenting to anything.

Rice started in. "Let me tell you what I think. I think you two had a sexual encounter."

"That what you're calling 'rape' these days?" O'Malley said.

Walker looked sideways at her, then back to Rice.

"And you know what my colleague thinks," Rice said, gesturing to O'Malley. "She believes him." Rice tapped the photo with a finger. "Maybe I should, too. But I don't like to leap to conclusions, especially not about what goes on behind closed doors between two adults."

O'Malley thudded her fist against the doorframe behind her. "Would you cut the boys'-club-consent bullshit?"

"Why don't you take a walk," Rice said.

O'Malley looked long at Walker, then slipped from the room. Rice got up and made a show of gently shutting the door. He sat back down in his seat and leaned toward Walker confidentially.

"O'Malley can get a little emotional about these cases. I think it's hard for her, as a woman. Don't get me wrong," he said with a wave, "she's an excellent detective. But there's a reason they give me the lead on cases like this."

"It's not right to just blindly believe whatever someone tells you because you have some chip on your shoulder."

"I know; I'm sorry about her."

"I've never hurt anyone in my life, Detective. Believe me."

"I do, to be honest. Not like this was some pretty little girl you could throw around." Rice chuckled as he spoke, and Walker smiled with relief. "He's a grown man," Rice said.

Walker nodded.

"Just help me understand what's going on here," Rice said. "Give me something to run up the chain."

"We never—" Walker stopped, like his tongue had snagged on a word.

"You two never what?"

Walker's gaze sharpened with defiance. He smiled with half his mouth. "That was good," he said quietly. "That was really something. Huh. I'm all done."

Rice wasn't ready to concede. "So we agree you knew him."

But it was too late. Walker's chair was already scraping back on the linoleum. "Goodbye, Detective."

Walker pulled open the door to the hallway. There was O'Malley, a thin stack of paper in her hands.

"Warrants," she said.

Rice had talked it over with the Assistant District Attorney and decided to secure the warrants for Walker's arrest and a DNA sample before the interview. He'd bombed over to the courthouse late that afternoon, gotten back just in time to interview Walker himself.

O'Malley circled a finger in the air. "Turn around, Mr. Walker. I'm placing you under arrest. We'll do your saliva at the jail."

16

As Nick talked to the detective, Tony studied his face. Tony knew Nick had gone to the police station earlier that day and had identified a picture of Josh. It was him—Nick was sure of it. Julia had told Tony all of this; when Tony got home, Nick didn't feel like talking about it. Now, standing in the hallway with the phone against his ear, Nick's face looked like he was getting bad news. He murmured "Okay" every now and then but said nothing more.

Nick hung up.

Finally, Tony said, "Well?"

"They found him," Nick said. "They arrested him."

Tony's first thought was a selfish one: *Thank God; I might actually sleep tonight.* Tony's attention had been divided since that first call from the hospital. It didn't matter if he was at work, eating breakfast with the kids, or trying to sleep: his worry for Nick was ever present. But now, it was over. They had him.

Julia moved to Tony's side and asked what the detective had said.

"Something about bail," Nick said. "He needs $100,000 to get out."

Julia looked at Tony with wide eyes. "Wow. That's great."

"But there'll be a hearing on Monday, and it could get lowered. If he gets out, he won't be allowed to talk to me."

Bail. Right. It wasn't over. Now there would be court. Tony turned to Julia. She would know what came next.

"Are they gonna indict him?" she asked.

"I think he said something about that."

"Okay," Julia said. "Do you want me to call him back and ask?"

Nick shook his head. "He said someone would call me and I'd get to have a meeting or something."

"Oh, with the ADA?"

"What?"

"The prosecutor," she said.

"I think so." Nick's eyelids were drooping like he was exhausted.

"Sorry," she said. "I'm sure he just hit you with a lot of information."

"It's okay. I think they'll tell me more at the meeting."

"I'll go with you," Tony said.

"Okay," Nick said. He sounded annoyed.

"If you want."

Nick shrugged. "I'm gonna go to bed."

"Wait," Tony said. "Did he tell you the guy's name?"

Nick looked upward. "Yeah . . . I can't remember now. It's not Josh. Something with an R."

⟜

Raymond Walker. That was the man's name. It was on the paper's website the next day. Nick's name was absent.

Now, the man in the dim photo from the bar with the pale skin and dark hair had a name. Tony hadn't realized it before, but until that moment, the man in the photo had been a monster. He hadn't been a real person to Tony—he'd been nothing but the evil act. A name transformed him: Raymond Walker had an identity. He had a life. Tony had to know what it was.

He started by searching Walker's name.

Raymond Walker was a salesman at a company in Portsmouth, New Hampshire, where he sold waterworks products around New England. Under his photo on the company website, his brief bio read that he lived in southern Maine.

Raymond Walker lived in Salisbury, like Nick, according to a White-pages website.

Raymond Walker had graduated from the College of New England in 1998, making him thirty-eight, give or take. Thirty-fucking-eight, to Nick's twenty.

Raymond Walker had a private Facebook page. That was worse than him having none. All Tony could see was a profile picture: it was Walker flexing in a sleeveless shirt in front of a gym, grinning like a snake.

What Tony did not find was evidence of who he knew this man to be. There was no entry on a sex-offender registry, no other court cases, no news articles about prior victims.

Deep in the pages of a Google search, Tony found the 1997 obituary of one George R. Walker, who was survived by his wife, Darlene, and his son, Raymond. To say he found the obituary was a slight exaggeration— he found a link that was described as containing this obituary, but the link did not work. All he could do was read the description. It taunted him. An obituary might have divulged more personal information about Raymond's history, if it was even the same Raymond.

Now he searched the name Darlene Walker, and her Facebook page appeared. That morning, she had posted a long block of text on her page. In it, she wrote that her son had been arrested on "nothing more than a story, of which his side is completely different." She called Nick's accusa-tion "the made-up story of a boy who went willingly."

Something surged in Tony as he read the words, and his chest boiled. "You fucking bitch," he hissed at his phone. People had shared the post and written comments—people who were friends with the Walkers, clearly. Lots of shocked and angry emojis on behalf of Walker and his mother.

"Unbelievable," one man had written.

A woman wrote: "Ray is such a good guy, have faith Darlene."

"I know," someone added. "Did the cops ask literally anyone who knows Ray? Because they either have the wrong guy or the other guy's lying."

One comment nearly stopped Tony's heart: "Does anyone know the accuser's name?" There was no response to that one.

To the rest of the world, Ray Walker was a good person until proven otherwise. He had a job, a house, a gym, a mother who loved him. Tony, Nick, Julia, the detectives—they could see what he really was. They had seen the sickness inside of him. When would everyone else see it, too?

Julia was working in her study that weekend. She often worked a bit on the weekends—she always felt she was behind. On the weekends, the kids were largely Tony's responsibility. Now, he stuck them in front of the television and knocked on her office door.

"What comes next?"

"Hmm?" She was standing at her desk, typing something.

"What comes next in Nick's court case?"

"Oh. It sounds like they'll get an indictment." The question must have been apparent on his face, because she explained herself. "The prosecutor will present evidence to the grand jury. Nick will have to testify."

"What will it be like?"

"I've never been to one. The defendant and the defense attorney don't go. Nick will have to tell *me* what it's like," she said with a laugh. Then she grew serious again. "He'll have to tell his story under oath. There will be people in there—the people sitting on the grand jury, the prosecutor, some kind of court reporter. The point is for the prosecutor to prove she has enough evidence to bring the charges against him. The real point, I think any prosecutor will admit, is to test the case. See how the evidence looks so far. She might even want to see how Nick does testifying."

Tony thought for a moment. "I'm glad he doesn't remember."

Julia cocked her head like she was considering this.

"Don't you think?" he asked.

"I think it's bad he doesn't remember."

"Why?"

"It gives the defendant free rein to make up whatever he wants."

"I thought his lawyer would have to stop him."

Julia looked confused. "Where did you get that?"

"You," he said. "You told me once you couldn't let clients lie."

"If I knew they were lying."

"Anyone would know he's lying."

She shook her head. "Not just if you *think* your client's lying. You have to know—like if he tells his lawyer 'I raped him,' the lawyer can't let him testify and say 'he consented.' But I doubt he'll tell his lawyer the truth."

"Did you have clients lie to you?"

"Yeah," she said apologetically. "I'm sure I did."

Julia had only been a defense attorney for four years, but in that time she represented all kinds of people. Most of them normal people, maybe even good people who'd made bad choices. But she'd represented some bad people, too. A wife-beating professor. A teenage drug dealer. A long line of parents who abused and neglected their kids.

And apparently there had been rapists. Tony just didn't know anything about them.

The thought of her defending someone like Raymond Walker made him sick to his stomach.

"I'll let you get back to work," he said quietly, and he closed the door on her.

17

A week after Josh—or Raymond—was arrested, Tony drove Nick to a meeting at the District Attorney's office. It was around the back of a courthouse where the case would happen. That was all Nick really understood: *the case would happen*. But what that meant—what would actually happen—he didn't know. He felt clueless about what he had started.

The District Attorney's office reminded Nick of the police station; it actually seemed more secure than the station had. The woman at the front desk sat behind a thick layer of glass to their right and she had to buzz them into the building through a locked door.

She brought them down a hallway to a room where two women were waiting.

"Can I get either of you a drink: coffee, a soda?"

"You have Coke?" Nick asked.

"You got it."

Meanwhile, the women in the room stood up, and the older one reached out her hand to Nick.

"Nick, it's nice to meet you." Her handshake was firm, and Nick tightened his grasp. "I'm Linda Davis, your prosecutor." She was striking, with red lipstick and jet-black hair. Nick wondered immediately if it was dyed.

The younger woman had a softer handshake. "Sherie," she said. "I'm your advocate." She smiled, revealing a gap between her front teeth.

"And you must be Tony," Linda said, turning to him.

They all sat down around the table as the woman from the front desk returned with Nick's drink.

"How are you doing?" Linda asked.

Nick popped the tab. "I'm okay."

"You in therapy?"

Nick nodded as Tony said, "He is."

Sherie was staring at Nick. She was probably looking at the yellow bruises on his cheek and neck. They were fading but still noticeable, at least if you knew to look.

"Really," Nick said. "I'm doing fine."

"Well, that's great," Linda said. "We wanted to go over the court process with you, answer any questions you might have so far."

"And I'm your girl when you have questions later," Sherie said, "because you will." She pushed two business cards across the table. Nick and Tony each took one. Beneath her name were the words *VICTIM WITNESS ADVOCATE*. "My job is to help you understand what's going on and to be there for court. And I can help you advocate for yourself."

"Are you a lawyer?" Tony asked.

"No," she said. "I'm just there to support Nick. But I work with Linda—we're always in touch—so when Nick has questions he can call me." She turned to Nick.

Sherie's voice went apologetic. "It's going to be a lot of information all at once, but then it's gonna be slow. It normally takes a long time for a case to end."

At the same time, Nick and Tony asked, "How long?"

"It can take a year," Linda said.

A year. The word was small, but it held a lifetime: Christmas. His twenty-first birthday. The summer. Next school year, his senior year. *This* might still be the center of his life?

"That's ridiculous," Tony said.

"I know," Linda said. "But this is a high-priority case," Linda continued, "so I'll do everything I can to make sure it goes before the grand jury in November. But the court gives the defendant time to hire a lawyer, do an investigation, get an expert. There's a lot that goes into a case like this."

An investigation? What was there for Josh—Raymond—to investigate?

Linda went on. "A month or two after we get an indictment, we'll have a court date where the defense attorney and I talk about the case and try to come up with a deal."

Right. Plea deals.

"So it could be over then," Tony said.

"It could be over then," Sherie said, "but you should know it usually isn't."

"I thought most cases ended in plea deals," Tony said. "My wife's a lawyer."

"Many do," Linda said. "But cases involving sexual assault go to trial more often than others. Plea deals are still common, just not *as* common. But if we can get a conviction and a sentence we like, we absolutely want to avoid you having to testify."

Nick had felt Sherie's eyes on his face again when Linda said the words *sexual assault*. She was looking for a reaction from Nick.

"Is that something you're willing to do, Nick?"

He turned to Linda. "What?"

"Are you willing to testify?"

"Oh, yeah," he said.

"It's important for me to know if you don't want to."

Nick was confused. Obviously he didn't *want* to. "Don't I have to?"

"Well, if you want a trial, yes. I can't have a trial without you. But it's your choice. If you don't want to testify, I'll do what I can to get him to plead to something. I just need to know where you're at."

This was confusing. Nick didn't know what to say.

"Your name will stay private," Sherie said.

"Is it private now?" Tony asked.

"Yes," Linda said. "I filed a motion. That's why the criminal complaint calls him 'John Doe.'"

Nick didn't know anything about that.

"I didn't know you could do that," Tony said.

"We have to have a reason," Linda said. "It depends on the case. I wanted to maintain *some* privacy for Nick." She turned and began addressing him. "Your case is open to the public, which means reporters or anyone else can come watch the court dates. They just don't learn your name, so it shouldn't get published anywhere."

"I know it's still a huge invasion to have to testify about this," Sherie said. "There's no judgment if you don't want to. You've been so brave to even report this."

"It's not a big deal," Nick said. They were acting like testifying would kill him. He didn't want to, obviously, but he could do it.

Linda was studying him. "It's your choice, Nick. Just tell me if there comes a time when I *need* to settle the case. I won't go to trial if you aren't testifying."

"It's fine," he said. "I'll do it."

"Okay," Linda said. "Let's hope he'll take a deal and we'll avoid that.

But even if it does settle, it normally happens a lot later on, closer to trial."

"Okay," Nick said.

"A year," Tony said again. He glanced at Nick.

There was an in-breath of silence, like everyone was expecting Nick to say something. He didn't know what else to give them.

18

TONY HALL, 2015

A year. The words kept repeating as they walked down the hall, out of the DA's office. They might be doing this *a year* from now. Tony looked over at Nick.

Nick was wearing Tony's clothes. He'd brought a pair of jeans from his apartment, but that morning before they left for the meeting, Nick had grown anxious about his outfit.

Tony thought Nick looked good when they met in the hallway upstairs.

Nick grimaced. "I look like I'm not taking this seriously." He gestured down at his cotton-and-denim ensemble.

"You look great," Tony said. He'd taken the day off work to go with him.

"I should have brought something nicer," Nick said.

Tony tried to understand. "Are you worried they won't respect you?"

"Do you think we have time to stop somewhere?"

Tony looked at his watch. No chance. "What size are you?"

"Thirty-two/thirty-two."

Tony smiled. "You got Dad's waist. Hold on."

Tony went to his bedroom closet and dug for a pair of pants he was sure hadn't gone to Goodwill yet. He'd had Ron Hall's waist once, too, but those days were gone. With parenthood came dad weight, and no amount of ab work seemed capable of scraping off the last of his new inches. He found the tan pants hanging in the far back of the closet. He selected his smallest dress shirt and a tie, just in case.

When Tony came out of the bathroom a few minutes later, Nick was opening the door to Seb's room. His tie hung open on his collar.

"Can you tie this?"

Tony stepped up to his little brother. He wasn't so little anymore—Tony's shirt was snug on his shoulders. He'd seen Nick in his hand-me-downs many times over the years, but never in clothes from Tony's adulthood. The juxtaposition of this moment against his five-year-old son's bedroom made his chest feel tight.

He grasped the tie and began. Tony brought the knot up close to Nick's throat; Nick gasped, stepping back as Tony let go.

"I'm sorry," Tony said, overlapping Nick's rushed "It's fine."

Nick brought his hands up to the tie, fumbled at the knot.

"I can get it," Tony said.

"Let me," Nick said. He worked at the knot, his eyes welling, and finally it came loose.

He handed the tie back to Tony.

"Just give me a minute," Nick said, and closed the door.

That was the thing. Sometimes Nick seemed fine. Looked like his old self. And Tony would forget what had happened. In that outfit, Nick looked like a man, but to Tony he was a kid again.

Tony held the door as they left the DA's office. "I'm proud of you."

"For what?"

"Being so brave," Tony said. "You could be like 'this isn't fair' and not do anything. It wasn't your fault, but you're still doing something."

Nick groaned loudly. "Would you stop saying that?"

"Saying what?"

"That I'm brave; it wasn't my fault. Do you know how many people have said that to me?"

"We're saying it because it's true."

"But it doesn't matter." Nick tilted his head back and drained the last of his Coke.

"It *does* matter," Tony said. "It wasn't your fault, Nick."

Just off the walkway, there was a large, covered trash can with RETURNABLES written on the side, and Nick walked to it.

"You're not helping," Nick said as he lifted the lid.

"Okay, so how can I help?"

Nick tossed in the can and turned to face Tony. "How about you let me speak for myself?"

"What?"

Nick pointed at the building. "You couldn't have talked over me more if you were trying."

"You *weren't* talking! Someone had to."

"I didn't have the chance."

"Fine. I'll sit there in silence next time."

"Great. Now tell me I'm not a victim." There was something in his voice that sounded like a taunt. Like he didn't expect Tony to say it.

"You're not," Tony said.

"Then stop acting like I am."

Tony didn't know what to say.

Okay, he was babying him. But what was he supposed to do? Pretend it hadn't happened? When Tony did that, he did stupid shit like hand Nick a tie after he'd been choked by a guy. Nick *was* a victim, something awful had happened to him. Was it such a big deal, that he had been a victim? Just in that one moment?

"It was just a single moment," Tony said. "I wish I'd been there."

"God*damn* it." As Nick spoke, he pushed the trash can beside him, tipping it over and spewing cans onto the lawn.

"Nick!"

"You think *you* would have stopped him."

"I would have *killed* him."

"Shut up, Tony, just shut up!" The vein in Nick's forehead was bulging. He kicked a can at his feet and crouched down, sat in the grass.

Nick groaned, angry and raw, and buried his face in his hands.

Tony stood for a moment, shocked at Nick's display. He'd never seen Nick get angry like that before.

Above Nick, he could see a pale face in the window, looking out at them from the DA's office.

He walked to Nick's side and stooped down, pushing handfuls of cans and bottles into the trash can. Then he righted the bin and offered Nick his hand. They walked to the car in silence.

———

They were almost home when Tony apologized.

Nick had been staring out the window, maybe watching the fields roll by, maybe stewing. He turned to Tony. "For what?"

"I should have just shut up when you said I wasn't helping. I'm acting like I think I understand, and I don't."

Nick nodded. "I know you just want to make it better."

Tony said nothing. He wanted to tell Nick he was right—tell Nick it was killing him not to be able to just undo what had happened. Frustrating him beyond explanation that he couldn't understand what Nick was feeling. He and Nick had always understood each other. Yeah, Nick was gay and he wasn't—there were pieces there that Tony could never truly *get*. But on a base level, they understood each other like no one else did. It was pretty simple: they'd had the same dad. Heard the same slurs, felt the same cuff to the ear, been told—in Ron Hall's varied but persistent ways—that they were worthless. So they understood each other. They even had a simple message in code. When Nick was little, Tony would take his hand and squeeze it three times: *I love you*, it meant. Nick would return four squeezes: *I love you, too.*

To feel so clueless about this tragedy, so separate from Nick, made Tony's chest ache.

But he didn't say any of that. He seemed to be getting everything wrong. And all of that might just make Nick worry about how this was affecting Tony when he should be worrying about himself.

"I'm sorry, too," Nick said. "I don't know why I flipped out like that."

"It's okay." Tony paused. "It's okay, and that's all I'm gonna say."

"Ha," Nick said. "Thank God."

—◦—

That weekend, Nick moved back to his apartment.

19

Julia had always fought against the addition of a second television. "One in the living room is *plenty*," she used to say to Tony every six months or so when he would mention how nice it would be to watch a movie in bed, or how he wished he could keep an eye on the game as they made dinner. When Chloe was born and Julia started nursing her, however, she quickly changed her mind about the TV in the bedroom. She and Tony had made a deal that he would pick up a small one at Target, and it would move out of their bedroom and into the kitchen whenever Julia stopped breastfeeding the baby. It sat on a small table in the corner beside the hamper and entertained them with episodes of *Lost*, *CSI*, and Tony's secret favorite, *The Bachelor*. Then one day Chloe was done breastfeeding, but Julia said nothing, and eventually Seb was born, so the TV stayed. Tony had the luxury of a TV in his bedroom for four years before Julia finally moved it one day while he was at the office. He had feigned devastation when he came home to find it in the kitchen, collapsing on the floor to the giggling glee of his children.

This was how, three years after that, Julia came to be packing lunches for the kids with the television on a local news program the morning that Raymond Walker made bail. She was shaking baby carrots into plastic baggies when she heard the words behind her: "A man from Salisbury who is accused of sexual assault posted $100,000 surety bail today." Julia spun toward the television and moved closer.

One of two local anchors looked grave as she spoke. "Local business-man Raymond Walker was arrested for gross sexual assault for an alleged incident on October second of this year. The victim is a twenty-year-old male from the York County area. *His* name is private in the court records at this time."

Julia's heart pounded in her ears, and she exhaled hard at this line.

"This morning, Mr. Walker was released after filing proof of a $100,000 bail lien on his home in Salisbury. The State plans to seek an indictment of Mr. Walker next month."

Julia heard heavy feet on the stairs. She unclenched her damp palms from the counter's edge and switched off the television before Tony could see.

⌐

That evening, Julia left the TV off when she started dinner.

All day she had resisted the urge to call Detective Rice and ask him how Raymond Walker had been allowed to post bail at all. If she'd known the prosecutor she would have called her to talk about it, but their paths had never crossed during Julia's brief time in practice. Detective Rice was the only person on Nick's case she felt any real connection to. But there would be nothing for him to say to her. Of course Walker had made bail. Unfairly, it was only the poor who had to wait out their case from a jail cell. Walker had offered up his house as collateral for his continued at-tendance in court. There was nothing abnormal about it, really. Under other circumstances, Julia would have acknowledged that it was a good thing: a defendant was supposed to be innocent until proven guilty. There was supposed to be a balance: the government couldn't punish you without proving that you'd done something wrong. In theory, the public could be protected by bail conditions while the defendant awaited trial. But now that this was happening to her family, suddenly the whole concept of due process seemed dangerous.

She knew there were bail conditions in effect now; she had texted Nick earlier that day to see how he was. When he didn't answer, she called and he picked up. Nick promised her he was okay, not that she fully believed him. In the weeks he'd lived with them, she never felt he was showing how he truly felt about the situation. But yes, he should at least be safe. Walker would not be allowed to speak to Nick, let alone come near him, but court orders did not always prevent violence. And what if he ran away? What if he disappeared, leaving Nick frightened? Leaving Walker free to hurt other men?

Tony got home while she was chopping root vegetables to roast. He had barely stepped both feet in the kitchen when Chloe came running in, followed closely by Seb. Both were hollering "Dadaaaaaa" as though they were missiles screaming by.

Julia set the knife on the cutting board and turned to Tony with a grimace.

"Enough, beasts!" he shouted. "Let me kiss your mother!"

Tony waded over to Julia, one child on each leg, and kissed her hello.

She looked at her ridiculous, precious family and breathed deeply. *This is perfect. Be happy.*

—◦—

After the kids were asleep, Julia and Tony stood on opposite sides of their room, undressing for bed. As Julia pulled off her earrings at the dresser, she contemplated whether she should tell Tony about Walker. He'd been in a good mood all evening, and now he stood behind her, humming. There was no way he knew. Was it patronizing to hide it from him? She'd saved him from one day of ruminating on Nick and Walker. Selfishly, she wanted to spread some of the bad news to someone else and to relieve herself of the guilt of keeping this secret from him. But she could carry this for him—the burden of knowing that the man who assaulted Nick was free again, for now. *Christ, listen to yourself. Not telling your husband something that's public news makes you some kind of martyr? Get over yourself.*

She turned to face him. "Ray Walker made bail this morning."

Tony finished pulling his shirt off. His hair was a pile of static; he looked electrocuted.

"Oh, honey." Julia laughed and moved toward him. "Your—"

"He made bail," he cut in, leaning away from her hand.

"It was on the news earlier. He had to put up his house; it's not like he's going anywhere."

"That's not . . . he—" Tony fumbled for words. "Have you talked to Nick? Does he know?"

"Yeah, I texted him earlier to make sure."

"But not me."

Julia waved her hand at him. "I thought you'd get upset, and I was right." She heard herself sound defensive, but Tony seemed unfazed by her tone.

He was looking out their window, fists clenched, a tight frown clamped on.

"Honey," Julia said. "Nick knows, and he's okay."

"He should come here, tonight, just to be safe."

Julia shook her head. "He doesn't want that. There's a no-contact order; that man can't talk to Nick or go anywhere near him. He doesn't know where Nick lives." She had closed the distance between them and smoothed down his wild hair. "Nick is gonna be fine."

Tony hung his head.

"I've had some of these same thoughts," she said. "I have. But I talked to him, and he's actually good. He's happy to be back at school, hanging with his roommates. He just wants to get back to normal. We have to let him have that." Her voice went to a whisper. "Okay?"

Tony nodded.

She kissed him deeply and guided him to their bed.

20

NICK HALL, 2015

When Nick moved back to his apartment, the scab came with him. That weekend, he realized it had been two weeks since it happened—two weeks since that night—and still the small wound hadn't healed. He resolved to leave it alone.

The first couple of days he was restless, quick to tune out his professors' voices in class. His mind was a tangle of thoughts: Why had he left with Ray? Why was he living like this? What had he expected? And his fingers were on the scab, rubbing, flicking, but each time he realized—*goddamn it, I'm picking at it again*—he sat on his hands to stop himself.

On Wednesday morning, he awoke to a text from his sister-in-law: Hi honey. Hope you're hanging in there. Just thought I'd give you a heads up that RW posted bail, better to hear it from me than the news. If you need anything we're here for you. His hand reached back, and his fingers dove beneath his hair; this time, when the sting alerted him to what he was doing, he scratched harder. As he pulled the loosed scab through his hair, a couple of strands came with the skin. Maybe if he pulled out some of the hairs, the wound would breathe and heal faster; if it would just heal, he would stop picking at it. He pinched his fingers around a couple strands and pulled; his scalp stretched and released the roots, which came free with a painfully satisfying pop. Nick looked down at his hand. The nail of his index finger was rimmed in light red blood, and a small tuft of his own hair was pinched between his fingers.

Oh my God. I just pulled out my hair.

It had all happened so fast. Nick crept from his bed to his door and listened. He didn't hear any of his housemates outside, so he opened the door and scuttled across the hall to the bathroom. Mary Jo's hand mirror was in the cabinet where Nick remembered it would be; he leaned toward the mirror over the sink, using the hand mirror to inspect the back of his head. There was nothing—wait, yes, there was something. "Oh shit, *shit*, what did I do?" Nick hissed aloud. The pristine landscape of his dark hair was marred by a pock of white scalp and red wound.

His phone was ringing in the bedroom. He hurried back across the empty hall to his room. Julia was calling him.

Was he okay, she wanted to know.

Yes, he told her.

Had he seen her text, she asked.

Yes, he had, he said. He was fine—good, actually. Nice to be getting back to normal. He wasn't even thinking about Josh. Raymond.

Okay, she told him. Her voice was light, and she believed him. She didn't know him well enough, apparently. She couldn't hear the strain in his voice.

The rest of the week, he wore a Red Sox cap his dad had given him years ago. It wasn't his style, but he'd kept it out of sentimentality—a good day with Dad. It came in handy now, not that anyone seemed to notice the little patch of skin when he did remove the cap. The rest of that week, Nick occasionally found himself touching the spot, rubbing at it mindlessly, but he resisted damaging the area further.

But then Ray gave a public statement.

It happened on the last Sunday of October, a miserable bookend to the worst month of his life. Somewhere in the early-morning hours of that day, Nick had finally shut his laptop and gone to sleep. He awoke bleary-eyed and disoriented, unsure of where he was. The room was bright with sunlight. There was his bedside clock: it read 11:27. There was a knocking behind him, and he realized he was in his bedroom and someone was at his door.

"Yeah," he croaked, his vocal cords coated with sleep.

"Can I come in?" The voice was dulled by the door, but he recognized it was Elle.

"Yeah."

He rolled toward the door as Elle pushed it open. She took two reserved steps into the room. "Are you just waking up?"

"Yeah." Things had been awkward between them since the morning after it happened. He didn't blame her for any of it, but he knew she blamed herself. She kept apologizing. Was painfully careful around him. It made Nick tired.

"You haven't been on your phone?"

Nick rolled back and reached for his phone on his bedside table.

"Hold on," Elle said as she came toward him.

Nick's screen overflowed with notifications.

"What's going on?" Nick felt immediate despair.

"Um, that guy, Ray, he sent, like, a statement into all the newspapers."

Nick had missed calls and texts from Tony and Julia, Tony's mother, friends, even Chris. He hadn't spoken to Chris since he stood Nick up that night. He opened the message.

I'm so sorry.

Nick looked up at Elle. "What did Ray say?"

Elle looked like she was going to cry. "Um, basically that you two went home together and you were, uh, basically that it was all, like, consensual and you . . . Well, he said it in a weird way, but he made it sound like you wanted him to do what he did."

Nick shook his head, trying to process Elle's gibberish.

"Like rough sex. Like you wanted him to be rough. And now you're lying."

Disbelief rolled upward from deep in his stomach. At first Nick couldn't speak: he felt his mouth hang open in a horrified smile. No one would believe that . . . would they?

Inexplicably, his first question was, "Which newspaper?"

"All of them. Or, I don't know." Her voice cracked. "Like, the Maine papers."

Nick sat up higher in bed. "Wait, does he name me?"

Elle's eyes filled with tears. "He said you went to school here."

Nick looked back at his phone. Chris knew it was Nick.

"Do people know it's me?"

Elle began to cry.

Wait. Wait, no.

"Elle?"

"They know," she sobbed.

"How?"

"The letter. He said your major."

No. No.

"And." She paused. "And I guess Mary Jo's boyfriend told some people."

"How does *he* know?"

Elle stepped closer to Nick, her shoulders drooping. "I told Mary Jo. I'm so sorry. You were gone and you didn't answer my texts, I thought I could tell her. And she told him. I never would have told her if I knew he'd be so stupid."

His mind raced. If Chris knew . . . Chris didn't hang out with Mary Jo or her boyfriend. How many people had her boyfriend told for Chris to find out?

"How many people know? What are they saying?"

"I don't know," she said quietly. She was lying.

"Do they believe him?"

"Mary Jo's boyfriend?"

"*Ray*," Nick said.

Elle shrugged with a grimace. That looked like a yes.

"They do," he said.

"Just trash people who post in the comments on newspaper websites," she said as she sniffled against her hand. "People are commenting, that's all—it doesn't mean anything. It's too ridiculous to believe. Anyone who knows you believes you."

Nick looked down at his phone again. Pulled up the internet browser. Elle snatched the phone from his hands.

"Hold on, you're not reading it."

"Are you *fucking kidding* me? *Of course* I'm reading it. *Give* me my *fucking* phone, *Elle*." Nick forced the words out of himself in a voice he'd never heard before; pushing harder with each word felt good. He could let his anger out on Elle—she deserved it. That night hadn't been her fault, but this was. Her face was wet, but she had stopped crying. Her eyes were wide, like a sad baby deer. *Perfect, make me feel bad when I'm the one whose life is ruined, that's just classic Elle.*

"Please promise not to read the comments," she said quietly, handing the phone back.

"*Bye*" was all he said.

Elle turned and left quickly as Nick reached back into his hair and dug the scab off. It was smaller and drier from its days of respite, and it came off clean and fast. *There.* He quickly decided to check the local paper, *Seaside News*, though it sounded like it was in the larger papers, too. *Seaside* felt the most personal. There it was on the main page. MAN ARRESTED FOR SEXUAL ASSAULT SPEAKS OUT IN A LETTER TO THE EDITOR. As Nick clicked the link with his right hand, he felt the fingers of his left twirling a small section of hair next to the patch. *STOP*. He sat on his left hand and read.

It began with a paragraph in italics. The letter, it said, did not reflect the views of the newspaper. It was an opinion piece from a reader about the criminal justice system. He began to skim Ray's letter. Read the words without processing them: *brought the wrong man home, he had been drinking hard, rough play*. Rough play. Nick's stomach turned into a hot, solid mass, and adrenaline swept through him in a tidal wave. Rough play. Ray was saying Nick wanted it: the whole thing. Saying Nick pursued Ray, not the other way around. Nick asked to be hurt—asked for what Ray did to him. The slap, the punch, the hands on his neck—*stop it, stop it, don't think of that*.

Nick curled into a ball in his bed, barely able to breathe. Blood pounded in his ears. His mind was rushing, swirling, bursting, but he was too paralyzed to move. It had happened. Ray had hit back. Of course he had. He'd already proved he wasn't weak like Nick. And the prosecutor's motion to protect Nick's name hadn't mattered. Everyone knew it was Nick. His story to be weighed against Ray's. Nick would be proved one of two things: a victim or a liar. Finally, his hand began to reach for his head. *Stop. Too visible.* Nick reached below his sheets for his right thigh. He pinched a tuft of thin leg hair between his fingers and pulled slowly. His skin released the small bulbous hair roots with a collective *pop*.

21

The view from the front porch had changed. The hay laid down on the field had lost its golden color, looked more gray-green after weeks in the dipping temperatures and occasional rain. On the horizon, the tree line had gone gray too: the colorful leaves had dropped to the ground, where they would eventually rot. Tony stood on the porch in his robe, the air cold on his bare ankles. Was the end of fall always this ugly?

He heard Chloe come down the stairs. He turned and watched through the door as she drifted by and down the hall. He'd closed the inner door behind him when he stepped out onto the porch. The bottom half was screen, the top half glass. Through the glass, he could see Seb down the hall, standing in the kitchen, watching Julia make pancake batter.

The furnace had kicked on, but the house was still warming up. The incident with Nick had thrown off their usual rhythm, and Julia hadn't yet renewed their annual debate about the ideal thermostat setting. For now, that left Tony in charge, and layers were much needed in the morning. Chloe's hair was in its usual after-sleep form—something like a rat's nest disasterpiece—and seeing it spilling from the blanket she was bundled in sent warmth through his bones.

Get out of the cold, he thought, *and go in to your family.*

Tony went down the porch steps and stooped to grab the newspaper on the front walkway. In truth, his subscription to the Sunday paper stretched their budget. But the tradition had grown too important to abandon; it was almost integral to his sense of self. He'd started reading the paper the summer he dropped out of law school—the same summer he started dating his former classmate, then Julia Clark. While Julia toiled on in school, Tony dropped out. He would never admit it out loud, but reading a physical paper made him feel like he was still an intellectual. Still able to match her in conversation, or at least keep up.

Tony slid the paper from its plastic sheath as he climbed the steps. The past few weeks, Tony had combed the paper for mention of Nick's assault. There had been short articles online following Walker's arrest, but the incident had not made the Sunday paper. He straightened the pages. There was no need to comb the paper today. It was on the front page.

In the bottom right-hand corner was a headline: MAN ARRESTED FOR SEXUAL ASSAULT SPEAKS OUT IN A LETTER TO THE EDITOR. Tony heard himself suck in air. *Something else*, he thought. *Another case, please.*

But it was not another case. Beneath the title was Raymond Walker's name. Tony began to read.

I started writing this letter from the jail in Salisbury. One of the guards gave me paper and a dull pencil that I had to use in the common area. He didn't want me stabbing anyone or digging at my wrists, apparently. Overnight I was stripped of my humanity,

assumed I'd act like an animal in a cage, perhaps because I was put in one.

Take a moment, from the comfort of your home, and imagine yourself in my shoes.

So now you are in a cage. How did you end up there? Simple. You brought the wrong man home with you.

You met him at a bar. He sat beside you, offered you a shot, asked your name. He asked about your job, said he was in school for business, asked if you might teach him something. All you could see was that this young, dynamic man, to your lonely delight, was making a move on you. What you failed to see was that he had been drinking hard when you arrived, and he doubled your pace as you sat together talking.

You waited for him to grow tired of your graying hair and uncool style. Instead, to your delight and your destruction, he asked you to take him home.

He must have lived nearby for school, but you failed to think through why he didn't want you seen at his place. You were simply too eager, so you brought him to a hotel.

There, he surprised you again with an invitation you hadn't expected from the sweet-faced boy at the bar: one for rough play. It was an invitation you'd accepted with other partners, and you welcomed it that night. A conversation ensued in words and touches. A back-and-forth that climbed and crested.

Tony's vision blurred and doubled. With each line it grew harder to read. He cried out, a strange "gah" dragging from deep in his throat, and he ripped the front page off the paper, and the second, and third. He threw the paper down the steps and spun, trying to register something, anything he could strike. *Let it out. Let it out.* He turned to the house. *The door.* Tony lashed out with a tight fist and put his hand through the glass at chest-level. His foot went through the screen panel and he fell, scraping his arm down the broken glass.

"Jesus Christ!" Julia's voice echoed down the hall.

He staggered upright to see his wife rushing toward him, his children standing in the kitchen behind her.

22

Some smart-ass defense attorney had dropped off a couple dozen doughnuts at the station that morning, and Rice found O'Malley standing over them in the breakroom.

"I'm a goddamn cliché," she said with a mouthful of Boston cream.

"You're disgusting is what you are," Rice groaned. "Keep your mouth shut." He selected a plain, cakey doughnut.

O'Malley gulped to swallow her mouthful and pointed at Rice's selection. "You are also cliché."

A plain doughnut? "I'm classic!"

O'Malley rolled her eyes. "Just take your coffee and your plain doughnut and go play cop." She made a goofy, bug-eyed face at her own doughnut. "Leave us be."

"Gladly."

Rice made his way to his desk in the bullpen. For such a serious detective, O'Malley could get playful sometimes. Rice didn't mind, though. Unlike some, she could turn it off like she was flicking a switch. She was always professional when she needed to be. Her sense of humor was just her coping mechanism—humor, long-distance running, and apparently

Boston-cream doughnuts. Irene used to be Rice's favorite grounding force—sinking into her arms after a long day eased him like nothing else ever had. He still had mass and yardwork. Breakfast with his old friends. Visits from the grandkids; calls with his daughter.

Rice had spent a lot of his weekend thinking about the Hall family. It hadn't been the first time he'd struggled to leave the work at the office, so to speak, and it wouldn't be the last. In a small way, all the sadness that happened to the victims in these cases happened to him, too, and it had a way of building up in his mind. With decades of experience, Rice had learned to firmly tell unpleasant thoughts to leave him alone while he was off duty, but it didn't always work.

On Sunday, Rice opened his paper to see that Santa had dropped off his gift early this year. On the front page was a letter to the editor from Raymond Walker, admitting that he was, in fact, the man Nick met at the bar that night. Calling what had occurred at the motel "rough play." It was everything Rice had wanted, everything Walker wouldn't give him at the station two weeks ago: an admission and an unbelievable defense. Rice nearly kissed the paper.

But then it started to bother him. He'd even thought about calling Nick on Sunday, to check on him mostly, but also to talk to him. He prayed for the Halls at mass instead.

Now, he dragged his chair forward at his desk and pulled up the letter on the station computer. He scrolled to the words that had lodged in his brain.

There, he surprised you with an invitation you hadn't expected from the sweet-faced boy at the bar: one for rough play. It was an invitation you'd accepted with other partners, and you welcomed it that night. A conversation ensued in words and touches. A back-and-forth that climbed and crested. You parted from him feeling understood, feeling like the luckiest man on earth.

A week later, the police call you at your work and ask you to come to the station. They show you a photo of the man you met at the bar. Your stomach flutters, and you wonder if he committed a crime. You say nothing, unsure if an acknowledgment would betray him.

Then the police say that this man has told them that you raped him.

To say you are shocked is an understatement.

They want your side of the story, they say. You almost give it to them, but you can feel the trick in it, and you hold back. They arrest you.

For the first time in your life, hard metal handcuffs are tightened around your wrists. You are sat down in a police car and driven to the jail. You are strip searched. You are given a uniform to wear, and you think, *Just like on television*. Because you were arrested on Friday and don't happen to have $100,000 in the bank, you spend the weekend in jail.

You have to wear the uniform when you go to court, and they add shackles, as if you'd be stupid enough to run. You meet with the free lawyer for the day, who looks about eighteen years old, in the holding cell with all the other prisoners. There's no privacy, not that the lawyer has time to talk about much with you. Still, she says enough to make your cellmates raise their eyebrows.

"They've charged you by complaint with gross sexual assault," she says. It's the beginning of a long morning of gibberish that will only occasionally be translated for you.

"They're going to indict you," she says, "so you don't have to enter a formal plea today. The only thing worth focusing on is getting your bail lowered."

In the courtroom awaiting you is the same judge who granted the arrest warrant. The same judge who told the police they could cuff you, swab your mouth for your DNA, and put you in a cage for the weekend. And why did she let them do all that? Because she

read a story about you. A story the man from the bar told the police. This judge already hates you, has already chosen a side. She
leaves the bail so high that you'll have to use your house as collateral.

"First you have to get it appraised," the free lawyer explains,
"and you'll need to record the lien, there's a form; if you forget you
can call the clerk's office."

Instead, you call your mother from the jail and tell her what's
happened, because you need to ask her to arrange the appraisal. You
need her to drive the papers around until the court is satisfied that
it effectively owns your house if you violate your bail conditions.

In all, you spend twelve nights, thirteen days, in a cage, waiting to bail out. You are so obsessed with regaining your freedom
that you don't realize the depth of what is happening until you walk
out of the jail. You've tasted what it's like to lose your freedom. To
sleep behind a locked door across from a toilet. To feel prisoners—
and you're one of them—look at you sideways. You've heard your
name on the news followed by the words *gross sexual assault*. You
know that, if you cannot disprove a cry of rape, not only will you
go to prison, but when you are out, you will never be free again.
Your name will go on a list, and until you die, every person who
sees that list will think that they know you. "Know" what you've
done. "Know" that you are something less than human.

You will be reassured when you recall our experiment: this is
my situation, not yours. My impossible battle to fight against a
story. My life that will hinge upon who is more believable: me or
the man from the bar. The man I found so charming, so trustwor-
thy, that I went to bed with him.

His story might ruin my life. I don't understand it, this man's
decision to lie. I can make educated guesses. Self-hatred. Shame.
It's not easy for many of us to accept ourselves, as gay men. Add to
that the taboo of what he likes in bed, and, well, I can say I hadn't
planned on sharing my predilections with the public.

I fear I will never know why this damaged young man has done
this to me. My only hope is that the truth will come out in time,
but my introduction to our system has left me with little faith.

A defendant dissatisfied with his arrest, Rice thought. *Newsworthy, in-deed*. Another defendant who wanted to pretend the police were without physical evidence. They had the damage he'd done to Nick's body. Nick's blood left behind at the motel.

People wouldn't believe Nick had asked for that, would they? He dragged his chair closer to his desk and pecked at his keyboard to pull up the letter on the station computer. Rice scrolled to the comment section of the page. The top comment read:

Shame on Seaside for publishing this vitriol.

Good, Rice thought.
Another read:

It's probably true. Boy's crying wolf. Let's waste taxpayer money sorting this out.

Bad.
Someone had replied:

God hates f*gs. Hope this sets that boy straight lol.

Disgusting. Rice copied and pasted the link into an email to the ADA, Linda Davis, and wrote:

You see this?

At least Nick's identity was concealed. Still, it probably stung like hell, reading this. Someone should explain to Nick that this was a good thing. Rice pressed his finger into the doughnut crumbs on his desk, then scraped them from his fingertip with his teeth. Mostly a good thing.

His cell buzzed on the desk. It was Linda.

"I can't believe it," she said.

"Merry Christmas," Rice said.

She laughed. "Don't get cocky."

"I know."

"I got a call from Eva Barr yesterday." Linda's voice was tinged with anxiety Rice was certain she'd intended on hiding.

"Really."

"Yup. At least we know what we're dealing with."

Walker had hired Eva Barr, then. Better the devil you know, people often said, but Rice might have taken his chances elsewhere. Eva Barr was trouble in a rape case. It should have been an obvious tactic, but jurors always seemed to give Eva's clients extra credit just for having a pretty woman defending them. Eva was good at looking like she believed in her clients' innocence. She brazenly tried ugly, nasty cases that some attorneys would have bent over backward to settle, and she usually got an acquittal on the higher count or at least a mistrial. Rice had seen it in action himself: Eva had a charming, conspiratorial way about her that made the jurors lean toward her. In short, juries loved her and showed it with their verdicts. This also meant that her plea offers were better. Particularly from those few prosecutors afraid of a good fight. This was not Linda as a rule, but Linda didn't like to lose, and she'd lost hard to Eva around a year ago.

"Want me to forward her the letter, too?"

Linda laughed again. "I'm dying to know if she knew he was doing this."

"Giving us all these admissions? I doubt it."

"But it's well-written," Linda said.

And she was right. If he'd written it himself, the man could write a letter. Hopefully Walker wasn't as eloquent in person.

"Not believable," Rice said.

"No," she answered. "He was strangled."

"And the SANE report."

"Right, the trauma to his rectum."

In spite of himself, Rice's stomach clenched. So much of the horror he encountered went dull and flat with repetition. Hearing words like those ones always felt sharp.

"We knew this was coming," Linda went on. "I just wasn't expecting it this early."

"The gap in Nick's memory was always going to set him up. You worried?"

"No more than I already was," she said.

These cases were always troublesome in court. Nick Hall's was less than perfect. He'd been drinking. He didn't remember the assault itself. But they had his testimony that Walker attacked him, knocked him unconscious, and they had physical evidence to speak for him from there.

Walker's letter was bringing something else up for Rice, but he wasn't sure yet what it was. Walker sounded like a narcissist. But clearly intelligent. Well-spoken. He was holding down a job. And he'd been so controlled in their interview at the station, before the arrest. Neither of O'Malley's profiles seemed to fit him.

"You have time to do a quick follow-up today?" Linda asked.

"Sure."

"Can you get me more about Nick's boyfriend, or whatever he was?"

"The guy he was supposed to meet that night?"

"Yeah."

A blinking light started on Rice's phone.

"I've got someone on the other line. What do you want to know about the boyfriend?"

"Whatever you can get me."

"Easy enough."

Rice pressed the second line. "Britny Cressey," the receptionist said, "calling with information about Raymond Walker."

Who? "Put her through."

The receptionist did, and Rice introduced himself.

Her voice sounded young. "Hi, I'm calling about Ray Walker?"

"And you are?"

"Uh, an old girlfriend, kind of."

That was unexpected. "All right, and your name was Cressey?"

"Britny Cressey, sorry." She laughed cheerfully.

"That's okay."

"I just saw that Ray was arrested and charged with this thing, and I wanted to call and talk to someone."

Was this another report? Maybe Walker didn't stick to men when it came to assault. "How can I help?"

"I just wanted to tell you a little bit about him, since it seems like you're only getting one side of the story."

Ah. This was not a second report. "I don't know if you've seen the paper, but I do have his side of things."

"Ray was my best friend all through high school," Britny said. That made her Walker's age: thirty-eight or so. Her voice sounded about eighteen. "We dated for, like, a minute before he told me he was never gonna be into me."

She giggled. It was strange that she introduced herself as his ex.

"Well, I appreciate the historical information, but—"

"Ray was always such a nice guy. So smart and clever. Really mature. I wish we'd stayed close after graduation, but he went away to college, and that was kind of that."

"Okay."

"I reached out to him again when I saw what was happening on his mom's Facebook—that you guys arrested him. Ray and I have talked. He's really the same guy he used to be—he wouldn't have done this."

This was a waste of time. She didn't seem to know it, but who she really wanted to talk to was Walker's lawyer. Not Rice's job to help her figure that out. "I appreciate having your view, Ms. Cressey. Thanks for sharing."

"If I could just explain," she said.

"Explain what?"

"How well I know him, how I know he wouldn't have done what that guy says he did."

"I don't mean to be rude, but there's no way for you to know what happened in that motel room."

"No, but I was in his house every day for four years. I spent every second I could at Ray's house—they had cable, and he was an only child. My sister was so annoying then, I couldn't get a break from her if I was home. The only thing that sucked about Ray's house was his parents. His mom is crazy. Like smothering and kind of weird, I don't know how to explain it. She hated me. Thought I was trashy, and, like, I was, but I was sixteen." She laughed again. "She thought we were, *you know*, not like he was remotely interested in that. His parents didn't know then. His dad probably would have beat the shit out of him. His dad was a dick. And gross—he thought I was trashy, too, and he liked it, if you know what I mean?"

Rice's stomach tightened in disgust. "Help me see how this is related to the assault."

"Ray isn't violent," she said plainly. "He just isn't. There were a million times I'd have liked to punch his dad for being a creep, his mom for being *so* annoying. He never so much as yelled at them. I don't remember him having a single teenager meltdown *in four years*. I used to scream at my mom for no reason, didn't you?"

"I can't say I did, but I appreciate your point." Rice had never screamed at his mother, but he and his own daughter, Liz, had gone toe-to-toe on several occasions in her high school years. "I'll make a record of your call, Ms. Cressey. I've got a full plate today, so I need to sign off, all right?"

She repeated some of what she'd already said as Rice unpried her from their conversation and they hung up. He'd bet his house that Walker had put her up to that. Did Walker really think some old friend claiming Walker was a patient teenager would make one lick of difference to Rice? Even if she was credible, her observations were twenty years old. And she said it herself—they hadn't been sleeping together.

Rice grabbed his coat. There were more important questions to chase.

23

Julia had been meaning to reach out to Charlie Lee for months.

The main reason Julia left her law practice after they had the kids was to gain stability, which her trial work had never given her. When Chloe was born, Julia decided to get off the court-appointed roller coaster, at least temporarily, and find steadier money and shorter hours. It took her about a year to understand the stupidity in her decision to go into grant-funded policy work. She loved what she did, loved studying problems and recommending solutions. And just like when she was a defense attorney, she believed her job was important. Huge bonus points that working from home meant they didn't have to pay for day care. But a hallmark of grant work was recurring instability. Her job was always finite: when the money ran out, the job was over. She was always applying for a new grant, always thinking about what came next. Over the years, she became excellent at leaving a thought simmering on the back burner of her mind while she worked on something else in the foreground. It was the only way to do her job.

Her current project was to write a report about how juvenile records worked in Maine. What records were created when a kid was accused of a crime. What record was left behind, depending on the outcome of the case. Who could access the records. To what extent the records created would hold kids back later on in life.

In the spring, Julia had started in on her research. That summer, Julia began interviewing professionals in the system. Now, she would reach out to former juvenile defendants and ask them to anonymously answer questions about how their records had affected their lives. Some would be her own former clients. Some she would get from other attorneys. Months ago, when Julia laid out her plans, the institute she was working with approved a modest budget for a private investigator to help locate the former clients, who'd all grown up by now. There was only one PI she was interested in hiring, if she could have him: her favorite, Charlie Lee.

A day ago, while Tony was at urgent care, she'd thought of Charlie for another reason.

The sounds of that moment—the noise Tony made, like a dog roaring a warning before it attacked; the glass shattering; Seb's wail—she couldn't shut out the memory of it. But there was no use thinking about it any longer. She'd thought it to death throughout the night, and none of the obsessing had given her a better idea than asking Charlie Lee to do some digging on Raymond Walker. Tony wouldn't like it—when he was upset about something, he wanted to fix it himself. So she wouldn't tell him. Not unless Charlie found something that would be helpful to Nick's case, and then how could he be mad?

Now, her family gone, Julia stepped into her study and set her morning cup of tea on the windowsill. She normally chased her coffee with something herbal, but that morning she'd gone with Earl Grey; she needed the extra caffeine after her restless night. There was a door at the back right of her tiny office, and behind the door a narrow set of stairs stretched up to the attic. To the side of the door, Tony had hung shelves for her. She pulled down an accordion file where she kept articles and other scraps related to the report. From it, she retrieved her old client list. She sat on the stool at her desk and flipped through the pages, ticking with a pencil the names marked *JV*.

For the report, she wanted to interview people whose records ran the gamut, from essentially no record at all to a public felony record. She scanned the list, but she could only remember the precise outcome in three cases. Jin Chen: not competent, no record. Kasey Hartwell: hilarious case, driving record. And Mathis Lariviere—that was a name she'd never forget. He ended up with a private juvenile record, against all odds. The rest of the names bore some familiarity but the details were fuzzy, so she drained her tea, collected her things, and went up to the attic.

—◦—

Julia checked her phone—1:45. No wonder she was ravenous.

Even in late October, the air in the attic was thick and warm compared to the rest of the house. She wiped her brow but found no sweat. She simply *felt* clammy. She put Mathis's file back into the drawer marked *L–Q*. Closed the metal cabinet where she kept her old files. She had narrowed her list to fourteen names she wanted Charlie Lee to try to find. She'd written down each of their last-known contact information to give him a starting point.

She took the stairs back to her office, the cooler air kissing her forehead. She set down her things and pulled up Charlie's contact in her phone. He didn't answer, so she left a message.

She picked up her client list to put it away, but she paused. Her mind was snagged on the name at the center of the page: *Mathis Lariviere*. His name, and his mother's.

About a month into working on Mathis's case, Julia met with the seventeen-year-old at her office one evening. His license had been suspended because of his charges, and his mother, Elisa, had driven him to

Julia's office. When their meeting was over, Julia sent Mathis down the hallway. She assumed he and his mother were gone until she saw Elisa in the doorway.

"Do you have a moment, Julia?"

"Please, sit down."

Elisa closed the door behind her and sat across from Julia.

"You know Mathis is here under my visa."

"Yes. I've been working with an immigration attorney, doing everything we can to protect his status here."

"Mathis cannot return to France."

"Why not?"

"It should be enough that I tell you he can't."

Julia pulled a notepad out from under Mathis's file.

"No notes," Elisa said. Her posture was relaxed. She leaned back into her chair, her fingers interlaced in her lap.

"Is there something I can do for you?"

"I have a question. What happens to my son's case if the arresting officer doesn't testify?"

"Cops don't miss trials. That only happens in traffic court."

"Humor me."

Julia thought for a moment. "I don't know how the ADA could prove the drugs and gun were Mathis's without the first officer's testimony. But I don't know, I'd have to look into it. It's a weird hypothetical."

Julia smiled. Elisa didn't.

"Why are you asking?"

"Just curious. I don't know much about court, evidence."

That wasn't true, not according to Mathis. Mathis had told Julia that his mother was well-versed in criminal cases. That his whole family was.

Oh God. This woman was talking about . . . was she talking about paying this man off? Something worse?

"I don't like what you're implying."

"I'm not implying anything."

Julia's voice went shrill. "I think you are."

Elisa raised a hand. "Relax. We have the same goal here."

"I don't work with people who break the law."

Elisa narrowed her eyes a fraction. "Are you so sure of that?"

"Yes, I am."

Elisa shrugged and stood.

When she reached the doorway, Julia spoke again. "Elisa. I will drop your son's case if I even think you've done something."

"No need to grandstand," Elisa said. "You've made your point."

Julia heard the distant thud of the front door shutting, and she went to the window. She parted the curtain and watched Mathis and his mother cross the street to their car. Her hand shook against the lace.

As far as Julia could tell, Mathis's mother never meddled in his case. She came to every court date but never spoke to Julia like that again. And after more than a year of therapy, two hundred hours of volunteer work, and a clean report from his juvenile community corrections officer, Mathis earned an excellent outcome. Even some high praise from the judge on his last day in court.

In the hallway after the hearing, Elisa rested her manicured hand gently below Julia's elbow. They walked to a bank of windows away from the others outside the courtroom.

"Well done," Elisa said.

"It was a team effort."

"I like you, Julia." She smiled, the corners of her eyes crinkling under gray eyeshadow. "I am not so proud as to wish you ill. But if you had been in my place, with your own son, you would understand how I felt, that night we spoke at your office."

This woman, Julia realized, was bothered by the possibility that she had lost Julia's respect.

"I know it wasn't easy for you to trust me," Julia said.

"It is harder to play by the rules when it's your own family. And I hope with all my heart that you never, ever have to understand that."

That was true, Julia supposed. She didn't know what Elisa had felt, having her son face such serious charges. Even the possibility of deportation, back to a place where she believed he wasn't safe.

But Julia would never have been like Elisa, even if she had been standing in the woman's chic black shoes.

"I know you don't see it like I do," Elisa said, "but I feel like you've saved my son's life. If I can ever repay you—"

Julia cut her off. "Just pay your bill."

Elisa eyed Julia dryly, then let out a loud laugh.

Julia folded the client list closed. It would be nice, she thought, for Mathis's mother to see her now. See she'd been wrong about Julia. Just like there had been for Elisa, there was a young man Julia loved dearly whose life was, in a way, in the hands of the criminal court. And Julia was keeping her head down and trusting the system. Not hounding her old colleagues for gossip or favors.

But was Julia being as good as she thought, or was she simply not bothering to beat her head against a wall? Because in truth, there was nothing to do but wait for Nick's case to end, one way or another.

Below her office window, Julia could hear the telltale sound of the postman treading on the porch. She tidied up the desk, then went downstairs to the kitchen.

She put on the kettle for tea and got some bread out of the pantry. She heard the postman come back up on the porch. Now he was knocking on the door. Oh God, the door. Maybe he was going to ask about the broken window; she'd tell him Tony fell through it, like Tony had told the urgent care staff. Was that even believable? Julia opened the door and found she was out of time to assess the quality of her lie, because it wasn't the postman, after all. Standing on her porch was Detective Rice.

24

Rice parked on the road in front of the Hall house and checked his cell. It was just after two. He hadn't heard back from Nick yet, though he could have been in class. As the hours churned on he started to feel antsy. Walker's letter was so invasive. It wasn't uncommon for a victim in a domestic violence or sexual assault case to just drop away overnight, unwilling to prosecute. That letter—it would have made a lot of people think about giving up. He'd feel better if he could just talk to Nick. Assure him that the letter had helped his case. Make sure he was doing okay and knew this was just part of the process. And ask about Chris.

Someone was home: there was a red Subaru Baja—a distinctly hideous vehicle—in the driveway. But was Nick there? As Rice climbed the front steps to the porch, it occurred to him that he didn't know if Nick was still staying with his brother or if he'd moved back to his apartment. He could have tried Tony or Julia when Nick didn't call back. Instead, he'd driven to Orange without much thought at all.

Something was off about the outer front door . . . the glass was broken. And the bottom screen was ripped. Rice opened the door slowly, examining it. There was dried blood on the inside of the thin metal door. He knocked hard on the solid inner door. He heard muffled footfalls approaching.

The door creaked open to Julia's face. "Detective!"

"Good afternoon, miss. I was in your neighborhood and had a few minutes to spare, so I thought I'd swing by, 'case you were home."

"Sure, no problem, did you want to come in or . . ."

"I'll step in a minute, if you don't mind. Don't wanna cool off your house talking with the door open."

Julia smiled and stepped back from the doorway so that he could enter. "It's not that much warmer in here, I'm afraid."

Rice scuffed his shoes on the mat outside. "Say, what happened to your door here?"

"Oh, ah, accident," she said as she ushered him in. "We had an accident over the weekend, I just haven't had a chance to clean it up yet."

"What happened?" he asked again.

A kettle in the kitchen began to whistle, and Julia turned away from him. "Tony fell into the door yesterday, coming up onto the porch." She removed the kettle and switched off the burner with a snap. "He got to spend two hours of his Sunday at urgent care and now he's got this cast thing on."

Rice groaned. "Went clean through the glass? He all right?"

"Oh yeah, I'm sure it looks much more dramatic than it was. He did break a finger, but it sounds like it should heal fine." She turned to face him directly and asked, "Tea?"

"Ah, I'm not really one for tea, but thanks for offering."

"I could put on a pot of coffee for you, if you'd like?"

"No, dear, I don't want to trouble you. I'll just be here a minute."

Julia spooned what looked like loose tea leaves from a canister into a little clay teapot.

"How can I help, Detective?"

"Well, I'm assuming you saw the letter in the paper."

Julia nodded and breathed a sad yes.

"I'm so sorry for it. It's a terrible thing to have put out there like that."

She shook her head. "I just feel so sad for Nick. The . . . thing itself was already such an invasion, and now this."

"He doing okay?"

"I guess. We ended up going to see him last night. He wasn't answering us, so we just showed up." She paused. "He seemed kind of out of it, but he kept saying he was all right."

Rice felt some relief that it wasn't just his calls Nick was ignoring. And that Nick's family was on top of things, taking care of him.

"Well, I'm sure you know the letter's good for Nick's case."

Julia didn't speak; she looked like she was trying to work out how that could be.

"He's admitted we've got the right guy," Rice said, "and now we know the defense. It's all about consent."

"Huh," Julia said with surprise. "You're right. It's funny, I didn't even think of that. We were both so focused on how this would make Nick feel right now, we hadn't looked forward yet. But you're right."

Rice nodded.

"These are admissions," Julia said. "And he's screwed, don't you think? No one will believe someone would consent to what happened to Nick, right?"

Rice nodded. "Surely hope not. Do you know Nick's class schedule? I need to get in touch, but he hasn't gotten back to me, but clearly I shouldn't take it personal."

"No, I think he's just overwhelmed. It's not you. I don't know it off the top of my head but—"

Julia paused when her phone on the counter started to vibrate and ring.

Rice looked down at the screen, hoping it might say Nick's name. Instead, it read

Charlie Lee.

Charlie Lee? The PI?

"Oh, sorry, that's work. Do you mind if I take it quickly?"

"Be my guest."

Julia walked away down the hall as she answered the phone. "Hi, Charlie. I actually have company right now, maybe—yes—okay, let me just read you the list quick." Her voice grew quieter as she climbed the stairs.

Rice stood in the kitchen, listening to Julia's muffled voice above him, but he couldn't decipher a word. Why would she be working with a PI, if it was in fact *that* Charlie Lee? The Charlie that Rice knew had a pretty good reputation, at least for a PI who'd never been a cop. He came from insurance. They'd been on opposite sides of a couple cases; Charlie was usually hired by defendants.

Rice gave up trying to listen and leaned against the counter across from the stove. Checked his email until he heard a door shut somewhere above him and footfalls on the stairs.

"Sorry about that," Julia said as she reappeared at the end of the hall.

"That's fine, I've interrupted while you're on the clock."

She waved a hand.

"I have to ask, was that Charlie Lee the PI?"

"Yeah." Julia looked at him brightly and crossed her arms. "Yeah, I used to hire Charlie when I was a defense attorney, so I reached out to him on a project recently."

"I thought you worked more in policy now."

Julia set her phone back on the counter. "I do, I need him to track down some old clients for interviews."

"I see. Interesting."

She nodded.

"So, Nick's schedule," Julia said. "I think he's done with classes by three or four every day. I know he doesn't have any evening classes this semester." She picked up the teapot and swirled it gently, then tipped it into a mug on the counter.

The rush of liquid filling the cup sounded like music, and Rice regretted declining her offer for a drink.

"What do you need to talk to him about?"

"I just wanted to touch base after the letter. And, well." Rice adjusted himself against the counter. "Since I'm here, has Nick told you anything about the guy he was supposed to meet that night?"

Julia looked surprised. "Chris?"

"Yeah."

She considered his name. "I don't think I know anything about him, actually."

"Are he and Nick in a relationship?"

"No. Nick's liked him for a while, he mentioned him over the summer, I remember."

"Okay," Rice said.

She frowned. "What does this have to do with anything?"

"Probably nothing. I'm just making sure I've done my homework. Making sure we have all the information."

"I see," she said slowly. "You'll have to ask him."

⁓

Rice sat in his car for a minute before he drove on.

He had glazed over the issue with that vague due diligence talk. Maybe Julia sensed what he was getting at. She'd been a defense attorney.

Walker knew how to tell a good story. They knew that now, from the letter. He'd made admissions, but he'd also hit back against the charges. And as Linda had feared, the fact that Nick was a male victim seemed to make the media think this case was more newsworthy. Walker had hired Eva Barr, who would hire her own PI. It would only be a matter of time before the defense knew about Chris, and Chris was a problem. Chris gave Nick a reason to lie about the nature of his encounter with Walker. Chris was another thread for the defense to pull at.

25

NICK HALL, 2015

Nick's stomach pitched at the sound of his phone. The short vibration meant a text message, not a phone call. He paused the show on his computer and rolled toward his bedside table. Tony:

You doing okay?

Nick groaned. It was just the daily check in.
As he always did, he wrote back:

Yeah.

Thank God he wasn't staying with Tony anymore. At least Nick didn't have to deal with him in person. Tony was texting and sending Nick snaps all the time now, more in the last week than ever before. It was exhausting, reassuring Tony that he was fine. And every time Tony reached out, before Nick saw his name on the screen, Nick couldn't help but worry it was *another* classmate texting him because they'd heard about the case. Or worse: texting him because something new came out about that night. But that couldn't happen—only he and Ray knew what happened in that room, and they had both already talked.

There was a knock at the door, and Johnny stuck his head in.

"The detective is here. The guy."

"Why?"

"He didn't say."

Nick's phone buzzed in his hand.

Tony:

> Need anything?

He typed quickly.

> Yeah. Listen when I say I'm fine.

—⊘—

Detective Rice was standing at the bottom of the stairs, in the messy entryway.

"Do you have somewhere private to talk?"

"Not really," Nick said. He didn't want this man seeing his bedroom.

"Go for a walk?"

Nick grabbed a jacket and beanie and followed him outside.

They went down Spring Street and toward campus. The detective brought up the letter first.

He was fine, Nick told him.

It was helpful to his team, the detective said. Now they know the defense, so they can prepare, he went on. And, they can use the letter against Walker in court.

Okay, Nick said.

Detective Rice moved along quickly.

"Hey, I meant to ask you, what's the situation with you and Chris?"

"Nothing," Nick said with a shrug.

"You're not together?"

"Nope." Nick had never responded to any of Chris's texts since the night it happened. He was probably the last person on the planet Nick wanted to talk to about this.

"Were you that night?"

"No," Nick said. "He stood me up."

The detective shook his head like Nick wasn't understanding him. "Were you in a relationship with each other that night?"

"No," Nick said. Did he have to spell it out? "He didn't want to date me."

The detective nodded. "Would it have mattered to him for any reason if you slept with someone else?"

But I didn't, Nick thought. His eyes must have betrayed his shock at the question, because the detective spoke again.

"I know you didn't *sleep with* Walker. What I mean is . . ." He paused. "The ADA just wanted to know more about your relationship, thinking it'll come up in court. You saw what Walker's saying. Him and his lawyer will probably try to make it look like you didn't want Chris to find out. Like you cheated on him."

"How would they know about Chris?"

"Well, he's part of your story. His name's in my report, your statement, other places. They'll get all that."

"Wait," Nick said. "Are people gonna talk to him?"

"I don't know," Detective Rice said. "Probably. They might interview him. I might need to."

"He has nothing to do with what happened."

"I know it's confusing from where you are. I just don't want to sugarcoat it. Court can end up reaching into all kinds of places you wouldn't expect."

Nick thought again of something his therapist said during their first session. Jeff was talking about confidentiality, almost going through a mental checklist, and he said something about how a court could order a therapist to turn over records.

"How can whether or not he raped me have anything to do with Chris?"

"Because if he can't come up with a good reason you'd lie, he's fucked."

Hearing Detective Rice speak so crassly was jarring. The man looked rough—he was big and old and wore a gun under his jacket. His face was pocked and wrinkled. But he'd never spoken to Nick like that.

"He's gonna do everything he can to make you look like a liar, Nick. He's facing years, decades even. And lifetime registration as a sex offender."

Nick's breathing had gone shallow. He felt like they were fighting, but over what he wasn't sure.

The detective was still talking. "He's gonna come for you, hard. Has anyone told you that?"

"You could have," Nick said.

Detective Rice's eyes opened in surprise. He lowered his voice. "You were hurting."

Meaning, I didn't want to hurt you more. The detective had been babying Nick. Just like Tony. Just like everyone who talked to him about this goddamn case. They were treating him like he was a child. And it was working. Every time he had to talk about the case, he felt himself sink backward, further away from the man he'd been before that night.

The detective was watching him as they walked on.

"We weren't dating. I wanted to; he didn't. He wouldn't have cared if I did sleep with someone else. That's it. There's nothing there."

Detective Rice's voice was calm. "Okay. If there's anything you're not telling me about you and Chris, you should do it now."

"Why?"

"Because it doesn't look good when you change your story later."

Something was happening. Deep under his eyes, he could feel tears threatening to well in the cool air.

"I don't get to keep your secrets," the detective said. "You tell me, the ADA tells him. Everything is fair game for him, that's how due process works."

But he can't have what the police don't have, Nick thought to himself. *You know this. Ray can't have it if you don't give it to anyone.*

The urge to cry faded.

"I don't know what you want from me," Nick said.

"Just the truth."

Nick shrugged. "You already have it."

26

There was a hole in Tony's sneaker, where his big toe rubbed against the mesh. The shoes were gray with white detailing, originally, but now they were grass-stained and dingy with mud. He mostly wore them to play with the kids and mow the lawn. He couldn't remember the last time he'd gone running. He laced up and left the house. At the end of the driveway he went right, away from town center. He would turn around, he thought, at the small bridge around two miles down the road. The air was cold and dry in his nostrils, and a dull ache thrummed up his shins with each footfall.

The first time Tony went for a run outdoors was the summer after he graduated from college. It had been a summer of change, and he remembered it well. The last summer he threw a punch. With one exception, the last summer he had a drink. It was all connected.

Drinking was where he was weak: more than a couple and it was like the "restraint" switch in his brain flicked off. Tony's limbs got loose, and his laugh was too loud and he was funny and fun, usually, unafraid to sing or dance or hit on a beautiful girl. But sometimes he was not funny; his jokes got too sharp. And sometimes he was not fun. Sometimes a guy looked at him wrong, like he thought he was tough shit and he wanted

Tony to agree. There were a few drunken fights in college, always spurred on by that kind of thing, the posturing, a heavy-handed "What are you looking at?" Twice there were fistfights. His friends recounted these incidents with dramatic glee, like Tony was Rocky. Tony tried to see himself as they did: a take-no-shit badass. What he remembered of the fights, though, was the sensation that his arms were flailing, just barely within his control. Like he and the other guy were puppets thrashing against each other.

His last fight happened in the summer after college. That his then girlfriend called it a fight was barely accurate, actually, but his memory had logged it as one because of her. He and the guy went hands-on for seconds, really. The guy grabbed him by the shirt; he shoved the guy off. That was it.

The morning after, she was still mad. "You're too old for this."

"He grabbed me," Tony said in disbelief.

"You were yelling at him."

"If you think that was yelling—"

"You could see that he was a drunk asshole."

"He called that guy a fag."

"That guy didn't hear him."

"So?"

"You don't get to police everyone. What if you'd been arrested for fighting? What if he went crazy and hurt you, or me? You don't think about what you're risking, you just jump into some bullshit hero mode for people who aren't asking for your help. I don't like being out with you, wondering who might set you off. You're not like that when you don't drink."

"You don't think I would have said something to him if I'd heard that sober?"

"I don't think you would have gotten into a shoving match over it, no."

For the fight and other reasons, they broke up. She sent a goodbye email to his mother, apparently. Tony never got to read it, but in it she talked about his drinking. He knew because his mom brought it up the next time he saw her.

"You know your dad has quite a quick fuse when he drinks."

"Are you seriously comparing me to him?"

"No, honey. I know you're not just going around picking fights. Maybe you even have good reasons. But reasoning can get slippery when alcohol's involved."

Tony had spent his life watching his dad get worked up over something a sober person might not have noticed, let alone attached meaning to. Glances Ron perceived as disrespectful or unfaithful. With each popped tab came the potential for jealousy, anger, distrust.

Tony softened his voice. "I'm not an asshole like he is, Ma."

"I know you aren't." They were sitting at her kitchen table, eating the lasagna she'd made for his visit. "Sober, you're just about the best man I've ever known. Sometimes I can't believe you turned out like you did. Especially with your brother, my God you're good to him. I stayed with your dad as long as I did because I was worried that a divorce would ruin your life. I guess I was drinking the 'broken home' Kool-Aid. If I could have seen what an amazing man you'd become, I wouldn't have worried. I would have put you in the car and left years earlier. You are nothing like him." She paused. "You're nothing like him sober. But the drinking . . . nothing goes from zero to sixty. It's a slide. When I met your dad he was charming. Such a good dancer. He wasn't perfect, always a bit of a hothead, but he was different. There was a slide. And I think alcohol made it steeper and faster."

That month, Tony went to see a drug and alcohol counselor.

"Do you think you have a drinking problem?" she asked.

"No," he said. "But is it possible to be *pre*-drinking problem?"

"Like you're standing at the precipice of a problem, you mean?"

"Yeah."

"Absolutely." She said nothing. She wanted more from him.

"I think that's what my mom thinks. She's not, like, a dramatic mom. She doesn't helicopter. Or guilt trip. And she's seen it, serious alcoholism in my dad. So the fact that she thinks—" The words were too painful. He exhaled sharply, and the urge to cry passed. "The last thing I ever wanted was to turn out like him. She doesn't deserve that. And my little brother— he already looks up to me. And I want that, it makes me feel like I matter. I don't want him to think our dad is normal. I want to be that for him. And if I go over the ledge . . ."

She nodded. "So step back."

He decided to give up drinking, just for the rest of the summer, to see what he thought. The counselor gave him a list of local AA meetings, but he never went. She also told him to find a hobby that let him process what he was feeling. He started running that summer. It was his time to burn off nervous energy and useless thoughts. The summer ended, but he kept running. His runs got longer, and his highs got stronger.

He stopped a few months into dating Julia. He fell out of the habit so quickly—suddenly he hadn't gone out in a month. It wasn't that running had been bad; wasn't bad now. The stiffness in his ankles was loosening, and his strides grew longer. He remembered this, the kinks working out as his legs warmed up.

Maybe he stopped needing the run. By then he was used to not drinking. Happy with the person he was becoming. And who needs a runner's high when you've got a new girlfriend? He got higher off Julia than anything else. She made him feel blissed out and self-assured. Calm and strong. Not that he became flawless. He had, in fact, punched through a window in anger ten days ago. Broke his pinkie finger. It felt like a cosmic insult: *Think you're a tough guy, big man, punching glass? Now your wittle finger is broken.*

He passed a neighbor's house. They had a barn and an old grain silo that was falling to pieces, big hunks of metal missing from the sides and top. His lungs began to ache in the cold air. It was November now, thank God. October had been miserable all the way through. As much as he'd wanted Nick under his roof, the long visit had exhausted him, and then Walker's letter swept him off his feet. Tony had been doing so well for so long. Fifteen years—was that right? It was. Fifteen years since he'd made all those changes. And they had worked, he thought.

Once, on a run, he passed a fallen tree and it reminded him of a fable his mom used to read him as a kid, about an oak tree and a reed. The tree, with its thick trunk, looked indisputably stronger than the wispy reed on the riverbank, but when a fierce windstorm came, the tree was ripped out by the roots and fell, while the reed survived because it could bend. And suddenly he got it—the point his mom had been making. His father thought he was as tough as they came, and he wanted everyone to know it, but in truth he was the weakest person Tony knew. Ron Hall couldn't function in the morning without a fresh can of Bud. He broke things to scare his wife. He hit his sons. He was pathetic. Tony's mother, by comparison, was outwardly soft and gentle, but her inner strength was abundant. That day on the run, he'd gotten it. He'd learned the lesson. And he'd gone on for fifteen more years working at himself. Working at learning to bend.

But in spite of it all, the anger could rush him so easily. He'd read Walker's letter, read those sickening words, and he was blinded. Felt certain that hitting something, anything, would relieve the excruciating pain he was feeling. His father's method of coping was always going to be there, offering itself up to him. "Don't be a little pussy; be a man. Hit back. Don't take that." Fifteen years and it was still there. And what had it given him? A broken pinkie, damaged pride, and worst of all, two terrified children. Seb had wailed first, then Chloe. The shame he felt in that moment plagued him.

And yet, in spite of his shame, he had stayed angry. After all, Walker was the cause of his behavior. Tony was even a bit angry with Julia, for her shock. Yes, what he'd done was not rational. It was frightening. Violent. Fine, it was all the things he normally wasn't. But could she not forgive him, after reading what he had? Not only had this man assaulted Nick, but now he had reached them in their homes. Shoved his lies in their faces. Made up a bullshit story and twisted it all back around on Nick.

Tony ran faster, his feet beating the pavement. The ache in his lungs thickened, and his mouth began to water. Fuck Raymond Walker. Fuck him and his lies and his smug, self-important letter about truth and justice. Fuck him for doing this to Nick.

Nick.

A stitch began to stab the underside of his ribs, and he slowed to a walk, panting and grasping for the pain in his side. Nick told him to let it go. Nick was okay. He hadn't believed it at first; it didn't seem possible that Nick cared so little about the letter. But he said he was fine, and it seemed to be true. He answered Tony's texts. Sent Tony snaps on Snapchat. There was a bored selfie sent from class one day. Another day, a picture of the TV, his roommate off to the side watching with him. His life was going on like it had before. If anything, the only thing that seemed to be bothering him was Tony's constant checking on him.

Tony wasn't making anything better; he was only making himself sick. He turned and began to walk home. He hadn't reached the bridge, but he didn't care.

27

In mid-November, when Charlie Lee's name lit up her phone screen, Julia hurried to her office to take the call away from Tony.

Charlie rattled through the list of her former clients' names, pausing long enough for Julia to record the address or phone number he'd confirmed. When they'd finished, Charlie lowered his voice playfully.

"So, the side project." The way he said it smacked of secrecy. And to be fair, it was a secret. She didn't want anyone knowing that she'd hired Charlie to look into Raymond Walker, to see if he could drum up anything to help secure a conviction. Not even Tony.

Charlie only told her two things that she hadn't already heard from either Nick or the detective.

The first was that Raymond Walker wasn't the one who rented the room at the motel where he took Nick. The man working the front desk told Charlie he booked the room to a woman who'd paid cash. Motel 4 didn't make patrons put down a credit card, so long as they paid for the room and had a driver's license staff could photocopy. Charlie hadn't located the woman who paid for Walker's room, but based on search results that came up for her name, she was probably transient. Walker had probably offered her cash to book the room. "Happens more often than you'd think," Charlie said.

Julia didn't know if the police knew Walker had paid someone to book the room under a different name, but she suspected they did. They must have checked at the desk when they were still trying to track him down. It was hard to think of an innocent reason to do something like that. The term *malice aforethought* floated up in her mind. It was a term lawyers didn't use much in Maine but she'd learned it in law school. It stood for something like internal recognition of the evil you would later perpetrate. Booking a room under someone else's name before you bring someone there . . . that sounded like Walker had planned to do this to someone. It was strange to think that Detective Rice knew about something like that without sharing it with them—or at least with Nick. But that was a silly way to see it. It wasn't his job to tell them things.

The second surprise Charlie delivered was that Raymond Walker had no criminal or PFA history come up in his database searches.

"Not what I expected," Charlie said, "but I do think we're dealing with a crime people are less apt to report. I'm gonna call around out of state, since he travels for work."

"There's no way I've paid you enough for any more of your time."

"Don't mention it, seriously. It's been slow. And I'm interested. No one's as clean as this guy seems right now." He chuckled. "Except maybe you."

28

NICK HALL, 2015

From his bedroom window, Nick saw Tony pull up on the street. Nick paused at his mirror one last time. Light blue button-down, Tony's tan trousers, scuffed brown dress shoes. He looked respectable and adult, albeit boring. All three seemed right for testifying at a grand jury.

Outside, it felt cold enough for snow, but the sky was clear.

Nick climbed into Tony's SUV. "Thanks for the ride."

"No problem," Tony said. "I wanted to bring you."

"I didn't give you much notice."

Tony looked away and began to drive. "It's fine. I know I've been a bit much."

"No," Nick said.

That was a lie—Tony *had* been a bit much. After Walker sent the letter to the paper, Tony started texting him almost daily.

How you holding up, Just checking in

just checking, checking, it was exhausting. So Nick had dealt with Tony as he had done before: Nick gave him quick, perfunctory answers.

Fine; Good; Can't talk, busy; In class.

Basically, he would say enough to reassure his brother, and he'd withhold enough to stifle conversation. It had worked, and eventually, Tony backed off. Now Nick felt guilty. Tony just wanted him to be okay. Was that so bad?

Back when he was tired of Tony's concern, he told Tony he wanted to go to the grand jury himself. Tony asked a few times, but Nick said no, and Tony gave up. Then that morning, Nick woke up gasping for air, clawing at his throat, and it had taken seconds, long seconds, for him to realize he was safe in his own bed. For the sound of laughter to fade from his head. He was safe. Safe, but alone. He texted Tony. Asked if he wanted to come after all.

When they got to the courthouse, Nick used the bathroom for the fourth time that morning. His stomach was killing him. He'd eaten some toast, but even that wasn't sitting well.

A marshal told them where to go, on the second floor of the court-house. Linda came out into the hall and met Tony. Told them they could sit on the bench against the wall. Said it would be a while as she ducked back into the room down the hall.

They sat together talking about television, Nick's classes, a funny story about his niece, anything but why they were there. Tony was trying to distract him, and right now, Nick didn't mind.

The toast and acid in Nick's stomach were rioting, and the noise was getting obvious. A couple of times, he noticed Tony's eyes flick toward his stomach and back up again.

Finally, Tony said, "It sounds like a barrel of snakes in there."

Nick burst into laughter, shocked and delighted at the absurdity of it.

Tony laughed, too, clearly pleased with himself. "You must have been shitting your brains out earlier."

"I'm nervous," Nick groaned, still smiling. And he was nervous, but the laughter was settling his stomach.

The door opened. It was Linda again. "Ready?"

Suddenly, Nick felt Tony's hand close over his own. Three squeezes: *I love you*, like when Nick was little. Nick returned four squeezes. He did love Tony. He might have loved him more than any other person. His brother was a pain in the ass, but he took care of Nick like no one else did.

When he stepped into the room, first he noticed the people. Sherie, the advocate person for the case, had called him last week to talk about the grand jury, and she said there would probably be twenty-three of them. Twenty-three grand jurors who would vote on whether Linda had enough evidence to charge Ray with raping Nick. Twenty-three strangers who would decide what they thought of Nick.

There was wood paneling and Maine and American flags in the corner, but the room was a little unlike a courtroom, too. There was no judge, no seating for an audience. He sat down in a little booth, like he'd seen in court movies before. Linda stood to the side of him, and he faced the grand jurors.

Linda started off easy. His name, his age, where he lived, what he was studying.

"Now I have some questions about October second of this year."

The *thud-thud-thud* in Nick's chest quickened. He nodded.

Why did he go out? Who went with him? Did Chris show up? Was he dating Chris? What did he and Elle do at the bar? How many drinks did he have? How quickly? But over how much time? So he wasn't drunk, right? When did he notice the man who introduced himself as Josh?

"When I went up to the bar. Elle wanted another round."

"What time was that?"

He couldn't remember. Was that bad? Sweat broke out on his hairline. "I don't remember."

"Would you remember if you looked at your statement?"

Nick nodded.

Linda pulled a stapled set of pages from a folder on the table beside her. She folded over a page and underlined something with a pencil from the table. She handed it to Nick.

It was a police report. It read *DETECTIVE JOHN RICE* at the top. A sentence was underlined in pencil: *Nick told me it was sometime after 10:30 and before 11:00 that he met the man he would later identify as RAYMOND WALKER at Jimmy's Pub.*

"Do you remember now?" Linda asked.

"Yeah," he said. "It was sometime after ten thirty and before eleven."

"Okay. Was he at the bar when you went up?"

Nick's eyes drifted to the carpet. He pictured it. "No," he said. "He sat down beside me when I was already there."

"Who initiated the conversation?"

He didn't have to think about that one. "He did," Nick said quickly. Nick hadn't wanted to think back on that night—he wanted to let the memory of it wither and die in the dark. But Ray had written that letter, and he'd made it sound like Nick had been pursuing him. Nick couldn't help remembering, comparing his version to Walker's. That part just wasn't true.

Linda's questions went on. What name did the man give Nick? What did they talk about? How long did they talk? How many drinks did Nick have? How many did "Josh" have? Who invited whom to leave?

"He did," Nick said. He could hear it: "Wanna get out of here?" It should have been cheesy, but Josh—Ray—had the perfect voice for the line.

"How did you decide where to go?"

"He said he had a room, so we just went there."

"Where was the room?"

"Motel 4."

"How did you get there?"

"We took a cab?"

"What happened in the cab?"

Nick felt his face flushing.

He had liked Josh so much. He'd felt loose and pliable from the liquor, Chris's rejection. Josh was so handsome, mature, with crinkles by his light eyes. Josh had been so relaxed about himself. They'd gotten into the taxi, a male cabbie up front, Josh had said, "Motel 4," and he'd leaned into Nick. Josh didn't care what the cabbie thought, and in that moment, Nick didn't, either.

"We made out."

He was really getting into it now. Not just that he was gay—that alone was probably a problem for some of the people in the room—but that he'd been willing. *At first*, he reminded himself. *You were only willing at first.*

He looked out at the group of them, and he accidentally locked eyes with a man in the front row. The man looked away quickly.

"Just kissing?" Linda asked.

Nick's hands were in his lap, and he began to rub at his right forearm. It was dark in the cab, their breath had been fast, and Josh had brought a hand to Nick's groin. Nick hadn't told that detail to anyone yet.

"Yeah," Nick said.

He worked his thumb up under his sleeve.

⁓

When Nick came out of the double doors, Tony was standing at the end of the hallway.

"Hey," he said, and walked back to Nick quickly.

"Linda said I can leave if I want," Nick said.

"How did it go?"

"Okay." Slow and fast at the same time. Exhausting, stressful, but better than he'd worried it would be. He'd stuck to his story. Didn't fuck anything up. "I think I did okay," he said.

"Is he indicted?"

"She's not done."

Tony looked over Nick's shoulder, at the door behind him. "You don't want to wait, just in case?"

Nick shook his head. The adrenaline that had rushed him as he testified was draining. "I want to go home."

In the parking lot, Tony offered to take him to lunch first, but Nick was too tired.

He climbed into the front seat and sank back against it. He might fall asleep on the drive, he thought. As he brought his seat belt over his torso, the soft inner flesh of his forearm stung where it rubbed against the inside of his sleeve. He clicked the buckle into its lock, then turned his wrist upward. He looked down, as subtly as he could. A pinprick of blood had soaked through his sleeve.

29

Julia had said nothing in response. She just kept sipping at her tea. Even now, Rice couldn't help but be reminded of Irene when he looked at her. Irene had been solid as a rock. Julia used to look solid, too, but today her hands were shaking.

"You've never been to a grand jury," Rice said.

"No."

"Generally pretty boring, but Nick's was interesting."

"Why?"

"Well, for one, the victim doesn't always testify, but you know that. Linda wanted to give him a practice run, see how he did."

"Yeah," she said.

"Did you know he made a mistake?"

"No."

It was subtle enough that Linda Davis, the ADA, hadn't even noticed it, and she had pretty good attention to detail. Something about it, though, had bothered Rice. The boy had reached the part of his story where he and Raymond Walker entered the hotel room. He testified that he shut the door, and Walker hit him over the head. He said he fell to the floor, then Walker turned on the light, and that was where Nick's vision and memory faded out. Rice remembered looking at the boy's face as he said it. Nick was looking down, which was not abnormal; it wasn't easy stuff to talk about, let alone to a room full of strangers. But suddenly Rice felt itchy under his collar and like he needed to stand up. Rice had waited until the boy left and Linda began speaking to the jurors, then he leaned back in his chair as casually as he could and opened his folder. He pulled out his notes from his interview of Nick, but he would have to listen to the recording to be sure.

Back at the station, he sat at his desk, put on headphones, and pulled up his interview of Nick. Hunched forward, hands in his lap, he listened to the entire thing. Yes, it was small, but there it was. Nick had never mentioned Walker turning on the light before.

In the interview, Nick had said it was dark when Walker hit him, and that was the last thing he remembered. Now he said he fell to the floor and Walker turned on the light. Such a sensory detail. The kind of thing you couldn't help but picture: the black hole of a dark motel room flooding with yellow light. So why hadn't Nick mentioned it before?

"He changed something," Rice said.

"At the grand jury?"

"Yup. And as crazy as it sounds, that was the moment. That was when the case slipped away from me."

A case was never fully in the state's control start to finish—that was impossible. That wasn't what Rice meant. He walked into that grand jury feeling as good as he could about a case like Nick's. The story had been consistent. The physical evidence was on their side. Even Chris Gosling seemed to be less of a problem than they'd worried—Chris told O'Malley the same thing Nick told Rice: they weren't dating. As far as Rice knew, Nick didn't have a motive in the world to make up a sexual assault.

And then at the grand jury, Nick fumbled on the strangest point.

"What do you mean it slipped away from you?"

Rice shrugged. "I knew something was wrong, and I sat on it."

Julia stared at him, wide-eyed and miserable.

There was no way to atone for the sins he had committed. But at least he could confess.

"You know why I called you here, don't you?"

30

L ast week, Raymond Walker was indicted. They hadn't gotten many details about the grand jury proceeding: just that it had been successful. This good news was followed swiftly by what felt like bad news: press coverage.

Linda had been smart to make Nick's name private, because the press seemed hooked on the rape case with the male victim. Even a paper up north had run an article on the case following the indictment. Julia couldn't remember any of her cases making the news like this, with statewide coverage or regular updates.

The articles discussed the procedure thus far—the arrest, Walker's bail, the indictment—and contained a couple quotes from Walker's lawyer, Eva Barr. The quotes were the same across the articles—she must have sent them by email. "We're unsurprised by the indictment, given that the grand jury only hears the prosecution's version of events. We're confident that when a jury has the chance to hear from Ray, he'll be acquitted." The article then recapped Walker's letter: according to him, "the alleged victim had been drinking, pursued Walker at the bar, and then the two consensually engaged in 'rough' sex."

That was hard enough to read, but Julia's primary anxiety, unfounded as it was, was that Nick's identity would somehow get linked to the case, destroying what little privacy he had in this mess. Julia wasn't a fan of reporters, per se, but she trusted them not to publish Nick's name, given that the judge had ruled it should be confidential in the court proceedings. It was the active comment sections of the articles that worried her. For whatever reason, people felt compelled to take to the internet and give their view of the case. The only people who knew "the victim" in these articles was Nick Hall were other Halls and a couple of Nick's best friends, save for the professionals. That someone might out him online seemed far-fetched, but even the possibility bothered her. The day after the indictment, she skimmed the comment sections of each article she could find. She tried to look only for capital *N*'s and *H*'s, but it was impossible to resist reading. Many of the comments were anti-Walker. Some were not.

There was the sexist:

> I might be able to swallow this if the "victim" were
> a smaller female, but a 20yo male gets knocked
> unconscious in a single blow? It's just very hard
> to buy.

And the bigot:

> Is this not how two dudes get down?

Mostly, the negative commenters questioned Nick's story.

> TBH this sounds like a kinky hookup?
> Do we really want judges, i.e., taxpayers, sorting out

levels of consent when this much alcohol was involved
and two adults went to a hotel room?

So can we just get straight that this guy blacked out,
wasn't hit on the head or whatever nonsense . . . just
doesn't want to own that he drank himself dumb. If he
doesn't remember what happened, that doesn't mean
he wasn't consenting to it.

⁓

The comments bothered Julia for hours after she read them. They bothered Tony for days. He kept trying to show her new ones. Fresh grenades
of hate lobbed at anyone who read them.

"I'm done with that stuff," she said.

"Why?"

"It's too painful. It's nothing new and it just—people suck. I don't
need to keep reading all the ways that people suck."

"What if Nick is seeing this shit?"

They were in bed, Tony on his phone, Julia setting down the book he
was distracting her from.

"He might be seeing it," she said.

Tony looked at her like, *exactly*. As if she could do something about
Seaside News's comment section. He was all revved up at the faceless
users who'd left the comments, and the only person he could reach about
it was Julia. She got that. But it was starting to piss her off.

"It is terrible," she said emphatically. "But I don't know what else
to do."

"I wanna kill all these people."

She snuggled against him. "That is *super* reasonable."

He laughed softly.

She added, "We could fit some bodies out back."

—◦—

Tony seemed to calm down about the whole thing for a couple of days, but apparently not enough to stop looking for news online. Julia was showering when Tony came in.

"He fucking did it again."

She pushed back the curtain. "Who did what?"

"Walker." Tony shoved his phone in her face.

It was a Facebook page. She read aloud. "'Confirmed: My son's accuser has a boyfriend.' Oh, Christ," she groaned. "Is this his mother?"

"Yup," Tony said. "Keep reading."

"I'm in the shower." The most self-evident statement she'd ever made. "Can it wait?"

Tony read on. "'Anyone think of a reason he doesn't want to admit to sex?'"

Julia turned off the water. "That's awful."

"He must have told her to post it."

"Can you pass me a towel?" Julia squeezed the water from her hair.

Tony handed her one through the curtain. "Can they use it against him in court?"

She wound the towel around her torso and secured it. "A statement by his mom? They can ask her about it, but I don't know what good it will do."

"Why don't you sound more upset?"

She pulled back the curtain. "I guess because we knew this was gonna happen. We knew they'd try to make something out of Chris."

"Can't the judge make him stop talking?"

"It's not his post."

"But isn't that a thing a judge can do?"

She sighed. "A gag order?"

Tony's mouth pulled into a tight line. "I'm annoying you."

"Kind of. I'm trying to get ready; I need to go to the store."

Thanksgiving was that coming Thursday. The grocery store would be a mob scene.

"I can go," Tony said.

"No," she said quickly. "I know this is hard. He's your brother. It sucks. I'll take care of the store."

In truth, she wanted the excuse to get out of the house and take a breather.

—◠—

Julia's list was long, encompassing a normal week of meals and a dinner for ten, since Nick was bringing his roommate Elle. In a few days they would host Thanksgiving, as they had for years now. Julia considered their unit—herself, Tony, and the kids—to be the hub of the family. Her widowed mother, Tony's divorced parents and Jeannie, and Nick were the spokes they connected. One year Nick would have a serious boyfriend, and he might go to another family's dinner, but she hoped that once he was married, and if he had kids, he would continue to celebrate the holiday with them. She loved Nick. There had been moments that fall when Tony acted like he didn't believe she did. She had been heartbroken when he was assaulted. She felt miserable for him with each new invasion the process brought. Her feelings just didn't have the same staying power as Tony's. This was all much more personal for Tony. Maybe she would have understood if Nick were her brother, but it seemed to be more than that. Their relationship was different than most siblings she knew. Tony felt responsible for Nick.

Hopefully Tony would cool off in the hours she and Seb were at Shop 'n Save. Bless him, Seb was obsessed with the grocery store, and while Chloe would usually pass on the chaos of a weekend shopping trip, Seb would throw a fit before he'd be left at home. Though she was merely guessing, Julia assumed people who tripped on acid looked something like her son as he stepped through the automatic doors of their local Shop 'n Save. Every week, Seb was visibly in awe of the colors, smells, and busy sounds that inundated him on arrival.

The storefront of the Shop 'n Save in Orange hadn't actually worn that name in more than a decade. A big corporation bought it out and changed the name long before Julia even moved to Orange, but her neighbors still called it by the old name. The store's products and prices catered more to the inhabitants of the town center—mostly liberal, mostly wealthy, mostly that southern Maine mix of bougie and hippie. Sometimes Julia's neighbors in the country griped about what the store had become, and Julia felt like a fraud for feigning her agreement with them. With her creaky farmhouse and stay-at-home job, they didn't know she came from affluent stock by way of her parents in Yarmouth. They didn't know how much she liked to buy six-dollar loaves of rosemary bread, herbal face oils, and all organic everything, right down to the canned beans. "Shop 'n Overpay," her neighbor Willie called the store. Julia soothed her guilt by buying eggs from Willie every week. She always noted the irony that they were quite expensive.

This weekend the store was a madhouse, and Seb was in heaven. He cradled sweet potatoes in his arms, dropping one with a thud as Julia tried to intercept him on his way to the cart. He selected a purple onion and inspected it with a severe look on his face before holding it up to an older gentleman riffling through the pile to his left.

"Good choice," the man said with a nod, and Sebastian beamed. As they made their way through the store, her chatty son greeted neighbors and strangers alike. In the cereal aisle, Julia was crouching for a canister of oatmeal when she heard her son exclaim, "Detective!"

She turned to find Detective Rice standing over her. She must have looked startled, because he opened with an apology for sneaking up on her.

"It's fine," she said as she stood. "Hi."

"Hi," he said with a smile.

A woman came up next to the detective with her cart, and he moved out of her way in the cramped aisle.

"I didn't realize you lived over here, too," Julia offered.

"Oh, I don't, but my sister-in-law and her kids do. I'm due there for lunch, and I was stopping to grab bread." He held a single, fresh boule in his hand. It was from the bakery section across the store—had he followed her?

"Are you making sandwiches?" Sebastian asked brightly.

"I think so, little man."

"Is your wife here, too?" Julia asked.

"My wife passed away, actually, little over five years ago."

Julia winced; he continued before she could speak.

"It's all right, really."

"That's so sad," Sebastian said. "Do you miss her?"

Julia put a hand on Seb's shoulder; she felt an urge to shush him, but there was a sweetness to his innocent concern that didn't deserve to be silenced.

"Very much," the detective said.

"How did—" Seb began.

"Honey, Detective Rice needs to get to his family's house."

Detective Rice took the hint and nodded. "I just saw you and wanted to check on you quick. Lot of business in the news lately." He spoke in code for Seb's sake. "Hope you and your family are doing all right."

Fatigue crept over her shoulders. "We are." She let his eyes hold hers for a beat. What did he expect her to say? There was nothing to do but survive it. The wheels of justice were grinding along slowly, and there was no way for Detective Rice or anyone else to shut down the public chatter in the meantime.

Detective Rice departed with a quiet goodbye to Julia and a wave to

Sebastian, who had wandered to the end of the aisle, bored with the adults talking about the news. Julia watched the detective amble away, slightly hunched, looking older and maybe smaller now. Was it her new knowledge that he was a widower, and one who still wore his wedding band? Or was it the image of him, just a man on the weekend, off the clock, worried about what her family was going through? Julia had felt that way a thousand times before at her old job—like she couldn't do anything real for people who desperately needed help. She had assumed a man of Detective Rice's experience would be immune to such feelings of failure, but now she suspected she didn't know him as well as she had thought.

31

At least twenty minutes had passed since he heard the change in Julia's breath and knew she was asleep. Tony, on the other hand, could feel his mind revving up instead of settling for the night. Thanksgiving was a matter of hours away, and there was so much to do in the morning. Tony would handle the oven: the turkey, mashed potatoes, and pie; Julia would take the salad, hors d'oeuvres, and table. The kids would "help," meaning they'd double the time it took to do everything. People would start arriving at noon. Their mothers would be on time; Nick would not; Ron and Jeannie were a crapshoot. The first time Tony and Julia hosted the whole family for Thanksgiving, Ron showed up with a buzz on. Ron polished off a six-pack as they ate, and Tony ended up asking him to leave early. He and Jeannie left with less fuss than Tony had expected, but they didn't show up the next two years.

It was debatable whether Tony and Ron's relationship had improved or deteriorated with time. To Ron, he suspected, Tony had grown into a disrespectful man who'd adopted some soft-minded view that his father had been abusive. To Tony, he had finally grown too strong for his dad to control with his hands or his words. Over time, Ron had backed down, and eventually he became tolerable enough that Tony didn't mind him being around Chloe and Seb, so long as Tony or Julia was there. There was always a tension between the two of them, teeming under the surface of their uneasy truce. Neither respected, or even much liked, the other.

If Nick hadn't existed, Tony probably would have been long done with Ron Hall. But Nick did exist, and that kept Ron in the loop. As difficult a person as Jeannie was, Nick loved her, and she and Ron came as a set. Nick probably even loved Ron, too. He'd gotten a slightly modified version of him—he was still a shit dad, but he would have been worse if Tony hadn't stepped in.

It happened the same summer that Tony stopped drinking. The same summer he threw his last punch.

Nick was five then. Tony had just graduated from college. He moved back in with his mom while he figured out what to do next. He got a job waiting tables, usually working dinner shifts. Sometimes he went to see Nick during the day.

One day, he dropped by to find Nick playing outside by himself. Nick sat in front of the single-story house, smashing action figures together in the grass. When he saw Tony, Nick ran up to the car and yanked the door open. "Tony, Tony, Tony!"

He climbed out of his mom's car and swung Nick up, hooking an arm under his rear.

Simultaneously, Tony smelled a foul odor and felt something against his arm. Tony put him down. Nick had soiled himself.

Squatting down at his level, Tony asked quietly, "Did you have an accident?"

Nick smiled at Tony, placed a hand on his shoulder, and ignored the question.

"Can I look?" Tony spun Nick around and realized he had a diaper on. *What the fuck?*

Tony took his hand and brought him into the house.

Ron and Jeannie were on the couch, each holding a beer, a few emp-
ties at their feet. The TV was blaring.

"Nick needs a diaper change," Tony said.

"'Kay," Jeannie said.

Tony watched them for a beat. Obviously they knew Nick was wearing diapers, not like Nick had snuck that by them. Tony wasn't sure what
he was expecting. An explanation.

He brought Nick to his room and changed him.

"Can you make cheese?" Nick asked. That meant mac and cheese.

It was late afternoon. "It's too early for dinner," Tony said.

Nick pouted.

"What did you have for lunch?"

"Um, nothing."

"Did you have lunch?"

Nick shook his head.

What was going on?

Tony walked out into the living room. "Has he had lunch?"

"Not yet," Jeannie said.

"It's almost three."

Jeannie looked up at Tony for the first time. "I tried at noon, but he
wasn't hungry."

"So you just skip a meal?"

"He's old enough to decide when he's hungry, Tony."

Ron spoke. "Just feed him if he's hungry."

Tony wanted to lay into them both—*still in diapers but old enough to
skip meals?*—but Nick was standing right next to him. He chewed the
inside of his cheek and went into the kitchen to put on the water for
pasta. He found a box of Kraft and a can of green beans.

Tony sat with Nick while he ate. Nick polished off the pasta but left
the beans untouched.

"Can I have more?"

Ron got up to grab a beer from the fridge.

"Once you eat your veggies," Tony said.

Ron chuckled behind him. Popped the tab with a *crack*. "Not so easy, is it?"

"Much easier than you make it look," Tony said.

"What'd you say?"

"I don't like them," Nick said, pushing his plate away from him.

Ron stepped forward, saying, "Shut up and eat 'em," as he cuffed Nick's ear.

Tony didn't even feel himself stand up, he did it so fast. His hands were on Ron's shirt and *bam*, he walked Ron backward and slammed him into the fridge. Ron's beer can hit the floor, and cold liquid sprayed Tony's legs. The memory was blurry from there—Jeannie was yelling, "Stop it, stop it"; Ron was saying something; Ron's hands were up, and Tony punched him. It wasn't a clean hit, but he knew he made contact because Ron's teeth scraped his knuckles. More yelling, more noise, Tony stepped back, and Ron let him.

"The fuck out of my house."

At the table, Nick was wailing.

"It's okay," Jeannie said. "It's okay, it's okay."

Tony tried to move toward Nick.

Ron stepped toward him, his hand clutching where Tony had struck him. "Get. The fuck. Out."

Tony went back to his dad's the next day. He parked, and Ron came outside.

"You're done here," Ron said when Tony got out.

Tony walked partway up the walkway.

"Leave or I'll make you," Ron said.

"I just want to see him."

"Too bad."

"I don't need to see you or Jeannie. I just want to see Nick."

Ron shrugged. "Deal with it."

"I'll call DHS."

The words hung in the air between them.

"For what?"

"He's not potty-trained; he's fucking hungry; you *hit* him."

"You assaulted me; I could call the cops on you."

"Do it. I don't care. They'll still take him from you."

"Okay," Ron said with an ugly grin. "Call. Let them put him in foster care."

"You know what I learned?" Tony felt his face spread into the same smile. "They'll check for family first."

"They wouldn't give him to you."

"Maybe not, but they'd give him to my mom."

Ron's face went dark. "She ain't his family."

"She's the mother of his brother. And she'd take him." He hadn't discussed any of this with Cynthia, but Ron didn't know that.

"She knows better than to fuck with me."

"She *hates* you." He hissed the word between gritted teeth. "You know how *hard* I had to work to be able to see you after she left your ass?"

"You wanted to see me." Ron said it like it was an insult. A pathetic trait of Tony's, to want to be near his own father.

"I didn't know better. I do now."

"Then what do you keep coming back for?"

"Him." Tony pointed at the house. "I know how badly he needs me because I needed it, too. I was so desperate for it, I settled for a piece of shit like you."

"You're pissing me off," Ron said.

"You touch him again and I call. I show up and he's hungry or cold or sitting in his own shit, I call. You do right, I don't."

The change hadn't been night and day, but Ron must have known there was truth in the threat. Tony never saw Ron hit Nick again.

Tony checked the time on his phone. Almost midnight, and he was wired. He needed to turn off his brain and go to sleep or he'd be useless in the morning. Seeing Nick would make him feel better. They'd texted a bit since the grand jury last week, but it would be good to see him in person. Make sure he really was doing as well as Nick said he was. And then, Tony thought of Darlene Walker's Facebook post, and he decided to check her page on his phone.

Tony tilted the phone to keep the light from falling on Julia beside him. He pulled up Darlene's page. This was a mistake.

"Lesson to all," she had written on her wall on Tuesday of that week. "Have sex with a kink, make sure to film it, in case they call it rape later."

Tony's blood boiled. He crawled out of bed. Crossed the dark hall to the bathroom. Closed the door and read the words again.

There was no reason to think Nick had seen either of her posts, but it worried Tony. Nick would feel attacked if he did see them. And even if he didn't, Walker was poisoning people against him. Tony stood in the bathroom, staring at the sentence on his phone. Worst of all, it scratched at something problematic.

Walker's whole defense was unbelievable, but it was 2015, and there were still people out there who thought gay men were sex-crazed lunatics. There were people who believed that Nick had been complicit in what Walker did to him. People who believed it was more likely that Nick had wanted to be hit, choked, made to bleed, than it was that he'd been raped.

What if one of those people ended up on the jury? What if Walker stirred up people enough that the ADA got scared; what if it ended in a bullshit plea deal? Court couldn't change what had happened to Nick, Tony knew that, but Nick's name needed to come out of this clean. And Ray Walker deserved to suffer for what he'd done.

On his phone, he went to Google. He typed the words he'd thought of over a month ago—a search he hadn't bothered to run. He clicked through the link. There was another search bar. A drop-down menu. "Search by owner." There was a creak in the hallway, and Tony started. He stuck his head out of the bathroom. No one was there—just a house sound. He'd felt, for a second, like he was about to be caught doing something wrong. And maybe he was. He was getting himself all worked up again about something everyone else, Nick included, seemed to have accepted. Walker was going to blame Nick to try to save himself. Nick was going to have to wait, maybe a year, for the noise of the case to be over. And Nick's identity was private, at least for now. Tony closed the browser on his phone. He needed to get some sleep.

—◦—

"Can I be excused?"

Blobs of mashed potatoes and gravy clung to the corners of Seb's mouth.

"Holy moly," Tony said, motioning for Seb to use his napkin.

Tony had woken up that morning with a nervous energy he'd only fueled by drinking two cups of coffee and fasting until they sat down to eat around one. As the massive meal settled into his stomach, he finally began to feel how tired he was. Tired and calmer. Everything was going well. The food had turned out great—his best turkey yet, Julia said—and everyone was getting along. Julia's mom, Marjorie, brought out his own mom's fun side, and the two of them had been laughing together all afternoon. Ron and Jeannie had shown up sober and friendly. Nick seemed to be doing okay. He brought his roommate Elle. The one who'd been there that night. Tony had felt anxious about seeing her for some reason, but when Nick asked if she could come, of course he'd said yes.

"Me too?" Chloe asked. They'd all been at the table for nearly an hour now.

"First," Tony's mother said, "could we go around and share what we're thankful for?" Cynthia was holding her handwritten name tag in one hand, clearly thankful for her grandchildren. Julia had had the kids make place cards for the guests. After Julia set up the folding card table against the dining room table and covered them with a long cloth, Tony noticed that she had set his parents' cards as far apart as possible.

He looked to Julia, who held up her glass. "Go for it."

"Well, I just wanted to say how thankful I am to have all of you in my life. I just love you all so much." She reached to her right and squeezed Chloe's cheek. Chloe grinned and squirmed away. "I have the best family in the world, and I'm so glad we're able to be together. All of us." She made a point to look at Ron and Jeannie at that moment. It was actually pretty sweet.

Julia's mom went next, and then Elle as they moved clockwise around the table. Tony couldn't help but notice that Nick looked a bit pained as his turn to speak drew nearer—he was wringing his hands together under the table.

Even more pained was Seb, who had already grown bored with being at the table. He began to slide, slow motion, out of his chair.

"Bud, stay in your seat," Tony whispered, but Seb kept sliding.

After Elle thanked the Halls for letting her join in their family event, she moved on to Nick. "I'm thankful for you, Nick. You're my best friend, and the best person I know. You've just been so brave."

"Seb, honey, come back up here," Tony said full volume.

A muffled voice under the table said, "What's that?"

Nick banged his hands against the underside of the table, making the silverware rattle over its surface. His face was white.

"Honey, come back to your seat," Julia said to Seb.

"What's what?" Elle asked, lifting the table cloth.

"What's on your arm, Uncle Nick?" Seb said.

Jeannie was looking at her son now—Nick was tugging at his sleeves.

"What *is* on your arm?" She reached over and yanked his left sleeve up.

From his seat, Tony could see a long, blotchy red wound running up Nick's forearm, continuing under his sleeve.

"The fuck is that?" Tony said involuntarily.

"*Tony.*" Instantly, Julia chastised him for swearing in front of the kids.

"Oh my God!" Jeannie pulled at Nick's sleeve, leaving the gashes on his arm visible.

Nick ripped his arm away and stood, knocking into the windowsill behind him. "Mom!" He pulled his sleeve back down and pushed past his parents' seats to run through the living room.

Tony shoved backward in his chair and followed.

"Tony!" he heard Julia call after him.

He made it up the stairs to the bathroom door just in time for it to slam in his face. The noise woke him up to what had just happened. He hesitated, then said, "Nick?"

"Go away, Tony." Nick's voice was sharp, punctuating each word.

Tony fought the urge to turn the knob—their old-house doors didn't lock. Instead, he leaned forward, resting his forehead on the door.

"Please," he said quietly. "Please let me in. I'm so scared." The relief that came from saying those words aloud nearly overwhelmed him.

After a pause, he felt Nick moving on the other side, and the door creaked open.

Nick's face dissolved into tears first, and Tony pulled him into a hug. Nick shuddered and sobbed wet, hot breath on Tony's neck.

What was that?

Tony clamped his teeth around the question. He knew what it was. He began to cry, and he held Nick tighter.

—◦—

They stood, holding each other, until their surroundings came back. They were standing in the hall, excited voices downstairs in the dining room. Jeannie's voice was rising above the others.

Nick shifted to release himself from the embrace.

"Can we please talk?"

Nick nodded.

They sat on the bed in Tony and Julia's room, and Nick sighed a shaky breath. Tony didn't want to see the marks again. But did he have an obligation to look closer? "So that's— You— When did you . . . start doing that?"

Nick shrugged. "I guess not that long ago."

Was *Why?* a stupid question? Tony didn't know.

An obvious statement would be easier. "You're not doing okay."

Nick shrugged. His arms were crossed over his torso, and his legs were crossed, too. He looked like he was trying to shrink into a little ball. Tony realized he was unconsciously doing the same thing. He released his legs to sit wide.

"Does your counselor know?"

"Not yet."

"I need you to tell him."

"I will," Nick said quickly.

That was hard to trust, since Nick had been in counseling all this time. But how was he supposed to explain that to Nick?

"I don't want to say the wrong thing," Tony said.

Nick looked up at him. "Just say it."

"I'm afraid you won't tell him."

"I promise."

Tony looked down at Nick's covered arms. "I feel like you've been lying to me."

Nick frowned and looked away.

"You're cutting yourself?"

"No," Nick said. "Just . . . I'm not cutting."

"Then what is that?"

After a long pause, Nick said, "More like scratching."

"Nick," Tony whispered. Nick *was* in pain. Even more than Tony had worried.

In a quiet voice, Nick said, "I have been lying to you."

About hurting himself, or something else? Tony said nothing. Waited for him to speak.

"Everyone knows it's me."

Tony was confused. What did he mean? "That you're the victim? In the case?"

Nick nodded. Fresh tears began to run down his cheeks.

"How?"

"It doesn't matter."

"Who knows?"

"Everyone on campus."

"Fuck," Tony hissed.

"Yup," Nick said. He dragged his hands down his face and dropped them in his lap.

"What do I do? Fuck, Nick. What do I do for you?"

Nick stared at the floor in front of them. Tony reached for Nick's hand. Squeezed it three times.

Nick sighed. "Can you get me a tissue?"

"Okay. Can I get Julia, too?"

"Yeah."

⌒

Maybe an hour later, Tony, Nick, and Julia rejoined Marjorie and Elle, who were with the kids in the living room. Julia had told them upstairs that the rest were going home, to give them privacy. Tony had heard Jeannie earlier. She'd left angry. Julia had probably told her to stay downstairs, to not overwhelm Nick.

"Sorry about that," Nick said awkwardly to Julia's mom.

Marjorie shook her head and pulled Nick in for a hug. She whispered something inaudible to him.

Elle was on the couch, flanked by the kids, who were each just about sitting on her lap. She had turned to face the adults, her silhouette over *The Jungle Book* playing on the screen behind her. She said nothing, and Nick didn't look at her at all.

Upstairs, Julia had approached the situation with the calmness of an EMT. She knelt down low, below Nick's eyeline, and said that she needed him to call a crisis hotline with her. Nick had resisted at first, explaining that he wasn't suicidal, that he wasn't actually cutting himself, but Julia had worn away at him, and he eventually agreed to call. The woman at the hotline scheduled an emergency counseling session for Nick for the next morning, as his own counselor was on vacation until Monday.

Nick had declined their offer to stay over, and Tony was ashamed at the relief he felt when Nick said to Elle, "I'm ready when you are."

Tony stood in the window and watched the pair get into an unfamiliar car and pull away.

"Dad, you said the f-word," Chloe said behind him.

Tony turned. Seb's eyes were glued to the movie, but Chloe's were on him.

"I'm sorry, honey. I shouldn't have said that."

"Why did you say that?"

"I got scared."

"Scared how?"

A bone-tired fatigue washed over him. He didn't know what to say to her. Julia could take this one.

"Just scared," he said. "I need to go clean up, we can talk about it later."

He left her to find Julia and Marjorie in the kitchen, washing and drying dishes.

"You don't need to do that," he said to Julia's mom. "We can do all this."

"Nonsense," Marjorie said. "I stayed to help."

Julia stepped toward him. "Are you all right, honey?"

"Honestly, I think I could go to sleep."

"Oh, do," she said. "Really. We've got this. That was a lot."

"I'll just help for a minute," he said in spite of himself.

Tony walked across the kitchen and into the dining room, where the plates and silverware had all been cleared; cloth napkins were rumpled across the table and in chairs, and glasses of wine and water stood all about.

He stacked the water glasses into a tower, then started to grip two wineglasses with one hand. One of them—Julia's—was a third full. It would spill if he took it with another glass. Obscured by the French doors and the wall, Tony glanced around the room and drained the glass down his throat.

—◦—

The room was dark.

"How long can we do this?" Tony said in a sleep-laden voice.

Julia was getting into bed next to him, and he felt her pause. "What?"

He felt himself wake up more, his eyes registering his bedside table, the clock, the lamp in the dark. "Hmm?"

"You said something."

"Sorry, was dreaming." He tried to hold on to his sleep, but it was slipping away from him. "What time is it?"

"After eleven. My mom finally left," she said with a laugh. "I tried to wake you earlier, but you were out."

He'd thudded upstairs and collapsed into bed sometime around four that afternoon. He couldn't even remember falling asleep.

Julia snuggled into the nape of his neck and kissed his ear. "You doing okay?"

No talk, not now. I'm so tired.

"I wanna keep sleeping," he said as he rolled away. "Love you."

She rubbed a hand over the back of his head. "Love you, too."

He tried to sink away, gently, not forcing the sleep to come.

Nick's scabbed, picked arm flashed in his mind.

Shh, go away.

Nick's tear-soaked face on his neck.

Stop. He tried to breathe deeply. The air he inhaled whistled down his throat, disturbing something like the taste of alcohol. He'd drank a glass of wine before he came to bed. Or was that a dream? Had he really done that?

This was all taking too long. Someone had to do something. A year of this? A year of articles and comments and letters and Facebook and everyone that mattered to Nick, everyone who saw him every day, knowing it's him? His body, his story, his reputation? A year of Nick trying to survive that? No. He couldn't. Something had to be done.

Nick was getting help in the morning. It would be fine.

But Nick *had* been getting help, and still he was digging his own skin off.

Soon Tony was pounding with adrenaline. He couldn't keep trying.

Slowly, he pushed his feet from the bed and found the floor. He slid from under the covers to stand. *Just walk, like you're going out to the bathroom.* Tony strode purposefully from the room, and Julia said nothing.

Down the stairs he crept, across the hall into the living room. It wasn't there. He circled the downstairs until he found it in the kitchen—his phone. He leaned against the counter and pulled up the browser. He would finish what he started a night ago. Town of Salisbury's Assessor's Office. Online Database. Search by Owner. Walker. And there it was. Raymond Walker's address.

32

Julia woke up to Chloe's face inches from her own.

"Oh, jeez!"

"Seb's in the cookies and he hasn't had breakfast yet." Chloe frowned at her bitterly.

Julia wiped the grit from her eyes. "What time is it?" She turned and saw that Tony was already out of bed. According to her phone, it was 8:23. How had she slept so late?

"Honey," she said. "We don't tattle. Only when someone's being unsafe."

"But you said it's not healthy to eat dessert before breakfast." Chloe raised her eyebrows and looked at Julia like they were standing on opposite sides of a courtroom.

Damn that clever child. She hadn't been awake long enough to enunciate a better definition of tattling. It was like SCOTUS on pornography: you just know it when you see it.

"Why are you blessing me with this information instead of Dad?"

"Dad's gone," Chloe said.

Another run, Julia thought, *finally*. Maybe he'd sweat off the emotional hangover he no doubt woke up with. Just remembering the day before made a fresh lump rise in Julia's throat. Poor Nick.

"Come snuggle me," she said.

Chloe climbed into bed, and Julia wrapped her arms around her, buried her face in her hair.

Chloe's voice was muffled. "Can I have a cookie, too, then?"

Julia squeezed Chloe tighter. "Yeah, let's go have cookies for breakfast."

They climbed from bed, and Julia followed Chloe from the room.

Down in the kitchen, her eyes skimmed over Tony's sneakers at their usual station, sitting in the corner by the door to the mudroom. Had she paused to register what she was seeing, that Tony was not on a run, it might have all been different.

33

Tony had been sitting on the street in front of Raymond Walker's house for hours, waiting to see what would happen. At some point, he would make up his mind, or Walker would force a decision by emerging from the house.

Tony had checked the website again to be sure, but there was no question this was it. It was a gray bungalow on a quiet street in Salisbury, a way from Nick's apartment, across town from the bar where they met. The house looked wrong, not the way Tony would have pictured it. There were flowers out front: tall purple ones; white globes of petals on thin stems; bursts of orange and yellow. The driveway was empty and the door was down on the detached garage.

Tony knew what he wanted to say: his wife was a lawyer, and if Walker and his mother didn't stop posting stuff about Nick online, they'd sue him for invasion of privacy or libel. Julia had already said they probably couldn't sue him, but Walker didn't need to know that. Tony would stand tall, look him in the eye, and tell him he was done bullying Nick. Tell him he was lucky court was taking care of the situation instead of Tony.

But now that he was there, something was stopping him from getting out of the car. As soon as he knocked on the door to that house, there was no going back. As the morning sun climbed his windshield, the thought grew stronger that it was pointless to threaten a lawsuit. Walker was shameless. He took pleasure in hurting others—Tony would only be showing Walker that it was working. And what would happen if Tony pissed him off?

Then, the side door opened. Raymond Walker, clear as day, stepped from the doorway. Raymond Walker. The man who'd made Nick hurt so badly he'd gone on hurting himself. Walker turned to shut the door. Turned back to the driveway. Started to walk to the garage. Wait, he was leaving.

Tony fumbled his door open and stepped into the street. "Hey!" he yelled.

At the top of the driveway, the garage door was climbing upward; Walker was standing in front of the garage, waiting for the door to open. He turned toward Tony's voice.

"Raymond Walker," Tony said as he crossed the street. His voice was strong, commanding.

Raymond Walker tilted his head incrementally. "Yes?"

Tony was in the driveway now. His legs carried him faster than he could think. He was approaching Walker, who took a step back toward the truck in the garage.

"Hey—hey—*hey*," Walker yelped.

Tony grabbed him by the jacket and slammed him against the bed of the truck.

"You stay the *fuck* away from Nick Hall you piece of shit." His voice had gone shaky.

Walker raised his hands, squeezed his eyes shut. "Done," he said. "Done."

Spittle had flown from Tony's mouth, and it glistened on Walker's forehead. He could see the pores on his nose, he was so close to him.

Tony released the lapels of Walker's jacket and stepped back from him. He turned and strode down the driveway. What did he do? What did he just do?

He reached the street as Walker spoke.

"Hey, for future reference, are you the brother or the boyfriend?"

Walker was goading him; Tony needed to get in the car and leave. But his feet stopped. He swayed in the street. He didn't turn. *Just walk forward. Just get in the car.*

"He talked about his big brother." Walker's voice was edged with a strained cheeriness. "You certainly look big."

Just take a step forward and the other will follow. Get in the car.

"Maybe when all this blows over—"

"Open your mouth again and I will *kill* you." Tony turned to Walker. Gone was his strong voice or even the shaky one. Hot tears had sprung up as he spoke, and his voice went to a whisper. "I will *kill* you. You leave him alone."

Walker grinned, ugly and satisfied.

Tony turned back to the car, strode to it, climbed in, slammed the door, started it, pulled away, as Walker stood and watched.

34

JOHN RICE, 2015

D etective, call for you."

Rice had barely made it through the unit door when Officer Thompson called out to him.

"Take a message."

"Sorry, sir," Thompson said. He was new, painfully young, and a little clueless about station etiquette. Rice had been called in at four that morning for a burglary and aggravated assault and was just getting to the station; he didn't need to be jumped the second he walked in the door.

Rice continued across the bullpen, toward the breakroom, slow enough to hear Thompson say, "Sorry, Mr. Walker, I'll need to take a message for when th—"

"Hey!" Rice spun and waved his free hand at Thompson, coffee sloshing up onto the lid of his Styrofoam cup. "I'll take it," he mouthed.

"Oh," Thompson said as he watched Rice. "Why, there he is. I'll put you through to his line."

Rice set his coffee down on his desk at the edge of the bullpen and elected to press Speaker so he could stand. The unit was relatively quiet, and his back was aching—he'd forgotten to pop an Aleve before he left the house that morning.

"Detective Rice here."

"Good afternoon, Detective. So glad I was able to catch you." Raymond Walker's shit-weasel voice almost sounded sarcastic, he was trying so hard to sound charming.

Rice matched his tone. "What can I do for you, Ray?"

"I just wanted to make a report that Nick Hall's brother just came to my house and threatened to kill me."

Rice picked up the receiver. "He did, did he?"

"Yes, sir. I understand this must be hard for him, not knowing his baby brother is lying about the whole encounter."

Rice bit his tongue; Ray could easily be recording the call. In this day and age, never say anything on the phone you wouldn't want played back in court.

Ray continued. "I really do empathize with the family. But I can't have someone coming to my house, putting his hands on me, throwing me around."

Rice grimaced; was Tony Hall that stupid?

"I have to draw the line somewhere, don't I? Compassion must have its limits."

How much would Rice mind hearing "compassion my ass" played back in court? Instead, he said, "You sure this was Nick Hall's brother?"

"Oh, yes, so many of the same features. And I'm sure you know he drives a gray Ford Explorer."

Shit. What was Tony thinking? Tampering with a witness was a felony, not to mention assault and terrorizing charges. This would only complicate things. Julia would be a wreck. Rice felt almost dizzy, and he shook his head as though to scatter the thoughts.

"All right, Ray. Can you come in to give your statement?"

"Oh, I'm not pressing charges."

What?

Ray continued when Rice didn't speak. "I will if anything like this happens again, but for today I just wanted to make the report. He frightened me, Detective. He said he'd kill me. But I'm a reasonable man. I know he's grieving. And he doesn't have reason to believe me over his little brother . . . yet."

What was his game? Rice pulled a pen from his breast pocket and found a clean sheet on his desk. Wrote: *11-27-15 Call from RW. TH threatened to kill RW. RW not pressing, just reporting, knows he's grieving.* Rice paused then added quotation marks around *just reporting.*

"Well, I'll leave the choice with you, to press charges or not."

"And I'm choosing not."

"What time this happen?"

A pause. "This morning, around nine fifty."

"Well," Rice looked at his watch, "it's nearly two. Why'd you wait till now to call?"

"I went to brunch first. I was on my way out the door when he surprised me. He was waiting in the street."

"Mm. And where'd you go to brunch?"

"Why?"

"For your report. Better if I ask the details now so you don't have to remember them later if you change your mind." The whole thing reeked of ulterior motives. Rice scribbled down the times on his sheet.

"Fork and Napkin," Ray said quickly, then: "I need to get going." There was something to his voice. He just wanted Rice to write down exactly what he wanted . . . and he didn't want to linger on the restaurant.

"Over in Ogunquit? Great little diner. No problem, Ray, you go about your business today. I'll log your report and close it out."

"Thanks," Ray said flatly, and hung up.

Rice hung up the receiver slowly. What was he after?

When Rice called Fork & Napkin, a young voice told him that they'd had a pretty busy morning, the day after Thanksgiving usually was. She did remember a man coming in, though, whose name she did not know.

He was somewhere around thirty, maybe older, maybe younger, she was terrible with ages. But this man stood out to her.

"He said he was late for a ten o'clock, and he said a few different last names to check for, and I found the reservation but no one had shown up. Besides him, I mean." She told Rice the name the reservation was under—it was meaningless—and continued. "He seemed sad when I said no one else was there. I think he was stood up."

Rice thanked the girl and hung up. So at least some of Ray Walker's friends had the good sense to distance themselves. If only the idiots agreeing with him online had done the same.

Tony Hall needed to be set straight. If any part of Walker's story was true . . . how could he have been so foolish? Rice knew Tony and Nick were close. Tony was a father figure, in a way, to Nick. Clearly this was all driving Tony crazy. But he had simply given Walker ammunition: *See? The Halls are unstable.* He was hurting the very person he was trying to protect. Not to mention risking what could happen to Tony—how that would harm his children, his wife?

His mind paused on Tony's wife for a moment. Whenever Julia's face came into his mind he pushed it away, but today he let it linger. Her hair bathed in sunlight, like the first time he saw her at the kitchen sink. The longer he pictured her, the more her resemblance to his departed wife dawned on him. The hair was wrong, and the nose, and build, but the eyes, the smile, the warmth. That's what it was: just like Irene. They bore the markings of supremely *good* women. Good women who had married men who had to work to be good.

35

Tony's cell rang in the kitchen. Julia turned up the TV and left the kids on the couch, walking quickly to meet Tony as he answered the call. Tony had gotten home late that morning and told her what he'd done: found Walker's home address on Salisbury's registry, gone to Walker's house, pushed him, threatened him. Julia had laid into him, he'd cried, she'd holed up with the kids in the living room, ignoring him as she tried to process the insanity he had just confessed to.

Then nothing had happened for hours. She was certain the quiet wouldn't last.

And she was right. It was the detective on the phone.

"I just got a call from Ray Walker," Detective Rice said.

Julia's heart fell into her stomach. Tony was going to be arrested.

Tony opened his mouth to speak, and Julia held up a hand. Whatever Tony was going to say, she didn't want the police to hear it. No admissions.

After a beat, Detective Rice said, "You there?"

Julia nodded at him.

"Yup," Tony said.

"And Julia?"

"I'm here," Julia said.

"Okay," the detective said. "Tony, Ray Walker says you assaulted him at his house this morning."

Julia's gaze moved from the phone to her husband's face. His puffy eyelids were closed and his brow was furrowed with worry.

"Says you threatened to kill him."

A chill squirmed up her spine, and she shuddered.

"So it's assault, terrorizing, tampering with a witness."

Julia brought her hands to her face. The whole mess they were already living was going to start again, this time with Tony as the defendant. Her brain started listing potential outcomes: probation, jail time, a record. Tony's office would find out—lawyers were the biggest gossips. *The media* would find out. They were already all over Nick's case. Everyone would know.

After a long pause, Detective Rice said, "That's what you might have been charged with."

Julia lifted her face from her hands. Tony looked at her in confusion.

"He's not pressing charges," the detective said.

"What?" Julia asked.

"Yup. Not sure how you got so lucky."

Tony handed Julia the phone and laid down on the kitchen floor.

"So . . . that's it?" she asked.

"For now," he said. "Tony. I don't know what you were thinking. But this isn't going to help anyone. You hear me?"

On the floor, Tony nodded. His head lolled on the tiles, his arms down at his sides.

"I'm not a big fan of the *Boondock Saints*, you hear?" Rice said. "You let us take care of this."

"Thank you," Julia said.

"Don't thank me," he said. "This would have been a different conversation if Walker wanted to press charges."

They hung up.

"I don't know what I was thinking." Tony stared up at the ceiling. "I don't know."

Julia did.

Tony had always been a fixer. He liked to fix problems: mostly other people's.

It took Julia a while to notice it, but once she did, it bothered her. The porch light at her apartment burned out: he showed up with a bulb, screwdriver, and stepladder. She caught a cold: he brought take-out soup and encouraged her to nap. She was moody: he wanted to talk about it. Her best friend, Margot, told her it was romantic. Julia felt disrespected, like he thought she couldn't take care of herself. Julia may have had the perfect childhood, with all the financial and emotional security a kid could ask for, but she'd been dealt a tougher hand in college. Her dad withered and died in the span of a month. Her mother had to give up her business. Julia started bartending to help pay for school. By the time she met Tony, she'd grown confident in her self-sufficiency, and proud of it.

Then one night during their first winter dating, one of Julia's coworkers got mugged. The woman was walking to her car after she closed up the Ruby, the bar where she and Julia worked in Portland, when a white guy in a hat and scarf showed her a switchblade and demanded her purse. She wasn't hurt, she told Julia after, just shaken. Julia told Tony on her way to work. She regretted it instantly. In the span of their five minutes on the phone, he told her not to go in, asked her if she'd get a different job, grew angry, and told her she should quit. She hung up on him. She'd never even heard of a mugging in Portland before. The odds of it happening to her seemed low, her coworker was fine, and Julia didn't have much worth stealing. Near the end of her shift, Tony showed up at the bar. He started by apologizing for being so crazy on the phone. She almost believed him, until she realized he was there to walk her to her car.

When the last barflies buzzed off at closing time, she locked the door and turned to Tony. All the things she hadn't said came up at once, like she'd been keeping a list to lob at him. She could see what he was doing. He didn't trust her to take care of herself. He didn't respect her decisions. And then she upped the ante.

"You're possessive."

Tony shook his head in confusion. *"Possessive?"*

"Yes."

"You're being crazy. The girl who does the same job as you got mugged last night. He could have done a lot more than show her a knife."

"It's not just this, it's everything! You think I can't change a light bulb! You suffocate me! I'm not your child!"

"What the fuck, my *child*? You're my girlfriend, and I love you, why is that so hard for you?"

"Why is it so hard for *you* to let me take care of myself?"

"It's what I do!" Tony shoved the barstool back and stood. "I take care of the people I love." He was breathing heavily, like he'd just sprinted. "My love suffocates you?"

Julia crossed her arms, tried to collect herself. Instead, a sensation of terror washed over her. This might not be a fight. This might be the end.

"There is so much that I love about the ways you love me," she said. "But if you need to be saving someone all the time . . . that doesn't work for me. I don't need that, I don't want it. And I hope you don't, either—I hope you don't need to be with a weak woman to feel like a man."

He opened his mouth, and she held up her hand.

"I don't think you do," she said, "consciously at least, but you need to listen to what I'm saying. How you're acting right now, it's not how I want my boyfriend to be. I need you to change." She inhaled. Exhaled. Goddamn it, her tears had pooled and spilled anyway. "Or I need you to go."

She'd said what she had to, and she met his gaze now, defied him to call her wrong. His dark hair went black in low lighting like this, and he came toward her, sharp features on a pale face. He wound his arms around her middle, rested his face against her neck. He kissed the hollow of her collarbone and released her.

"Okay," he whispered.

He reached behind her, turned the dead bolt, stepped around her, pushed through the door and onto the street.

He was leaving. He was leaving her.

He turned back. "This isn't me leaving," he said, as if he could hear the voice in her head. He narrowed his eyes, angry but playful. "I'm letting you walk to your car." He shook his head, then he turned and left.

She'd been right to take a stand that night, but wrong, too. So much of love was contradiction. For Tony, loving Julia was letting her be her own hero, even though his self-worth seemed to be founded on what he could do for the people he loved most. For Julia, loving Tony was letting him take care of her, as much as it scared her to start needing what she could lose.

And right now, Tony wanted to take care of Nick. His little brother, the boy he'd saved again and again. He had nowhere to put all that anger and despair.

Julia laid down on the cool kitchen tile beside Tony and took his hand in hers.

⌒

The next afternoon, they found themselves playing a game that resembled football in the side yard. Chloe's version of the sport included throwing the Nerf ball at the participants and touchdowns by either team at the same apple tree. It was confusing to say the least, but each time Chloe announced a new rule as the game progressed, Julia found her too charming to reason with, and so they complied. The kids had Julia laughing so much that her mood had lightened, and Tony seemed to be trying his best. He ran the yard, bickered playfully over the rules, glanced at her with eyes that seemed to measure whether she was having fun. He was apologizing.

"Wait, Seb," Chloe said to her brother.

Seb paused midsprint for the apple tree, squeezing the ball between his two small hands.

"The tree is ghouls now."

Tony shook his head. "What?"

"Ghouls, Dad," Chloe said, like Tony was an idiot.

"Why would we have ghouls in football?" Julia laughed. Tony held his hand out toward her in a gesture that said *Thank you!* She smiled at Tony and held his eyes. Even when it was against their own children, it felt good to team up with each other.

"It's not football, it's tag-football-dodgeball," Chloe said.

"Dodgeball," Seb chortled as he threw the ball at his sister.

Julia's cell trilled in her pocket. There were only a handful of people she'd answer a call from right now—Charlie Lee was one of them.

"I've got to take this, but I'll be right back," Julia said as she jogged toward the house and out of earshot. She paused at the front step and sat beside the jack-o'-lanterns they'd left moldering there since Halloween.

Charlie apologized for calling over the weekend.

"Are you kidding? I've been dying to hear from you."

"Ah," he sighed.

And just like that, she wished she hadn't answered. "What? Nothing?"

"I'm sorry, Julia. If he did this to anyone else, I didn't find them."

Shit. "That's okay."

"I thought I was on to something at one point, but . . ." He paused.

"What do you mean?"

"Ah, it was a dead end. A bartender in Providence thought it was possible he saw Ray Walker one weekend at his bar, *two years* ago."

"Providence, Rhode Island?"

"Yeah, Walker's company sells all around New England. So I reached out to a bunch of gay bars in some of the bigger cities."

Julia's heart pounded in her ear against the phone. "And?"

"And nothing, really. He remembers a real handsome guy coming in two nights in a row, talking to a shy young regular. On the second night, the kid left with the guy. The bartender was planning to ask the regular about it the next weekend, but the kid never came back."

A yelp from Chloe drew Julia's eyes to the backyard. Tony was chasing her with the ball.

"Long time after that, the bartender saw the kid at a farmers market with a girl. He called her a 'beard'—I guess they were acting like boyfriend, girlfriend. Bartender thinks she got wise to things. He never thought anything bad had happened. Until he got my email."

"Does he remember the regular's name?"

"No, not his last name, anyway."

"So . . ." So it really was nothing.

Julia studied her boots. Rolled her ankles to see the bottoms. Her treads were filled with mud and strands of grass.

"I'm really disappointed," Charlie said. "What he did to your brother-in-law, there must be others out there. Just hard to find them."

"It was sweet of you to look for me, really."

"I still might hear back from some other bars. If I do—"

"Yeah, just give me a call, but don't spend any more of your time on this."

Charlie paused. "I know you're worried about court, but try not to be."

Julia pulled back her jacket sleeve to wipe her nose on her flannel beneath. She was starting to feel like crying.

"They have plenty to nail him," Charlie said. "If I had to put in my vote, I'd say Raymond Walker is a man whose lifetime of good luck has finally run out."

After they hung up, Julia sat by the pumpkins and turned her phone over in her hands. A lifetime of good luck, that could explain it. Charlie was good, but if no one had reported Walker, if no one had pictures of him, or DNA samples—she shuddered. A lifetime of good luck. She looked up across the lawn. Tony was swinging Chloe around by the waist while Seb leaped at her, trying to grab the Nerf ball from her hands. The kids were chattering and whooping. Tony laughed, set Chloe down, rolled his shoulders, dropped his smile. Watched the kids run for the tree, some kind of wistful look on his face. What about their long run of bliss? Had that run out, too?

36

It had snowed on the last day of November that year. They woke up one morning to find that the fall was over. The winter that followed buried them.

That was the winter where Julia learned that you could lose yourself in the snow. You could lose sight of where you were if you didn't keep your wits about you. You were closer to spring than you'd been in the fall, but the low light, the mounting snow, it blinded you to the promise of spring. Just like the plants outside, you had to strip yourself down and harden to survive.

She glanced sideways at Detective Rice.

If she'd never seen this man again, she might have died happy.

"You know why I called you here, don't you?"

Yes.

"No," she said.

Could he see the sweat at her hairline?

"I look back on Nick's case," the detective said, "and I see all the mistakes I made. What I sat on. And what I missed. When Walker called and told me what Tony had done . . . I look back on that day, and I wish I'd seen what was coming."

Detective Rice was taking his time, offering up his memories like they were apples he was plucking from the trees on a lazy stroll through an orchard. Like they were just occurring to him and she might like to see them. But he was moving chronologically—methodically. He'd walked her through the fall, and the winter would come next.

For a moment, Julia indulged the voice of her inner victim. *I shouldn't have to remember all of this. It's not fair.* Then she silenced the voice. The voice was a fake. In truth, she thought of that winter frequently, with or without detectives calling her to their apparent deathbeds. She had learned to control the strong feelings tied to that time—the memories still existed, but she viewed them with the cool detachment of a researcher, perhaps, observing the actions of unknown persons. That hadn't been them, Tony and Julia. That was some other couple. And when her mind drifted to that couple—on winter nights; or in the early moments of her waking from a nightmare; or, for some reason she could not recall, whenever Tony made BLTs—she would watch that strange couple for a moment and then release them.

Today, a long-sedated emotion had reawakened in the pit of her stomach as she sat facing the detective, the embodiment of the criminal justice process. His sagging skin and ill coloring were a distraction; a fortuitous ruse on his part, but she knew what he was. A cop was always a cop: retired or not, dying or not. And history always demanded justice, didn't it?

Because she knew why she was here. She knew what came next. The detective had taken his time, but they were approaching it now: the winter that Raymond Walker would go missing.

III.

DECEMBER

—⟶

"We are nearer to Spring
Than we were in September,"
I heard a bird sing
In the dark of December.

Oliver Herford, "I Heard a Bird Sing"

37

NICK HALL, 2015

Jeff's office was small and toasty. The wall behind Nick's seat on the couch was brick, and the window there cast the bright light of early winter onto the counselor's warm brown face. Per usual, Jeff was wearing a sweater and slacks. Every now and then, he hooked a finger under the band of his silver wristwatch and stretched it as he listened to Nick. Nick had taken off his boots at the door, and he rubbed his socks back and forth against the plush carpet as they talked.

"So it feels like a relief," Jeff said.

"Yeah." They were talking about what Nick had been doing to himself. The picking, or whatever.

He'd already talked about it in the emergency counseling session he had with some woman after Thanksgiving. Talking about the same stuff with Jeff wasn't going to help. He knew why he was doing it, picking at his skin. It was a distraction from the truth. He'd almost told Jeff once before. Almost told Tony, on Thanksgiving. He thought he could change the truth if he told himself the false story over and over, but it was only getting harder.

Jeff was saying something, and Nick cut him off.

"Can you explain again how it works with us, like with court?"

"What do you mean?"

"Like I know you can tell someone if I'm going to hurt myself or someone else, but you said something about court once."

"I did?"

Nick nodded. "The first time we met, you said a judge could make you give him my records."

"Oh. Well, that's possible. I guess it would depend—I like to tell clients up front that there are a few limits on confidentiality. As much as I want you to know I'll keep your secrets, I also want you to know that there are a few times when I can't. I think it's really important that I say so *before* something has happened."

Nick raised his hand to his head. The scab was still there. Drier and smaller, but he was still picking at it too often to let it heal all the way.

"Nick," Jeff said, and nodded in his direction.

Nick lowered his hand.

"I can't see a scenario where Ray gets your records, if that's what you're worried about." They called him Ray in Jeff's office. Nick didn't like to call him "Walker," like the prosecutor or Tony did. "What do you want to talk to me about?"

Nick's arm began to itch, and he rubbed at it.

"Nick."

Nick clasped his hands in his lap. He wasn't strong enough to keep the secret anymore. He'd tried to clamp down on it, shut it out, but he was too weak. If he didn't tell someone, he didn't know what he'd do.

"I want to tell you what really happened."

⁓

Nick heard Johnny's rusted-out Volvo before he saw it. Johnny had gotten there early and was waiting for him, just as he had been after each session since Nick left Tony's house.

Nick craned to see the car idling on the street behind the new snow-bank, courtesy of the storm a day before. His face was puffy from spending so much of the last hour crying; as he stepped onto the sidewalk, the cold air stung his eyes. There was a swelling of hope in his chest unlike anything he'd ever felt. Back in Jeff's office, he'd finally done what he had pretended to do so many times that fall. He gave someone the whole truth, and nothing but. When he was done, Jeff leaned forward in his chair and said Nick's name. Nick lifted his head and met Jeff's eye, and then, Jeff said the three most unexpected words.

"I forgive you."

Jeff said lots after that, but those three repeated in Nick's mind as he reached Johnny's car.

"I forgive you."

He could be forgiven for what he'd done.

Nick opened the door and slid in beside Johnny. The Volvo looked like shit from the outside and roared above forty miles an hour, but it was warm and clean and smelled like strawberries. Johnny was always swapping out air fresheners, and the latest was a pink jelly thing that clipped into the passenger heating vent. It always made Nick crave buttery toast with jam.

"How was it?"

"Fine. Good, actually." Nick pulled the seat belt over his lap and smiled at Johnny. "Thanks for picking me up."

Johnny smiled back as he drove. "You don't have to say that every time." Then the smile dropped from his face. "At least not as long as you're pitching me gas money."

Nick exhaled a soft laugh. As the only one with a car, Johnny was stuck chauffeuring his roommates on a regular basis. After the first two weeks of living together he'd started to get annoyed, but then they started paying him gas money and it became less of an issue. By now the system was simple: no payment, no Taxi Maserati—Nick had come up with that name back in September. He hadn't called the Volvo by that name in months.

At home, Nick handed Johnny a five and went straight up the musty stairs to his room, closing the door behind him.

He sat on his bed and pulled out his phone to look up the number for the DA's office. Jeff had said Nick should try to talk to the victim advocate person, Sherie. Sherie would probably be the best to deal with this. Nick pressed the number on the DA's webpage. If he didn't call now, while he was reeling with confidence that it was the right thing to do, he might never pick up the phone.

Nick pressed his way through a menu to reach a human.

"District attorney's office, this is Jodi speaking."

"Hi, um, I'm calling to talk to Sherie. The advocate, please."

"Sherie's out this week. Are you a victim in an open case?"

There was that word again. "Yeah, I— Yes I am, yes."

The voice softened. "Sherie's had a death in the family, she should be back next Monday. Would you like to speak to the attorney assigned to your case?"

Would he? No. She was intimidating. Sherie's whole job was to be there for Nick. She would be easier to talk to.

"Is the attorney the right person to talk to about your story, or your testimony? I mean, if I needed to . . . if . . ."

What am I doing?

"Never mind, I'll call back next week, thanks."

"Can I—"

Nick hung up. He needed to talk to Sherie. Not anyone else, not yet. He could make it a week. It wasn't his secret alone anymore—he'd told Jeff, and that counted for something.

Nick gently pushed his sleeves up one after another, careful not to scratch them down against the scabby wounds. They ran all over the undersides of his forearms, dry, brownish-red and pink rimmed. They itched to be picked at. Instead, he just observed them. They kind of looked like islands. He pictured Tony's face when he saw what he'd done to himself. Nick pulled his sleeves back down and stood up from the bed. *Enough of that*, he thought. *Redirect yourself, like Jeff said.*

Nick walked downstairs and popped an ice cube out of the tray in the freezer. He held it in his left hand, squeezing it tightly. The cold ached against his palm. He held out his throbbing hand and let the melt dribble into the sink. The pain in his hand was all he could feel, just like he wanted.

38

J ulia could hear the kitchen from the bottom of the stairs. The sizzle of bacon, the sputtering of the coffeemaker, the familiar voices of local news personalities on the television. Channel eight's anchors hosted an inane show called *Saturdays with Michelle and Miguel*, which Tony sometimes turned on as he made breakfast. It was the cookie-cutter morning-show template of overcovered local news split up by segments on recipes and shelter pets. She'd never knock the show too much, though—any time she heard it, it meant breakfast was underway.

Julia paused at the doorway to the living room, where the kids were playing. Down the hall in the kitchen, a third voice chimed in between Michelle's and Miguel's. Julia didn't recognize the voice, but she knew immediately what they were discussing.

"What makes this case so interesting is that we have an adult male victim," the voice said. "I don't want to call it unheard of, but it practically is."

Julia hurried to the kitchen, where Tony stood motionless in his sweats. A heavy man in a suit was on the screen before him.

Julia moved to Tony's side. "What's this?"

"Shh!" Tony hissed.

On the screen, the man sat in a chair across from Michelle and Miguel. "It will be fascinating to see how a jury responds to the situation."

Julia stepped forward toward the TV. "Why are you watching this?" She reached out a hand to turn it off.

Tony pushed her hand down. "Leave it, I'm trying to watch."

"Why are you doing this to yourself?"

He widened his eyes in annoyance but kept them on the screen. "Can you stop talking?"

Julia settled back on her heels and crossed her arms.

Miguel leaned toward the man. "And what *is* the situation, as we know it?"

"The two men met at a bar, Jimmy's Pub, in Salisbury. Somehow they determined that they were mutually interested, and they left the bar together and went to Mr. Walker's hotel room. The State will be looking to prove that Mr. Walker essentially clobbered the victim at the hotel, and that the sexual assault followed while the man was unconscious."

"Now, why would it matter that the victim is male?" Michelle asked.

"It will really matter more in terms of the stories that the defense and the prosecution tell, and it may affect what the jurors believe happened. It could go either way. Will a jury believe that a strong, healthy man was essentially knocked out and has no memory of the event? There's a lot of speculation about how much alcohol the victim consumed, but as a male, his tolerance is higher, of course. And there probably won't be questions about what he was wearing," the man said with a gross little smile.

Julia shot out a hand and flicked off the TV. Tony stood motionless, staring at the black screen. She reached for him as he stepped away, and her hand passed through the air where he'd stood.

Without a word, he strode from the kitchen into the mudroom. After a pause, the door slammed. She heard the crunch of shoes on gravel, and Tony was gone.

—⌐

Tony was sitting in bed with a book in his lap, staring at the window across from him. He'd been reading the same book for a month. Barely reading it, really—Julia kept seeing him like this, holding the book but off in his head somewhere. She climbed into the far side of the bed. She reached for the book at her bedside, but he spoke.

"That fucker needs to be put away."

He was talking about Walker. He was always talking about Walker. "He probably will be." She had more to say, but Tony cut her off.

"Probably?"

"You just never know. But even if he does go to prison, that's not going to make Nick stop hurting himself."

"It might."

"I think you're oversimplifying what Nick's going through."

"Meaning?"

"Walker going to prison isn't going to help Nick come to terms with whatever happened that night."

A small smile crept over Tony's face. It was an ugly smile—as though he'd thought to himself, "There it is." Like she'd just proved him right about something.

"What?"

Tony opened his book. "Nothing."

"That's not passive aggressive."

"Fine." He shut the book. "Sometimes I feel like you don't believe Nick."

"What? Where did you get that from?"

"I just feel it, the way you talk about him."

"How do I talk about him?"

"Just now, like he doesn't know what happened to him."

"I'm saying where he blacked out we don't know—"

"Stop." He flipped back the comforter and climbed from the bed.

"Whoa!" Clearly this had been a mistake.

He was at the dresser now. "Before you say what I think you're going to, I want you to remember what he looked like at the hospital. In our home. What the nurse said. You know what, I don't want to know what you think."

"Tony—"

"I won't be able to look at you if you think—"

"Tony—"

"No, just stop, I'm done with this."

They were talking over each other.

She didn't want to raise her voice with the kids down the hall. "Tony. *Tony.* Listen to me. I'm telling you I think Nick is telling the truth, but *he said* he doesn't know what happened. Don't you think it's weird there's no one else Walker's done this to?"

Tony eyed her meaningfully. "There's a first time for everything."

"What, us disagreeing?"

"We don't know there aren't other people out there."

"What if we do know that?"

"How would we? The police don't have time to look for others."

"Not the police."

"What are you talking about?"

Did she want to tell him about Charlie Lee? She'd thought she wanted to keep it private—keep him from being disappointed that Charlie hadn't found anything to help secure a conviction. But clearly she did want to tell him—she'd led him right to it.

"I asked Charlie Lee to look into things for us."

"Who's Charlie Lee?"

"That PI I used to work with."

Tony stared at her for a beat. "You hired a PI?"

It wasn't much money, but she'd leave that out entirely. "I was already using him for the juvenile records report."

"When did you talk to him?"

"Which time?"

"So you're *working with* a PI and you didn't tell me."

"I didn't think I *should* tell you—I called him right after you put your fist through a door in front of the kids."

Tony frowned and suddenly his face was all Sebastian, teetering on the brink of tears. That was harsh; she shouldn't have said that.

She softened her voice. "I'm sorry. But I think we need to be realistic about what court can give Nick. I know there's some other evidence, but it's really going to be Nick's word against Walker's, and Nick is going to say he doesn't remember what happened. That's not great. So I asked Charlie to see if he could find anyone else, and he couldn't, and he's really good at this."

"So what, he called *all the men in the world* and asked them, 'Hey, were you ever—'"

"Obviously not," Julia cut in. "But he tried a bunch of gay bars in New England, where Walker might have gone on work trips. Only one of them even thought it was possible he'd been there."

Tony's face lit. "Someone recognized him?"

"No, maybe, he wasn't sure. Just that he looked like a guy who went home with a younger regular once, but that was it. Charlie can't find who the regular was, so literally all we know is someone who looks like Walker went home with a young, shy guy, and the bartender never got to hear what happened."

"Are you listening to yourself? He has a type. He has an MO. This needs to go to the DA for court."

"God no, absolutely not! If I were Walker's attorney I'd have a field day with that. 'Where'd this information come from?' 'Nick Hall's family hired a private investigator.' 'And *all* he found is that someone who looks like my client went home with a guy at a bar two years ago?' It's worse than not having looked at all."

"Right there," Tony said as he pointed at her. "That's your problem."

"What?"

"'If you were his attorney.' You've been his attorney before, Julia. You've defended scumbags like him."

"So what?"

"You're looking at it from his point of view when you should be looking at it from Nick's."

"That is *so* insulting. That was work. This is personal—this is *family*. I just want you to be realistic about how this part of the whole thing might end. Walker might go to trial, and if he does, Nick will have to testify, and Walker could win."

Tony held up his hand. "I need a walk."

"Right now?" The window across the room was a black mirror. "It's dark; it's freezing."

"I'll wear a jacket."

It was too cold to go out on foot. And would he walk, or would he get in his car and drive? And where could a drive lead him but back to Walker's?

"Please don't go out right now." If she said what she was thinking, she would only entrench them further in *this*, this fight, whatever it was. But she had to know he wouldn't do something else he'd regret. "Please don't go again."

Maybe he feared the same thing she did, because he relented. "Fine." He snatched his pillow from beside her and retrieved the book from under the covers. He didn't look at her.

"Fine," she said.

He paused in the doorway. "Can I just point out, for all your talk about what you think I'm not saying, that was a pretty big secret you kept, hiring that guy."

She reached for an apology, but it wouldn't come. She wasn't sorry.

"Good night," she said, and she stretched her hand for the lamp at her bedside. She flicked it off, sending Tony into the darkness.

39

They'd finished the tea and time was getting on. It seemed strange to Rice that Julia had let him drag her through the fall into the winter—*that* winter—without complaint. Without asking where he was taking her. Her face looked about as pale as his did every time he caught his reflection in the bread box (he'd removed the mirrors weeks ago). Was it the standard civilian compliance he enjoyed when he asked questions on his home turf? Normally home turf meant the station—this was his first interrogation on Maple Street. It could be that. Or it could be that Julia didn't need to ask where he was taking her; perhaps she already knew.

"Here I am talking about what I was feeling, but I had no idea what your brother-in-law was going through."

Julia nodded. "I didn't either, really."

"Did you ever learn why he . . ." Rice paused.

Julia's voice was unapologetic. "Tried to overdose."

"That."

"I think it was a lot of things, all piling up on top of each other." She turned her head and thought. "I remember he had had a really hard week."

40

The week went like this.

On Saturday night, Nick drank alone. He finished off Mary Jo's Stoli and an old jug of cranberry juice from the back of the fridge. He wondered if Mary Jo would ask him about it when she noticed the empty bottle, or if she'd avoid the topic like she had the assault, since her boyfriend broke the news to the whole campus. Nick still caught people staring at him, even fucking whispering, because Mary Jo hadn't been smart enough to see that her boyfriend was a douchebag.

Nick ended the night in the bathroom. He knelt on the floor and made himself vomit into the stained toilet bowl, hoping to stave off a hangover. Then he stood, rinsed his mouth out, and locked eyes with the reflection above the sink. Was that person really him? The lines of his face were harsh, his eyes wet and empty. The image was sharp, but his mind was melting, blurring. He wished he could dissolve into the cold water and wash down the drain.

‑‑‑◦

On Sunday, he was hungover anyway.

‑‑‑◦

Sherie called on Monday. At first he thought she knew, somehow, that he was the one who called looking for her the week before. But she immediately started talking about court, and Nick realized it was just a coincidence. She told Nick there would be a court date next Tuesday. She said she was reminding him of the date, but he didn't remember being given it.

"The dispositional conference," she said, "is what we call it when the prosecutor and the defense attorney meet at court, talk about the case, and try to come to an agreement to settle it."

"So it could all be over next Tuesday?"

"It could be, but please don't get your hopes up."

Right. Nick remembered the meeting at the DA's office. If the case did settle, it would probably happen closer to trial. Two months had seemed like a lifetime to Nick, but apparently they were still early on in the case.

"How does it work?"

"At court? The defendant goes, and there's a judge for part of it, but a lot of it is just the lawyers talking alone. Linda will tell Eva—that's the defense lawyer—Linda will tell her why she thinks she would win at trial, and what she thinks a fair sentence would be. Eva will tell Linda why she thinks Linda will lose, and what sentence they would accept to make the case go away."

"What kind of sentence would it be?"

"Linda wanted to know what you thought of him serving four years in prison, with a total of ten years he could serve if he violates probation."

Nick didn't know what to say. Four years in prison sounded like a long time. But maybe not. If they settled the case now, without Nick telling Sherie the truth, that would mean everyone would see the four years as Ray's payment for what Nick said Ray did: invited Nick to a hotel, knocked him out, and assaulted him while he was defenseless. Four years didn't sound so long, then.

"That's just an offer to get him to settle," Sherie went on. "If he won't settle, if Linda wins at trial, she would argue for way more time."

"So it would be four years if we skip the trial."

"Exactly," Sherie said.

If there was no trial, there was no reason to tell the prosecutor the story—the actual story. Was there? Would he be any freer, truly, just for having said it, if saying it would be pointless?

"That sounds good," Nick said to Sherie. And he didn't tell her.

—◦—

On Tuesday, he had therapy. He went into the session ready to tell Jeff what he'd decided as he spoke to Sherie: that he would wait until after the coming court date to tell anyone else what he'd told Jeff a week before. But when he saw Jeff in person, it hit him how much he liked Jeff. Jeff had shown him, over the last couple of months, what it looked like to be a man who had also been a victim. Proved to him that you could be a victim without it defining you. Jeff was married. He was funny, but also gentle. He was sure of himself. He was the kind of man Nick wanted to be. And this man might lose respect for him if he knew Nick wanted to wait and see if the case went away. Might find him cowardly—might even think, *I guess he's not as brave as I thought he was.* So Nick changed his mind and decided to lie.

"Have you talked to the advocate yet?"

"I called last week but she was gone for a family emergency." *Not even a lie*, he thought, but he still felt guilty.

"Oh. Did you talk to the prosecutor, then?"

"No. I'm just gonna wait and tell the advocate this week." *Definitely a lie.* "I'll try her again when I leave here."

Jeff hooked a finger under the band of his watch.

"You don't have to if you don't feel ready," he said. "You get to make the decisions. No one else."

Nick could hear the soft *tick-tick-tick* of the clock on the wall behind him.

"And as I said last week, I'm more than happy to be there when you call."

When he did tell Sherie—if he had to, if the case didn't settle next week—that would feel good. Familiar.

"Maybe," Nick said. Maybe it would feel good, or maybe it would feel like more of the same. Like he was a kid who'd spilled a glass of milk, and he was watching someone else clean it up.

Nick left Jeff's office feeling even worse than when he got there. As Johnny drove him home, he wished for an accident. He pictured a car slamming into theirs, hitting the passenger side of the Volvo and snapping him out of consciousness and into a coma. It would leave Johnny unscathed, somehow, and no one upset—everyone could know that the coma wouldn't last. His mom, Tony, Johnny, and Elle—none of them would have to worry. And Nick could sleep through it all. He could wake up after the case was done, after everyone had forgotten they were so interested in his life.

⌐

As it went sometimes after a bad day, Wednesday was okay.

⌐

On Thursday, he dreamed that Elle was knocking at his door, asking to come in, asking if he'd seen the news. She handed him a phone but the words were blurry.

"You lied," Elle was saying. "You lied. You let me believe you. You let me see what I wanted to see. Everyone knows now. Everyone knows what you are." She was sobbing. Nick was sobbing. And then he woke up.

He reached for his phone. Googled his name. Nothing new. Googled Walker's name. Nothing new. He should have stopped there, but he didn't. He was sick with guilt. He wouldn't pick at himself. Instead, he would read.

He scrolled to the bottom of the most recent article on *Seaside*. There were no new comments, so he reread what was there.

> I might be able to swallow this if the "victim" were
> a smaller female, but a 20yo male gets knocked
> unconscious in a single blow? It's just very hard
> to buy.

> So can we just get straight that this guy blacked out,
> wasn't hit on the head or whatever nonsense . . . just
> doesn't want to own that he drank himself dumb. If he
> doesn't remember what happened, that doesn't mean he
> wasn't consenting to it.

Nick was right not to tell Sherie. Not if he could help it. People already thought he was a liar. Already thought he was less of a man for the story he told. He didn't want to know what people would say, what they would think of him, if they knew the truth.

He could make it a week—less than a week—to hear if, by some miracle, the case would go away on its own. Only if it didn't would he need to make a decision. Would he tell the truth and watch the case fold and his reputation crumble? Or would he split himself in two: the real Nick only Jeff was allowed to see, and the fake Nick who'd appeared in the car on the way to the hospital and told the story no one seemed to believe?

⌒

Sherie called again on Friday. Court was pushed off, she said, until January 12.

Wait. January 12. That was a month away.

"Why?"

"His lawyer has a scheduling conflict next week."

So what? Why did that cost Nick another month of his life?

"So . . ." What could he say? What could she do?

"Right," she said. "So, there's really nothing to do at the moment. I'll call you after court in January to let you know where we landed. And now," she said like it was good news, "you can just focus on the holidays. Any special plans?"

The only thing Nick had thought about the holidays so far was that maybe, just maybe, all of this would be over by then.

⌒

On Saturday, he was drinking alone again when Elle knocked on his door.

His stomach rolled as he remembered his dream.

She opened the door and stuck her head in.

"Ooh!" she squealed. "We drinking?"

41

On December 13, Rice stepped out of mass feeling calm and centered. He sucked the cool air in through his nostrils and let it out his mouth, sending a white cloud of frozen breath out before him.

His Sunday morning ritual consisted of mass at eight sharp and breakfast with the boys downtown at ten fifteen. Bob Lucre and Jim Allen would be waiting for him in their usual booth at Dorothy's Diner in Cape. Hot coffee, a short stack, and a recap of the week. Most people seemed to feel filled up by their worship. Rice usually left feeling hollowed out, like all of the burdens he'd been carrying, all the negative thoughts, had been stripped from his head and given up to God. All his mistakes and bad choices, big and small, had been left behind in the rafters of the church. As freeing as it was to feel so light, his Sunday breakfast grounded him again.

Rice crunched down the cathedral's salted steps and made his way to his car. It had snowed earlier that week, enough that the lot had been plowed. Rice had parked right up against a low bank of snow, already dirty with grit.

He sat down into the car and reached for his phone. This morning he had two missed calls from the station, a voice mail, and a text message from Brendan Merlo.

Nick hall at YCMC. Suicide attempt. Heading there now

The message was time-stamped 8:03 a.m.

Rice read the message over again.

He shot off a text of his own—he wouldn't be making breakfast—then headed for the hospital.

—◦—

Brendan Merlo was just reaching his patrol vehicle when Rice pulled into the lot next to the emergency department, giving his horn two quick taps. Merlo stopped and waited for him to park.

He whistled as Rice shut his door. "Don't you look sharp."

"Mass," Rice said. "What's going on?"

Merlo moved leisurely to Rice's side. "Didn't mean for you to come over, we're all set."

"What happened?"

"Kid's roommate Ellen called it in, sometime around three this morning." Merlo fished a small notebook from his jacket as he spoke. "Elle, I mean. Said they were at their apartment, drinking last night into this morning, thought they were having a good time, blowing off steam. Elle said he told her he was going to the bathroom and he was gone long enough she went looking for him. Found him passed out on the floor with an empty bottle of his psych meds. Hard to say whether it was a genuine attempt or not."

"What does *that* mean?"

"Just my phrasing," Merlo said. "Nick says he can't remember doing it is all, and he doesn't feel suicidal now. Obviously swallowing a whole bottle of pills looks like suicide, I just meant I don't know if he *really* wanted to die."

"What pills he use?"

"Fuck if I can pronounce it; it's the generic Zoloft. He says he doesn't want to hurt himself now." Merlo shrugged. "I believe him."

Rice didn't. Instead, he felt a panicked frustration rising up. "They're not letting him go home, are they?"

"Don't need to. His sister-in-law really worked him over on staying at a hospital-type program. He's going up to Goodspring in Belfast."

He needed to get inside. "Thanks, Brendan," Rice said, patting Merlo's shoulder as he passed him by.

"No problem," Merlo called after him.

Rice waved his hand in the air without turning back.

For the third time, Rice found himself walking down a sterile hallway in York County Medical Center headed for Nick Hall's room. This time his steps were propelled by an urgency not present for his first two visits.

Stepping into the ER was like waking up. He was at the ER. Off duty. To see a boy who'd tried to kill himself.

A nurse behind the large desk at the center of the unit looked up from the chart in his hands. "Can I help you?"

It was all wrong. The intrusiveness was clear: no one had called for his help. Nobody had invited him in.

"No," Rice said. "No, I—"

"Detective Rice?" Julia Hall was standing in the doorway of what must have been a bathroom on the far side of the unit.

Shit.

"Julia, hi."

She came toward him, not quite smiling. "Are you here for Nick?" She eyed his church clothes. "Or . . . something private?"

"Well, I was here for a personal matter, and I ran into Officer Merlo just now. Thought I'd stop over just in case . . ." He trailed off. *Just in case what? What could he do for them?*

For a second, Julia looked as though she was thinking the same. Then she half smiled and said, "That was sweet of you, but I think we're okay."

"Well, great. I'm glad. I heard he's going up to Goodspring?"

She frowned. "Uh, it's not set in stone yet, but it looks like that's gonna work out. Why?"

"Oh, no reason."

Julia crossed her arms over her chest and nodded. "If it affects the case, it affects the case, I guess is how I see it."

"Julia I—I wasn't even thinking of that. I want Nick to take care of himself, truly."

Her face softened, but her arms stayed crossed. "Me, too. Thanks for coming by, Detective."

"No problem," Rice said, and he turned away before she could beat him to it.

42

*H*ouse Hunters is good," Tony said.

"Maybe when you're old," Nick answered.

Tony stood on his tiptoes, flicking through the channels on the TV mounted high in the corner of the room.

A woman in a wedding gown appeared on the screen.

"Pass."

"Oh, how about a dog show?" Tony asked with genuine enthusiasm.

Nick turned the dead remote control over in his hands and nodded. "That could work."

"We don't have to—"

"No, keep it here."

Tony rolled his shoulders as he came back to the chair next to Nick's bed.

Before that awful silence could creep in on them, Tony asked, "Should we get a dog?" It was a question he might have asked Chloe or Seb; it wasn't real. It was just a game.

Nick looked at him, then up at the screen. "Yeah," Nick said. "You should get . . . that one." Some kind of miniature Doberman–looking thing was being manhandled on a table.

"Christ. Probably more dangerous than the big version."

Nick chuckled softly. "Why *don't* you guys have a dog?"

"Julia's allergic."

"Oh yeah, I knew that." Nick turned the remote over and over. "Literally her only flaw."

That wasn't quite true. To most people, Julia looked perfect. She was pretty and kind and endlessly thoughtful. She never showed up empty-handed, always remembered birthdays and anniversaries, always asked how you were doing and meant it. But she could be headstrong and critical when she thought she knew better than someone else. Especially when it came to Tony. Sometimes she just didn't get him—didn't trust that he knew what he was doing. Until she was in college she'd been rich, at least compared to Tony's family, and then, abruptly, she wasn't. Her dad died and the floor fell out from under her and her mom. When Tony met Julia, it was only a few years after that, and she was *obsessed* with taking care of herself. Every time Tony tried to do something for her, she questioned and critiqued and pushed him away. It was equal parts enraging and arousing, figuring out how to get her to let him in. Even now, sometimes they'd have a standoff.

"Speak of the devil," Nick said with a faint smile as Julia appeared in the doorway.

"You boys talking about me?"

"Just your allergies," Nick said.

She squinted. "Scintillating. I'm gonna go down to the cafeteria—I just came back to take orders."

"Yes!" Nick said with the most enthusiasm he had mustered since they'd arrived earlier that morning to see him. "A coffee, with cream and sugar."

Julia winced. "You know, caffeine might be something to cut back on right now, it can kind of feed anxious feelings."

"Oh—"

"Christ, Julia. Let him have a coffee." Tony pressed his fingers into his temples. He could feel a splitting headache coming on.

Her voice was deflated. "Yeah, sorry, that was stupid."

"No, it wasn't," Nick said. "I could have tea instead."

"No, you can have a coffee." Tony pointed a hand at Nick.

"Well, if I should—"

"A coffee will make absolutely no difference," Julia said as she stepped farther into the room. "I don't even know why I said that. Do you want anything to snack on with it?"

Nick paused. "A cookie, if they have any. Or something else sweet."

"On it. Tony?"

"I might come with you," he said as he stood. "We can figure out what the plan is today, with the kids."

Julia backed out of Tony's way as he came through the door. She had this antsy energy around him, like she was afraid to stand too close to him. It was exhausting.

"We're running over to the cafeteria," she said to the nurse at the desk.

The man nodded. "You're good; I got eyes on him," he said quietly as they passed by.

They walked in silence most of the way down the hall. Tony wondered if Julia was preparing an apology. That would be just like her, to apologize when he had been snippy. She was too quick with her sorries, betraying that she didn't always mean them.

Instead, she said, "Detective Rice came by."

"Where, the house?"

"Here, in the ER."

"When?"

"Just now, I ran into him on my way back from the bathroom. It was kind of strange."

"Wait, was he in the ER for himself or—"

"No, to see Nick."

Tony considered this as they crossed the atrium, their boots crunching on the salt and dirt dragged in from outside. "But he didn't come in."

"I told him we were all set. I didn't think there was any use in Nick talking to *another* cop about it. And it's not like the two of them have a relationship outside of why he's here in the first place."

Tony nodded.

She went on. "I just couldn't tell if he was here out of concern or if it was more about, like, checking in on an important witness, you know?"

That was perfect. Just fucking perfect. He probably *was* here to check on his star witness, make sure he wasn't getting too *unstable* to testify. The ADA would probably drop by next.

"Fuck him if it was," Tony said.

Julia said nothing for a beat, and then: "I'm just so glad he agreed to go to Goodspring."

"Do you know anything about what it's like there?" Tony thought she may have, from her old job.

"Not Goodspring specifically, just enough to know he's better there than at home."

"Not even our home?"

Julia stopped walking and grabbed his arm. "Honey, we can't take care of this ourselves. We need real help. He needs to be . . . kept an eye on right now."

"We could do that. You're already home, and I could take a week off."

"No," she said. "I'm sorry, but no, I don't want to take this on, and with the kids."

"The kids? He would never do anything in front of them, he loves them."

"I know that, but clearly this is out of his control."

"He doesn't even want to hurt himself, it never would have happened if he hadn't been drinking on his meds! And he knows never to do that again."

Julia started walking again. "I'm not having this conversation right now."

Tony followed her. "He's gonna miss Christmas if he's stuck up there, did you even think of that?"

"Christmas?" She nearly shouted the word as she turned to face him, and he involuntarily took a step backward. "Tony, he almost missed *all* the Christmases! What do you even—he could have died last night."

"The doctor said—"

"That's not what I'm talking about. He could have done it differently. I don't care what he would have done sober. He wasn't sober. He was drunk out of his mind, and he tried to kill himself."

She was right, but she continued.

"I am *so* sick of you acting like you know better than everyone else. Christ! Nick needs to be with professionals, *wants* to be with them, and for some reason you can't stand that. You aren't the only one who can take care of him."

Tony's chest was tight, and he could feel his face flushing with heat. His eyes began to burn.

"I know that."

Julia's face softened, but she didn't move toward him. "Do you?"

A man passed by them in the hall and Julia fell silent and smiled at him. Can't have a stranger knowing they're fighting. Another thing about Julia: she was ashamed by the appearance of conflict.

When he was gone, she said, "I know you're terrified." She brought a hand to her chest and her voice choked. "*I* can barely stand it. I can't believe we could have lost him."

He was going to cry if she didn't stop talking. He wiped his eyes, stopping his tears before they started.

"I hate being powerless as much as you, but the only thing we can do for him is get him to Goodspring."

He didn't know what to say, so he said nothing.

They walked the rest of the way to the cafeteria in silence. Julia's words replayed in his mind like a sad song.

Nick had almost died. He'd almost lost him.

They were in a new place now: a place where Nick's life was at risk. Not just what people thought of him at school. Not just what would come of the court case. His life.

Julia didn't like to feel powerless, and neither did Tony. But Tony wondered if he was as powerless as she thought.

$\sim$

The drive to Goodspring was long and quiet. Tony tried to get Nick chatting a couple of times, but he couldn't keep him distracted from whatever it was that kept making him fall silent. Nick kept looking over at the GPS, like he was watching the minutes scrape off the time left in the car with Tony. Eventually, Tony stopped trying to make chitchat, and they drove in silence.

How did they get here? Two months ago, Nick had been like any other junior. Solid grades, living with his friends, too funny for his own good. He was born great, and Tony had managed to keep him that way. It sounded stupid, but it was true: it had been Tony. How else did you explain him being so functional after being raised by *two* alcoholics? Tony had been there from the beginning. When he was little. When he was suffering through the horror that is male puberty. Tony had been the one Nick came out to first. When Nick was sixteen, Tony and Julia took him into their home for weeks—with a three-year-old and a baby in the house!—after Ron caught Nick kissing a boy in the living room and threw Nick out. Later, Tony mediated between his dad and brother to get Nick back into the house so he could finish high school without transferring schools.

Had he really managed to ferry Nick out of their father's house and into well-adjusted adulthood, only to have him obliterated by someone else?

As they pulled off the highway and drove onto Route 3, a sign pointing them toward Belfast, Tony felt Nick grow tense. It was a shift in the air, like a swell of humidity. From the corner of his eye, he saw Nick fiddle with his sleeves, touch his hairline, and stop himself from doing more than that.

Goodspring was a flat, industrial-looking building at the end of a long driveway in the woods. There were walking trails around it, according to a nurse at the hospital. Nick would get to go on walks while he was there for the month. Tony thought about saying something about it, anything at all, as he pulled into a space in the lot.

"I need to tell you something," Nick said.

Tony put the car in park. "Okay."

Nick rubbed at his sleeves, then crammed his hands under his thighs.

"You can tell me anything," Tony said.

"I haven't . . ." Nick stopped. He breathed.

Tony's heart began thumping so hard it seemed to move his whole torso back and forth in his seat. "What is it?"

Nick breathed out of his mouth in a thin stream, like a kid learning to whistle. "I haven't been honest with you," he said. "About that night."

Chills spread down his spine as some part of Tony's brain warned him that something terrible was about to happen.

"And I know that's not the only reason I'm having a hard time. I know that." He sounded like he was trying to convince himself of something. "But the lie, the lie has made everything so much worse."

The lie. What did that mean?

God forgive him, Tony thought of Julia and what she said about Nick.

And just for a second, Tony wondered if Nick had made up the whole thing.

43

NICK HALL, 2015

Tony was staring at him like he could see into Nick's head—like he could read the words Nick was about to say on a marquee behind Nick's forehead. So he said the words out loud.

"I remember everything."

Tony shook his head like he didn't understand.

"I made up the blackout."

Nick brought his hands up to his face and sobbed sharply. It was the same as when he told Jeff—the pain of it rushed him at once, overwhelming him. What Ray had done to him. What he'd done to himself. The shame he felt, and the anger that he felt any shame at all.

"I remember everything he did." His own voice was a wail in the cavern between his hands. "I thought I was going to die."

"Nick!" Tony was saying his name like Nick couldn't hear him, like Tony couldn't reach him. "Nick!"

Tony's hands were on his shoulders, pressing, squeezing, pulling him against Tony's chest.

"I'm so sorry," Nick sobbed. Snot poured from his nose onto Tony's shirt. "I'm so sorry, Tony."

"What are you sorry for?"

"Lying, fucking everything up."

Nick pulled himself back to look at Tony's face. "You didn't fuck any-thing up," Tony said.

"I did," Nick said. "I've lied so much. I lied *under oath*. When they find out—everyone will hate me. Even the prosecutor and the detectives. They'll all hate me."

Tony shook his head. "They'll understand. You were in shock."

"Yeah and it wore off. I kept lying. I kept pretending I didn't remem-ber what happened in the middle. What happened in the room with him."

Tony frowned. Held something back. Nick knew what it was. Tony wanted to ask the obvious: Why *had* he lied? Nick decided not to make him say it.

"I decided on the way to the hospital," Nick said. "Everything was happening so fast, I got so upset, I couldn't breathe—I couldn't think. And then I got really calm, and I thought, I'll just tell them he knocked me out. He did hit me."

"I know," Tony said.

"It was such an easy lie. And telling it was easy—it was easy to say I didn't remember. I didn't want to."

"It's okay," Tony said.

"By the time you came . . ." Nick stopped to wipe his nose on his sleeve. "I'd already lied to the police. And I thought, *Okay, I won't tell anyone, ever, and eventually it won't feel like a lie.*"

Tony reached across the console and rubbed Nick's arm. "Why did you—you just didn't want to have to talk about . . . what he did?"

"No. I . . ." Nick paused. "I was bleeding."

Tears began to run down Tony's face.

"People were going to know he raped me. I didn't think I could hide that. I just didn't want anyone else to know what happened before that."

"What?"

"I was so ashamed," Nick said. "It was so confusing. With Ray. One minute it was one thing and the next . . . I barely had time to think. I didn't want it."

"It's not your fault," Tony said quickly. "Whatever you did or didn't do. That doesn't mean—"

"That's not what I'm saying," Nick said. "I told him to stop. I tried to make him. But I didn't . . ." Nick paused. And he let himself remember.

They went into the room. He was nervous but eager, his hands trembling and restless. Josh—Ray—shut the door. Nick sat on the bed, and the springs bounced under him. Ray smiled, came toward him, stood him up. Kissed him. It was good, a little awkward, a rougher kiss than in the cab. Ray pulled his face back from Nick's. And then he hit Nick.

Not like Nick told the police. It was weird, there was no other word for it. It was open-palmed, slow-motion, not hard but jarring in its wrongness.

"You like that?" Ray asked.

Nick said something stupid, he couldn't remember what. Something like "I don't know."

Ray's eyes were playful. "Bad boy," he said.

Nick's stomach went hot.

Ray slapped him again, hard this time.

Nick's eye watered and his ears rang. It was awful, and horribly familiar. An old humiliation.

"Don't," Nick said. His voice was small, childish, and his breath hitched. He had made a mistake. This was a mistake.

"No?" Ray leaned forward and kissed his neck. "Sorry, baby."

Nick held still. He wanted to leave. He wanted to shove Ray back and walk out the door, but he held still. He didn't know why he had held still. But he did.

Ray started pushing him back toward the bed.

Nick planted his feet, slowly brought his hands up to Ray's shoulders. He started to say something. He couldn't remember what it was. Maybe if he'd told the police right away, he would remember it now. He didn't know. All he knew was it happened quickly after that. Ray hit him again; Nick hit back. Ray forced him down; Nick scratched Ray's arms, cried out, tried to headbutt him, but Ray won. And Ray raped him.

"I didn't see it coming," he told Tony. "I mean I did, I felt it the second he hit me—that he wanted to hurt me, but my body, it was like I froze." Hot tears ran down Nick's face, soaking into his collar. "But then I fought, I did, I tried to stop him, but I couldn't get out from under him. I thought he was going to kill me." Nick brought a hand to his throat. Ray had pressed into his neck so hard, it felt like Nick's throat would collapse. "I wasn't strong enough. I fought back, and I lost."

When Tony spoke, his voice was hard. "I'm gonna kill him."

Nick shook his head. "When I tell the prosecutor what happened, she has to tell Ray and his lawyer. It'll change everything. He'll use that I lied against me. It'll be in the papers. Everyone will know."

"I'll kill him," Tony said again.

"Don't be stupid, Tony," Nick said. "Don't talk like that. I just need to decide whether to tell them at all."

Tony shifted a bit in his seat. "What else would you do?"

Nick shrugged. "Give up the case. I don't know if I ever cared to begin with."

"Don't do that. You told the police the part they needed to know—that he'd done it at all."

"I didn't tell them, though. Elle did. It was already done when they asked me what I wanted to do."

"Don't let him win," Tony said.

"You're not listening. No matter what, I lose."

They sat in silence for a minute. Through the windshield, Nick watched a woman come out of the building and get into a parked car.

"I wish you hadn't kept this from me."

Guilt cut through Nick's belly. "I'm sorry."

"No, I'm not blaming you. I mean I wish I'd been there for you."

"You have been," Nick said. "I just . . . I should have told you, but I didn't want to."

"Why?"

"I don't know." There were emotions tied to it, overwhelming feelings he could vaguely categorize. Pride, shame, fear, protection. He just didn't know how to talk about it yet.

"Why'd you tell me now?"

Nick shrugged. "Honestly, I'm just tired of keeping it from you."

"It's why you took all your meds, right?"

"I still don't know why I did that. I wasn't thinking straight."

"Nick." Tony's eyes were dry now. "You know there isn't a thing I wouldn't do if it meant saving your life, right?"

44

I was using that!" Sebastian shouted.

"Not so loud, Seb!" Chloe said even louder.

Julia stuck her head into the dining room. Chloe was holding the cereal box at arm's length from her little brother, who was stretching across the table.

"Nope," Julia said as she swiped the box from Chloe's grasp. "If you're still hungry, there's extra oatmeal in the kitchen. No seconds on the cereal." One of them must have grabbed it from the cupboard while Julia was occupied.

"Seb already got some," Chloe whined.

Julia leaned down to Chloe's eye level. "Honey, I don't like tattling." She kissed Chloe's forehead to show her that she was forgiven. "And, Seb, if you can't follow the rules, we won't do cereal for breakfast at all."

Seb's face burst with shock. "What!"

It was all she could do not to laugh in his adorable face. "Do either of you want oatmeal?"

Each grumbled a no.

"Backpacks," Julia prompted, and she cut through the living room for the stairs. She'd take the kids to the bus stop in a minute, but first she wanted to swap her pajama bottoms for warmer pants. Wind was pushing against the windows that morning, and it looked frigid outside.

At the top of the stairs, she heard Tony's voice in her study. He used the space every now and then, mostly for phone calls when he wanted to block out the background noise of the kids. He'd used it last night, too. Something for work, but Julia didn't know what.

"I just think you should wait until after that," he said. "Yeah."

She paused in the doorway of the bedroom, curious to know who he was talking to so early in the morning.

"Right," he said. "If you tell them before, it doesn't— Exactly. Okay. I just woke up thinking about it and wanted to ask. You're making the right decision."

She didn't have a clue who it could be until he signed off. "I love you too, bud."

It was Nick. That was odd. What were they talking about?

She opened the door to the bedroom closet and paused. The inside of the closet door was covered with pieces of the back-and-forth love letter they'd been writing for longer than they'd been married. There were notes from her to Tony, notes from Tony to her, the occasional note from the kids. A smattering of photos and concert tickets were scattered through the mix, and Tony's tie rack hung down the middle. Over the years the collage had nearly overtaken the door.

Her fleece-lined jeans were folded on the top shelf. Julia dropped her pajama bottoms and stepped into her pants. As she buttoned them closed— a little tighter every winter, it seemed—she took in the collage of her life with Tony.

Julia's girlfriend Margot had seen it one night after she came over for dinner. She'd asked what Julia would be wearing to a mutual friend's wedding, so Julia brought her upstairs and swung the closet door open.

Margot had stepped forward and sighed. "Are you kidding me? Could you two be any cuter?"

"Ignore that," Julia said with a grin as she dug for the dress.

"Impossible." Margot's eyes scanned the collection, and her voice went syrupy. "Aww, you're so romantic, Julia." Margot shoved her with a soft hand.

In truth, though, it was Tony's collection. She'd added the stray piece here and there, but he was the true curator. He was the one with a roll of tape in his sock drawer. Some mornings she'd find Tony standing in the closet, half dressed for work, staring at the door. She might watch him for a full minute before he turned to her, his eyes a little misty.

Tony's softness was one of his greatest qualities. He was so handsome, his body so strong, that even after more than a decade together, she could still be caught off guard by his tenderness. The way he'd touch her back so gently as he passed by her in the kitchen while they cooked. The way he pecked the kids on the head. The fatherly voice he used with his younger brother.

Tony was shutting the door to the study as she left the bedroom.

"Was that Nick?"

He looked surprised, like he'd been caught. "Yeah."

"What's going on?"

"Nothing," he said quickly. "Just—we were talking about court yesterday on the drive."

Tony had driven Nick to Goodspring a day ago. He said Nick had been quiet. They hadn't talked about the overdose or anything else.

"Oh, you were?"

"Just for a second. Barely. He's just nervous to testify. You know."

Julia nodded. It would be awful. The chance that it would settle in January seemed fleeting, but sometimes the possibility was the only thing that gave her any peace about what Nick would otherwise go through.

"Were you telling him not to tell the ADA that he's nervous? She'll understand."

"Not that he can't tell her, just that he doesn't need to think about it really." There was a defensive edge to his voice. "Until the next court date. Since it might settle. That's all."

Julia nodded. That made sense. Tony must have been so upset about all of this—Nick trying to overdose, going to the program. She replayed their fight—was it a fight?—at the hospital and regretted how harshly she'd spoken to Tony. But he needed to understand the severity of the situation with Nick's mental health. That they couldn't take on keeping him safe themselves.

And now both of them, Nick and Tony, were already back on court. Although they were premature, Nick's fears weren't misplaced. If there was a trial next fall, it would be awful. Eva Barr would try to make Nick look like he'd been drunk and willing. Photos of Nick's body would be shown in court. Eva would argue that the graph of Nick's actions only had one logical landing point: a consensual sexual encounter with her client.

And at the end of the trial, a jury of Mainers would decide what the situation looked like to them. The court would try to control for prejudice—would try to remove from the jury pool anyone who held a bias against gay people or male victims. But surely they would squeeze through: unspoken inclinations and unrealized beliefs. People who would watch the evidence for proof of their preheld beliefs about what a man like Nick or Walker would be like, and what must have happened between them.

It was too early to worry about that. She stepped forward and pecked Tony on the cheek. She was glad he thought so, too.

45

Tony was greeted by warmth as he opened the front door of the Portland Public Library. His face had gone stiff with cold on his walk from his office. His ears began to ache as he crossed the atrium with the bubbling fountain.

He took the stairs to the lower level and made his way to the nonfiction section, keeping his face turned away from the circulation desk. He remembered from the past two days that he was looking for the general range of 363–364. Eventually he would move into the pharmaceutical section, but he was going to take this one topic at a time.

It seemed the odds were higher that he'd run into someone he knew in Portland, but he was tired of using up most of his lunch break driving to and from libraries farther away. Besides, he had rehearsed for the possibility earlier in the week on those very drives.

"Oh, this?" (Sheepish laugh.) "I'm trying to write a murder mystery—how embarrassing is that?"

Maybe it was stupid to be using the library like this at all, but using his phone or a computer to plan anything seemed a dangerous idea. He'd deleted the history on Julia's computer earlier that week, but he couldn't shake the vague idea he had that for the police, everything electronic was traceable.

Tony walked around the edge of the room, reading the numbers on the sides of the shelves until he found the right range. With relief he quickly spotted the spine of a promising book he'd found on an earlier trip. *Now take it and go sit down.*

"Tony?"

Tony jerked his hand and sent the book pitching forward off the shelf. He caught it awkwardly, splaying the pages open between his hands.

"Whoa, sorry!" the voice said.

He turned to see it was Walt Abraham, a classmate from his first year in law school.

"Walt, hey!" They met mid-aisle and shook hands. "How've you been?" Tony folded his arms over the book against his chest.

Walt launched into the same chitchat Tony heard every time he ran into a former classmate. How long had it been? What was he up to? He was smart not to be a lawyer, what a slog. (As if human resources *at a law firm* was any better.) How about Julia? How old were the kids now? Tony squeezed the book to his chest and kept his answers short. In spite of Tony's decision to leave law school after the first year, his career and marital choices had left a foot firmly planted in the world of attorneys. He generally didn't mind running into a guy like Walt, but at the moment he wanted nothing to do with him.

"Well," Walt said at last. "I've gotta get moving, but I just had to stop when I saw you. I'm so glad to hear you and Julia are well. You know," he said, stepping closer to Tony and lowering his voice, "a lot of guys I run into after seven years, I might not expect they were still married to the same woman. But look at that—you even sound happy!"

Walt had gotten divorced the year after Tony left law school, then married again a few years after graduation, Tony had heard. Judging by his bare left hand, that one hadn't gone well, either.

"How do you two do it?"

"Oh, just lucky I guess," Tony said.

"Great running into you," Walt said as he walked away.

"You, too," Tony said. His heartbeat thudded against the book. Walt hadn't even noticed it. And why would he have?

He looked down at the book, nestled against his chest; there was a splash of coffee or tea spattered across the top edge of the pages. *Just go sit down and read. Standing here, staring at it is way more obvious than sitting down and reading it.* He strode across the collection room, sat in an overstuffed armchair, and read.

⁓

As he walked back to the office, Tony probably should have mulled over everything he'd read in the last forty minutes, but instead he couldn't distract himself from Walt's question. How had they stayed happy—save for the present blip—for so long?

His first and only year in law school, Tony had noticed Julia Clark, sure, but he noticed other pretty classmates, too. She was reserved in class, like a lot of them were that first year, and he hadn't thought too much at all about her. He was too busy bombing his classes. At the end of the first year, he dropped out. Then one night that summer, he walked into a bar with a friend and found Julia there, slinging drinks.

The bar was called the Ruby, and Julia looked different there. Her wild, curly hair was up in a ponytail. It swished against her neck as she wiped out the glasses with a cloth. She was wearing a tight tank top and high-waisted jean shorts that made her ass look ample—it wasn't, he'd snuck quick glances during the school year, but the illusion still excited him.

Struck by how *cool* she looked behind the bar, he worried what she would think of him ordering something nonalcoholic. When she greeted them and took their orders, Tony asked for something off the chalkboard behind her. It did not taste like alcohol—instead like vanilla and something spicy—and he drank it far too fast.

She stood behind the bar giggling and talking to him for an hour before his friend saw he'd become the third wheel and left. They'd covered their classmates, Tony's drop-out, and had started in on television when she asked if she could make Tony another.

What had felt like the warm fuzzies of infatuation suddenly went numb.

What number was that?

"Hold up," he said.

She turned to him, standing against a backdrop of liquor bottles—blue, green, amber. A loose curl had fallen to her collarbone, and in the dim lighting, her features were pronounced and beautiful.

"I don't drink."

"Oh." She looked down at the clean glass in her hand. "But you just drank."

"I mean, I do—no, I *can*." He felt his face flushing. "I just don't really like to." This was the part where she'd ask why—was he an alcoholic, or just afraid of becoming one?

"Okay," she said skeptically. "Can I get you a water?"

And just like that, everything changed. They stopped flirting and started talking. Over the next three hours, they laid themselves bare to each other, knowing that if either pulled away after this, it didn't count as real rejection, because it hadn't been a date to begin with. Tony told Julia, as best he could, why he didn't drink. About his father who did and the brother who still lived with him. How badly Tony wanted to fight whenever he drank, as stupid as that was.

"Are daddy issues sexy on a guy?" Tony asked.

Julia raised an eyebrow. "Wanna hear mine?"

Tony leaned forward. "Please."

She leaned down onto her elbows so her face was inches from his. "My dad was perfect."

Tony laughed and sat back.

She smiled. "Perfect for the first twenty years of my life. Then one day I went to my parents' for dinner, and my dad told me he had pancreatic cancer, stage four, and a month later my mom was giving his eulogy."

"Fuck."

"Yup. It sucked, big time. And the worst part?"

Tony shook his head.

"He refused treatment."

"Why?"

"He didn't want to spend all the money, didn't want to take medicine that would make him even sicker. I was never sure which reasons were real and which were bullshit, because none of them were good enough not to try to stay with us."

Tony didn't know what to say to that.

"For the record," Julia said, "I will never marry a man who isn't a fighter."

Tony leaned toward the bar again. "As you know, I fight too much to trust myself drinking."

She smiled and nodded. "I noticed."

As the memory played out in his mind, Tony felt a resolve swelling in his chest. He and Julia had compared their emotional baggage that night and found it compatible. He'd driven her crazy a few times over the years, and she him, but they worked together *because* of their pasts. Julia had always wanted a fighter.

And that, Tony was.

46

John Rice, 2015

Rice and O'Malley were in the break room making their morning coffees when Merlo poked his head in and told Rice he had a visitor.

"Britny Cressey?" Merlo said.

Rice groaned.

"Britny who?" O'Malley asked.

"She called me a couple months ago—Ray Walker's old friend. Or girlfriend, but not." He shrugged.

"Right," O'Malley said as Rice followed Merlo out. "'He's not a violent guy, I just happen to want you to know that,' et cetera."

"Yep," Rice said. He had actual work to do today. She was just going to waste his time.

He set his coffee on his desk, then met the woman with the girlish voice in the lobby.

"To what do I owe the pleasure?"

"I don't even know where to begin," Britny said. In spite of her voice, she looked her age. Late thirties.

"Why don't you give it your best shot."

Her long hair was dyed an unnatural red, and she pulled a handful of it in front of her shoulder. "I told you Ray and I were friends in high school but we lost touch."

"Yes."

"I reached out to him when I heard about all this, and at first we just chatted a bit but not much, but we've started to get close again. I think he's losing friends because of everything, getting lonely." She pushed her hair off her shoulder and smoothed her part.

"All right," Rice said.

"We've had drinks a couple times and talked on the phone a lot, and at first I really did feel bad for him, but I've started to feel like he's hiding something."

"About this?"

Britny nodded and raised her eyebrows. She brought both her hands up and smoothed her hair again, then shook it over her shoulders. "Like, I think maybe he did hurt that boy."

Goose bumps spread over the back of Rice's neck. Had Walker confessed to his friend?

"Has he said anything to you about Nick or that night?"

"No, but I think he would if I asked the right way. He's talked about nearly everything else with me. He's so stressed about money and court. He tells me everything about his lawyer. She just wants him to take a plea deal and go on the sex-offender registry. He borrowed *so* much money to pay for her, and he fights with her constantly and can't afford to get someone new. I guess he wanted to testify that you wouldn't arrest someone who assaulted him?"

Of course. The call about Tony Hall, where Walker said he didn't want to press charges. "He's saying I wouldn't arrest someone?"

She nodded smugly. "He told me he *told* you *not* to arrest him, but he was going to testify different. He was gonna say it was just more proof you all decided he was guilty. To show you were wrong about the rape, too. But his lawyer won't let him lie in court. He's all pissed off about it.

I guess they're having huge problems, and she pushed court off because of it."

"Stop," Rice said, and held up a hand. "I—I'd be lying if I said I wasn't interested in all this, but I don't think you should be talking to me. I mean, I guess he's waived any privilege about these conversations by telling you, but—" His mind was racing. What Walker and his lawyer talked about was supposed to be privileged, confidential. But if Walker told Britny, Rice could let Britny talk, couldn't he? But why was she doing this? "Aren't you friends with him?"

Her gray eyes went wide. "Not if he's a rapist, which now I think he is."

"Okay, well—"

"I think I can help you."

"How?"

"He's telling me so much. He's so stressed. Even his mom is driving him nuts. I'm the only friend he has left. I think I can get him to tell me whatever you need to know."

"I don't want you to do anything for me."

She dropped her hands to her side. "What?"

"Hold up, let me be clear, Ms. Cressey—I've never asked you to do anything for me."

"I know that, I—"

"Let me explain something to you. He has a lawyer. He's asserted his rights. I cannot and would not try to get a statement from him by working around his lawyer, through you. You got that?"

Her lip trembled. "Yes."

"I know you're trying to be helpful. But don't be helpful for me." It was more than helpfulness—she was one of those people. The limelight people. She wanted to testify. It was probably why she reached out to Walker in the first place—to worm herself into the news or something.

And she didn't care whose side she was on, so long as some of the spot-light hit her.

"I think you should go." Rice waved toward the front doors. "I don't want any part of this."

Rice turned and strode for the stairs.

Her childish voice was a whimper behind him. "You don't want a confession?"

"Not like this." Rice let the door slam on the lobby without waiting to see if she was leaving, too.

His coffee was still warm at his desk. His mug read: "If you run, you'll just go to jail tired." It had been a parting gift from the last admin to retire from Salisbury. Something about filling that mug with coffee, hold-ing it in his hand, drinking from it, even just seeing it at his workstation—it made him feel good. More competent, somehow. O'Malley was on the phone across the room, but as soon as she hung up she'd be asking about Britny Cressey. What a viper of a friend. Rice didn't need to be accused of making a civilian into his agent, trying to get a confession from Walker. They didn't need one.

But was that true? He sipped at his coffee and watched O'Malley absently. Her desk was much messier than Rice's, but she never seemed to lose things in the snowdrift of files and loose papers atop it. She laughed into the phone and crossed one leg over the other. Something was going on with Nick Hall. The suicide attempt. That could have to do with trauma, yes. But could it also speak to something else eating away at him? An attempt at escaping something besides a night he couldn't remember? An escape from something *he'd* done?

At this point, it wasn't his place to question whether he believed Nick Hall. The case was Linda Davis's, now. The system would have to do its best to sort it out.

47

"That was another regret I had," Rice said. "I didn't make it easy for Nick to tell me the truth."

Julia looked surprised. "I don't think it was your fault."

"I do," he said. "A better detective would have done it differently. Would have known how to make him feel safe. I should have told him from the beginning that it was never too late to tell me new information."

"Doing a job like yours, you make mistakes with people. It's awful but there's nothing you can do."

"I could have done better. I shouldn't have been so concerned with getting everything up front and it staying the same."

Julia shook her head. "I don't know what happened between the two of you. What exactly you did or didn't say. But I know you're a good man, and he knew you were doing your best by him. And your job is to get the story up front. You do have to hope for consistent statements, because those statements get cross-examined. The press plays them on repeat. That's how our system works. It's not designed for sexual assault cases."

"We never got to find out, though."

"What?"

"In Nick's case. We never got to find out if the system would have done right by him."

He studied her face. She looked at her mug on the table between them.

"Because the defendant went missing," Rice said. "*Weird*, right?"

Her mouth twitched: a smile was threatening to break through.

It was wild how often people smiled while they were being interrogated. In his earlier years on the force he assumed it was an attempt at nonchalance—an oversimple idea that someone guilty wouldn't be smiling. Later he wondered if it was some kind of psychological hiccup—the brain smiling at the strangeness of being interrogated, like on TV. He eventually learned another possible explanation at a body language training: an evolutionary holdover where we smile out of fear.

"Yeah," Julia said, and she cleared her throat. "We just assumed from the beginning he skipped town."

He held her eye.

His voice was soft. "Did you."

48

Julia was in her office, trying to work on the records report. It had grown too complex to wrangle into a single readable narrative. Her bewilderment with the project was bleeding over, and she kept slipping sideways into other worries.

In the last few weeks, a low-level anxiety had kicked up in her chest, unrelated to the report. Tony had been off lately. The cause seemed obvious enough: Nick's overdose had rocked him. She didn't blame Tony for being upset, but something more than that was going on. For one, he had lied about going to visit Nick on Saturday.

At the end of Nick's first week at Goodspring, Nick was feeling lonely. Tony went up to see him for the day on Saturday. Tony told Julia all of this, and she believed it until a day ago. A day ago, she called Nick to find out how visiting hours were going to work on Christmas Day, which was fast-approaching.

Nick sounded anxious about them bringing the kids to see him at Goodspring.

"You don't want us to bring them?"

There was a long pause. "I guess I don't know. I don't want them to think I'm crazy."

"You aren't, honey. We could approach it so many ways, including just telling them you're there to feel better. We could even say it was a school you were at or something if you'd rather. But we'll do whatever sounds good to you. I guess I just want you to know that we don't have any thoughts about hiding you from them."

"Thanks," Nick said quietly. "It would be good to see you all."

"I want to see you, too. And the kids will be bonkers for you, you know that."

"But not Tony?"

Julia laughed. "Obviously he'll want to see you, but he just got to."

"Oh," Nick said. "I guess. This week has felt like a month."

"Will it blow your mind if I tell you it was yesterday?"

"What was?"

"That you saw Tony."

There was a pause. "I didn't see Tony yesterday."

That night, she tried to get the drop on Tony. She waited until he was undressing for bed, and she asked him, as casually as she could, if Nick mentioned anything he wanted for Christmas at their visit. No, Tony said, he didn't.

"Did you ask?"

Tony said nothing.

"Because he mentioned today that you weren't there at all yesterday."

Tony stammered a second, then told her she'd caught him.

"Christmas shopping," he said. A two-word explanation that was beyond cross-examination.

Even if she believed that he'd been occupied with some Christmas surprise for her all day Saturday, that didn't explain his behavior on the other days that had passed since Nick's attempted suicide. Every day, Tony had left early for the office and gotten home late. When he was home, he seemed absent, zoning out while the kids were talking to him. It wasn't like him at all.

There were other things that bothered her, too, harder things to name. The rehearsed quality of his voice, for example, when he answered a question about his day. It was the same voice she'd heard him use when he gave a toast at a friend's wedding. The tone of his voice was different when it was material he'd practiced.

She could barely focus on the work before her, and she was relieved when she felt her phone buzz on her desk. It was Charlie Lee.

She'd completely forgotten that Charlie was still looking at Walker for her.

She answered quickly, longing for some kind of good news about the case.

His greeting was defeat: "There's nothing I want to do more than tell you I found something."

"Oh, Charlie, that's okay. I didn't even remember you were still looking."

"I just wanted to circle back. Heard back from the last of the bars I'd contacted. Nothing helpful. He's been careful before, that's my guess. Careful and lucky. And now, he's on his best behavior, as far as I can tell."

She thought about telling Charlie what had happened with Nick—about the overdose and the hospitalization. But what was the point? It would probably only frustrate him to hear, since he hadn't found anything. "Thanks for trying, Charlie."

"I know he's been a real jackass in a public way, with the news and stuff, but at least he isn't confrontational. With your husband, I mean."

"Yeah," Julia said as she tried to process what he might mean.

"He isn't, is he? He wouldn't still be out on bail if he were being threatening or anything at the gym."

"What gym?"

"The gym they go to, him and your husband."

Tony didn't go to the gym. "The one in Orange?"

"No, the Weight Room in Salisbury."

"Tony doesn't go there."

Charlie paused. "I saw him in his car in the lot there. I drove by last week when I was over that way."

The hair on Julia's neck prickled.

"It certainly looked just like him," Charlie said. "I remember him from the photo at your old office. He was in a gray SUV in the gym's side lot."

"What day?"

"Would have been Thursday."

The chill in her neck went hot. "Must just be someone who looks like him," Julia said. "Tony doesn't really go to the gym, and Salisbury's too far a drive."

"Must be, that makes more sense. Figured you would have mentioned if they were running into each other."

"Thank you so much for trying, Charlie. You can stop looking now, really."

"Things're still slow, I'm happy to keep at it for a bit—"

"Please stop. Please just leave it."

"All right."

"Promise me you won't look into Walker anymore."

"Fine, I promise." There was silence, and Charlie said, "He'll get his justice, Julia. I know it's hard to wait, but it'll come in time."

Tony had been home late on Thursday. Said he had an emergency at work. What were the chances it was his lookalike in a gray SUV at Raymond Walker's gym all the way in Salisbury?

There was no way to tell Charlie how wrong he was—how sure she felt that the time for waiting was over.

～

It wasn't until she saw the receptionist through the glass doors at Tony's office that Julia realized it might seem a bit nutty of her to drop in on him in the middle of the workday. She could give two shits what Tony thought about it, but there were other people at his office. Shirley, the receptionist, for one.

If she knew the thoughts running through Julia's head at that moment, Shirley would have fainted.

Shirley saw Julia and slapped the folder in her hand down on the desk. "Julia Hall," she singsonged. "What a surprise! What are you doing here?"

Julia felt called out immediately. She looked overbearing. She smiled but could feel it was a lame one. "I just need to see Tony quick."

Shirley frowned. "Did he come in today?"

"What?"

"He took the day off, or have I lost my marbles?" Shirley sat down and started clicking at the computer. "I always check everyone's calendar when I come in, and he's off today and all next week. Unless he popped in for something and I didn't see him. There he is, yes, he's out today."

Julia white-knuckled the lip of Shirley's desk. "Can you call down and make sure he isn't in?"

"Sure, hon." Shirley pecked out a number and let it ring on speakerphone. It rang and rang and rang until Tony's voice mail picked up.

"I must have misunderstood," Julia said quietly.

"Oh, shoot," Shirley hissed. "I probably just spoiled some kind of Christmas surprise."

"Maybe," Julia said. "I'm sorry to run, but I've got to go."

Shirley's face fell with friendly disappointment. "Oh, all right. We'll have to catch up next time!"

Julia nodded as she left. Shirley might not have even seen the nod, but Julia couldn't offer anything more polite—she couldn't speak.

She made it to the elevator. The air around her felt as though it was pressing in from all sides. She hit the button and it lit up. Heat rose up through her stomach, chest, neck, face. She kept walking down the hall, found the stairwell, and stepped in as she heard the elevator ding behind her. She walked halfway down to the next landing and sat on a step. Put her head between her legs. Breathed in through her nose. The smell of her jeans, like chemicals. Breathed out through her mouth. Another round, and another. The air thinned and her skin began to cool.

Julia pulled out her phone. Pressed Tony's cell number. On two rings he answered.

"What's up?" His voice was clipped. He sounded interrupted.

"Where are you?"

"At work?"

"Perfect, I'm out front. Meet me in the lobby."

She relished the pause.

"You're at my office?"

"Yup, I'm heading up."

"Wait."

There was silence. If he lied again—

"I'm going into a meeting, I can't see you now."

"Bullshit," she hissed. "*Bullshit*. I've already been up. You're not here."

"What are you doing at my office?"

"*Great* question. I show up to my husband's job expecting him to be there on a Tuesday after he kisses me goodbye in the morning and tells me he's going to work. Great question. *I'm* the one who owes an explanation? But I've got one, Tony, and since you're *not* at work, meet me at home in an hour and I'll tell you why I came looking for you."

Tony was silent for a bit. She'd really unleashed there.

"You want to do this at home?"

"We're out of time to do it anywhere else. I've gotta get Seb from the bus stop."

"What about Chloe?"

"My mom is picking her up for girl time, we talked about this last—"

"Right, right, I forgot. I'll get Seb."

"I can get him."

"Please. Let me get Seb, and we'll meet you at home."

She wanted to say no. Not until he told her where he'd been, what he was doing, what the fuck was going on. But this had nothing to do with Seb. This would not bleed over onto the kids.

"Fine."

She hung up without waiting to see if he'd say anything else. She'd given him time to prepare now. He was going to come up with some explanation for playing hooky, so she'd keep what she knew about the gym to herself until she had eyes on him. When had this happened? When had he started—whatever this was, scheming?—behind her back? And where was he now?

49

Julia had said he could pick up Seb. He needed to see his son. Tousle his hair, squeeze him tight. Because whatever was coming—a fight, a full-blown marital storm—was going to be a big one. Julia sounded ready to go up one side of him and down the other.

Tony did some quick math and determined he could, in fact, beat the bus home as long as he left now. He was glad—calling her back to admit otherwise would have been brutal.

He took one last look at Walker's house and put the car in drive.

⟶

Tony could see Julia through the living room window when he and Seb pulled into the driveway. He wondered, pointlessly, if she might have cooled off since she found he wasn't at work. Doubtful.

Seb went running into the house ahead of Tony. He was already chattering at Julia when Tony made it inside. He could hear them in the kitchen as he pulled off his boots in the mudroom.

"Dad said I could play with the Wii," Seb announced.

"Did he," Julia said.

Tony stepped into the kitchen. "Thought we could talk while he did."

Julia nodded, releasing the smile she'd put on for Seb.

"Just while we wrap some extra presents," Julia said to Seb. Christmas was in a matter of days. "That means you stay downstairs, got it?"

Seb nodded, wide-eyed and grinning like a maniac. The kids had all but forgotten about the Wii until a week ago when they saw an ad for a new game, and now they were obsessed with the stupid thing all over again.

Tony set Seb up with his game. He stooped to kiss the top of his head through his soft curls. When he straightened himself, Julia was staring at him from the stairs. She beckoned him with an impatient wave.

He knew what was coming, and they barely made it to the top of the stairs before she started.

"So, what's up with your day off?" She paused at the landing and turned to face him.

"Can't a man have some privacy around Christmastime?" He smiled as he moved past her and toward the bedroom. It could have been breezy, but he'd practiced it too much.

Julia shut the door to their room and took a deep breath. She looked tired. "Can you please, please not lie to me? Apparently I can't expect you to just offer me the truth yourself, but don't give me an outright lie. And don't look at me like that."

"Like what?"

"Like I'm hurting your feelings."

"How should I feel when you call me a liar?"

"What should I call you when you put on a tie and tell me you're going to work when you have the day off?"

Everything he hadn't said was welling up in his throat. He turned to their closet and fought to avoid looking at the door as he reached to pull down the last of the unwrapped gifts. Their notes from all their years together flooded his peripheral vision to his left, reminding him of all the things they'd said before. "Can we just do what we need to do before Seb gets restless and comes up here?"

"No, *this*"—she pointed at the two of them—"is what we need to do right now. You got dressed for work this morning. You carried your bag out. You went to his gym."

Tony started so violently that he dropped a plastic box to the floor. He dumped the rest of the presents onto their bed.

"Yeah," she said.

He turned to her. She didn't look angry. She looked like she hated him. For a second, he thought she knew the whole thing.

"Have you been following me?"

"Fuck off," she whispered. "How was I supposed to know following Walker meant following you?"

"You're following him?"

"No," she said. "Charlie was just giving him one last look."

Charlie Lee again. "When did he see me?"

"So you've been there more than once." She didn't sound angry. She sounded tired.

She stared at him with eyes that skimmed left and right, surveying the landscape of his face. Searching for something. Yes, he was guilty of that. But he was guilty of more, too, and that needed to stay his guilt alone. He said nothing.

"You're scaring me. You *need* to start talking to me. I can't—I'm losing my shit." Her voice cracked. "I don't know what to do with myself." Tears brimmed in her eyes and spilled. "I can't have *you* scaring me like this on top of everything else."

She wrapped her arms around herself and hung her head.

He was torturing her. Tony reached out to pull her into his chest. He kissed the top of her head and shushed her quietly. The urge to comfort her with the truth, all of it, was overwhelming. But it wouldn't comfort her, that was the problem. It would only put her at risk. If anything went wrong, it was better if she'd known nothing at all.

"I'm following him, too," he said finally.

She pulled her head back from his chest and looked up into his face. "Why?"

"I—" he started, and stopped. "I thought I could catch him doing something to get him in trouble. To make them send him back to jail."

Julia released from his embrace. "Swear."

"What?"

"Swear that's all this is."

"I do," Tony said quickly. He'd never lied to her like this before. Never sworn on a lie. He couldn't remember her ever asking him to swear he was being truthful. All of this was new. And he needed to sell it, to keep her innocent. "I swear," he said. "I'm just watching him."

"I want you to stop," she said. "I told Charlie to stop, and I want you to, too."

"Okay," he said.

"It can't get out that we were stalking him."

"It won't," Tony said. "We're done. We're done."

"Promise we won't keep secrets," she said.

"I promise," he said. What he was really promising was to keep her protected, but she had no way of knowing that. And to himself, he made a second promise: after this, he'd never keep a secret from her again.

50

Rice had struck a nerve, that much was obvious. Julia sat in her recliner, squeezing her hands together. Her mind probably going a mile a minute, trying to decide what to say next.

"I think I'm confused about where this is all going," Julia said. "Why wouldn't we think he had run away?"

Her question hung in the air.

Rice could say nothing, and his silence would compel her to say everything. She would talk against herself, trying to explain away whatever she thought he knew, and in doing so she would reveal everything to him.

"I feel like I'm missing something," she said.

It was already starting. The whole bit folded out in front of him now. He could see it, clear as he could see her. She was utterly terrified, and she would go wherever he might take her. It was all over, if he wanted.

He hummed quietly before he spoke. "Did you miss it then?"

Her voice was hoarse. "Miss what?"

Rice sighed. *Enough.*

"*I* know what happened," he said. "I've always wondered if you knew, too."

51

The visiting room at Goodspring was wide and bright. The hard walls were painted white and covered in patient artwork. It reminded Nick of a school cafeteria. There were groupings of tables and chairs all around the room, for patients to visit with whoever had come to see them. It was Christmas. The holiday seemed to lose more of its magic with each year as he aged, but this year was different. This year, Tony and Julia had packed up the kids on Christmas morning and driven two hours to come see Nick. This year it felt special again.

"I'm gonna hit the bathroom," Tony said as he stood up from their table.

Julia turned to Chloe. "Why don't you pick out a game for us to play?"

"I want to pick," Seb whined.

"There's no need for that," Julia said as she eyed him with a raised brow. "You can each pick one, but no whining. Especially on Christmas!" she added as the kids crossed to the far end of the room.

She smiled at Nick and leaned on a fist. "Are you hanging in there okay?"

He was a weekend shy of two weeks in the program now. "Yeah," he said. "At first, after I told Tony, I felt better than I had in months. It was like everything was going to be good again and I felt like my old self. But then it wore off, and it was awful—I'm so glad I was here."

Julia looked confused.

"My therapist here said I was probably just finally starting to process things. I told Jeff about the overall lie, you know, at the beginning of the month, but we still hadn't talked about what happened in detail. We were going to do it slowly over time, but it's all started to come up anyway. You know what I mean?"

She shook her head. "What lie?"

Did Tony not tell her? "What I told Tony."

"When?"

"When he drove me here."

"He didn't tell me anything."

Tony appeared in the doorway across the room.

Nick began to whisper. "Please don't ask him."

Julia whispered back. "What didn't he tell me?"

"Please, Julia—please not today."

They fell silent as Tony reached the table. "What's going on?"

Julia looked at Nick. He pleaded with his eyes.

Her voice was cautious. "The kids are picking games."

Tony sat down. "Cool."

Julia was staring at him. What was he thinking, not telling her?

Two game boxes slammed onto the table.

"Ea-sy," Tony cautioned with a frown.

"Connect Four," Nick read. "Love it."

Chloe beamed at his approval.

"One thousand— No, Seb, this is what you chose? A thousand-piece puzzle?"

Sebastian grinned at Tony so wide that Nick wondered whether he'd intended it as a joke.

"He liked the picture on the front," Chloe said with a shrug.

Nick kept looking back at Julia, whose eyes hadn't left Tony's face.

52

I can't believe it." Julia was lying on her side in their bed, turned to face Tony. "He remembered everything."

Tony nodded.

"He's been so alone, all this time."

"I know."

Snow was falling outside the window across from the bed. Julia was doing what anyone would—she was processing what she'd just learned about Nick. Tony was just waiting for the other shoe to drop: why hadn't he told her?

"I don't know if I understand what he said about the fight," she said.

"He didn't want to tell anyone that he couldn't stop him."

"But isn't that . . . obvious? Even in the version he first told?"

"Yeah but . . . it was different. At first he told it, like, single cheap shot, he's out. What really happened made him feel powerless." Tears began to well. "He was awake for all of it—for the moment he was overpowered. Do you get it?"

Julia nodded. And maybe she did, to some extent. But Tony didn't know how to explain what it meant to Nick—what it would have meant to Tony—to be dominated by another man, in spite of being conscious when it happened. What it was like to spend your whole life hearing you were supposed to win fights, be strong. And if you couldn't do those things, you weren't a man.

"What are you going to do about it?"

There it was. Her eyes were steady on his face.

"Nothing."

"You always do something. You can't help yourself. What are you going to do about this?"

Tony rested a hand on her shoulder. "Nothing."

53

Two days after Christmas, Julia caught up with Margot. They'd become friends during law school and grown closer over the years. On paper they'd always looked quite different. Margot was engaged when school started; Julia was fiercely single. Margot was outspoken and confident; Julia usually had to be forced to give an answer in class. They had study carrels in the library near each other, and they bonded over their love of caffeine and TV shows that kept them up at night. Over a decade later, Margot was divorced and childless and Julia was married with kids, but the important stuff had stayed. They still met for coffee at least once a month, they still texted about *Criminal Minds* after every episode, and they still loved each other.

"Hey, I keep forgetting," Margot said, "send me that cauliflower rice recipe."

"Oh God, I haven't made that in so long."

"I tried to make it up myself and it was awful."

"I mean, it's cauliflower," Julia said.

"But it was so good the time I had it with you. Can you email me the one you used to make?"

Julia walked into the study and shook the mouse to wake up the computer. "Yeah, I'll find it for you."

"You're the best."

They hung up, and Julia opened Google. Typed *cauliflower rice*. There were so many results, and none of the hyperlinks were purple. She scrolled but couldn't tell which recipe was the one she'd been using in the spring.

She opened the internet history. Typed *cauliflower*. No results. That didn't make sense. She'd probably gone to that page ten times.

She clicked back to the main history page. Scrolled. The list of pages she'd visited ended on December 14. There were no results before that date.

There were searches and page titles from the fourteenth—the work she'd done that morning. Everything before that was gone. The history had been cleared on the thirteenth. The same day, she now knew, that Nick told Tony what Ray Walker really did to him.

She closed the history and returned to Google. Typed *How to restore history*. The page filled with links to articles. She clicked the first one. She could run a "system restore," apparently, and it should recover the lost history. She saved all her most recent work to a flash drive, just in case, and then followed the prompts in the article. She selected 12/13/ 2015 as the restore date and sat back on her stool to watch and wait.

She was being crazy. But why would Tony have deleted the history? He had come home from dropping Nick at Goodspring and gone into the study for a long time—at least an hour. He'd said that night he was working, but he wouldn't have deleted work stuff from the computer. She was probably just going to see where he'd bought her Christmas presents. Oh God, or pornography. She laughed softly. Her stomach was so upset with worry that she was sure she'd be glad to see he'd just been watching porn that night, even if she'd been reading in the next room.

After a few minutes, the computer rebooted. She opened the browser and clicked history. The most recent entry was a page titled "How to Delete Your Internet History."

Before that was a Google search: "Delete history."

Before that, a blog post titled "Ice Knives & Stone Fruit." What the hell did that mean?

Before that, a page that froze Julia in place.

A page called "Forum: How Would You Commit Your Perfect Murder?"

And before that one, "Forum: What Are the Main Causes of Unsolved Murders?"

And before that, a news article: "Why So Many Murders Go Unsolved."

And before that, a Google search: "Unsolved murder causes."

He was going to kill him.

Tony was going to kill Ray Walker.

54

He found Julia in the bedroom. It was just after four, and she was under the covers.

"Honey?"

She didn't stir. What was going on? She took a call from Margot and went upstairs. Over an hour had passed before Tony noticed she hadn't come back down.

Something was wrong.

He sat down on the bed gently. "Honey?"

Without opening her eyes, she said, "I saw the computer."

"What?"

"I know what you're doing."

Dread spilled into his stomach. "What are you talking about?"

She sat up with her eyes clamped shut, a hand on her head like she was woozy. Then she opened her eyes, kept them on the bedspread. "Just tell me I'm wrong."

No. No, please, she doesn't know.

"About what?"

"What the fuck are you thinking?" she whispered violently as she shoved him.

"Hey!"

"I saw what you were looking at. Murder. *Murder?*" She pounded her palms against his chest again, and he brought his hands up to catch her wrists.

Fuck. Oh, fuck.

"How did you see it?"

"It was easy. Nothing you do on the computer is *ever* gone." She wrenched her hands from his grip.

"I'll get you a new one."

"So when you kill him and they take our computer, they won't be suspicious that it's brand-new?"

"Shh," he hissed. "Keep your voice down."

"Tell me what you're doing."

"I can't tell you."

"Why?"

"I don't want anyone knowing anything about it, not you or Nick or anyone."

"So you'll get me a new computer." She nodded, wide-eyed and tight-lipped. "And we'll be good."

"That was a one-off. I haven't done anything like that again."

"Everything is traceable, Tony."

"No, I've been careful."

"Besides this, besides using the computer in our house."

"Yes. I swear."

"So you're gonna do this."

Tony broke her gaze.

"Explain it to me. Explain why you think you're entitled to do this."

"Entitled?"

"Yeah. Nick's doing everything he's supposed to. He told the police, he's willing to testify, he's killing himself to get through court. Why do you think you get to—just—do this insane fucking thing?"

"He can't go on like this. You know that—he tried to kill himself."

"He's safe. He's getting help. You're pretending this is about him, but it's really about you."

"If you can't see how this would help Nick, I don't know what to say. He's our family."

"You want to talk about our *family*? You're talking about killing someone and our fucking kid is downstairs."

An awareness struck him, suddenly, of what Julia was missing. A simplicity to how he might help her see.

"One of our kids is downstairs," he said quietly. "But my first kid is in a hospital in Belfast."

She looked at him wide-eyed, then at the bed.

"If it were Seb or Chloe, maybe then you'd understand. He's like my kid."

Julia laid back down and rolled away from him.

"He's always been my kid to me." Tony walked around the bed and knelt before her. "Don't you see that?"

She didn't move. Her eyes looked strangely faraway, but her gaze rested somewhere near his back foot.

"He tried to kill himself." Tony's voice cracked and he shrugged at himself. "If he tells the rest of it . . . if the case doesn't settle, he's going to tell them what Walker did to him. When that comes out, it'll all get so much worse." He waited a while to go on. "We almost lost him. You said that; you know. He's part of your family, too."

She looked up at him then. "I know that."

"Then let me save him," Tony said.

Julia dropped her eyes back to the floor. Tony stood. Neither of them spoke. He walked around the bed and reached the door when he heard her voice.

"Promise me," she said quietly behind him.

He turned back.

"Promise me you'll wait to see if it settles in January."

He nodded. That was fine. January was a good month for it.

55

JOHN RICE, 2015

Depressingly, the week after Christmas was always a busy one at the station. Crime usually spiked around the December holidays: money problems, alcohol, too much time with family. Rice was just getting ready to leave on a domestic violence case when the receptionist paged his desk phone. Julia Hall was calling for him.

"I'm sorry to bother you," Julia said. "I'm sure you're busy."

"It's fine. Is everything all right?"

"Oh, yeah. I'm just calling to ask, ah." Her voice was all defeat. "Something I think I already know the answer to."

"Okay?"

"Is there any way that, um, Ray Walker's bail would be revoked because of anything that's happened?"

"What, with Nick?"

"Well, yeah. With him and his mom contacting the press so much, and all of it just having such a negative effect on Nick's mental health."

He was going to fail them again.

"No, I don't think so. He hasn't violated bail, he's had no contact with Nick. Nothing he's done has been criminal. It's terrible, what Nick's going through, but no judge would let us hold him just because Nick is struggling. I talked to Linda, and she thinks we'll get into a pissing match, pardon my French, if we try to do anything to stop him or the press from running their mouths. Technically, they haven't released anything they weren't allowed to. Probably just end up drawing even more attention to the case."

Julia paused for long enough that Rice thought the call had dropped.

"Yeah, I figured. I just felt like I had to ask."

"You guys doing okay over there?"

It was a stupid question. He doubted she'd be calling if everything was coming up roses.

"Going a little crazy," she said softly.

"I'm so sorry, Julia. I wish there was something I could do, but unless he violates his bail, we're waiting out a plea or a trial."

"They told Nick they thought it could be a year. Was that just . . . you know, them managing his expectations? It could be sooner, right?"

"Anything's possible. But, I mean, I'm set for trial next month in a case I closed three years ago."

Julia was silent. Why was she so surprised? She'd been a defense attorney.

"You know how it is. Court's backed up, DA's backed up, and time hurts a case like Nick's, so Eva will push it out as far as she can."

"What if he can't wait that long?"

"Nick has to just live his life, try to forget about the case."

There was another long pause.

He started again. "Look, ah." She was a professional, in a way, even if she wasn't on this case. "Between us, Julia?"

"Yeah?"

"I'm not sure there'll be a trial."

"Really?"

"I just heard from a faux friend of Walker's that he knows his goose is cooked. I think he'll take a plea. Probably not until the eve of trial, you know how it goes, but then I bet he'll take it. I think some of his bravado is for show. He's scared shitless."

"Really? Did it sound like it would be soon?"

"Well, no, he seems the type not to roll over until it's really showtime. But Nick might not have to testify. Don't tell him that, don't get his hopes up, but I don't think you need to worry so much about the end result. I think it'll settle. It's the waiting we can't do anything about."

She paused. "Okay." Her voice was high and quiet. She sounded like she was trying not to cry. "Thanks for your time, Detective."

"I'm sorry I couldn't be more helpful, Julia." She'd already hung up, but he needed to say the words anyway.

56

JULIA HALL, 2015

Julia hadn't slept the past two nights. There were moments where it seemed she had fallen into a light sleep, but the whole time she was dreaming she was awake. Awake and obsessing over what her husband was going to do.

She asked him how he would do it. He wouldn't tell. When he would do it, and where. He wouldn't tell. How he would ensure he was free from suspicion. He would be sure, he said. He just kept repeating his mantra: "It's safer if you don't know."

Julia didn't feel safe. She felt frantic. He promised he would wait until the dispositional conference, when the case might settle. If Walker agreed to plead guilty, Nick wouldn't tell the prosecutor the truth, and maybe Tony would let this go. So she had until January 12. Two weeks. Two more weeks to try to figure something out.

She could go straight to Nick—try to get him to give up the case—but would that solve the problem? Or would Tony do it anyway, because giving up the case meant Walker went unpunished? And if something happened to Walker after Nick abandoned the case, would they be even more suspicious of Tony? Would it look like Nick had given up the case so that Tony could enact justice of his own?

She'd already tried calling Detective Rice the day before. It was pointless, just like she'd expected. Walker had done nothing to get himself thrown back in jail, out of Tony's reach.

She'd tried to reason with Tony: What about the kids? What about Nick? What about *her*? It was like he couldn't hear her. He thought he had the moral high ground—he was so far up there he had altitude sickness.

And morals—she was surprised by how little of her desperation to stop him came from the immorality of it.

So much of her identity, as a lawyer, as a mother, as a wife, friend, person, had been focused on *being good*. It was such a vague goal, but she never questioned it, maybe because it came easily to her. Do the right thing. Treat people well. What was *right* was usually easy for her to identify. The first time she met with Mathis Lariviere and his mother, she had to convince both of them, not just the boy, that he should have a substance abuse evaluation and start therapy immediately, long before he was sentenced.

"The better he is," Julia said, "the better his result in the case will be."

"You mean the better he *looks*, the better his result," his mother, Elisa, said coolly.

"No," Julia said. "He can't just sit through a year of therapy with his headphones in. He'll need to change. The judge will see through it, otherwise."

"I'm not so sure," Elisa replied. "Some of us are good at looking good."

At the time, Julia wrote off the woman's comment. They hadn't seen eye to eye on much, she and Elisa Lariviere, whose son had told Julia things about his family that gave her chills. For Elisa to insinuate that Julia's morality was an act had been laughable.

But now she wondered. Maybe Julia had just been good at *looking* like she was good. Acting like she believed in doing moral things. Because in this moment, she cared far more about looking good than being good.

Everything that kept her awake and squeezed sweat from her hairline had to do with Tony being caught. Not what he wanted to do in the first place.

If Tony was caught, she'd lose him. The *kids* would lose him. He was a good man. That sounded impossible, given what he was doing right now, but Tony Hall was a good man, and a great father, and her kids were going to lose him if he wasn't careful. And she'd told him from the start—from the first night they talked, she told him she would never marry a man who wasn't serious about what that meant to her. Who wouldn't fight like it was life or death to keep whatever they made together. She'd been so sure he was that man. How could he do this to her?

There was only one thing she'd thought of that might work.

She texted Charlie Lee.

> I need one last thing

she wrote.

And Charlie responded,

> Anything.

57

JULIA HALL, 2015

J ulia leaned over her dresser as she worked mascara through the upper lashes of her left eye. Nina Simone crooned softly from her cell phone. She stepped back to survey her work—all that was left was lipstick. She selected a tube of brick red. It wasn't her favorite, but Tony loved it, and it would vamp up her plain black dress. She applied the color to her open mouth and took her hair back down. The grays at the crown of her head caught the low light of the lamp on her dresser; she was due for a touch-up. She scrunched her fingers into her roots and refocused on the music. Nina wouldn't worry about gray hairs—and she'd probably call them silver. Julia swayed a little to "Feeling Good" as the brass came in, letting the song seduce her. Sometime after they'd had babies, she'd come to feel that the act of *getting ready* for a date with her husband was the night's first opportunity for foreplay. She was forcing the magic tonight.

If they hadn't made a reservation months in advance, they probably would have stayed in. One of the side effects of their decision to get married on New Year's Eve nine years ago was that reservations were a necessity if they wanted to eat out on their anniversary. Julia had booked the table long before she knew she'd be spending all her free time wondering if her husband really was capable of killing a man.

Julia picked up the small purse she'd abandoned on the bed earlier. She snapped the clasp open, and the envelope of her card peeked out. The words inside were imperfect, and mostly stolen, but she was satisfied that she had captured what she was feeling at rock bottom, beneath all the other emotions. This card might go onto the collage in the closet, and it might not. Would either of them want to remember this time?

She knew what her notes meant to him, but this year she had been at a loss for what to put on paper. Earlier that evening, the card was still sitting blank in her office when she climbed into the shower. It was there that she'd thought of their first dance song: Barry White's "You're the First, the Last, My Everything." She'd slung a towel around herself and darted down the hall to write her favorite lines into the card. He was the sun and the moon, she wrote. "My first, my last, my everything."

Nine years ago today, they'd danced to this song. Everything had seemed so simple then. She had imagined their vows would be tested over a long life together, but not like this. She read the lines over again. The words seemed empty in the face of where they stood. But she had to say something, and there was still truth in the song. He was still everything to her. That's why it hurt so much.

Now, she pushed the tube of lipstick into her purse, next to the card.

"Wow," Tony said from the doorway. She caught a glimpse of him in the mirror as she turned—clean lines and dark hair.

"Wow yourself," she said. "I love that blazer."

"I know you do," he said, and he spun slowly for her to the music. "Notice anything . . . new?" he asked as he thrust his arm out in time with a trumpet's bleat. His new watch popped from his sleeve, and Julia laughed in spite of herself. She was holding on to something angry, sad; it was palpable. She would let it go. At least for tonight, she would let it go.

She bent to pull her heels on, and when she stood he had come to her. They were closer to eye level now with her added inches. He wrapped his hands around her waist and leaned in to kiss her gently; she sunk into him with a soft sigh. When her husband pulled away, his lips were smeared with melted red. She giggled and wiped them with her thumb, her fingers under his clean-shaven chin.

"Maybe when my mom comes for the kids we should skip dinner," he murmured, holding her close against his waist.

"She's watching them here—they'll be asleep when we get home." She pecked his cheek and stepped back.

"Stay a minute," he said with a wolfish grin, and pulled her back to him.

"No," she said flatly as she pushed his hands away and stepped back. He looked surprised, confused. She was, too. Something about him telling her to stay—holding her so firmly against him—had infuriated her, just for a split second. She crossed the room and paused at the door. She was being so cold to him lately; sometimes by choice, other times by impulse.

"Grandma's here!" Chloe shouted from the living room.

Julia took the stairs quickly, leaving Tony behind.

⁓

Julia scuffed her feet as she stepped into the warmth of Buona Cucina, grinding slush and salt into the welcome mat.

"Happy New Year," the hostess said as she collected menus from her post. "Coatrack's behind you."

Buona Cucina was a small, expensive Italian restaurant in downtown Orange where they'd celebrated a few anniversaries and birthdays over the years. With its exposed brick, hardwood floors, and decor, it reminded Julia of several places in Portland, including the Ruby, the bar she used to tend. Part of why she favored Buona Cucina for romantic nights was because it felt so much like the places she and Tony went on their first dates.

They crossed a landing into the smaller of two dining areas. As they walked, Julia reached out and squeezed Tony's hand: an unspoken apology for pushing him away earlier. Tony squeezed back.

They ordered a bottle of sparkling water for the table, and a glass of pinot noir for Julia.

"Will you at least tell me how you're going to do it?"

Tony looked surprised. "What?"

Julia lowered her voice. "You know what."

He sighed. "Why do you want to talk about this on our anniversary?"

"I can't get it out of my system because you won't tell me anything. Just tell me how."

"I want you to be safe. I need you to be, the kids—I think not telling you is what I have to do."

"But you can't plan something like this alone. You keep saying you're being careful, but how can I know that if you won't let me ask you questions—test your plan."

"They're not even going to know it was anything but an accident."

"Okay, so—" She shook her head. "Right there. That sounds like wishful thinking."

"It isn't." He adjusted the fork next to his plate.

"You're really going to do this?"

He looked surprised. "I thought you were okay with it."

"When have I *ever* said that?"

Tony frowned. "Well, I need you to *get* okay with it."

"Or what?"

"Or, nothing, I guess," he said as he straightened up in his chair. "I've told you what I'm doing."

"Where does that leave me?"

"Supporting me, I thought."

"Cornered," she said. "You've cornered me."

"I don't know how to make you understand."

She shook her head. "I do understand about you and Nick. I didn't grow up taking care of someone else. But I have you, and we have the kids. So what about us?"

His face went soft in the candlelight. "I promise you we'll be okay. I *know* it. Like I've known so much about you and me."

He put his hand over hers and went on. "I knew I'd marry you the day we went ice fishing with Margot and her ex, remember? And you dropped the flask in the hole, then snatched it out and took a sip?" He laughed softly. "I knew then, in a weirdly calm, almost psychic way, that we would be married, and everything would be okay. I feel the same now. I'll be careful, and we'll be fine."

Julia wanted to pull away from him, but she left her hand in his.

The waiter appeared in her peripheral vision, sidling up to the table like he knew he was interrupting something. He took their orders and left. They sat for a moment in silence, unsure of where to pick up.

Tony laid his napkin back on his plate. "I'm gonna hit the bathroom."

Julia was alone. She watched the flames flicker in the frosted glasses at the center of the table. Between the two candles was a single blossom in a thin glass. It was orange, with thin petals unfolding from the center.

She had lost. There was nothing more to do but admit that she was not, in fact, as good as she thought. All of Tony's talk about leaving her out of it was meaningless. When this was over, she would be complicit in what happened to Ray Walker.

Tony talked about the moment he knew he'd marry her. Hers hadn't been a moment so much as a day: a day they had a picnic with Nick. She'd met Nick before, but she'd been dating Tony for long enough on this day that they'd all dropped the pretenses of impressing each other. Instead, they were just being together. She watched how Tony talked to the boy. She listened to the strong warmth in his voice. Saw him put an arm around Nick at one point and squeeze him close. She saw all of this and thought, this is the man I want to make babies with. My children will have this man as their father. She had missed that he already was a father, in a way.

And as much as Tony had driven her crazy at times in the beginning, always trying to do things for her, she had liked how he was a fixer and a fighter. He wouldn't watch idly if their marriage grew stale. He would do anything for his family. And if he got sick one day, he would fight like hell to stay with them. As much as she loved Nick, loved him so much, she had missed how much a part of their family he was, by way of Tony. Tony was everything to her, but that didn't mean she didn't love the kids. Maybe even more than she loved him. The soul has room for competing loves. She had three. Tony had four.

She looked out the window beside their table. She could make out the shape of snow on the ground, but otherwise it was nothing but darkness. If they could just make it to spring, maybe everything would feel different. The sun and the crocuses would lighten up Tony's heart. He would see that the world had not, in fact, gone pitch black. But spring was months away, and between here and there, Nick would tell the ADA his story, and the ADA would be forced to tell Walker. There would be media again, more talk, more public opinion about things people knew nothing about. And that was the clock that Tony was racing against. It would all be over long before spring came. When the light came back, would they be able to face what they'd done in the dark?

Julia reached forward across the table and brushed her fingertips over the orange blossom's broad face. She tipped the bloom down into the flame and watched the petals singe.

58

TONY HALL, 2016

Things got easier after their anniversary. After she found his stupid search on the computer, Julia kept surprising Tony with questions and arguments ad nauseum, every time they were away from the kids. He could feel her eyes on him when he looked at his phone or even just moved around the house. Tony wished she didn't know anything at all about Walker—he wanted her in the dark, just to be safe. If something ever went wrong, she would *not* be an accomplice to him. But still, she knew almost nothing. He had stood firm in the face of her questions, and finally, after their anniversary, she stopped asking.

At times he wondered if she was on his side, but the storm truly seemed to have passed. A day ago, Julia's phone rang and Charlie Lee's name lit up her screen. Tony locked eyes with her over the phone, then she answered on speaker and asked Charlie what was up. He said he had the contact information she needed for the records report. She gave Tony a withering look, and he put up his hands in surrender as she took the phone to the study. So it was true—she wasn't using Charlie Lee to investigate Raymond Walker anymore. Still, there was something in it all that Tony wanted to analyze. He took the first couple of days of January off, and the kids were on school break. He'd expected to spend the days hanging out with her and the kids, but instead she'd been working on her records report most of the time. It was like she was subtly punishing him for lying about going to work by working while they should have been together as a family.

At the moment, though, the four of them were together, sitting in the living room. Tony and Seb were lying in the recliner together, Seb's tiny body wedged against his. Julia sat on the couch; Chloe perched behind her on the couch's arm, her legs sticking out on either side of Julia. Tony was reading aloud from *Swallows and Amazons*, a gift that year from Julia's mother. The inscription showed it had been Julia's as a girl: *Dad used to read you this*, Julia's mother had written. *C & S will love it, too.* Tony wished, in moments like these, that he'd met Julia's father. He had been a wonderful parent, Julia told him. She desperately wished he'd made different choices at the end of his life, but until that moment, he had been perfect to her.

Chloe braided Julia's hair as Tony read the old adventure book, and he occasionally glanced up at their progress. First it was two braids, the left one thick and straight, the right one thin and wonky. Then the braids came out and Chloe started a single one down Julia's back. This time when he looked up, Julia was wiping her eyes. She held his gaze, then sighed and shook her head.

"I need to make a phone call," she said as she stood.

Tony stopped reading. "Right now?"

"Mom, your braid fell out!" Chloe groaned.

"Sorry, honey," she said to Chloe, then she turned in Tony's direction. "It won't take long, and I'll bring a hair tie back down when I'm done."

Chloe nodded with satisfaction and slid into Julia's spot on the couch.

Julia retrieved her cell phone from the coffee table and disappeared up the stairs.

⌐

Tony was making sandwiches when Julia came back downstairs.

"BLTs," he said in a dramatic voice, waving his hand over the spread as if it were a magic trick. The sandwiches were splayed open with lettuce and fat slices of ripe tomato; beside them was a container of bacon left-over from breakfast.

"They smell delicious," she said. "One for me?"

"Of course, my jewel," he whispered, wagging a strip of bacon at her. She smiled absently. "Tea?" she asked.

"No, thanks." He felt an annoyance bubble up; she was still holding out on him, pushing off his playfulness. That was unfair of him, though. He'd had longer to process all of this. "Who were you calling?"

He heard the gas burner snap behind him and the rush of flame catching.

"Just people for the report."

"Today, though?"

"Just voice mails today." She came back into view and leaned on the counter next to him.

He handed her a plated sandwich. "You'll eat with us?"

"Yeah." She checked her phone, then pushed it into her sweatpants pocket. It immediately trilled. She dug it back out and looked at its face.

"I gotta take this," she said as she left the kitchen. "I'll come back for my tea," she called as she went down the hallway. "Take it off when it boils, please, but I'll come back for it!"

Her voice quieted as she said, "Hi, Elisa."

Tony heard the study door close, shutting out Julia's voice. The itch of an incomplete memory thrummed in his brain when he heard the name, but whoever Elisa was had faded into the recesses of his memory.

59

W hat's this worth again?" Nick tipped his hand forward to reveal four spades to the man across the table.

"Four," David responded.

Nick laid his cards down. "Shit," he whispered. That was right. That was the hand that seemed like it was worth more. And he couldn't make fifteen from any of them. He pegged four on the cribbage board. "I think you're gonna smoke me again."

"Skunk," David said as he pegged twelve. He pushed his glasses up the bridge of his porous nose and grinned. "Probably."

David had only been there a week and a half. Nick was a day shy of a month. His counselor at Goodspring, Anne Marie, had written a letter to get permission for him to stay at the program for a little longer. She convinced insurance or whoever to give him extra time so he could be here for a while after the next court day, which, incidentally, was today.

Nick was glad to have David. He was fortysomething, dry and funny, and loved playing games like Nick did. Before David showed up, Nick hadn't really connected with anyone besides the staff. There was a guy there named Kedar who might be cute if he had a haircut and looked like he'd slept at all in the past year. But cute probably wouldn't do Nick any good right now. Cute had gotten Nick into this, in a way. He shouldn't blame himself, his counselors had been firm on that and they were right. But he'd gone home with a stranger. But he'd done that before. He wanted a boyfriend, but instead he was taking whatever he could get. He was a million miles from being ready for sex again, and yet if this cute program guy wanted to go there, he wasn't so sure he wouldn't follow. So he'd continue to give Kedar a wide berth.

Most of the people at Goodspring didn't want to be there. They either admitted so out loud or their actions said it for them. Some didn't think they needed the help; some hated the broken-in beds, the bright lights, the vegetable-heavy food, the windows in the bedroom doors for staff to do safety checks all night. But Nick liked being at Goodspring. It was so strange, so foreign to anything he'd experienced before that it made him forget his life outside the place. There was no DA in here. No criminal case. He was in a bubble.

At least, it normally felt like that. Today, even from the safety of the bubble, he felt the presence of the outside world pressing in on the walls. Out there, life was going on. Tony was stressing out over him. His parents were probably fighting. The winter semester had started. The ADA was at court, right now, with Walker and his lawyer. Real life would be waiting for him when he left Goodspring. He'd be right back where he started— standing in the middle of the mess he had made. His forearms started to itch under his sleeves.

"Nick?"

He looked up, and his counselor Anne Marie was standing in the doorway to the common room.

"You have a call."

⌐

It was Sherie.

"So there's no deal," she said. "I'm sorry."

It was what he expected, but his heart sank anyway. "Are you allowed to tell me what happened?"

"Oh, of course. The lawyers were just too far apart to come to a deal. I told you what she was going to offer him, right?"

"Yeah," Nick said. "Four years in jail but he could end up doing ten?"

"Right. It would be prison, not jail, but that's more of a technical thing. And Linda offered to change it from gross sexual assault to aggravated assault."

These were words he'd heard before, but it still felt like he was jogging to keep up with her.

"So the defendant and his lawyer didn't like that," Sherie said. "They wanted simple assault and six months in jail. His lawyer was acting like it was impossible to get him to even consider six months, but that's always how attorneys act when they negotiate. She and Linda couldn't get there. At least not today."

Simple assault, whatever that meant, and six months in jail. He wondered if that's where the case would end up, once he told them that he'd been lying. That it was worse than he'd said—but he'd lied about it. He would talk to Anne Marie and make a plan about telling them the truth.

"So now what?" Nick asked.

"Technically, jury selection is next."

"Already!" It wasn't going to take nearly as long as they made it sound.

"So, your case will get scheduled for jury selection in March. But the defendant will probably file a motion to push it out further than that. And when the next court date does happen, it's just a scheduling day where the judge tries to sort out what cases can have trials that month."

She paused. "Anything's possible, I guess, but you should still be prepared for the long haul. Okay?"

"Okay."

They hung up, and Nick sat for a moment. Anne Marie had left him alone in her office to take the phone call. He wanted to just skip this part—telling his family there was no deal. He wanted to go to bed. But they were all waiting for the news. And going to his room and sleeping wouldn't change the fact that the case still existed.

Nick stood and stuck his head into the hall. Anne Marie was nearby, talking to Kedar.

"Yeah?" she asked when she saw him.

"Can you get me my sister-in-law's cell number?" He wasn't allowed to have his cell phone for most of the day here, and he didn't have Julia's number memorized. He'd call her. She could pass on the news to Tony and his parents. It would be so much easier to talk to her than to Tony.

60

JULIA HALL, 2016

Julia and the kids were doing a Paw Patrol puzzle on the coffee table when her phone buzzed. It was Nick. She groaned as she stood from her seat on the floor.

"Hey, just give me a minute." She left the room and took the stairs quickly. "What happened at the hearing?"

"There's no deal."

"Shit," she hissed, and she meant it more than Nick knew. "That really sucks."

"Yup."

She closed the door to her office. Checked her notes. "Uh, you doing okay?"

"Yeah, just disappointed. Would you mind telling Tony?"

"Sure." No deal meant Tony went forward with his own plan. "Actually. This reminds me. He was saying he wants to come see you."

"He does?"

"Yeah. Friday. He wants to come Friday this week."

"Okay," Nick said. "Do you know why?"

She sighed and leaned against the closed door. "I think he misses you."

61

TONY HALL, 2016

There was a large envelope jammed into the mailbox when Tony got home. It was addressed to Julia *Clark* and bore a Michigan return address. He would have guessed it was junk mail if it hadn't been handwritten.

He could hear Julia coming down the stairs as the kids mobbed him in the kitchen.

"Someone doesn't know you're married," Tony said as he handed her the package.

Julia looked at the envelope and smiled. "She knows I'm married. Just doesn't respect that I changed my name."

"Seriously?"

Julia rolled her eyes. "I'm positive."

"Who is she?"

"A lady I'm working with on the records report." She started to walk back to the staircase and stopped. "Before I forget: Nick wants you to go see him on Friday."

Tony frowned. "This Friday?"

"Yup. The hearing about a settlement got pushed out another week. He wants to see you before then."

Tony motioned, and they started to climb the stairs together.

"Did it sound important?"

"Important to him, yeah."

"Shit," Tony said quietly. They'd reached the landing. Julia held up a finger, walked down the hall, and put the envelope in her office. They moved into the bedroom.

"What's wrong?"

"Nothing," he said. "I was just hoping to go see him and have something . . . *good* to tell him, finally."

Julia's eyes widened. "That Walker is dead?"

"*Shh.*"

"Don't shush me, no one can hear me. You were hoping you'd have . . . taken care of Walker before you saw Nick again."

"Fine, yes."

"Nick wants to see you and court's in a week. You'll just have to go."

"I guess so."

Julia crossed her arms. "Once they have the hearing, if there's no deal, how soon are you going to do it?"

"Would you stop?"

"I will if you give me *something*. Anything. Tell me when. Not even a date—what time of day?"

62

On January 15, 2016, at 6:00 p.m., clad in a bathrobe and scratching the stubble on his face, Raymond Walker came down his stairs and wondered, absently, why the lights were out in the living room below. He flicked the switch to his right as he stepped from the stairwell. The lamp in the living room snapped to life. In the same way one's peripheral vision might register the vague shape of a spider on the wall, out of place and threatening, Ray saw the figure of a man standing in the dark of his kitchen.

63

On January 16, 2016, Rice was pecking out a report at his computer when the receptionist paged him.

"Detective, there's a Darlene Walker calling about her son, Ray Walker, I thought you or Megan would want to take it."

"Yup," Rice said quickly.

"This is Detective John Rice."

"Yes, hello, Mr. Rice—Detective Rice—this is Darlene Walker. I'm calling regarding my son, Raymond." Her voice was full of nervous energy.

"Yes, ma'am."

"Well, something's happened to him, and somebody needs to get over here immediately."

Rice straightened. "What's happened to him?"

"I don't know, but I can't find him! I'm at his house, he gave me a key, and I let myself in when he didn't answer my calls or come to my house today—we were supposed to have lunch this afternoon, and he didn't show, didn't call, didn't answer when I called—"

"Ma'am, can you slow down a minute? You're—"

"No, *you* need to hurry up and get over here, you can't treat him any different just because you've made your mind up that he's a criminal, which will be cleared in the courts, by the way, I'm confident of that. I tried calling the police where I live, but they said I had to call the police in Raymond's town, even though it seems like an obvious conflict of interest."

"All right, ma'am—*ma'am*." Rice paused until she finally stopped talking. "I'll be over shortly."

—◦—

Rice pulled up outside the small, gray house numbered *47*. So this was Raymond Walker's house. They'd never had probable cause to get a search warrant for anything besides Ray's DNA, which of course had been a match to the sexual assault kit. They'd also been able to do an inventory search of Ray's car, after towing it from the station lot after he was arrested. The search had yielded nothing of apparent value to the investigation involving Nick Hall.

Rice could see a light on inside as he walked up the short driveway to the back door—the front steps were unshoveled, and there was no discernable walkway to them. Ray's car was parked in the driveway.

Rice hadn't reached the door before it opened.

A woman around his age, give or take a few hard nights, leaned out toward him, immediately shivering in the cold. "Are you the detective I talked to?"

"Yeah." He offered his gloved hand to shake. "Should we go inside?"

"I'm not consenting to a search of the house." She pursed her lips and looked at him like a hundred people had before: like she thought she was a law professor.

"Understood. Just cold out." He smiled.

Darlene Walker turned back into the house, and Rice followed.

The mudroom was small but well organized. Tall shelves housed shoes and a box of scarves; heavy coats hung on a stand. Rice's boots squeaked on the floor as they moved into the kitchen.

"Ms. Walker, you said on the phone that you can't reach Ray and you expected to see him today."

"Yes, I was expecting—"

"I'm sorry to cut you off, but if I could ask a few specific questions. When did you last talk to Ray?"

"Friday morning, on the phone."

"Friday as in yesterday, or Friday as in a week ago?"

"Yesterday."

Rice noted *Friday, January 15*, on his pad.

"We made plans *yesterday* to have lunch *today*. He was supposed to pick me up."

"And he didn't."

"Nope."

"Do you have your phone with you?"

She narrowed her eyes in suspicion, like he might snatch it from her. "Why?"

"Some specific times would be helpful. Like what time you talked on the phone, what time you tried to reach him and couldn't."

She stood and pulled her cell phone from her purse on the counter. "We talked at ten sixteen yesterday."

"In the morning," Rice said as he wrote.

"Yes," she said like he was stupid. Sure it sounded like an obvious question, but people were always jumping around while they talked to him. Better to get it right and lock her in than wish later he'd been more thorough.

"Any contact since then?"

"No. I've tried, but he hasn't responded."

"When did you try?"

"Last night I texted him about something else, and then I texted him this morning about lunch."

"Times?"

She sighed. "Last night at eight twenty-seven I texted him. Nothing. Then this morning at eleven fifteen I texted him about what time he was getting to my house. Nothing. Then I started calling."

"Okay," Rice said. "He usually text you right back? My daughter isn't exactly reliable when it comes to answering my texts, is all."

"Same," Darlene said quietly.

"What time was he supposed to pick you up today?"

"Noon."

"How many times you call this morning?" This he asked more out of curiosity than anything.

She looked down at her phone. "Thirteen."

Seemed about right. "And what time you come here today?"

She continued to study her phone. "I can't drive right now, so I called a cab here at twelve thirty, and I must have been here before one."

"Why can't you drive?"

She looked up at him then and said tersely, "That's private."

"All right," Rice said with a shrug and smile. "Will you walk me through the house?"

Again, suspicion fell over her face. "I said I don't consent to a search of the house. There's nothing out of place."

"I don't need to open any drawers or touch his computer." *That will come later*, he thought with ugly satisfaction. "This is my job. I might see something you can't. If you really think something's happened to him."

Darlene stared at him. She looked like she was going to cry—for a moment he actually felt for her. She didn't know what to do, whether to trust him. Ray might have been her fault; her mistake unleashed on the world, on people like the Halls. But he was still her son, and Rice couldn't help pity her for that.

He used the pity to soften his face. "I give you my word," he said. "I'm not playing you."

Raymond Walker's mother walked Rice through the house. The first floor was largely an open space that kept going back: the kitchen flowed into a living room with a small dining area, which stretched on into a room that looked like a sunroom that had been opened up and better insulated. There was a bathroom, a spare bedroom, and a couple closets on the first floor as well. All was clean and orderly; there were no signs of an altercation, or an abrupt departure.

Darlene took Rice up the stairs to the master bedroom and bathroom. The second floor was smaller than the first, but the suite was quite large. It occupied the whole floor. All appeared quiet here as well.

At Rice's request, Darlene opened the closet to show him her son's suitcase. Rice also noted what looked like a gym bag in the corner of the room, next to the hamper.

"He have any other bags?"

"No, I got him the suitcase for his birthday two years ago. He wanted to get rid of his old one—it had a broken wheel, or it was squeaky or something. I think it wouldn't roll. So this is the only one—it's the one I bought him." Not quite what he'd asked, and way more detail than he needed, but it was hard to say whether it was suspicious. It seemed to be how the woman talked in general.

She stood next to her son's bed with her arms crossed, rocking heel to toe. "So now do you believe me?" Her face was oddly smug. Was it because she thought she was pulling one over on him, or because she was the kind of person who would take some satisfaction in being proven right about anything, including her son's disappearance?

Rice stepped into the bathroom. Toothbrush on the sink. Darlene was in the doorway behind him with her eyebrows raised up, as though she were asking, *Well?*

"He say anything to you about going away?"

"He's followed all your little rules."

"Anyone else who might know where he is? His lawyer?"

Darlene expelled a laugh like a cough. "He wouldn't tell her."

"Why not?"

"She's part of the whole racket. She's in on it as much as you are. At least you don't pretend to be on his side."

He thought of Britny Cressey's phone call. Walker was fighting with his lawyer, unhappy with how she was handling things. Maybe he'd skipped town. If he had, Rice needed to move. He needed to freeze the house and have a crew come in—and Darlene needed to go. "Let's head downstairs, I need to call the station."

He motioned for Darlene to take the stairs first.

"What are you going to do?"

"Try to find your son." He motioned again.

"And you'll be looking into all the people who've been threatening him online and in the papers and on the radio, and all the real sex offenders who live around here, and that boy who lied about the rape in the first place?"

"Yes, we'll look into all those things. But you need to leave now."

"I'm going to wait here in case he comes home."

Rice took a step toward her, and he towered over her. She stunk of stale smoke. "No, Ms. Walker. You need to leave the house."

"Actually, Detective, you can go to hell." She'd inexplicably held up her fingers in air quotes as she'd said *Detective*. Her body jerked strangely as she pounded over to her son's bed and sat. "You're just using this as an excuse to search the house. It's illegal, and I *will* be calling your supervisor."

"You're more than welcome, but you need to get up from that bed and leave this house immediately, or I'll arrest you for obstructing." There was no time to do this gently. If Walker had run, every minute was going to count. And if he hadn't . . .

Darlene stared at him, her eyes brimming with hatred.

"You want to wait for Ray, that's fine. You pick: do it from your house or a jail cell."

She jerked up from the bed and blew past him with a flurry of threats of getting a lawyer and suing his department and taking his badge, her voice hoarse with tears.

Rice reached the ground floor just as Darlene was making her exit. She held her coat in one hand and her purse in the other. She waived the purse at Rice and shouted, "You're treating my son like a goddamn criminal!" She slammed the door behind her.

Rice strode to the door and locked it. From the kitchen window, he could see Darlene walking down the driveway, doing something with her hands. At the base of the driveway she turned, a fresh cigarette between her lips. She frowned at the house bitterly, said something, then began to peck at her phone as she walked up the road. He'd forgotten she needed to wait for a ride. Well, there was a gas station and a coffee place out on the main drag, she could wait there. He felt sick to his stomach. Was it Darlene? No. It was this house. Something had happened here. Ray could have made a run for it, but he was too arrogant to do that, wasn't he? Not to mention that he seemed to have left everything behind.

And of course, there was the trouble of the threat. Someone with every reason to hate Walker had been to this house and threatened to kill him. Tony Hall didn't seem the type, but when it really came down to it, no one ever did.

64

Detective Rice came unannounced this time. He'd done that before, Julia supposed as she welcomed him in, but this felt different. The police must have known Walker was missing. He didn't want to give them time to get their stories straight.

The detective arrived after breakfast on Sunday. Julia and Tony hadn't slept at all on Friday, and she'd spent Saturday obsessively watching her phone and starting violently each time it buzzed. Tony begged her to try to relax, but it was pointless. Then Sunday morning came, and their detective was at the door.

He rejected Julia's offer of coffee as he pulled off his heavy winter boots. Tony took his coat and sent the kids upstairs to read in their rooms. The three of them sat in the living room—Julia and Tony together on the couch, Detective Rice in a chair beside them.

He sat, apparently thinking for a moment, then reached into his pants pocket and produced his silver tape recorder.

"Ray Walker is missing."

The bluntness of his approach startled Julia, and she hoped it showed on her face. She looked at Tony, who looked back at her. "What?" she asked, as Tony said, "Missing how?"

"Missing like missing." He studied them overtly. "I need to ask you some questions, and I'd like to record it."

"All right," Tony said.

Detective Rice fingered the recorder and set it down on the coffee table.

"Like I said, Ray Walker is missing. I'd like you to account for your whereabouts Friday and Saturday of this week. Yesterday and the day before."

Julia looked to her husband. All three of them knew that Tony was the "you" he'd addressed.

"Um," Tony said with a shake of his head, "Friday I left work early and went to see Nick up at Goodspring, and yesterday we were home all day. Besides the library for a bit in the afternoon."

"What time were you at work Friday?"

"From about eight to two." Tony looked at Julia, and she nodded. A jolt of adrenaline rocketed through her—did he see her nod? Did they look rehearsed?

"And Goodspring?"

Her veins hummed as Tony answered. "Four to eight. A little after eight, actually. Maybe eight ten or something."

"And then?"

"Then home." Tony nodded at Julia. "I was here a little after ten, right?"

She cleared her throat. Her face was numb. "Yes, a little after ten."

Detective Rice looked her in the eye, and miraculously she held fast. He nodded and wrote on his pad.

"As for yesterday," Tony started, but the detective interrupted him.

"Make any stops on the way home?"

"No," Tony said. "No, I left a little after eight and came straight home. It's like a two-hour drive back from Belfast."

"Goodspring make you sign in for visits?"

Tony paused. "Yeah, they do."

"And work?"

Tony said nothing. He was staring at the coffee table.

Julia rested a hand on his thigh. "Honey?"

"Sorry," Tony said. "What?"

"You have a way to confirm when you were at work?"

"I don't, like, punch in or anything," Tony said, "but I'm sure the receptionist can vouch I was there until two. She tracks our calendars."

"And yesterday it was just you two and the kids all day?" The detective's eyes flicked up at the ceiling, and Julia wondered if he was going to ask to speak to them.

"They went to my mom's for a sleepover on Friday," Julia said. "She dropped them off Saturday morning, I can't remember when."

"Maybe nine or ten," Tony said.

They both knew it had been 9:17 a.m.—they'd been watching the clock obsessively that morning. But knowing anything too specific would sound bad.

"We can't get everything perfect," Julia had whispered in the hazy hours between Friday and Saturday. They laid in bed, Tony's head on her chest, her shirt wet with his tears. Her voice had been so calm then. "They'll have to question us because they know you threatened him. You have Goodspring, though."

Tony had nodded against her chest.

"It will take time for them to decide you must have been with Nick. Before that, they'll question us. We can't look like we knew this was coming. We need to act unsure of things, but only in the smallest ways."

Detective Rice was circling something on his notepad. Maybe he'd call Marjorie to confirm that Tony was home when she dropped off the kids Saturday morning. Maybe the police didn't know yet that Walker was long gone by morning. Julia straightened her posture to mask the shudder that had wormed up her spine.

It would be okay. It would be okay. The sign-in sheet at Goodspring would place Tony there from 2:00 p.m. to 8:00 p.m. The drive back down south was two hours. For now, that left Julia as the only witness to Tony's late Friday night and early Saturday morning hours. It was far from airtight—she'd lie for him, anyone had to assume that. But the police would figure it out eventually: that Tony had an alibi for the time that mattered.

"Julia." Detective Rice turned his body with his attention. "You were home when Tony got in Friday night?"

"Yes," she said. And she had been. She'd sat in the dining room, television blaring in the next room, and waited. Even now her stomach tightened, remembering how near she'd felt to vomiting as she waited for him to come home.

"And when do you remember him home?"

"Just a few minutes after ten." He held her eye for a beat. Should she say more? "I only know that because I was watching normal cable. And a new show had just started, so it was probably, like, ten oh three? I was waiting for him to come home. So I could hear about how it went with Nick." Tony took her hand and squeezed it. She was talking too much.

"And from when he got home to the kids getting in, did either of you leave the house at any point?"

"No," she said. "We just talked about his visit with Nick and went to bed."

Detective Rice retrieved the recorder from the coffee table and stopped it. He pocketed the silver bar, along with his little notebook and pen.

She walked him to the door, where he pulled on his boots and coat. As she watched him trudge down the front walk, it occurred to her that he hadn't separated them, like she would have expected. He'd asked his questions of both of them at once, allowing her to hear Tony's answers and simply confirm them. He hadn't asked questions about her at all.

He thought they were innocent. Or maybe he just wanted them to be.

65

Julia walked the detective to the door. From the couch, Tony could see Detective Rice pulling on his boots, tying the laces in silence.

Leave leave leave leave LEAVE—it was filling Tony's mouth, straining against his teeth he was so close to screaming it.

The door shut.

Tony stood. "Jesus Christ. Oh, Christ."

"Shh," Julia hissed from the hallway. "Keep your voice down."

"I don't think it matters. I don't think anything matters."

Now she was in the doorway to the living room. "What are you talking about?"

Tony's mouth was running, tripping over hot breath. "I fucked it all up."

"You didn't fuck anything up, you did fine. You're just upset. Take a breath."

"No, not today. I fucked up that day."

"How?"

Tony walked through the dining room, bumping against a chair. "If they think he's dead, that's it. I'm it. They'll be after me."

Julia followed him into the kitchen. "Take a breath, I can barely understand you."

He groaned, ran his hands through his hair. "What good is an alibi if there's no time attached to it?"

Someone was pounding down the stairs. The kids were yelling over each other about movies they wanted to watch.

Julia's voice was low but laser-focused. "What are you saying?"

"At Goodspring," Tony whispered as the kids rushed down the hall. "I forgot to fill in the sign-out time."

66

As Rice drove away from the Hall home late Sunday morning, he called the unit's head evidence technician, Tanya Smith, for an update on Walker's house.

Smith's voice betrayed her tendency to polish off a pack of Marlboro Lights over the course of a single shift. "We've got a cell phone," she said. "O'Malley's getting a warrant, but I doubt it'll matter. It's an iPhone. It'll have a passcode. Unless it's his mother's birthday I doubt we'll get in."

Rice grunted. With the advent of the smartphone came a whole universe of juicy evidence, but only if you could get to it. Nothing would convince Apple to let law enforcement past a passcode, warrant or not. You could probably have someone producing child porn with the phone itself and they wouldn't budge. The phone was a dead end.

"We've covered the ground floor of the house at this point. Williams collected some prints; so far I've come up dry on fluids." She chuckled at the joke he'd heard her make at least twice before.

Rice started to sign off. He wanted to call Goodspring. "Thanks, Tanya."

Down the line he heard the scrape of a lighter. Smith talked around a cigarette. "I say I was finished?"

"You smoking all over my crime scene?"

Smith laughed her witch's cackle. "Fuck the fuck off." He knew she'd be out in the street, far away from the scene.

"Might be nothing," she said, her tone cautious. "Basak canvassed the street, and the lady next door says she saw two men walking down the street on Friday night."

"Really," Rice breathed.

"Yeah, around seven thirty. Going down the street, away from the direction of her house and Walker's."

"She make out any details?"

"Average height and build, maybe one a bit bulkier. Couldn't make out skin tone or hair color or anything like that. It was already dark, and I don't think she paid them too much attention."

"But she thinks it was seven thirty?"

"That's what she said."

By the time they hung up, Rice had parked himself at a Dunkin' Donuts. He called O'Malley, and she forwarded him to voice mail. A minute later his phone buzzed: she'd texted,

Call you soon.

He pulled through the drive-through and ordered a small: two creams, two sugars.

A night ago, O'Malley meticulously sent out Walker's identifying information and mug shot to all the cab companies, bus depots, train stations, and airports in New England, and now she was following up by phone. That Walker had gotten antsy and skipped town was the simplest explanation, but Walker seemed incapable of seeing how guilty he looked. He'd spewed confidence everywhere he could—to the newspaper, the radio, social media. In the last article Rice read on the case, sometime in the last couple of weeks, his lawyer sounded like she was armed for bear. But then, Britny Cressey said Walker was panicking. Someone who did what Walker did to Nick Hall—that kind of person was good at hiding his true intentions, wasn't he? Come to think of it, Walker's incessant chatter about his innocence could have been a distraction. A long-term plan to take off could even explain why he'd reported the incident with Tony Hall but didn't press charges—to muddy the waters of his planned disappearance.

A lanky boy passed Rice his coffee through the window. He drove around the building, back into the lot and parked.

Two men, one a bit bigger and bulkier. That could be two brothers.

But the men were seen at seven thirty. Tony Hall couldn't have been walking down a street in Salisbury then if he really was at Goodspring from four to eight. Even if the neighbor was a bit off on the time, it was something like a two-hour drive from Nick's program back to Salisbury. Rice found the number for Goodspring Psychiatric Center online, and his stomach fluttered as he pressed to call.

The man who answered wasn't working on Friday night, but he was happy to check the sheet.

"I have a Tony Hall here on January fifteenth at four p.m. sharp."

"And the out time?"

"It's not filled in."

"It's *not* filled in," Rice repeated.

"Correct, sir."

"So no way to tell when he left." A neat little alibi evaporating on the spot.

"You could talk to whoever worked the desk. I think it's Ida but I'll make sure. Or you could speak to the patient he saw, if you know who it was, but I can't give—"

"Is it normal to see the out time left blank?"

"Yeah, or at least not *not* normal. I tell people when they come in to sign out when they leave. At the end of the shift I go down the list and make sure everybody's gone. But sometimes people forget. I remind people if I notice them forgetting as they're leaving. It's really just record keeping and security, knowing who's in the building."

"Can a visitor duck out without you seeing?"

"I guess anything's possible, but unless I'm in the can, I'm at the desk. And if he came in a car, he'd need his keys back."

"You hold the keys?"

"Yup."

Rice asked the man to find out who was working on Friday and have that person call his cell. He asked about security footage of the entrance, but the man said he should call back during the week to talk to the right person about that.

Rice hung up and sipped at his coffee. At first the convenience of Tony's alibi had bothered him, but it wasn't shaping up to be so convenient after all. If it turned out that Walker simply took off, all this signing-out business didn't much matter. But if Walker turned up dead in the woods, well, Tony Hall was an obvious suspect. Rice set his coffee down in the cupholder. It was giving him a stomachache. That this all might spell trouble for Tony's family—Julia, their kids, Nick—didn't make any difference. That was the judge's job: to decide how to sentence a family man who'd snapped, done something monstrous, but maybe understandable to on some level. That wasn't Rice's concern. First it was the judge's problem, and ultimately it was God's. Rice's job was easier. He didn't have to weigh right and wrong—didn't get to. He just had to find the truth.

67

The sound brought Julia to her feet before she recognized that her phone was ringing. With it came a rush of acid up the back of her throat. She slammed her hand down on the phone on the table in front of her. *Please*, she thought, *please be anyone but—*

It was Nick.

"Is Tony there?" he asked.

"No, he's not." Julia walked into the kitchen from the dining room where she'd been sitting. Tony was upstairs taking a cold shower, still trying to calm down after the detective's visit. She didn't want him hearing her on the phone when he got out. It would just stress him out more.

"Is everything okay?"

No, she thought as she stepped into the mudroom and shut the door behind her. Far from it. "Why, has someone called you?"

"I tried him first, but he didn't answer. Where is he?"

"Nick. Tell me why you're asking."

"The front desk guy said a detective called asking about Tony."

Julia kicked the kids' shoes out of her way as she began to pace the length of the mudroom. "Have you talked to them yet?"

"The police?"

"Yes," Julia breathed.

"No, are they gonna call me? What's going on?"

There was no reason not to tell him, was there? It would look strange of her not to, if the police *did* talk to Nick and they found out he'd talked to Julia but she hadn't mentioned it.

Nick spoke again. "Is something going on with *him*?" It was a "him" reserved only for Raymond Walker.

"Maybe." She nudged a shoe against the wall with her right foot. "He's missing."

Nick's voice was quiet. "Ray's missing?"

"Yeah. Detective Rice came to the house this morning and told us. They can't find him."

There was silence.

"Nick?"

"Yeah?"

Her stomach rolled. She took a deep breath; the mudroom smelled like wet rubber and stale feet. "Tell me Tony was with you on Friday."

"He was."

"Until eight."

Nick paused. "Did he tell you what we talked about?"

Yes. He told her everything. Too late for her to do a thing about it, but he told her everything.

"I don't know how much we should talk right now," she said. The possibility that the program monitored residents' phone calls seemed slim, but there was no way she was going to risk it. They couldn't talk details. But there was one thing she *had* to say. It wasn't fair to ask a single thing of Nick. Not after everything that had happened to him; after everything that had been taken from him. But she had to make sure he'd give the right answer if he was asked.

"They might call you," she said. "To ask if Tony was there until after eight on Friday. It looks like they're checking up on him, because, you know. But like he told them, he was with you until sometime after eight on Friday."

There was a beat. "Yeah, he was."

"I guess he didn't fill in the sign-out sheet. So they might ask you when he left."

"Okay. I'll tell them."

Julia slumped against the door to the kitchen; it was cool on her back. What she would have given to get off the phone now. To be able to run out into the back field and scream. To collapse on the floor with the dirty shoes. To cry. Why couldn't she cry? Her belly was full of salt water—all the tears she had swallowed that weekend. She and Tony had always been good at calibrating: when one went up, the other came down. Tony was a wreck right now, so she was the anchor. She didn't even have to work for it. It just happened; she just was. She didn't want to be. She wanted to scream and cry and run. She wanted to expel everything that was inside her.

"What a mess," she said.

"What do I do now?"

What *was* Nick supposed to do? How could they burden him with this? He was in a facility, for Christ's sake. He'd tried to overdose on his antidepressants. He'd been cutting himself. Keeping a secret had nearly killed him. What the fuck was he supposed to do with this?

And then she thought of what Tony told her, about his last conversation with Nick. The last things they said to each other before he got in the car and drove south. Nick was tired of being babied. Tired of everyone handling him with kid gloves, acting like the rape proved he was weak. And she knew, maybe, how he could survive one more secret.

"It's your turn to protect Tony."

68

JOHN RICE, 2016

Rice pulled up to Walker's house late Monday morning. The driveway was taped off, deterring anyone from adding to the footprints in the snow there. The crew had been using the front door to get in and out. Searching a potential crime scene always meant causing some amount of damage to that scene. Because the front walk had been totally print-free on the day Rice met Darlene Walker at the house, that was the path they chose to walk.

Earlier that morning, Rice and O'Malley had met at the station first thing, and they ran through their plans for the day. Rice was going to check in with the evidence team finishing up at the house. O'Malley was going to keep calling all the travel spots, trying to keep the pressure on them to check their surveillance systems and passenger lists.

Before he'd had a chance to call Tanya Smith for an update, Smith texted Rice and asked him to meet her at the house—there was something he needed to see. Smith enjoyed the drama of an in-person reveal, but she'd have told him if he called and asked her what she found. Rice hadn't wanted to call—he hadn't wanted to know whatever it was any sooner than he needed to. He also didn't want to admit to himself how poorly he'd slept the night before, worrying about what Tony Hall might have done to Walker.

By the time Rice got out of the car, officer Mike Basak was waiting for him in the front door of the house. He was the uniform who had talked to the neighbor about the two men she thought she saw in the area on Friday. Now, Basak waved Rice up the front walkway.

"I collected some shoe prints in the driveway and at the side door," Basak said, "so I'll need to get a print of your boots at some point, since you were here with the mother. He's got a lot of shoes inside, so they could all turn out to be his, but you never know till you know." He shrugged and handed Rice a pair of covers for his shoes so he could go into the house. "Starting to look like we could have a crime scene, though. Smith wants you in the upstairs bathroom."

From the top steps of the stairs to Walker's bedroom, Rice could see Tanya Smith in the dim bathroom on the far side of the room. Smith had blocked the window over the tub, casting the space into shadows.

"You rang," Rice said.

Smith stood up and stepped out of view to grab something. Her voice echoed off the high ceiling as she said, "You know where this is going."

Rice's stomach did a slow barrel roll, and he pictured a tub filled with the glow of a body's worth of luminol. He forced the usual chitchat. "Bad cleanup job?"

"Yep," Smith said as she stepped from the bathroom. She held her camera in her right hand, the strap swinging. They met in the center of the bedroom, a faint waft of stale cigarettes on her hair. On the LCD screen of her camera, she pressed Play on a video. It showed the darkened bathroom with a hint of luminol glowing on the lip of the bathtub and a larger smear on the floor beneath.

"Fatal?"

"No," Smith said. The video moved up to the inside of the tub to show it spotless. "We found a bloody towel in the waste bin, so I swept the bathroom but this was all that flared. The smear is only about the size of a hand towel, not a fatal amount of blood loss here. It's more the location that gets me—don't exactly look like a shaving injury."

"No," Rice agreed as he moved to the edge of the bathroom. The glow of the luminol was long gone, but he wanted to see the tub. It was an old-fashioned claw-foot bathtub standing alone in the middle of the room—there was a separate shower in the right corner of the bathroom. Sink in the left corner. So there had been blood on the outer lip of the tub and on the floor beneath. Standard bathroom injuries were cutting yourself shaving like Smith said, maybe slipping in the tub and hitting your head—but not the *outside* of the tub, leaving you bleeding on the floor.

"He's got a basement with a utility sink and a washer/dryer," Smith said. "I thought you'd want to join while I check the rest of the hot spots."

Rice's cell buzzed and rang in his coat pocket. "Yeah," he said absently as he pulled out the phone—Belfast area code. He waved the screen at Smith and said, "Goodspring."

He crossed the bedroom and went down to the kitchen as he took the call.

It was Ida, she said, from the front desk at Goodspring. Her voice was friendly, if a little anxious. "They said to call you?"

Rice introduced himself. "Were you working the desk this past Friday?"

"Yeah."

"Did a man named Tony Hall come in to see his brother?"

"I'm not supposed to reveal who's a patient here—"

"Well, I just meant—"

"But," she said, "Tony Hall did come on Friday."

"Okay. He show you an ID?"

"He didn't need to. I've seen him here before. Not a face you forget." The woman laughed nervously.

"He's not bad-looking," Rice said.

"Nope. Is he in trouble?"

"Do you remember when he left on Friday?"

"They said you were asking about the sign-out time. He was here so late I had packed up to leave; I think that's how I forgot to have him sign out."

"How late was it?"

"Visiting hours end at eight, it was probably a few minutes after that."

"A few minutes meaning?"

"Eight ten, maybe."

So Tony was at Goodspring until after eight. A two-hour drive away. *Maybe* he could shave off fifteen minutes with a lead foot.

Ida went on. "He and his, uh, the person he was visiting, they were having a serious conversation, I didn't want to rush them, but eventually I had to kick him out."

"What were they talking about?"

"I don't know. What's going on?"

"Why do you say it was a serious conversation?" Rice said.

She paused. "The way they looked, I guess. I could see them from the desk. It looked like they were fighting, at one point."

"Did you hold his car keys when he signed in?"

"Yeah, we have to."

"And could you see him the whole time he was there?"

She paused. "Well, the visits aren't, like, supervised. So I wasn't watching them the whole time."

"But are they happening near your desk?"

"Mostly the visits are in the visiting room, which I can see part of. But Tony Hall went back with a staff person first."

Rice thanked Ida and asked her to call back if she thought of anything else. Someone might be in touch with her about a written statement. She sounded disappointed to hang up with him. Maybe he'd misidentified the tone of her voice when she first called. Instead of nerves, maybe it was excitement in her voice. She wanted to have something important to say—wanted something to be going on, like she kept asking. But if Tony Hall was at Goodspring until after eight, he couldn't have been one of the men on Walker's street at seven thirty. They might have had nothing to do with this, but it felt like *something*. Whatever it was, did it involve the blood in the bathroom?

"Smith," he yelled up the stairs. "Ready for the basement when—"

His phone started up again and he laughed aloud. It never ends.

O'Malley's name was on the screen this time. "Hold on," he yelled up to Smith.

Rice turned back to the kitchen counter. He answered gravely. "I've got blood in Walker's bathroom and nothing but questions."

"They'll have to wait," O'Malley said. "I've got Walker."

69

JULIA HALL, 2016

In the back seat, Seb's sweet voice was muffled by the cotton scarf he'd been sucking on. "Could we play tag when we get home?"

Julia eyed him in the rearview as she drove. There was a wet patch in the center of the scarf, where his mouth was.

"It's too snowy," Chloe said as she reached over and tugged his scarf down.

"So?" Seb replied.

"I want to make a fort," Chloe said.

Seb squealed. "Will you help, Mumma?"

Julia grimaced at the mirror. "I'm not feeling very well, honey. I think I need to stay in."

"What's wrong?" Chloe asked.

"I just have a headache. I'm going to put away the groceries and rest for a bit." Julia twisted her hands back and forth on the steering wheel. "You two can play outside, though." She wanted to give the kids some semblance of normalcy while she and Tony were so upset, but there was no way she could romp around in the snow today. She'd barely managed to pull on real pants and go to the grocery store before she got the kids from the bus stop.

Julia steered into the driveway and parked. The kids unbuckled themselves as she grabbed the two totes of groceries in the trunk.

Seb streaked by her, but Chloe paused at the gate. "Will you watch us?"

"For a minute," she said.

Chloe grinned and ran after her brother.

Julia paused at the fence and set the bags down in the snow. Chloe ran for the edge of the yard, to the spot where crocuses exploded from the earth every spring. They were buried now, sleeping deep under the snow. Julia felt, for a moment, that she had forgotten that the spring even existed. She had forgotten that everything, to some degree, was finite. Even the bleak winter that had, just days ago, seemed endless, would end.

Seb yelped as he ran after Chloe, trying to keep up. The two tracked their boot prints all over the backyard. Behind them, the rolling fields of Orange stretched until they touched the snowy tree line.

The earth would yawn and stretch in the spring, and everything would change again. Everything but one: what had happened would never change.

Complicit. It was such a persistent word. The sun came up that morning, white-yellow and cold, and they'd made it to Monday, and now she'd be complicit for the rest of her life. She'd never be *good* again. The kids dropped to their knees and buried their hands into the snow.

A dagger of a thought sliced down the center of Julia's brain, and *complicit* was a lie. *Complicit* was too soft, too quiet, for this. Her ears began to ring, an electronic hum that grew louder, the yard before her began to dim. Julia grabbed the fence post. Squeezed it as hard as she could. For a moment the sensation of wood against her palm was the only thing she could feel. Her knees buckled but she stayed on her feet. She hung onto the post, and the world came back in, slow and warm in her ears. When her head had steadied, she straightened up and looked back out at the yard. The kids hadn't noticed; they were scraping the snow into a mound.

Julia's heart pounded, but her stomach was settling, her vision was clear, and she loosened her grip on the fence. Her children were safe. Tony was safe. They were safe. They were whole. That was all that mattered. The rest would get easier. Spring would come, and she would forget who she'd become in the winter.

Julia turned to pick up her grocery totes. One of them had tipped over; she crouched to scoop the spilled oranges and bread back into the bag. As she stood, a dark car drove past the house and down the lane. She thought nothing of it and went into the house.

70

I know what happened," Rice had said. It felt like minutes had passed since he'd spoken, but it had probably been a matter of seconds. "I've always wondered if you knew, too." *Well, no longer*, he thought. The sheer shock on her face told him everything: for all these years, she'd never known that he'd figured it out. She had no idea that she'd made him an accomplice to her crime. She was responsible for the most colossal sin he'd committed in his days on earth, and she hadn't even known it. At least, not until this moment.

Julia sat beside him, bottom lip dropped open, revealing a trembling row of teeth.

What must she have been feeling? A small part of him wanted to punish her—to let her wither under his words. Compared to his years of burdensome knowledge, years of praying for forgiveness for a sin that was perpetual, Rice thought a moment of suffering was a short sentence indeed.

"Enough." The word was harsh, and she started. "I want to hear it."

"What?" she whispered.

"I want to hear it from you. Tell me what I already know. Tell me what happened on the day he went missing."

IV.

LUCKY

—◦—

Don't try to make life a mathematics problem with yourself in the center and everything coming out equal. When you're good, bad things can still happen. And if you're bad, you can still be lucky.

BARBARA KINGSOLVER, *THE POISONWOOD BIBLE*

71

TONY HALL, 2016

At 4:00 p.m. on the day Raymond Walker would go missing, Tony Hall arrived at Goodspring. The pretty woman at the front desk perked up as he came through the door. She looked like she was in her forties, with stiff blond hair she'd had back in a clip each time he'd come in. There was always an air about her, as if she knew everything going on with Nick and she wanted Tony to know it.

"Mr. Hall, right?"

"Yeah," Tony said as he pounded his boots on the mat.

"Your brother's primary worker said to expect you. She's here today."

"Is she not normally?"

"Oh, no, she is. I just mean she's here for your meeting with Nick."

The woman's face begged him to ask why. Instead, he said, "Oh, okay," and he slid his car keys across the counter toward her.

She scooped up the keys and pushed the sign-in sheet toward him. It probably made her feel important, working there, getting to dip her toes into the drama of other people's lives.

She pulled the sheet back and said, "I'll let Anne Marie know you're here."

A couple had come in behind him, and Tony stepped away from the desk. He stood to the side, fixated on the double doors the woman had motioned toward a couple of times as they spoke.

After a minute, a woman appeared at those doors. She looked just about Nick's age; too young to be his therapist, or whatever she was.

"Mr. Hall?"

Tony went to her quickly.

"I'm Anne Marie." They shook hands, and the woman turned to start walking down the hallway. "I'm Nick's primary mental health worker here. Nick is looking forward to seeing you."

"Is something going on?" Tony still didn't know why Nick had asked him to come visit.

"Well, since you were coming up, Nick asked if we could do a little group session. He wants to talk to you about something." She pointed to a door they were fast approaching. "I'm really just here for support. We won't be too long, and then you two can move to the visiting area."

She opened the door without pause. Nick was sitting in a small chair on the opposite side of the room, his curly hair glowing in the low sun of late afternoon.

He stood to hug Tony. Tony had grown used to Nick's new, tense embrace, and he began to release his arms after a single squeeze. Nick held fast, though, and Tony looked to the side of his face, brought his arms back around his little brother, closed his eyes, and hugged him deeply for the first time in as long as he could remember. It was the kind of hug that sank into his chest.

When they released each other, Anne Marie was sitting behind a small desk near the door, and she motioned for Tony to sit beside Nick.

"What's going on?" Tony said to Nick.

Nick looked at Anne Marie.

"Nick?" she said.

"I guess I wanted to talk to you about some stuff."

"About that night?"

"No. About us."

"Oh." The knot in Tony's stomach loosened. He looked over at Anne Marie. "Oh, are we doing therapy?"

Anne Marie laughed, and Nick smiled nervously. "If that's okay?"

"Yeah," Tony said. "Sure."

"I just wanted to talk to you about something, and I feel like whenever I try to, I get all jumbled in my head. But when I'm with Anne Marie, or when I was with Jeff, I could talk about it better."

"It's really fine. What do you want to talk to me about?"

"I'm so scared to sound like I'm blaming you."

The knot returned. "For what?"

"I'm not, though. Please try to listen, please try to hear me, because I don't blame you for a single thing. You have done more for me than Dad or my mom ever has. More than I think they could—I don't think they're capable of love in a normal way. But this isn't about them or what's wrong with them. I'm so lucky I have you—I'd be fucked without you."

"Okay," Tony said.

Nick looked at Anne Marie, and she nodded at him.

"Sometimes, I feel like you baby me."

Oh. This was not news. Tony felt his hackles going up.

"I know you were young when you started taking care of me. You were younger than I am now. And I *was* a baby. I was helpless. All a baby can do is rely on the people around it. But I'm not a baby anymore."

"I know you aren't."

"Tony," Anne Marie said. "If you could let Nick finish what he needs to say, that would be really helpful."

"Sorry."

"It's okay." Nick's eyes welled. "Please don't apologize for anything you've ever done for me. I just need you to know that I need to feel like I'm taking care of myself now. When Ray raped me, that was the most powerless moment of my entire life. I felt like every fear I've ever had was confirmed. I was weak. I wasn't a man. I couldn't stop whatever bad things people wanted to do to me—I could be used. I could even be killed, if he'd wanted to do that, and for part of that night, I thought he did. You remember how Dad was about me being gay. I felt like everything he'd ever said I was, Ray made me in that moment.

"And I'm never gonna get better if I can't start believing what Jeff and Anne Marie and all of you keep telling me. That it *wasn't* my fault. That it had nothing to do with who I am.

"And the more you say stuff to me like you wish you'd been there, you would have stopped him, you'll take care of me—the more you say that stuff, the more I feel like I'm still a victim. Like I can't save myself."

"Nick," Tony said quietly, and Nick nodded. Tony could speak now.

"I'm so sorry. I'm so sorry for how I've treated you. I swear, I know it doesn't change what I did, but I swear it doesn't match how I see you myself."

While Nick was talking, Anne Marie had gotten up to hand Tony a tissue. It was soaked through now, but he kept wiping his nose with it anyway.

"You are the best man I know. I am in awe of you." Tony hung his head. "I'm so stupid."

"No," Anne Marie said.

Tony looked at her in surprise. How could she not hate him after what she'd just heard?

"Nick and I have had a lot of time together," she said. "You want to know what I think?"

Tony looked at Nick. Nick nodded.

"I think you grew up in an unsafe home with a dad who was withholding, cruel, and unpredictably violent, until your mom took you away. And then, when you were a teenager, and you were figuring out who you were, you saw that same dad have another kid, and that kid didn't have a mom like yours. And you decided to be his hero."

Nick cleared his throat. "Jeff was talking about that one day with me. I asked him about, like, what would happen to me later. Like, would I become violent, because of what Ray did. And Jeff was saying that people who are hurt by other people, like abused, sometimes they have a hard time not getting hurt over and over after that. And sometimes they start hurting other people. But sometimes they get kind of obsessed with helping other people. And Jeff was talking about me and him, but I think that's what you did."

"I did think I was helping," Tony said to Nick. "I've only ever wanted to keep you safe."

"I love you for that. But you can't protect me from everything."

That was obvious. Look at what had happened.

"I want us to figure out a new way to be without me feeling . . . fragile every time I talk to you."

Tony blew his nose into the tissue. "Okay."

Nick reached for Tony's hand and squeezed it three times.

Tony squeezed back four.

72

At 5:30 p.m. on the day Raymond Walker would go missing, Tony and Nick entered the visiting room together. They went straight for the corner cabinet and selected a pile of games. Then they sat at a table and played checkers, then cribbage, then war, then Connect 4, then checkers again. Games had always been their favorite way to suspend reality when Ron and Jeannie were drunk or fighting, or when school felt like too much for one of them. Since that fall, *everything* had seemed too much, too heavy, too hard to do together. Nick hoped it would get easier.

"I've decided to go forward with it." Nick hopped Tony's checker piece and plucked it from the board. "At least for now."

"The case?"

Nick nodded.

"You're sure you want to do that?"

Nick eyed him.

Tony held up his hands. "Sorry, sorry. Your choice, and I trust you."

"If it gets too hard again, I can always tell them I'm done."

"But everyone will know."

That was true. Nick was sure his absence from the school had not erased everyone's memory that he was the one in the story. And the new story—the real story—would be in the news again. He would have to contend with what people thought of him. What they thought it said about him, as a man, to have failed to stop Ray. What they thought it said about him as a *person* to have hidden the truth. Whether they believed him at all.

"I know," Nick said. "But it's my fight to have, if I want it. And I do."

Tony rubbed a finger on a checker for a moment before he spoke. "You really want to go through it all? A whole year of this? A trial?"

"Yes," Nick said.

Tony moved the piece forward. "It's not what I would have chosen for you."

Nick laughed. "You're such a dad."

Tony's face lightened with surprise, and he laughed, too.

"It could settle," Tony said.

"I mean, it didn't, but it could later."

"I thought the court date got moved to next week."

"No, it was a few days ago. Julia didn't tell you?"

Across the board, Tony looked at Nick like this was news to him.

"Wow. You must have been being *insufferable* about my case."

Tony sighed. "You don't even know."

His brother didn't look angry, so Nick smiled. "I really meant for her to tell you." He'd called her the same day . . . wait a minute. The same day she told him that Tony wanted to come see him at Goodspring. "Why did you come visit today?"

"You wanted me to," Tony said.

Nick laughed. "Your wife is *sneaky*. I didn't ask you to come here. The second I told her the case didn't settle, she said *you* wanted to come see *me*."

"Really?"

"Guess she thought it would be good for me to tell you myself. That or she just didn't want to have to do it."

Tony sat back from the board and crossed his arms. "I don't blame either of you. I haven't exactly been . . . levelheaded about all of this. Did she say anything about me, or what we talked about today?"

"No," Nick said honestly. "I wanted to do this. We needed to talk."

Tony held Nick's eye for a minute then moved a piece forward on the board. "So there's no deal, and you *really* want to do this your own way, with court."

"Yep. Will you come with me the next time there's a hearing?"

"Of course. I'll do whatever you want me to."

"You sure you can take it? Is your head leveling out?"

"Yeah," Tony said. "You've set me straight."

"Thank God," Nick said as he jumped another piece of Tony's. "I was starting to worry you'd do something stupid."

73

At 6:00 p.m. on the day Raymond Walker would go missing, Julia Hall was standing in the kitchen of a man she didn't know, a single sweaty palm gripping his counter, when she heard him descending the stairs.

He stepped from the stairwell, and a lamp went on in the corner of the living room.

She only saw him for a second, probably, before he saw her, but that second stretched like a warm taffy pull. There he was: Raymond Walker. Just like his mug shot, but alive and real. Wearing a robe like Tony wore. Regret crashed over her, and if she could have blinked and made herself disappear, she would have. Raymond Walker's eyes stuttered as he took her in, and he stepped back, knocking his heels against the bottom step of the staircase he had just come down. He wavered, then sat with a thud.

His voice was pure bewilderment. "Who are you?"

She hadn't disappeared. He could see her and she needed to speak. She could do this.

"I'm not here to hurt you," Julia said, holding her empty hands up at shoulder height. She'd thought about bringing a gun to scare him into listening to her, but she'd been worried she'd have shot him before either of them said a word. Given the tremor in her hands now, she was glad there wasn't a trigger under her finger.

"Who the fuck are you," he said. "Are you—" He tilted his head, like he was trying to see her face better. If her clothing was doing its job, he might have even thought she was a man. Her hair was slicked back tight under her hat, and she wore an oversize men's parka.

"I'm not gonna hurt you," she said again. "My name is Julia." She took an incremental step toward him. "Hall."

He shook his head. "Nick Hall's sister?"

"Sister-in-law," she said.

"Shit," he hissed as he turned. Before Julia could react, Walker had crawled himself to standing and was pounding up the stairs.

"Wait, wait, wait!" Julia called as she rushed across the kitchen.

She took the stairs two at a time; her baggy pants would have tripped her if she hadn't thought to wear a belt. She pictured Walker waiting at the top of the steps, ready to kick her back down, but when she rounded the bend in the narrow staircase he was gone.

She burst out onto the landing. Walker was across the room, next to the bed, his back to her.

Julia ran at him, and he started to move toward the bathroom door, but the phone he was clutching was plugged in next to the bed. She slammed into him arms first, driving him into the doorframe with a yelp. The phone released from its cord and clattered to the bathroom floor.

Walker stooped toward the phone, and Julia grabbed for his arms, but he wrenched them free. She clambered onto his back, a strange cry emerging from her throat.

"Get off!" he bellowed in confusion, jerking his body to the right.

She clamped her limbs around him. "I just want to talk!"

He moved toward the phone again, and she released a leg to drag her foot along the floor in front of him. She felt the phone underfoot, and with a miraculous yank she sent it skittering under the claw-foot tub.

Walker bucked her off and she fell to the floor.

"Stop," she groaned. Her ribs thrummed where she'd landed on the lump of papers folded in her coat pocket.

She picked herself up and saw him scrambling for the phone on his hands and knees.

She rushed toward him and shoved her hands against his shoulders, driving him squarely into the side of the tub. His head drove up into the lip of the tub and snapped back against his neck. A metallic *thong* rang out and he slumped to the floor.

Julia Hall stood in Raymond Walker's bathroom, swaying, her heart pounding in her ears.

And Raymond Walker did not move.

74

At 8:10 p.m. on the day Raymond Walker went missing, Tony called Julia as he crossed the parking lot outside of Goodspring. She'd been all over him about his calling her whenever he finished meeting with Nick. For some reason she'd gotten herself worked up about this visit. She didn't answer. It was a shame—she'd be happy to hear the news.

Nick, and the therapist to some extent, had convinced Tony. Tony had taken control of the hand Ron Hall dealt him by making himself a hero: Nick's hero first, then anyone who'd have him. That was fine when the person actually needed saving, but Nick didn't need or want to be saved. And Tony had been stifling him for a long, long time. It was a fine line, it seemed, between helping someone you love and hurting them. A line Tony hadn't even been looking for.

He got into the car and rattled off a text—"Heading home, call me"—then started the engine.

The whole drive home, Julia never called. The mile markers on 95, then 295 South ticked off in a blur, while Tony mourned the death of his plans to kill Ray Walker.

75

JULIA HALL, 2016

At 6:15 p.m. on the day Raymond Walker would go missing, Julia Hall reached her hand out of the stairwell on the ground floor of Raymond Walker's house, and she felt blindly up the wall to her right. There was the light switch under her shaking fingers, and she flipped it off with a heavy sigh. Once again, darkness flooded the living room.

"All right," she said. "Follow me."

She glanced behind her, then started for the kitchen. His footsteps were hesitant, but he followed.

She turned back. The opening to the staircase was black and vacant.

"Come on," she said firmly.

His voice resonated in the stairwell. "You aren't going to stab me with a kitchen knife?"

She exhaled a soft laugh. "You can hear me all the way across the room, right?"

Raymond Walker melted into the black square that was the stairwell. After a beat he stepped into the living room and made his way toward her. He still held the washcloth against his bloody hairline.

She had started in with her old routine up in the bathroom. When she wanted to get her way with a client—earn their trust on something gravely important—she joked with them. It made her seem at ease, even when she was scared shitless, like now. She stood to the side of the refrigerator in Raymond Walker's kitchen, keeping her eye on him as she opened the freezer and grabbed a bag of mixed vegetables.

"You can really just relax now," she said as she shut the door. He was at the island, out of reach. "If I were here to kill you I'd have drowned you in that tub upstairs."

He looked at her incredulously. She stepped forward to hand him the bag. He snatched it and stepped back. "Who *are* you?" he asked as he swapped the cloth for the frozen bag.

"I've said I'm Tony's—"

"No, I—I got that." He waved the cloth in her direction. "Same style as him, you 'come over to talk' and I get beat up."

"I *am* here to talk, you just wouldn't—"

"You've said," he sighed, "as you cleaned my blood off the floor." He eyed her strangely, and she realized he was being funny. Was he just doing the same thing as her, or was her old trick working?

"I *am* sorry for your head."

"It would build trust if you'd give me my phone back."

She shook her head. His phone was wet in her sweaty palm. She was boiling with adrenaline. She wished she could take off the winter coat, but she didn't want to risk being seen without it. In the bathroom, Walker told her he thought she was a man when he first saw her in the kitchen. She knew the outfit was working to disguise her. It was just also cooking her to death.

"Let's go back upstairs," she said. "I'll explain everything."

"No, I'm staying right here."

She patted her pocket. "We'll need light to look at everything I brought."

"I'll turn on this light," he said as he leaned toward the wall at the end of the counter.

"No!" Julia lunged across the island and grabbed his wrist. "Someone will see."

"What?" he said as he shook his arm free. "What will they see?"

She took a deep breath and let it out. "I'm here to help you escape."

76

Good, sweet Julia. God forgive him, he'd judged her the second he crossed the threshold of that house. Doing the dishes, watching the children, round-faced, a picture of femininity. He'd judged her as good on nothing but his own ideas of what a woman like her should be.

She sat beside him now, looking just like she did the day he came to question them about Walker's disappearance: wide-eyed, stiff as a board with fingers that trembled. That first time, he'd mistaken it as fear about Tony: fear about what her husband might have done. Well, she'd fooled him. It made him feel pathetic. Would she have fooled O'Malley? No. O'Malley would have seen it. Everyone got the same messaging about men and women—what they're like, what they aren't. But O'Malley was from a younger generation. A generation that saw the world differently.

They'd been frantic to find Walker, and O'Malley had been busy putting in calls, so Rice had gone to the Hall house alone. If he'd brought O'Malley, she would have seen what Rice couldn't. Julia hadn't been frightened of what her husband might have done. It was guilt in her eyes. Guilt and self-preserving terror, just like now.

Rice leaned toward her. "Is this your invocation?"

Julia said nothing.

"Which are you trying to invoke, Julia? God, or your right to remain silent?"

Her eyes flicked in his direction. She scratched at her sleeve. The wind whistled at the window behind her, and she held her tongue.

77

At 7:00 p.m. on the day Raymond Walker would go missing, Julia sat with him on the floor of the living room, shielded from the window by the couch. Walker had taken the small lamp and set it on the floor, and its orange glow fell over the pages Julia had brought.

Already, Julia had gone over each sheet and talked him through his journey. They'd start by walking several streets over, to where she'd parked her car. She'd keep her hood up and her head down, and hopefully, like Walker had, anyone who saw her would think she was a man. Then Julia would drop him at the bus in Portland, which he'd take to Boston using a ticket under the name Steven Sanford. There was a small sum of cab money for him to get himself to the train station there, and he'd get on the train west with a ticket to Chicago, also purchased for Steven Sanford. His eyebrows had raised, impressed, when she explained he'd get off the train early in Toledo, Ohio, and use a third ticket bought under a different name to take a bus to Columbus.

"And your friend will pick me up there," he said as they talked through it again.

"Yes." She glanced at her phone. Still nothing from Tony; that meant he hadn't left Nick yet, but he'd be in the car within the hour.

"And her name is?"

Julia looked up from the phone. "I hadn't said. Elisa."

"Elisa what?"

She shook her head. "I'm not giving you that. Or your phone back, at all."

Ray was looking at the bank statement again now. Even as he'd looked back through the other sheets, he'd kept a tight grip on that one.

"Afraid I'll change my mind halfway to Toledo?"

"So you're going?" she asked.

His eyes narrowed. "What will you do if I say no?"

Her stomach clenched, but she forced a smile. "Nothing."

"And when I call the police?"

"No one will believe your victim's family tried to help you get away with it."

He smiled. "You think I'm guilty."

"I know you are."

"No one but Nick or I can *know* that. Actually, even Nick doesn't know, what with his *blackout*. Very convenient."

Julia wasn't going to dignify that with a response.

"I'm just curious," he said. "You think I'm guilty. So how do you feel about this?" He paused. "Letting me get away with it?"

He was picking at it—the scab that had formed over the questions she kept asking herself. If everything went perfectly: If Walker went, if she was never caught, if Tony and the kids were safe when this was over, what would it mean? What would she have done, on a grander scale? Would she be hurting Nick even more than Walker had already? More than he'd be hurt by news coverage of the case, the opinions of strangers on the internet, the gossip of his classmates, the system?

"I'd rather do something than nothing," she said at last. "Wouldn't you?"

Now Walker was silent.

"Do you really want to see if a jury believes you? Because if they don't, your life is over. I know you know that, because you can't seem to shut up about it. Have you thought about what happens if you're acquitted? You're not proved innocent, and nobody thinks you are. They just think you got away with it. Did you know Nick could still sue you? That you could be fired for this? That every time someone googles your name, for the rest of your life, the word *rape* is gonna come up?"

He looked back at the sheet in his hands.

"You're not fooling me," she said. "You feel just as trapped as I do."

Walker sifted through the papers between them to pull out the photocopy of the passport. Elisa had mailed Julia the photocopy and retained the actual passport. It belonged, apparently, to a man named Avery King.

"So your friend *Elisa* will give me the actual passport when she picks me up in Columbus," he said.

He was talking like he was going to go. Like she was right. He just didn't want to say it. Julia decided not to push him. "Right," she said.

Walker studied the photo. "He does look a lot like me. How'd she get this?"

"Didn't ask; don't wanna know." This had always been her approach to Elisa, including when Julia was representing Elisa's son, Mathis. Julia felt, then and now, that she was on the tip of the iceberg with that family, and she was terrified to duck beneath the water and open her eyes.

"Your friend sounds shady as shit," Walker said. "How do you even know someone like this?"

Julia shifted the cross of her legs. "I helped out her son, a long time ago."

"Avery King. I could get used to that name."

Julia smiled. "It is a great name."

"Much better than *Steve Sanford*," he said with a grimace. He picked up the fake ID from the floor. The picture was actually Walker's mug shot from his arrest. You'd never guess it without knowing: he looked calm, with the faintest crook of a smile. But Julia had recognized it from the paper instantly, when her package from Elisa arrived in the mail.

"When you meet Elisa, you become Avery. Steve's just a holdover until you get to her."

"Still," Walker said, and he smiled at her. She unpacked it in her mind: it was warm, teasing, genuine. He *was* starting to like her. Something deep inside her ached, and she spoke abruptly to break her train of thought.

"Are you with me?"

He looked back at the sheets in his hands. At the new life she was offering him.

He sighed. "Fuck it. Yeah."

The relief she felt at his words nearly overwhelmed her. "Okay," she breathed. "The last thing, then."

"Yeah?"

"Wait to call your mother."

His face went flat. He'd thought of it; why wouldn't he have? He could easily borrow a stranger's phone to make a call.

"It's in both of our best interests that your mother be genuinely unsure of what happened tonight," Julia said. "Whenever they figure out you're missing, they'll question her. Don't leave it to her acting skills—you need to make it to Elisa before they figure out that you left on your own."

Ray said nothing for a bit. Then he said, "That's actually a good point."

"I wouldn't want to leave my mom scared that something had happened to me," Julia said. "But I also wouldn't want to get her in trouble. And like I said, it'll help buy you time to get your money and get wherever you choose to go, before you tell her you're all right."

Ray nodded thoughtfully but said no more.

He looked around the living room. "Should we mess it up in here? Like a fight happened or something? So they go in the wrong direction, first?"

"No," Julia said quickly. "If we do a bad job of staging it, which I'm guessing we would, they'll suspect even faster that you're on the move."

Ray nodded slowly. "How long have you been planning this?"

In truth she wasn't sure—it had started subtly, like something she could see out of the corner of her eye that she didn't want to turn and look at too closely. The planning had been quick, but thinking about planning . . . that was harder to say. "I dunno. Long enough."

"You're a natural," he said.

She grimaced at him. "Really?"

"It's a compliment."

"Well, that makes me feel like a terrible person."

"I guess just get me to the bus, then, and you won't have to think of it again." He brought a hand to his chest. "I'll remember you fondly, though."

She grinned and pointed at the bank statement in his hand. "I'm sure you will!"

Terrible or not, Ray was right. She was good at this.

78

At 10:00 p.m. on the day Raymond Walker went missing, Tony pulled into the driveway behind Julia's car. From outside, he could see the living room bathed in that flickering, blue-white light. Maybe she'd fallen asleep in front of the TV.

He pulled his boots off in the mudroom and wandered toward the living room, through the kitchen and into the dining room. He jumped when he found her sitting at the table there, facing him.

"Christ, you scared me."

The look in her eye was familiar but hard to place. Her face was drained of color, and she shivered, then crossed her arms. She looked frozen.

"Were you outside?"

She shook her head.

"Are you okay?"

She didn't speak, and kept her eyes on the table before her.

"Honey," he said as he crossed the room to her. "You're scaring me."

She shivered again as he knelt beside her. He placed a hand on her thigh and rubbed up and down her leg.

There was a palpable electricity between them, and he knew she would speak if he waited.

Finally, without turning her eyes from the table, she did.

"Before I tell you what I've done, promise you'll forgive me."

79

Still, Julia had not spoken. Rice would have given anything to see inside her head. Was she running over what she knew—what she thought safe to reveal? Was she planning a lie? Maybe. It would sting to hear her lie to him now, even if he knew she was doing so for understandable reasons. But she owed him the truth. She owed him after what he'd done.

⌐

The last time John Rice had seen Julia Hall, she was in her backyard, bundled in winter clothes, watching her children play.

Rice could remember January 18, 2016, more vividly than he could remember dinnertime yesterday, it seemed.

It was afternoon and bitterly cold. The sky was saturated with color— yellow sun on bright blue. He'd driven out to the pastures of Orange and found the Hall house deserted. He drove farther up the lane and parked the unmarked car. The Hall house was small in his rearview; he could have plucked it from the mirror and crumbled it between his fingers. Eventually he saw Julia's red Subaru Baja—unforgettably ugly—grow from a speck on the country lane in his rearview. The car pulled into the Hall driveway and parked.

How his heart had pounded as he watched that car. He'd recognized it on the grainy security footage from the Portland bus depot instantly. Two days after Raymond Walker disappeared, Megan O'Malley had called Rice to Portland to view a recording of Walker walking up to the depot at 8:11 p.m. on Friday, the day before his mother reported him missing. The video quality was poor, but he'd come right to the edge of the building, and his face was unmistakable. Then he boarded the eight fifteen bus to Boston, and he was gone.

O'Malley had directed the depot worker to pull up the footage of the parking lot. The first of his sins, Rice had shaken his head when O'Malley asked if he recognized "the truck" that dropped off Walker at the very edge of the screen. Only a hint of the car was visible, and the bed made it look like a small red truck. A ubiquitous vehicle in Maine. But Rice knew better. It wasn't a small truck—it was a Subaru Baja.

Guilty people were always trying to convince him that strange coincidences had caused their DNA to be at a crime scene, or stolen property to end up in their garage, or their make and model to happen to be the same as the getaway car. This was no coincidence: a Hall had driven Walker up to the bus station in Portland the night he disappeared, and Tony Hall was accounted for.

Watching her driveway three years ago, Rice had stared at that stupid car, waiting to see her face. He had been sure she'd done it to stop her husband from killing Walker. To keep her perfect life from collapsing with her husband's crime and inevitable arrest. Rice had craned in his seat, heart pounding in his neck, and strained to see her face. The face he had once compared to Irene's. She would look different to him now: selfish and vain, nothing like Irene. Nothing like who he made her out to be.

After a moment there was movement at the car, and the little girl climbed out on the passenger side. She ran ahead, and then Julia appeared in front of the car, walking toward the house. She was carrying two large totes of groceries, the little boy trailing after her. Rice had been too far away to be sure, but they looked like they were speaking. Her son had run past her, his smile wide enough to see from the street, and toward the yard behind the house. Julia had followed him, out of view. Slowly, Rice backed up until he was across from their driveway. Julia stood at the cedar fence, her back to the street. Her children ran in the yard, and she watched them. She'd put the groceries down at her feet, and one had tipped over, spilling groceries into the snow. She didn't care. She just wanted to watch her children.

In that moment, a realization washed over him slow and warm, like sinking into bathwater. He knew what she had done, but he had been wrong about why.

She'd saved her children from losing their father. She'd saved her husband from becoming a murderer. And she'd saved Ray Walker's life. Maybe she hadn't cared so much about that, but the purity of it all was overwhelming him. She had saved Walker's life. Not a good man, but a man nonetheless. Julia held the fence now and tilted her head down. Rice imagined what she might look like if he were facing her from the yard. A single tendril of her hair loose from her hat. Tears in her eyes, lips trembling in a smile. Overcome with joy, watching her children play and knowing they would be safe, knowing they would have their parents. Knowing she had committed a lesser sin only to halt a greater one.

Rice had watched her a moment longer, then put the car into drive. He'd driven down the country lane until it met an outlet, through the town center, onto the highway, and back to the station. And then he went inside, and he sat at his desk, and he said nothing.

Over the following months he and O'Malley had worked off of the 8:15 p.m. passenger list, trying to trace Walker's journey. The "truck's" license plate was only partially captured and totally indiscernible, so chasing Walker himself was the only option. The security footage confirmed that Walker had shown an ID to board the bus, and his real name was absent from the passenger list, so they meticulously moved through the names that had prepurchased tickets. They ran criminal and driving histories, searched social media, and compared pictures of the male passengers against the surveillance footage. It was slow going, and they were too bogged down with other work to make fast progress, but O'Malley was tenacious. She worked from a place of hell-bent rage that Walker had evaded justice and would move on to new victims. For his part, Rice worked alongside her, treating the horrific guilt he felt as penance for his sin. But he felt he, like Julia, had chosen the lesser of two evils.

They'd enlisted the help of the local FBI, in theory, but it was O'Malley who determined that Raymond Walker was the passenger listed as "Steven Sanford," and that "Steven Sanford" had also bought a train ticket from Boston to Chicago. The tickets were bought with stolen credit card information from the dark web, the federal agent told them. That was the sum total of his help.

As best they could tell, Walker never made it to Chicago. Where he'd gotten off early they never determined.

When the news broke that Walker had fled, Britny Cressey stepped into the light she'd been waiting for. She gave interviews to the local stations and papers, detailing what she'd learned from Walker before his flight. She was quick to qualify that she knew nothing about the escape itself or how he planned it. He'd never mentioned it to her, she said, but he had talked at length about the court process, the money he owed, the dread he felt that the game was rigged against him.

Eventually the story of the man who evaded his justice grew stale, and the news coverage stopped, and life moved on without Raymond Walker.

And then a month after Walker ran, Rice got a call from Linda Davis.

Nick Hall had called her and asked her to dismiss the case against Raymond Walker.

"He says he wants to just move on," she said. "He really didn't want to get into it. But he wanted us to know something: he was awake during Walker's assault."

Rice had been stunned.

"I know," Linda said. "He sounds like he wants to just move on from the whole thing. I can't say I blame him."

He'd been awake. Rice thought of O'Malley's work early on the case, about serial rapists. There was a second type of sadist that they'd ruled out initially: the type of person who didn't hurt their victims for the fun of it, but who fantasized about it. Maybe Walker was that type. Maybe he'd never had a victim fight back as hard as Nick, and it woke something up in him. Maybe that was why they never found anyone before Nick. He wasn't the first—he was just the first Walker had left unable to hide the violence that was done to him.

⌒

The silence had stretched on long enough.

"Julia," he said. "Say something."

80

JULIA HALL, 2019

He knew what happened. He'd always wondered if Julia realized it, too. He was saying he thought she might have known that *he* knew what she had done—of course not. She'd have lost her mind. He knew what she did. He knew? How? He'd always known. Why tell her now if not then? Why didn't he arrest her? What had she thought would happen? She would go to prison now. The kids—oh Christ, the kids. What did he want? What could she do? Julia's mind was barraged with thoughts, and she'd failed to piece together a coherent sentence when the dying detective spoke again.

"Julia. Say something." He sounded exhausted, like she was a child who wouldn't stop getting out of bed at night.

In all her years as a defender, she'd never met anyone guilty of a crime who was glad he spoke to the police, even to deny it or offer explanation. But then, a defense attorney wouldn't meet someone who successfully misled the police, would she? And her silence was damning. When she spoke her voice was miniscule.

"I don't know what you mean, about whatever happened."

She should have kept her mouth shut.

Detective Rice leaned back into his chair, and it squeaked under him.

He was calmer than she would have imagined, if this was a prelude to her arrest. If this wasn't a conversation but an interrogation. But then, what did she know of his self-control?

"You know," he said, "that depot's security cameras captured cars out by the road."

Shit. Her eyes went wider. *Oh, shit shit shit.* She'd thought of it just after, and a million times since, but no one had come asking questions. She should have called him a cab, or dropped him even farther away, but she had to see him get on that bus.

"I know it was you that dropped off Walker in Portland," the detective went on. "There weren't a lot of people driving those ugly Bajas." He laughed as he said the sentence, and when he finished, he was coughing hard. He reached for the mask at his side.

It gave her time to think. Why was he doing this? It had to be a trap. Without moving her head, her eyes scanned the room: no blinking light, no obvious recording devices. That recorder he used to use was so small, though; it could have been under her chair. Had he chosen her seat for her? Yes, he'd definitely told her to sit in this one . . . she'd gone for the other.

Julia drew a quiet, shaky breath and expelled it. If she didn't calm down she was going to have a panic attack. She breathed in. *Calm down.* She breathed out. *Calm down.* Detective Rice was reholstering his mask to the tank. He'd known for three years. Maybe this wasn't him coming after her, maybe it was something else. Because why now? Had something new happened?

Did they find Walker?

At the thought, the room began pressing in from all sides; an electronic hum rang in her ears. The light began to dim, and Julia felt the urge to tip forward to her knees. She did, and Detective Rice's voice was far away behind the hum.

She scooted backward against her chair and put her head between her knees. With each breath, the hum quieted and the rush of panic softened. When she opened her eyes, the room was light again.

"Julia." His warm hand was on her shoulder. "Julia."

She looked back at him then turned forward again. "Sorry."

"You all right?"

Julia nodded.

"Was that a panic attack?"

She nodded again. There was nothing to say. Her body had betrayed her guilt.

"Julia, I'm not—I didn't ask you here to arrest you or interrogate you. I've done this all wrong." He seemed to say the last bit more to himself than to her. "Please, sit so I can see you?"

On leaden legs, Julia pushed herself back up into the armchair.

"I'm not trying to scare you. Or, well . . ." He shook his head. "I dunno. Maybe I was."

She glanced at him sideways, then turned to him fully. His face was apologetic, and maybe something else.

"No one else knows," he said quietly.

"You said my car was on camera."

The detective smiled. "It looked like a truck. It was never identified as yours, not officially." He paused. "But I knew."

When Julia didn't speak, he went on. "I'm moving to hospice next week, and I didn't want to do this there. And, well, I don't want to die without having the conversation at all."

"Okay," she said quietly.

"I do think I get why you helped him run away. I didn't at first, and I meant to come out with it—expose what you'd done—but I wanted to talk to you before that. And then I went to see you, at your house. I saw you playing with the kids outside, and suddenly I understood."

"Understood?"

"That you did it for them. For your kids, and for him—for Tony. You thought he'd kill him."

She almost nodded.

"So you saved him instead."

Her eyes welled, and a heavy tear rolled down her cheek.

"You are so good," he said quietly. "It was always so clear about you. I was so angry when I saw your car on that tape. I felt like you'd betrayed *me*, isn't that strange? I wanted to scream at you, understand why you weren't who I thought you were. I drove to your house. Did you know that?"

She shook her head. She hadn't known. She couldn't even place the day.

"I was ready to rumble," he said with a laugh. "My mother would have called me *spittin' mad*. But then I saw you, in the yard with your kids. And it just hit me that I was wrong. I did know you. You *were* good. It was the only thing you knew to do."

The detective was looking at her with such tenderness that it seemed impossible he could be faking it.

"You sent him away," he said.

More tears slid down her cheeks. She still got upset sometimes, when she thought about what she did and how terrified she had been afterward.

Detective Rice had known all along. All the times she made herself sick wondering what would happen if he found out, he already knew.

"Was Tony angry with you?"

She was so tired.

Just a single word. It wasn't a confession.

"No," she said.

81

Sometime after 10:00 p.m. on the day Raymond Walker went missing, Tony held very still at Julia's side, his hand frozen on her thigh, while she told him what she had done.

When she was finished, Tony laid his head down on her lap. He only had a single thought: the only way forward was to tell her the truth.

"Jules."

"Do you hate me?"

"Jules, I changed my mind."

Her eyes went wide. "What?"

He told her everything that Nick had said. That Nick wanted to go through with the trial. That Nick needed him to stop trying to fix everything. That sitting in the visiting room at Goodspring, Tony changed his mind.

"Okay," Julia said. "Okay. Okay. Okay." Her mouth was a record, skipping on the word.

"We'll figure it out," Tony said quickly. He didn't have a clue how; he just wanted to take away whatever she was feeling.

"Okay," she said again. "I'll just call Elisa. I'll tell her to send him back."

"He's not gonna come back."

"She has everything he needs: the money, the passport. If she won't give it to him, he'll have to."

"Or he'll turn on you." Look what he'd done. Look what he'd fucking done.

"That was always a risk I was taking. We'll just have to deal with it."

"How?"

"I'll deny whatever he says. It'll get messy, but it already is. We have to get him back."

Tony stood. "Honey, the exact thing you were trying to protect the kids from could happen. You could get caught." His voice broke, and he finished in a whisper. "You could go to prison. Who knows how they'd punish this?"

Julia stood from the table and took his hands. "Take a breath. We'll figure it out."

"What if the police connect the tickets to the woman, Elisa," Tony said.

"They can't," Julia said. "And even if they did, she won't give them anything."

Tony spoke slowly. "Why blow it all up?"

"I've taken the one thing Nick had left."

"You didn't do that. I did."

"What if he doesn't forgive you? After everything he just told you."

She was right. Nick would have every reason to blame this on him—it was all his fault. But he would have to live with that.

"They'll figure out Walker got on a bus," Julia said. "It might take them a bit, but they'll have to figure that out."

"I think so," Tony said.

"So Nick will think he ran, too."

"Right," Tony said. "You're right."

"But what will he do? What will Nick do if he can't have a trial?"

"I don't know. But I don't think that's for us to figure out."

He walked around Julia and pulled out a chair. She sat back down beside him.

He leaned his elbows on the table and rested his chin in his hands. "I'm sorry I went so far away from you."

Julia pulled her chair closer to his. "It wasn't just you. I couldn't even see I was doing the same thing. If I'd just told you . . . we should have been doing it together."

They sat at the table talking it through. There was no way to unwind what was set in motion. The damage was already done. So they decided, together, to let Walker go.

82

A month after Raymond Walker disappeared, Nick sat on a couch across from his counselor. Not at a hospital, not at a program, but at an office in Wells.

"So, how are you doing?"

Today Jeff's sweater was navy blue with a fisherman-style knit. He started the session with the same question he always did.

Nick sat forward on the couch. "I actually wanted to ask you that."

"I'm doing fine."

"No." Nick laughed. "I mean, how do you think I'm doing?"

"Mm," Jeff said. "I don't like this game."

"I know how I feel. I know I'm not gonna just be 'better' or 'fixed,' but what's my prognosis?"

Jeff raised a salt-and-pepper eyebrow. "Prognosis?"

"You must have it written down somewhere. Or you have one in your head."

Jeff fiddled with the band of his silver wristwatch.

"When will I sleep normal? I mean, am I ever gonna go home with a guy I like again?"

Jeff smiled. "Your prognosis is good, Nick."

Nick leaned back into the couch. Jeff might have been humoring him, but he didn't care.

"When we look at the data, you have some factors working in your favor toward a good outcome. But you know I'm not only about that. This right here is the most important piece, and it's also the only one you have in your control. Keep putting in the work, and your prognosis is real good."

It was like a knot in Nick's stomach untied itself. A feeling of comfort spread through his body as he listened to Jeff's voice.

"We can keep working through what happened with Ray, the stories you tell yourself about what the assault meant. How those stories have been scripted by your society, your father, even your brother. And we can work on integrating your identity—who you are as a man—with this one thing that happened to you. And eventually, it's going to get better. There isn't gonna be a last day you *ever* have any symptoms. I still have nightmares about my abuse, and I'm old as dirt. But it *will* get better. And how you see yourself, how you see other people, romantic relationships—all that looks good to me."

"Cool," Nick said. Sometimes he didn't have the words to match how he felt when he met with Jeff. The future Jeff had just imagined for him was everything he wanted. But what it would take to get there—reliving that night, saying out loud the worst things he thought about himself, airing every stupid thing he had ever heard about what it meant to be dominated by someone else—it would be brutal. But he would do whatever it took to get to the future Jeff thought he could have.

"Any updates on court?"

"Yeah, actually. I've decided to dismiss the case."

"Really? Why?"

It happened last week, after Nick had moved home from Goodspring. At first, when Ray went missing, Nick couldn't stop thinking that Tony had done something stupid. Worse than stupid. He knew from Julia that the police had gone to interview his brother, and she seemed worried. But then the ADA herself called Nick: Ray had gotten on a bus to Boston. The coward had run away. Their next court date was in March, Linda said. She wasn't sure if the judge would let her go forward with a trial if Ray hadn't been found by then, but she wanted to try. Nick decided not to tell her the truth about his testimony just yet. It sounded like he had some time to think about it.

Then last week Julia came to his apartment.

It was snowing softly, and the city hadn't plowed Spring Street. They trudged down it anyway.

Ray didn't jump bail alone, she told him. She, Nick's sister-in-law, had helped his rapist escape.

Nick was stunned. It sounded like a joke without a punchline.

"I need you to know," she said, "you changed his mind. It was just too late."

"Ray?"

Julia shook her head. "Tony." The realization dawned on Nick as she went on. She didn't even need to say it. "I thought he was going to kill him."

Tony had said so himself, when Nick told him that he'd been awake during the assault. Tony kept saying he was going to kill Ray.

"I swear, Nick, you changed his mind. He came to see you at Goodspring and he came home, and he told me he wasn't going to do it anymore." She looked at Nick miserably. "But it was too late. I sent Walker away while Tony was with you."

Another piece clicked into place. "I thought you sent him to Goodspring because you didn't want to deal with his reaction when he found out the case hadn't settled. But it wasn't that. I was his alibi."

Julia nodded. "Just in case something went wrong."

They had stopped walking at the end of Spring Street. They stood in the falling snow in silence for a moment.

"Why are you telling me?"

Julia wiped her nose with the backside of her mitten. "Because I have a favor to ask."

Julia told Nick what she feared might happen if Nick went forward with the case and a judge let him have a trial without Ray: in short, it would be a media circus. The press had been all over Nick's case to begin with—a fugitive rapist being tried by the man he assaulted? That could make national news. And national news might mean someone, even in another state, making a phone call about a man they saw. National coverage could mean Ray's discovery, and therefore Julia's.

Julia's eyes were tired, and the snow had collected on her cap. "I don't deserve to ask a single thing of you."

"That's not true."

"It is, after what I took from you." She shook her head. "But I'm still asking."

"Oh," Nick said quietly. She wanted him to dismiss the case. Of course he would, if the case could get Julia caught. It was just . . . Ray. "What if he hurts someone else?"

"Nick?" Jeff's voice pulled Nick out of the snowy memory.

"Sorry, yeah?"

"Why are you dismissing the case?"

Nick took a deep breath. "Can I be honest?"

"Of course."

No telling lies this time, or partial truths. "The truth is, I really don't feel like talking about it."

Jeff's face broke into a smile. "Okay. It's your session."

Nick breathed out hard. That felt good.

"So what do you want to work on today?"

Right. His session, his choice. Maybe one day, Nick would tell Jeff why he made up his mind to dismiss the case, what Julia told him. Maybe not. Nick got to decide.

83

Julia felt hollowed out. Her mind was limping along, trying to keep up with where he'd taken her. Detective Rice seemed so genuine; it all felt real. And besides, he already knew it was her. If he wanted to turn her in, what did it matter if she talked or not? She might as well tell him the kicker.

"When I told him Walker was gone, Tony was heartbroken. Not because he couldn't kill him, but because he'd changed his mind."

The detective shook his head. "No."

She nodded. "Nick really wanted to have the trial. And Tony didn't want to take that from him."

"Then why did Nick ask Linda to dismiss the case? We could have tried to push forward, without Walker. It's not unheard of. His trial hadn't started, the court might not have let us. But Nick told Linda he didn't want to try. He told her the truth about his statement, but he didn't want to go forward. I just don't understand. I know he would have suffered more press at a trial, but he might have earned a symbolic victory, at least."

"Yes," Julia said slowly. "He might have won that. But the whole thing looped back on itself."

"What do you mean?"

Julia smiled. "He dismissed it to keep me safe."

A month after Walker left, Julia told Nick everything. The *whole* truth.

"If the court actually held a trial, it probably would have become a national spectacle—a male victim, a trial in absentia, a fugitive. And that kind of coverage . . ."

"It could have hurt Nick even more."

"No. Well, yes, absolutely. But I was being selfish. I wanted Nick to dismiss the case for me. I didn't want someone to see the coverage and piece something together that would get me into trouble."

"Oh," Rice said.

"Or for Walker to see it," she added. "And decide to come back."

"So Nick did it for you."

"And Tony," she said. "I felt awful about everything, but it actually seemed to be just what he needed. It, like, reset a balance between him and Tony. Nick dismissed the case, the news died down, and I was safe."

Rice was quiet for a bit.

"You said there was something else?"

"I've never been a perfect Catholic," he said slowly. "I've sinned a lot in my life, and I've always confessed it. But this time, it took me a long time to confess what I did. That I let a defendant get away by sitting on the only lead: that my victim's sister-in-law had helped him." He shook his head. "I almost went down to Boston to make the confession, to a different church. I was so ashamed to tell my own priest. I knew he'd lose respect for me. He'd deny it if you asked him, but how could he not?

"But I decided, fuck my pride, I didn't deserve to be proud. I confessed in my church. At first I felt better, then one day I started to feel it again: an itch in my stomach, like something needing to be let out. So I confessed again. It went away, then came back.

"And then the cancer. And now I'm dying. This spring might be my last Easter, if the docs are right. And I keep feeling this need to confess a sin. And I finally realized, it's because my sin continues. My sin is my silence. I'm a Catholic, but I'm a cop, too. I swore an oath, and I broke it, and I break it every day that I don't turn myself in.

"I've confessed my sins to God but I don't know if he'll save me, because every time I step out of confession, I'm already sinning again. Unless I die in that booth, I'll die sinning."

Julia felt stunned. "You don't think God would punish you for a single thing you did, just one single thing, do you?"

"I dunno. A younger, more romantic me might agree with you, but it feels different once you see the X-rays, these impossible shapes in your body, once you're calling the lady who did your will twenty years ago." Rice shook his head. "I hope—in my heart, I believe he'll forgive me. God is just and merciful. He gets to choose. I was always just. That was my job: uphold the law, let God worry about mercy. I let people off every now and then, but not like this. Real crime, I always met with justice. Only once did I choose mercy."

This was why she was here.

"You're going to turn me in."

He looked at her with surprise. "I can't."

"Oh. Why not?"

"It would undo everything else I've ever done. It would be just like these DNA scandals. Something as big as this—letting a woman, the family of a victim, collude with a defendant to escape . . . every case I ever worked on would be in post-conviction review. Every imperfect justice I ever achieved for other victims would be threatened. Every family that found some little bit of peace would lose it."

"I'm so sorry. I had no idea what I did to you. I'm so sorry."

"Don't be. Just tell me it was worth it."

"What?"

"Tell me what good it did, so if I go to hell at least I'll have something to smile about."

"Oh." She laughed, a snotty burst of air, and she wiped her nose with her sleeves.

The detective's arms were crossed over his stomach, and his shoulders sank away from his neck. He'd never looked smaller, sicker, sadder. But hopeful, that's what it was—his eyes brimmed over with desperate hope. Hope for what she might give him. Hope for solace. Just like Tony had trapped her, she'd unwittingly done the same to this man. And they'd each made their choice. All these years, he'd been her silent partner in crime.

She told him what their crime had bought. Told him about Chloe, who was now ten and precocious as ever. In the last few months she'd become utterly dedicated to learning karate, and she was hoping to earn her yellow belt that spring. Told him that Seb, at eight, had discovered a phenomenon on YouTube where people would film themselves making and manipulating slime, and he watched these videos religiously. Tony had tried to channel this obsession of his into a broader interest in science, but he'd recently remarked with grave defeat that Seb truly only cared about slime. (The detective laughed at this and took another hit of his oxygen for it.) Speaking of Tony, Julia told Detective Rice, he and she had celebrated their twelfth wedding anniversary at the New Year. In the wake of what she'd done, they had turned toward each other, and their bond felt even stronger now than it had when they were young and stupidly in love. And finally, she told the detective about Nick. He was twenty-three now, and as funny as he'd ever been. He moved to Boston after graduation and was working in advertising. Last Christmas, he came home with a boyfriend they'd all liked very much.

"So you think we did the right thing?"

She shifted in her seat. "I don't know if we'll ever know that. Or I guess, maybe you'll know before me." She pointed at the ground, and he laughed. Suddenly it was hilarious, the idea of them going to hell together.

"I'd have done it differently," she said. "If I knew what would happen that day. But I didn't know."

He was silent. He wanted more from her. He'd never talked about it, it sounded, with anyone but his priest. She was tiring, but she could go a little longer.

"For a long time I felt—*wrecked* isn't the right word, it was worse than that. At first I held it together, because Tony was a mess, but eventually he kind of calmed down, and then I fell apart. I didn't know myself. I felt untethered from myself. And like a terrible, terrible person. At first it felt like what I'd done had changed me, and then I realized maybe I'd never even known myself, my whole life. And I felt stupid, so stupid. When all the stress of what had been happening was gone, I could see options I hadn't thought of. Maybe I could have had Tony hospitalized. It's not a crime to *want* to kill someone. If I'd acted quickly, ah. I don't know. I could have hobbled him like in *Misery*."

Rice choked on a laugh.

Julia felt herself smile. "Trapped him in the house." Then she grew serious again. "I could have told you. That was a big one. I could have stopped him by telling you. And that one I didn't miss. I'd thought of it before I . . . sent Walker away. But I didn't know what you'd do with it. Would you have arrested him? I thought if I told you, I'd lose him, and the kids would lose him, and Nick. So instead I sent Walker away. I got what I wanted—Tony couldn't get at him anymore, Tony couldn't get himself in trouble—but I didn't like what I'd done. So I was a mess for a bit. But Tony took care of me, and I think the kids missed most of it, or I tell myself they did, and eventually I started boxing it away again."

Their eye contact was unbroken. It was deeply intimate, almost uncomfortable, but it made it feel true, and she wanted to give him this truth, even if she couldn't give him all of it.

She went on. "I figured out that I'd never know if I did the right thing. I know I did a bad thing. But can't it be more complicated than that? I think so. And I started to accept that. And when . . . what I'd done would start to creep in, or more like just blast into my head, and I felt horrible, or I was just absolutely sick with fear I'd be caught and go to jail and put my kids through just what I was trying to, you know, avoid happening with Tony—"

She reached her hand across the space between them and rested it on his arm. He was thin under his sweater, and she squeezed his arm gently.

"I would take a breath, look at the kids, look at Tony, look at Nick. They were the best answer I was ever going to get—to the question, did I do the right thing."

Detective Rice's eyes had welled over. Was it relief or disappointment?

"That's kinda what I figured, too," he said.

He frowned. "Did you ever hear from . . . ?"

"No." She shook her head. "Never."

"I wonder if he left the country."

Julia's eyebrows began to rise on their own, and she pushed them higher to match her sensitive tone. "Maybe."

"He just didn't seem like the type to stop hurting people, or even just attention-seeking all the time, and for nothing to ever turn up. Someone who does something like that, I don't think they just do it once. I always figured he'd get caught somewhere else, or we'd hear about his DNA matching a new crime. He must have gotten himself out of the country."

Julia said nothing for a moment. Could she give him—did she owe him—solace here? She thought of the day Rice had called Tony and warned him off of threatening Ray Walker again. "I'm not a big fan of the *Boondock Saints*," the detective had said.

She wiggled the hand that was on his arm. "You're thinking about the wrong things if you want to make peace."

He nodded.

"For what it's worth," she said, "he did know how close he'd come to losing everything. He knew this was his chance for a fresh start."

"Do you really think someone like him is capable of change?"

And there it was. The question that had bothered her most over the years. "What he did to your brother-in-law," Charlie Lee had said to her, "there must be others out there. Just hard to find them." Charlie's inability to find other victims—maybe there was a boy in Providence. Maybe not. Julia would never know if Walker had hurt others. One day, she would grow old or sick like the detective, or she would meet her end some other way, and she would die never knowing if Raymond Walker was the monster her family thought he was. She could lull the question to sleep again, but it would always be there, ready to crack an eye and ask: Just how bad was he, Julia?

"I'd lose my mind if I thought about him," she said truthfully. "That's why I focus on my family until I can get my brain to move on to the next thing."

Detective Rice sighed heavily. "I feel like an elephant just got off my chest."

She laughed and gave his arm a final squeeze. "I owed you. I had no idea what I owed you."

He shrugged. "Well, it was nothing."

"No, it wasn't." She shook her head. "It was everything."

They sat in silence together as the wind hit the window again. She looked at her watch, not that the time mattered—she was ready to leave. "I'm so sorry, but I need to get going. I really don't like driving in the snow after it gets dark if I can help it."

"Of course," he said, and he began making the motions of standing up. Julia stood and gave him a hand.

Detective Rice walked her down the narrow hall, back to the entryway. Julia sat on the bench to pull on her boots.

"Do you garden?" She nodded to the bookshelf.

"Oh, yes," he said with a grin. "It was always a hobby, but after I retired it was really what got me up and going most days. Maybe, well, if by some miracle I'm still kicking this spring, I'd love you to come see me again, wherever I am, if I'm well enough to grow anything."

Julia gave him her warmest smile as she stood from the bench. "I'd love to." An overt lie. She didn't think she could stomach another meeting with the detective. But there was no good in telling him that, especially if he'd likely be dead before he'd have reason to know.

She *would* go to his funeral. She owed him that.

Julia embraced Detective Rice goodbye and stepped out onto the porch. She turned to shut the door, but he was already pushing it closed behind her. He waved through the small window beside the door, and she waved a mittened hand back.

Overt or not, to lie to a man on his deathbed seemed especially sinful. But it was kinder than telling him the truth.

84

ELISA LARIVIERE, 2016

It was half past midnight on the day after Raymond Walker disappeared, and Elisa Lariviere was early. She preferred it that way, especially when there was nothing noteworthy about a car waiting around a place like this. She backed into a spot at the far end of the lot with the front end of her Gran Coupe facing the building. She'd left her home in Michigan three hours ago to make her way there, to the bus terminal in Columbus.

The night was frigid, and she left the engine running. The brutal Ohio wind outside gave the impression of heavy snowfall, but in truth it was only a light flurry. Still, she'd have traded her weather at home for this without hesitation. After living in Boston for more than two decades, Elisa thought she would be comfortable with winters in Michigan, but she'd been mistaken. Winter on the lake was longer, darker, and wetter than in New England. For tonight's purposes, of course, Michigan's climate would have certain advantages.

A song began to play softly from the public radio station she had on low volume. She hadn't been listening to the disc jockey—perhaps he'd said something about this being a fitting song for a late Friday night?—but the tune was immediately familiar. Softly twanging, a guitar picked out the melody and Elisa's chest swelled with bittersweetness. A man began singing, and Elisa only had to wait a breath for the famous line: "Whack for the daddy-o / there's whiskey in the jar." The song aligned with the memory, and Elisa smiled at the coincidence.

She'd heard the old Irish song in a movie a year ago. The movie was *Conviction*; it was the true story of a woman who went to law school and dedicated her life to exonerating her brother. It had been a quiet movie—Elisa had watched it at home one night, years after its uneventful release. The story was a slow burner, and it had scorched her. Her son Mathis's own legal case came to mind early on as she watched, and although the comparisons between the two cases were few, the themes of justice, vigorous defense, and family rang true.

Helpless as she felt in the wake of her son's arrest in early 2005, Elisa had been obsessed with ensuring Mathis had a zealous advocate, and that was precisely what he had gotten, in the most unexpected package. Elisa had hired Clifton Cook—Maine's answer to the proverbial eight-hundred-pound gorilla—and her gorilla had gone and hired a capuchin named Julia Hall. Elisa had been deeply disappointed with frizzy-haired, baby-faced Julia on sight. She chuckled now when she thought back on her first interactions with Julia, who'd smiled too much, espoused the values of cooperation with the prosecution, and recommended numerous social services for Mathis.

"She's not a lawyer—she's a social worker," Elisa had guffawed into the phone from the stark white kitchen of her Boston high-rise.

Her boy's voice answered from the detention center. "Clifton says juvenile court is complicated and we need her. She's nice, Maman."

Elisa rolled her eyes at Mathis's words. "And *cute*."

"Not even," he lied.

The snow began to build up on Elisa's windshield, and she activated her wipers. She checked the time. Ten minutes.

Mathis had been a fool to have even such a small quantity of cocaine in the car with him, especially while he crossed state lines as he drove to see friends in Maine. And the gun—Elisa had nearly crumbled when she learned he'd been caught with a gun. Against all odds, though, it was clean. Elisa had gone to see him at the detention center. They'd sat at a long table in a sterile room and they'd whispered to each other as they played rounds of Old Maid, an insufferably simple card game available at the facility. She'd shredded him with her words, then given him the story he needed to tell the lawyers.

There had been quiet work done in other places, of course, but over the year that Mathis's case worked its way through Maine's juvenile court, Elisa had watched Julia put in late nights and long hours for Mathis. Each time they returned to court, Elisa listened to Clifton update the judge about how Mathis was participating in the services Julia had arranged. Julia would sit with Elisa, uninterested in credit for what she'd done.

"He's doing really well," Julia said quietly at their last court date. "He's earned such a good resolution to his case."

Elisa leaned toward her. "Don't discount your part in this." In the beginning, Elisa hadn't trusted Julia's insistence on playing by the rules. But Julia's method had worked.

"I'm not," Julia said, "but he's worked really hard. He deserves what he's getting today." Julia paused. "He feels a lot of pressure."

Elisa glanced at her sideways. Julia's eyes remained straight forward.

Then she said, "I hope he has the freedom to figure out who he is and what he wants in life."

Elisa said nothing.

In the hallway, Mathis had embraced Julia goodbye. Call with any questions, Julia told him. When Mathis turned to Clifton, Elisa took Julia lightly by the arm and walked her aside. She had a few things to say.

She'd thought about Julia a fair amount over the past year, after watching the story of the lawyer who exonerated her own brother. The night Elisa finished the movie, she'd had a near-overwhelming urge to try Julia's old number, but she refrained. The next morning she'd googled Julia, and Elisa was disappointed to see that she appeared not to be lawyering any longer. It had seemed strange, almost serendipitous, when Julia called such a brief time thereafter.

Earlier that month, Elisa had left the hairdresser to find a voice mail on her cell. It was Julia Hall, rambling and nervous, saying nothing of substance.

Elisa had returned the phone call the same day she received the message, but later from the comfort of her sunroom. It had been a dreary winter day on the lake; the rain ran slow down the large panel window behind her, and beyond that was only gray and mist. Elisa sat by the small woodstove and made the call.

Julia had seemed distracted when she answered. She reacted slowly to Elisa's greeting and seemed to be moving away from someone. Elisa heard a door shut, and the quality of Julia's voice changed—her speech was freer.

"Thanks for calling back," Julia said.

"It's no problem. I'm pleased to be calling you."

"You've moved quite far from Boston!"

"I am a lady of the lake now." Elisa waved her hand for the benefit of an audience that wasn't there.

"How are the winters in Michigan?"

"They're shit. Did you really call to ask about the weather?"

"No, and I see you're direct as ever."

Elisa could hear the smile in Julia's voice, but she knew she'd sent her squirming.

"Out with it, kid." Elisa smiled back.

The silence was too long.

"Is everything all right, Julia?"

Julia's voice was quiet. "No."

Julia told her about a man, Raymond Walker, and what he'd done to her brother-in-law. She told Elisa about the press, the boy's problems, the unprecedented tension in her marriage.

"I'm sorry to hear all that. Truly," Elisa said. Still, it was strange. She doubted a woman like Julia had some dearth of close, female confidants to air her problems to.

After a long pause, Julia said in a low voice, "I think my husband is going to do something."

"Something?"

"Something I'll never be able to undo."

Elisa weighed Julia's words. "I'm not sure I blame him. Did you think I would?" She passed her hand through the steady rush of steam escaping the cup of tea on her armrest. Remembered the conversation they had in Julia's office one night. Remembered Mathis's anxious confession about the family history he gave his pretty lawyer. "I know the things Mathis told you."

"I know," Julia said. "Tony can't do this."

Elisa dropped her hand away from her cup. So there it was.

"And I can, is that it?"

"I was thinking I could convince him—Walker—to leave. Even setting Tony aside, he has to know he'll go to prison for years, decades maybe. He must have thought of running, but he'd have no help, no money, but if I helped him, I think I could convince him to leave." Her voice dropped away, like words falling off a cliff. "Just go, forever."

"This man will just go away. Forever," Elisa repeated.

"Maybe, if I got it—"

"This man who is obsessed with the spotlight."

"If I—"

"This sadist, you'll set him free. And he'll fade into oblivion, permanently and willingly—never to come calling on you for more."

At that Julia said nothing. Good. She was too intelligent to play stupid like this, and with Elisa of all people.

"So, what, you'd like me to rent him a room on the lake? Help him find a job? Apply for a passport?"

Still nothing.

"I'm happy to keep patronizing you if it makes you feel better, but we both know why you called me."

At that, Julia spoke.

"If—" She said the word and stopped. An exhale against the mouthpiece. "If I wanted your help . . . that kind of help."

"I meant what I said, the day you left my life. You saved my son—my very favorite son, at that."

A breathy laugh, like relief.

"I assume you have children now, you always loved them so. You know. You saved my child, and I would do anything for you. I'm guessing you thought then that you would never want anything from someone like me."

The inhale that shook through the phone was distinctly marred by tears. Perhaps of resignation, perhaps of relief. "Yes."

Elisa brought her finger back to her mug and trailed it along the rim. "It's easy to be good when things are good."

Julia said nothing.

The woodstove was pleasant, but the cold was radiating in on Elisa's back from the window behind her. She shifted in her chair to pull her feet up to rest before her, so that she looked out over her knees. Her joints protested and she slid her heels forward an inch.

"How much time do we have?"

"You mean, before Tony . . ."

"Yes."

"Not a lot. There's a court date on January twelfth. He promised me it won't be until after that. And if the case settles, that's it."

"That's it?"

"I won't need you," Julia said.

Elisa doubted that Julia could be so sure, but there was no point in saying as much. Elisa could begin preparing either way.

"But, assuming it doesn't settle so early in the process, I think I need it done that week."

"That is soon," Elisa said. "Do you really think you could convince this man to run? Temporarily, of course."

Julia cleared her throat. "Maybe, yeah. As worried as we've been about court, I've heard that he is, too. He's facing serious time, the sex-offender registry, all the stigma and trouble that comes with an allegation like this. I've heard he's starting to freak out about it, so if I could make the right promises . . . but I would need your help to make it look like I was offering him everything he could need to live as someone else."

"Passport, money."

"Right. And tickets to get out of Maine, without using his name."

"Why involve him in the equation at all? He could be dealt with in Maine."

"If something happens to him here, they'll still suspect Tony. Even if he has an alibi at the right time, obviously he could have hired someone."

Elisa chuckled. "Obvious enough to me." She continued tracing the rim of her teacup. "You need it to look like this man left on his own."

"Right," Julia said.

"Then, if you want *my kind of help*, send him to me."

"Right to you?"

"Not to my doorstep. A city nearby, in Michigan or Ohio. Don't send me driving all night. Tell him I'll pick him up and take him somewhere to lie low, as they say."

"And then?"

"And then you won't have your problem anymore. And this man will get what he deserves."

"I don't agree with that."

Elisa closed her eyes and exhaled a harsh laugh. "Are you so sure of that?"

Julia was silent for a moment longer.

Elisa might have registered this as weakness in someone else, and an obvious reason to hang up the phone. It was not weakness in Julia, though. She was at war within herself. The naive little house cat who believed in rules and order was being toppled by the puma who knew that some days, the only law is kill or be killed.

And she was an attorney. Thinking was her religion. She thought she could solve this like a logic puzzle, leaving her family intact and her morals unscathed. Julia did not understand what Elisa did: that all the thinking and weighing is meaningless, because in the end we are only as good as we are. And there are more important things than goodness.

"I'm not going to talk you into this," Elisa said. "You don't need my permission—you need your own. I'm not certain you have it yet."

"No," was all Julia said.

They spoke for a long while about what Julia believed she would need to get Raymond Walker on a bus out of town. She wanted counterfeit identification papers, travel tickets bought from untraceable accounts, the false promise of money waiting for Walker at the end of his journey, and, of course, the reality of an end to it all upon his arrival. And she wanted all of this from Elisa. Apparently Mathis had told Julia even more about his family than he'd been willing to admit to his mother.

Elisa sipped around the dregs of her tea as they sorted out the details of what Julia would need, and what Julia would do to get Raymond to Elisa. Julia occasionally interjected something like "if I even decide to do this," and Elisa would respond with a gentle "of course, of course." But she could feel her deciding.

Before they hung up, they agreed not to speak again by phone unless absolutely necessary—Julia had a clever explanation for their phone call, something to do with research for work related to her old cases, but it wouldn't explain multiple calls to the Midwest if her family fell under suspicion. Instead, Julia would send a postcard with the specifics Elisa needed to book the tickets, and only if Walker did not depart would Julia call Elisa again, to tell her that it was off.

In the days following their conversation, Elisa had put out calls in anticipation, collecting some of the pieces Julia would need. She only had to wait a week before the card came in the mail. It was postmarked Portland, Maine.

> *Dear Auntie Elisa,*
>
> *I'm excited to visit you this winter! I have quite a journey ahead of me. On Friday January 15 I'll be taking the 8:15 p.m. Concord Coach bus from Portland to Boston, then the 10:55 p.m. Amtrak train from the South Station to Toledo, though I think I might buy a ticket that could bring me all the way to Chicago, I've heard it's a lovely city. I'll arrive in Toledo on Saturday January 16 at 3:25 p.m., and from there I'll take the 3:55 Greyhound bus to Columbus, where I was hoping you'd pick me up. It would be around 12:25 a.m. on Sunday—I hope that is not too late.*
>
> *Looking forward to our visit. If there are any problems, you know how to reach me!*
>
> *Love,*
> *Your niece*

A couple of days later, Elisa overnighted a package to Julia: it held a fake driver's license; a photocopy of a dead man's passport; bank statements in the dead man's name, holding cash from one of Elisa's slush funds; and the bus and train tickets Julia had requested.

The baton passed back to Julia, Elisa had reviewed the postcard a final time before she flicked it into the woodstove.

Now, somewhere in the space between January 16 and 17, Elisa sat in her car and waited. Her foot drummed rhythmically against the floor in front of the pedals, sending reverberations through her body. She checked the time again.

The bus was two minutes late when it lurched into the station.

She thought back on the postcard. *If there are any problems, you know how to reach me!*

Julia did not want to know when it was done. She only wanted to know if it was not.

A young man stepped into view from behind the bus. The tall lights above the station cast shadows over his brow, pitting his eyes into holes as he scanned the parking lot.

Elisa flashed her lights, and Raymond Walker started toward the car.

She never did have occasion to contact Julia.

Acknowledgments

There are so many people who have had an impact on this story and its path to publication, and I'm afraid it's an impossible task to properly acknowledge each one of them. Fear of failure is a terrible reason not to do something, though, so here are the people I want to thank:

Helen Heller, the agent who blew up my life in the span of a week. Deciding to partner with you has been the best professional decision I've ever made.

My editorial team, Pamela Dorman, Jeramie Orton, Clio Cornish, Jill Taylor, and Marie Michels. You turned this novel into the story I was trying to tell. Erica Ferguson, copyeditor extraordinaire, who caught more mistakes than I will ever admit to making. Everyone at Pamela Dorman Books and Michael Joseph who touched this project and made me feel at home.

Editor and writer Clarence Haynes, whose notes on Nick's character and experience were invaluable.

Saliann St-Clair, Jemma McDonough, and Camilla Ferrier, who worked so hard to earn foreign deals for this book and then gamely answered my most inane questions about all of the weird tax forms. Ari

Solotoff, my former classmate who talked me through each contract because I cannot turn off the lawyer anxiety.

My early readers, including Melissa Martin, Anna Polko Clark, authors Maureen Milliken and Jeneva Rose, and my friends at the South Portland Public Library Writers' Group.

Taylor Sampson, Amanda Bombard, and James, who answered very different questions for me.

My aunt Cindy and uncle John Mina at Curry Printing in Portland, who printed many drafts of this novel over the last three years and cheered me on with each one.

Chloe, my best writing friend who let me steal her name, and who batted around query letters with me until I was brave enough to send them. Susan Dennard and Pitch Wars, for teaching me how to query agents in the first place.

My sister, Hannah, who told me to breathe deep and chase my crazy dream of publishing a novel. Mum and Dad, who encouraged reading and writing all my life. Mr. Ramsey, who told my dad I should stop worrying so much about what major I picked in college because I was just going to end up being an author.

And finally, Ben. You are the steady Julia to my spiraling Tony. Thank you for every single thing.